VICTORY OF EAGLES

Naomi Novik was born in New York in 1973, a first-generation American, and raised on Polish fairy tales, Baba Yaga, and Tolkien. She studied English Literature at Brown University and did graduate work in Computer Science at Columbia University before leaving to participate in the design and development of the computer game *Neverwinter Nights: Shadows of Undrentide*. Over the course of a brief winter sojourn working on the game in Edmonton, Canada (accompanied by a truly alarming coat that now lives brooding in the depths of her closet), she realized she preferred the writing to the programming, and, on returning to New York, decided to try her hand at novels. *Temeraire* was her first.

Naomi lives in New York with her husband and six computers.

By the same author

Temeraire
Throne of Jade
Black Powder War
Empire of Ivory

NAOMI NOVIK

Victory of Eagles

HARPER
Voyager

HarperCollins*Publishers*
77–85 Fulham Palace Road,
Hammersmith, London W6 8JB

www.harpercollins.co.uk

Published by Harper*Voyager*
An Imprint of HarperCollins*Publishers* 2009

1

A catalogue record for this book
is available from the British Library

ISBN: 978 0 00 725676 1

Set in Sabon by Palimpsest Book Production Limited,
Grangemouth, Stirlingshire

Printed and bound in Great Britain by
Clays Ltd, St Ives plc

Mixed Sources
Product group from well-managed
forests and other controlled sources
www.fsc.org Cert no. SW-COC-1806
© 1996 Forest Stewardship Council

FSC is a non-profit international organisation established
to promote the responsible management of the world's forests.
Products carrying the FSC label are independently certified
to assure consumers that they come from forests that are managed
to meet the social, economic and ecological needs
of present and future generations.

Find out more about HarperCollins and the environment at
www.harpercollins.co.uk/green

For Dr. Sonia Novik
who gave this book a home

PART I

Chapter One

The breeding grounds were called Pen Y Fan, after the hard, jagged slash of mountain rising like an axe-blade at their heart, rimed with ice along its edge and rising barren over the moorland. It was a cold, wet Welsh autumn already, coming on towards winter, and the other dragons were sleepy and remote, uninterested in anything but meals. A few hundred of them were scattered throughout the grounds, mostly established in caves or on rocky ledges, wherever they could fit themselves. No comfort or even order was provided for them, except for the feedings, and the mowed-bare strip of ground around the borders, where torches were lit at night to mark the lines past which they might not go. The town-lights glimmered in the distance, cheerful and forbidden.

Temeraire had hunted out and cleared a large cavern on his arrival, to sleep in; but it would be damp, no matter what he did in the way of lining it with grass, or flapping his wings to move the air, which in any case did not suit his notions of dignity. Much better to endure every unpleasantness with stoic patience, although that was not very satisfying when no-one would appreciate the effort. The other dragons certainly did not.

He was quite sure he and Laurence had done as they ought, in taking the cure to France, and no one sensible could disagree; but just in case, Temeraire had steeled himself to meet with either disapproval or contempt, and he had worked out several very fine arguments in his defence. Most importantly, of course, it had been a cowardly, sneaking way of fighting: if the Government wished to beat Napoleon, they ought to fight him directly, and not make his dragons sick to make him easy to defeat; as if British dragons could not beat French dragons, without cheating. 'And not only that,' he added, 'but it would not only have been the French dragons who would have died. Our friends from Prussia, who are imprisoned in their breeding grounds, would also have gotten sick. And it might perhaps even have spread so far as China; and that would be like stealing someone else's food, even when you are not hungry; or breaking their eggs.'

He made this impressive speech to the wall of his cave, as practice. They had refused to give him his sand-table, and he had no-one of his crew to jot it down for him. He did not have Laurence, who would have helped him work out just what to say. So he repeated the arguments over to himself quietly, instead, so he would not forget them. And if these arguments did not suffice, he might point out that it was, after all, *he* who had brought the cure back in the first place – he and Laurence, with Maximus and Lily and the rest of their formation – and if anyone had a right to say where it should be shared out, they did. No one would even have known of it if Temeraire had not happened to be sick in Africa, where the medicinal mushrooms grew.

He might have saved himself the trouble. No one accused him of anything, nor, as he had privately, and a little wistfully thought possible, had they hailed him as a hero. They simply did not care.

The older dragons, not feral but retired, were a little curious about the latest developments in the war, but only distantly. They were more inclined to reminisce about their own battles from earlier wars, and the rest had only provincial indignation over the recent epidemic. They cared that their own fellows had sickened and died; they cared that the cure had taken so long to reach them; but it did not mean anything to them that dragons in France had also been ill, or that the disease would have spread, killing thousands if Temeraire and Laurence had not taken over the cure. They also did not care that the Lords of the Admiralty had called it treason, and sentenced Laurence to die.

They had nothing to care for. They were fed, and there was enough for everyone. If the shelter was not pleasant, it was no worse than what the dragons were used to, from the days of their active service. None of them had heard of pavilions, or ever thought they might be made more comfortable than they were. No-one molested their eggs; the grounds-keepers took them away with infinite care in wagons lined with straw, and hot-water bottles and woollen blankets in the wintertime. They would bring back reports until the eggs were hatched and of no more concern; it was safer, even, than keeping them oneself, so even the dragons who had not cared to take a captain at all, would often as not hand over their own eggs.

They could not go flying very far, because they were fed at no set time but randomly, from day to day, so if one went out of ear-shot of the bells, one was likely to come too late, and go hungry. So there was no larger society to enjoy, no intercourse with the other breeding grounds or with the coverts, except when some other dragon came from afar, to mate. But even that was arranged for them. Instead they sat, willing prisoners in their own territory, Temeraire thought bitterly. He would never have endured it if not for Laurence;

only for Laurence, who would surely be put to death at once if Temeraire did not obey.

He held himself aloof from their society at first. There was his cave to be arranged: despite its fine prospect it had been left vacant for being inconveniently shallow, and he was rather crammed-in; but there was a much larger chamber beyond it, just visible through holes in the back wall, which he gradually opened up with the slow and cautious use of his roar. Slower, even, than perhaps necessary: he was very willing to have the task consume several days. The cave had then to be cleared of debris, old gnawed bones and inconvenient boulders, which he scraped out painstakingly even from the corners too small for him to lie in, for neatness' sake. He found a few rough boulders in the valley and used them to grind the cave walls a little smoother, by dragging them back and forth, throwing up a great cloud of dust. It made him sneeze, but he kept on; he was not going to live in a raw untidy hole.

He knocked down stalactites from the ceiling, and beat protrusions flat into the floor, and when he was satisfied, he arranged some attractive rocks and dead tree-branches, twisted and bleached white along the sides of his new antechamber, with careful nudges of his talons. He would have liked a pond and a fountain, but he could not see how to bring the water up, or how to make it run when he had got it there, so he settled for picking out a promontory on Llyn y Fan Fawr which jutted into the lake, and considering it also his own.

To finish, he carved the characters of his name into the cliff-face by the entrance, although the letter R gave him some difficulty and came out looking rather like the reversed numeral four. When he was done with that, routine crept up and devoured his days. He would rise, when the sun came in at the cave mouth, take a little exercise, nap, rise again when the herdsmen rang the bell, eat, then nap and exercise again, and then go back sleep; there was nothing more. He hunted for himself, once, and so did not go to the daily feeding; later that day one of the small dragons brought up the grounds-master, Mr. Lloyd, and a surgeon, to be sure that he was not ill. They lectured him on poaching sternly enough to make him uneasy for Laurence's sake.

For all that, Lloyd did not think of him as a traitor, either. He did not think enough of Temeraire to consider him capable. The grounds-master cared only that his charges stay inside the borders, ate, and mated; he recognized neither dignity nor stoicism, and anything Temeraire did out of the ordinary was only a bit of fussing. 'Come now, we have a fresh lady Anglewing visiting today,' Lloyd would say, 'quite a nice little piece; we will have a fine evening, eh? Perhaps we would like a bite of veal, first? Yes, we would, I am sure,' providing the responses with his questions, so Temeraire had nothing to do but sit and listen. Lloyd was a little hard of hearing, so if Temeraire did try to say, 'No, I would rather have some venison, and you might roast it first,' he was sure to be ignored.

It was almost enough to put one off making eggs. Temeraire was growing uncomfortably sure that his mother would not have approved of how often they wished him to try, or how indiscriminately. Lien would certainly have sniffed in the most insulting way. It was not the fault of the female dragons sent to visit him, they were all very pleasant, but most of them had never managed to produce an egg before, and some had never even been in a real battle or done anything interesting at all. They were frequently embarrassed, as they did not have any suitable present that might have made up for their position; but it was not as though he could pretend that he was not a very remarkable dragon, even if he liked to; which he did not, very much. He would have tried to pretend for Bellusa, a poor young Malachite Reaper without a single action to her name, sent by the Admiralty from Edinburgh. She had miserably offered him a small knotted rug, which was all her confused captain would afford: it might have made a blanket for Temeraire's largest talon.

'It is very handsome,' Temeraire said awkwardly, 'and so cleverly done; I admire the colours very much,' He tried to drape it carefully over a small rock, by the entrance, but the gesture only made her look more wretched, and she burst out, 'Oh, I do beg your pardon; he wouldn't understand in the least, and thought that I meant I would not like to, and then he said—' and she stopped abruptly in even worse confusion, so Temeraire was sure that whatever her captain had said, it had not been at all nice. He had not even had the satisfaction of delivering one of his cherished retorts, because it was not as though she herself had said anything rude. So, although he had not much wanted to, he obliged anyway. He was determined to be patient, and quiet; he would not cause any trouble. He would be perfectly good.

Temeraire did not let himself think very much about Laurence; he did not trust himself. It was hard to endure the perpetual sensation of deep unease, almost overpowering when he thought of how he did not know how Laurence was, what his condition might be.

He was sure he knew where his breastplate was at every moment, and his small gold chain, these being in his own possession; his talon-sheaths had been left with Emily, and he was quite certain she could be trusted to keep them safe. Ordinarily he would have trusted Laurence, to keep himself safe; but the circumstances were not what they ought to be, and it had been so very long. The Admiralty had promised that so long as he behaved, Laurence would not be hanged, but they were not to be trusted, not at all. Temeraire resolved twice a week to go to Dover, at once, or to London – only to make inquiries, to see they had not, only to be sure. But unwanted reason always asserted itself, before he had even set out. He must not do anything that might persuade the Government he was unmanageable, and therefore that Laurence was of no use to them. He must be as complaisant and accommodating as ever he might.

It was a resolution already sorely tried by the end of his third week, when Lloyd brought him a visitor, admonishing the gentleman loudly, 'Remember now, not to upset the dear creature, but to speak nice and slow and gentle, like to a horse,' which was infuriating enough, even before the gentleman in question was named to him as one Reverend Daniel Salcombe.

'Oh, you,' Temeraire said, which made Salcombe look taken aback, 'Yes, I know perfectly well who you are. I have read your very stupid letter to the Royal Society, and I suppose now you have come to see me behave like a parrot, or a dog.'

Salcombe stammered excuses, but it was plainly the case. He began laboriously to read to Temeraire a prepared list of questions, something quite nonsensical about predestination, but Temeraire would have none of it. 'Pray be quiet; St. Augustine explained it much better than you, and it did not make any sense even then. Anyway, I am not going to perform for you, like some circus animal. I really cannot be bothered to speak to anyone so uneducated that he has not even read the Analects,' he added, guiltily omitting Laurence; but then Laurence did not set himself up as a scholar, and write insulting letters about people he did not know, 'And as for dragons not understanding mathematics, I am sure I know more on the subject than do you.'

He scratched out a triangle into the dust, and labelled the two shorter sides. 'There; tell me the length of the third side, and then you may talk. Otherwise, go away, and stop pretending you know anything about dragons.'

The simple diagram had already perplexed several gentlemen, when he had put it to them during a party in the London covert, rather disillusioning Temeraire as to the general understanding of mathematics among the human populace. Reverend Salcombe evidently had not paid much attention to that part of his education either, for he stared, and coloured to his mostly bare pate. Then he turned to Lloyd furiously, 'You have put the creature up to this, I suppose! You prepared the remarks—' The unlikelihood of this accusation striking him, perhaps, as soon as he met Lloyd's gaping, uncomprehending face. He immediately amended, 'they must have been given to you, by someone, and you fed them to him, to embarrass me—'

'I never, sir,' Lloyd protested, to no avail, and it annoyed Temeraire so much that he nearly indulged himself in a very small roar; but in the last moment he exercised great restraint, and only growled. Salcombe fled hastily all the same, Lloyd running after him, calling anxiously for the loss of his tip. He had been paid, then, to let Salcombe come and gawk at Temeraire, as though he really were a circus animal. Temeraire was only sorry he had not roared, or better yet thrown them both in the lake.

And then his temper faded, and he drooped. He realized too late, that perhaps he ought to have talked to Salcombe, after all. Lloyd would not read to him, or even tell him anything of the world. If Temeraire asked slowly and clearly enough to be understood, he only said, 'Now, let's not be worrying ourselves about such things, no sense in getting worked up. Salcombe, however ignorant, had at least wished to have a conversation; and he might have been prevailed upon to read something from the latest Proceedings, or a newspaper. Oh, what Temeraire would have done for a newspaper!

10

During this time the heavyweight dragons had been finishing their own dinners. The largest, a big Regal Copper, spat out a well-chewed grey and bloodstained ball of fleece, belched tremendously, and lifted away for his cave. Now the rest came in a rush, middle-weights and light-weights and the smaller courier-weight beasts landing to take their own share of the sheep and cattle, calling to one another noisily. Temeraire did not move, but only hunched himself a little deeper while they squabbled and played around him He did not look up even when one, with narrow blue-green legs, set herself directly before him to eat, crunching loudly upon sheep bones.

'I have been considering the matter,' she informed him, after a little while, around a mouthful, 'and in all cases, where the angle is ninety degrees, as I suppose you meant to draw it, the length of the long side must be a number which, multiplied by itself, is equal to the lengths of the two shorter sides, each multiplied by themselves, added.' She swallowed noisily, and licked her chops clean. 'Quite an interesting little observation. How did you come to make it?'

'I never did,' Temeraire muttered, 'it is the Pythagorean theorem; everyone who is educated knows it. Laurence taught it to me,' he added, making himself even more miserable.

'Hmh,' the other dragon said, rather haughtily, and flew away.

But she reappeared at Temeraire's cave the next morning, uninvited, and poked him awake with her nose, saying, 'Perhaps you would be interested to learn that there is a formula which I have invented, which can invariably calculate the power of any sum? What does Pythagoras have to say to that?'

'You did not invent it,' Temeraire said, irritable at having been woken up early, with so empty a day to be faced. 'That is the binomial theorem, Yang Hui made it a very long time ago,' and he put his head under his wing and tried to lose himself again in sleep.

He thought that would be the end of it, but four days later, while he lay by his lake, the strange dragon once again landed beside him. She was bristling furiously and her words tumbled over one another as she rushed, 'There, I have just worked out something quite new: the prime number coming in a particular position, for instance the tenth prime, is always very near the value of that position, multiplied by the exponent one must put on the number p to get that same value – the number p,' she added, 'being a very curious number, which I have also discovered, and named after myself.'

'Certainly not,' Temeraire said, rousing with smug contempt when he had made sense of what she was talking about. 'It is not p, it is e; you are talking of the natural logarithm. And as for the rest about prime numbers, it is all nonsense. Consider the prime fifteen—' and then he paused, working out the value in his head.

'You see,' she said, triumphantly, and after working out another two-dozen examples, Temeraire was forced to admit that the irritating stranger might indeed be correct.

'And you needn't tell me that this Pythagoras invented it first,' the other dragon added, with her chest puffed out, 'or Yang Hui, because I have inquired, and no-one has ever heard of either of them. They do not live in any of the coverts or anywhere around breeding grounds, so you may keep your tricks. Who ever heard of a dragon named anything like Yang Hui; such nonsense.'

Temeraire was neither despondent nor tired enough to forget how dreadfully bored he was, and so he was less inclined to take offence. 'He is not a dragon, neither of them are,' he said, 'and they are both dead anyway, for years and years; Pythagoras was a Greek, and Yang Hui was from China.'

'Then how do you know they invented it?' she demanded, suspiciously.

'Laurence read it to me,' Temeraire said. 'Where did you learn any of it, if not out of books?'

'I worked it out myself,' the dragon said. 'There is nothing much else to do, here.'

Her name was Perscitia. She was an experimental cross-breed from a Malachite Reaper and a lightweight Pascal's Blue, who had come out rather larger, slower, and more nervous than the breeders had hoped for. Nor was her colouring ideal for any sort of camouflage. Her body and wings were bright blue and streaked with shades of pale green, with widely scattered spines along her back. Perscitia was not very old, either, unlike most of the once-harnessed dragons in the breeding grounds. She had given up her captain. 'Well,' Perscitia said, 'I did not mind him. He showed me how to do equations, but I do not see any use in going to war and getting oneself shot at or clawed up, for no good reason. And, when I would not fight, he did not much want me anymore,' a statement airily delivered, but Perscitia avoided Temeraire's eyes, making it.

'Well, if you mean formation fighting, I do not blame you; it is very tiresome, Temeraire said. 'They do not approve of me in China,' he added, to be sympathetic, 'because I *do* fight. Celestials are not supposed to.'

'China must be a very fine place,' Perscitia said, wistfully, and Temeraire was by no means inclined to disagree. Sadly he thought, that if only Laurence had been willing, they might now be together in Peking, strolling in the gardens of the Summer Palace again. He had not had the chance to see it during autumn.

And then he paused, raised his head and said, 'You made inquiries? What do you mean by that? You cannot have gone out?'

'Of course not,' Perscitia said. 'I gave Moncey half my dinner, and he went to Brecon for me and put the question out on the courier circuit. This morning he went again, and received word that no one had ever heard of those names.'

'Oh—' Temeraire said, his ruff rising, 'Pray; who is Moncey? I will give him anything he likes, if he can find out where Laurence is. He may have all my dinner, for a week.'

Moncey was a Winchester, who had slipped the leash at his hatching and eeled right out of the barn door, straight past a candidate he did not care for; and so made his escape from the Corps. Being a gregarious creature, he had been coaxed eventually into the breeding grounds more by the promise of company than anything else. Small and dark purple, he looked like any other Winchester at a distance, and excited no comment if seen abroad, or was absent from the daily feeding. As long as his missed meals were properly compensated for, he was very willing to oblige.

'Hm, how about you give me one of those cows, the nice fat sort they save for you special, when you are mating,' Moncey said. 'I would like to give Laculla a proper treat,' he added, exultingly.

'Highway robbery,' Perscitia said indignantly, but Temeraire did not care at all; he was learning to hate the taste of the cows, particularly when it meant yet another miserably awkward evening session, and he nodded on the bargain.

'But no promises, mind,' Moncey cautioned. 'I'll put it about, have no fear, but it'll take many a week to hear back if you want it sorted out proper to all the coverts, and to Ireland, and even so maybe no-one will have heard anything.'

'There is sure to have been word,' Temeraire said quietly, 'if he is dead.'

* * *

14

The ball came in down through the ship's bow and crashed recklessly the length of the lower deck, the drum-roll of its passage heralding its progression with castanets of splinters raining against the walls for accompaniment. The young Marine guarding the brig had been trembling since the call to go to quarters had sounded above; a mingling, Laurence thought, of anxiety, the desire to be doing something and the frustration at being kept at so miserable a post. A sentiment he shared from his still more miserable place within the cell. The ball seemed to be roll at a leisurely pace as it approached the brig. The Marine put out his foot to stop it before Laurence could protest.

He had seen the same impulse have much the same result during other battles. The ball took off the better part of the young man's foot and continued unperturbed into and through the metal grating, skewing the door off its top hinge before finally embedding itself, two inches deep into the solid oak wall of the ship. Laurence pushed the swinging door open and climbed out of the brig, taking off his neckcloth to tie up the Marine's foot. The young man was staring mutely at his bloody stump, and needed a little coaxing to limp along to the orlop . 'As clean a shot as I have ever seen,' Laurence said, encouragingly, and left him there for the surgeons. The steady roar of cannon-fire was going on overhead.

He climbed the stern ladder-way and plunged into the roaring confusion of the gun-deck. Daylight shining through jagged gaping holes in the ship's east-pointed bows, made a glittering cloud of the smoke and dust kicked up from the cannon. Roaring Martha had jumped her tackling, and five men were fighting to hold her long enough against the roll of the ship to get her secure again. At any moment, the gun might go running wild across the deck, crushing men and perhaps smashing through the side. 'There girl, hold fast,

15

hold fast—' The captain of the gun-crew spoke to the canon as if she were a skittish horse, his hands flinching away from the smoking-hot barrel. One side of his face was bristling with splinters standing out like hedgehog spines.

No one knew Laurence in the smoky red light, he was only another pair of hands. His flight gloves were still in his coat pocket. Wearing them, he clapped on to the metal and pushed her by the mouth of the barrel, his palms stinging even through the thick leather, and with a final thump she heaved over into the channel again. The men tied her down and stood around trembling like well-run horses, panting and sweating.

There was no return fire, no calls passed along from the quarterdeck, no ship in view through the gun port. The ship was griping furiously where he put his hand on the side, a sort of low moaning complaint as if she were trying to go too close to the wind. Water glubbed in a curious way against her sides, a sound wholly unfamiliar, and he knew this ship. He had served on *Goliath* four years in her midshipman's mess as a boy, as lieutenant for another two and at the Battle of the Nile; he would have said he could recognise every note of her voice.

He put his head out of the porthole and saw the enemy crossing their bows and turning to come about for another pass She was only a frigate : a beautiful trim thirty-six gun ship which could have thrown not half of Goliath's broad-side; an absurd combat on the face of it, and he could not understand why they had not turned to rake her across the stern. There was only a little grumbling from the bow-chasers above, not much of a reply to be making, though there was a great deal shouting.

Looking forward along the ship, he saw that she had been pierced by an enormous harpoon through her side, as if she was a whale. The end inside the ship had several curved barbs, which had been jerked back to bite into the wood. And when Laurence put his head out of the port-hole, he caught sight of the cable at the harpoon's other end swinging grandly up and up, into the air, where two enormous heavy-weight dragons were holding on to it: a Grand Chevalier, and a Parnassian, middle-aged, likely traded to France during an earlier peacetime, and a Grand Chevalier.

It was not the only harpoon: three more cable-lines dangled from their grip to the bow, and Laurence could see another two stretched from the stern. The dragons were too far aloft for him to note all of the details, with the ship's motion underneath him, but the cables were somehow laced into their harnesses. By flying together and pulling, they were pivoting the ship's head into the wind. The dragons were too far aloft for round-shot to reach them. One of them sneezed, from the action of the frantic pepper guns, but they had only to beat their wings to get away from the pepper, hauling the ship merrily along while they did it.

'Axes, axes,' the lieutenant was shouting; then the clattering of iron as the bosun's mates came spilling weapons across the floor: hand-axes, cutlasses, knives. The men snatched them up and began to reach out of the portholes to hack at the ropes, but the harpoon shafts were two feet long, and the ropes had enough slackness to prevent good purchase. Someone would have to climb out of a porthole to saw at them: open and exposed against the hull of the ship, with the frigate coming around again.

No one moved at first; then Laurence reached out and took a short cutlass, from the heap. The lieutenant looked into his face, and knew him, but said nothing. Turning to the opening Laurence worked his shoulders out, hands quickly beneath his feet to support him, and eeled out as the lieutenant started calling again. Shortly, a rope was flung down to him from the deck above, so he could brace himself against the hull. Many faces peered over anxiously, all strangers; then another man came sliding down over the rail, and another, to work on the other harpoons.

Making a bright target against the ship's paintwork, Laurence began the grim effort of sawing away at the cable, strands fraying one at a time. The rope was cable-laid: three hawsers of three strands, well wormed and thick as a man's wrist, parcelled in canvas.

If he were killed, at least his family would be spared the embarrassment of his hanging. He was only alive now to be a chain round Temeraire's neck, until the Admiralty judged the dragon pacified enough by age and habit that Laurence might be dispensed. That could mean he faced years, long years, mouldering in gaol or in the bowels of a ship.

It was not a purposeful thought, no guilty intention; it only crossed his mind involuntarily, while he worked. He had his back to the ocean and could not see anything of the frigate or the larger battle beyond: his horizon was the splintered paint of Goliath's side, lacquered shine made rough by splinters and salt, and the cold sea was climbing up her hull and spraying his back. Distant roars of cannon-fire spoke, but Goliath had let her guns fall silent, saving her powder and shot for when they should be of some use. The loudest noises in his ears were the grunts and effort of the men hanging near-by, sawing at their own harpoon lines. Then one of them gave a startled yell and let go his rope, falling away into the churning ocean; a small darting courier-beast, a Chasseur-Vocifère, was plunging at the side of the ship with another harpoon.

The beast held it something like a jouster in a medieval tournament, with the butt rigged awkwardly into a cup attached to its harness, for support, and two men on its back bracing the rig. The harpoon thumped dully against the ship's side, near to where Laurence hung, and the dragon's tail slapped a wash of salt water up into his face, heavy stinging thickness in his nostrils and dripping down the back of his throat as he choked it out. The dragon lunged away again even as the Marines fired off a furious volley, trailing the harpoon on its line behind it: the barb had not bitten deep enough to penetrate. The hull was pockmarked with the dents of earlier attempts, a good dozen for each planted harpoon marring her spit-and-polish paintwork.

Laurence wiped salt from his face against his arm and shouted, 'Keep working, man, damn you,' at the other seaman still hanging near him. The first strand was going, tough fibres fraying away from the cutlass edge and fanning out like a broom. He began on the second, rapidly, although the blade was going dull.

The roar of the cannon made him jerk, involuntarily, and the ball came whistling across the water, skipping two, three times along the wave-tops, like a stone thrown by a boy. It looked as though it came straight for him, an illusion. The whole ship groaned as the ball punched at the bows, and splinters flew like a sudden blizzard out of the open port-holes. They peppered Laurence's legs, stinging like a flock of bees, and his stockings were quickly wet with blood. He clung on to the harpoon arm and kept sawing; the frigate was still firing, her broadside rolling on, and the round-shot hurtled at them again and again. There was a sickening deep sway to Goliath's motion now as she took the pounding.

He had to hand the cutlass back and shout for a fresh one to get through the last strand. Then at last the cable was cut loose and swinging away free, and they pulled him back in. He staggered when he tried to stand, and went to his knees slipping in blood: stockings laddered and soaked through red; his best breeches, the ones he had worn for the trial, were pierced and spotted. He was helped to sit against the wall, and turned the cutlass on his own shirt, for bandages to tie up the worst of the gashes; no-one could be spared to help him to the surgeons. The other harpoons had been cut and they were moving at last, coming around. All the crews were fixed by their guns, savage in the dim red glow, teeth bared and mazed with blood from cracked lips and gums, their faces black with sweat and grime, ready to take vengeance.

Suddenly, a loud pattering like rain or hailstones came down: small bombs with short fuses dropped by the French dragons. Lightning flashes were visible through the boards of the deck. Some rolled down through the ladderways and burst in the gun-deck, hot flash-powder smoke and the burning glare of pyrotechnics, painful to the eyes. Then the cannon were speaking as they hove around in view of the frigate, and the order came down to fire.

There was nothing for a long moment but the mindless fury of the ship's guns going: impossible to think in that roaring din, smoke and hellish fire in her bowels choking away all reason. Laurence reached up for the port-hole when they had paused, and hauled himself up to look. The French frigate was reeling away under the pounding, her foremast down and hulled below the water-line, so each wave slapping away poured into her.

There was no cheering. Past the retreating frigate, the breadth of the Channel spread open before them. All the great ships of the blockade were as entangled and harassed as they had been. *Bucephalas* and the mighty *Gloucester*, both 100 guns, were near enough to recognize. They wore cables rising up to three and four dragons; a flock of French heavyweights and middleweights industriously tugging them every which way. The ships were firing steadily but uselessly, clouds of smoke that did not reach the dragons above.

And between them, half a dozen French ships-of-the-line, come out of harbour at last, were stately going by, escort to an enormous flotilla. A hundred and more, barges and fishing-boats and even rafts in lateen rig, all of them crammed with soldiers, the wind at their backs and the tide carrying them towards the shore, tricolours streaming proudly from their bows towards England.

With the Navy paralysed, only the dragons of the Corps were left to stop the advance. But the French warships were firing something like pepper into the air above the flotilla, in quantities that could never have been afforded if it were. It burned. Red spark fragments glowed like fireflies against the black smoke-cloud hanging over the boats, shielding them from aerial attack. One of the transport boats was near enough that Laurence saw the men had their faces covered with wet kerchiefs and rags, or huddled under oilcloth sheets. The British dragons made desperate attempts to dive, but recoiled from the clouds, and had instead to fling down bombs from too great a height: ten splashing into the wide ocean for every one which came near enough to make a wave against a ship's hull. The smaller French dragons harried them too, flying back and forth and jeering in shrill voices. There were so many of them, Laurence had never seen so many: wheeling almost like birds, clustering and breaking apart, offering no easy target to the British dragons in their stately formations.

One great Regal Copper, who might have been Maximus: red and orange and yellow against the blue sky, flew at the head of a formation with Yellow Reapers in lines to each wing, but Laurence did not see Lily. The Regal roared, audible faintly even over the distance, and bulled his formation through a dozen French lightweights to come at a great French warship: flames bloomed from her sails as the bombs at last hit, but when the formation rose away again, one of the Reapers was streaming crimson from its belly and another was listing. A handful of British frigates, too, were valiantly trying to dash past the French ships to come at the transports: with some little success, but they were under heavy fire, and if they sank a dozen boats, half the men were pulled aboard others, so close were the little transports to one another.

'Every man to his gun,' the lieutenant said sharply. *Goliath* was turning to go after the transports. She would be passing between *Majestueux* and *Héros*, a broadside of nearly three tons between them. Laurence felt it when her sails caught the wind properly again: the ship leaping forward like an eager racehorse held too long. She had made all sail. He touched his leg: the blood had stopped flowing, he thought. He limped back to an empty place at a gun.

Outside, the first transports were already hurtling onward to the shore, lightweight dragons wheeled above to shield them while they ran artillery onto the ground. One soldier rammed the standard into the dirt, the golden eagle atop catching fire with the sunlight: Napoleon had landed in England at last.

Chapter Two

The question sent out, Temeraire found the prospect of an answer almost worse. Before, the world itself had been undecided. If Laurence was still in it he might as easily stay alive as not, and so long as Temeraire continued to believe, Laurence *was* alive, at least in part. At best, the news would report that he was still imprisoned. As the day crept onward, Temeraire began to feel that certainty was a weak reward for the risk of receiving an answer to the contrary, a possibility Temeraire could not bear to envision. A great blankness engulfed him if he tried, like a grey sky full of clouds above and below, fog all around.

He wanted distraction badly, and there was none, except to talk to Perscitia, who was at least interesting, if infuriating also. Perscitia liked to think herself a great genius, and she was certainly unusually clever, even if she could not quite grasp the notion of writing. Occasionally, to Temeraire's discomfiture, she would leap quite far ahead, and come out with some strange notion, from none of the books Temeraire had read, that could neither be disproved, nor quarrelled with.

But she was so jealous of her discoveries that she flew

into a temper when Temeraire informed her that any of them had been made before, and she was resentful of the hierarchy of the breeding grounds, which denied her the just desserts of her brilliance. Because of her middling size, she had to make do with an inconvenient poky clearing down in the moorlands, about which she complained endlessly. It provided little more than an overhang to shelter from the rain.

'So why do you not take a better place?' Temeraire said, exasperated. 'There are several very nice ones directly over there, in the cliff face; you would be much more comfortable there, I am sure.'

'One does not like to be quarrelsome' Perscitia said being evasive and entirely false: she liked very well to be quarrelsome, and Temeraire did not understand what that had to do with taking an empty cave, either, but at least it diverted the subject.

The only event of note was that it rained for a week without stopping, with a steady driving wind that came in to all the cave-mouths and permeated the ground, and made everyone perfectly miserable. Temeraire was very glad of his antechamber, where he could shake off the water and dry before retreating to the comfort of his larger chamber. Several of the smallest dragons, courier-weights living in the hollows by the river, were flooded out of their homes entirely. Feeling sorry for their muddy and bedraggled state, Temeraire invited them to stop in his cavern, while the rain continued, so long as they first washed off the mud. They were, at least, loud with appreciation for his arrangements.

A few days later, when he was once again solitary and brooding over Laurence, a shadow crossed over the mouth of his cave. It was the big Regal Copper, Requiescat; he ducked in through the antechamber and came into Temeraire's main chamber, uninvited. He gazed around the room with an impressed air, and nodding said, 'It is just as nice as they said.'

'Thank you,' Temeraire said, thawed a little by the compliment. He did not feel much like company, but remembered he must be polite. 'Will you sit down? I am sorry I cannot offer you tea.'

'Tea?' Requiescat said absently. He was busy poking his nose into the corners of the cave, even putting his tongue out to smell them, as if he were at home; Temeraire's ruff began to bristle.

'I beg your pardon,' he said, stiffly, 'I am afraid you have found me unprepared for guests,' which he thought was a clever way of hinting that Requiescat might go away again.

But the Regal Copper did not take the hint; or at any rate he did not choose to go. but instead settled himself comfortably along the back of the cave and said, 'Well, old fellow, I am afraid we will have to swap.'

'Swap?' Temeraire said, puzzled, until he divined that Requiescat meant caves. 'I do not want *your* cave,' adding hastily, 'I am sure that it is very nice, but I have just got this one arranged to suit me.'

'This one is much bigger now,' Requiescat explained, 'and it is much nicer in the wet. Mine,' he added regretfully, 'has been full of puddles all week; wet clear through to the back.'

'Then I can hardly see why I would change,' Temeraire said, still more baffled, and then he sat up, outraged and astonished, and let his ruff spread fully. 'Why, you are a damned scrub,' he said. 'How *dare* you come here, and behave like a visitor, when all the time it is a challenge? I have never seen anything so devious in my life; it is the sort of thing Lien would do,' he added, cuttingly. 'You may get out at once. If you want my cave you may try to take it. I will meet you anytime you like: now, or at dawn tomorrow.'

'Now, now, let us not get excited,' Requiescat said sooth-ingly. 'I can see you are a young fellow, right enough. A challenge, really! It is nothing of the sort; I am the most peaceable fellow in the world, and I do not want to fight anyone. I am sorry if I was ham-handed about it. It is not that I want to take your cave, you see—' Temeraire did not see, in the least, '—it is a question of appearances. Here you are a month, with the nicest cave, and you nowhere near the biggest either.' Requiescat preened his own side, a little. He certainly outweighed any dragon Temeraire had seen, except Maximus and Laetificat. 'We have our own little ways here, of arranging things to keep everyone comfortable. No one wants any fighting to cut up our peace, not when there is no need. It would be a nasty-tempered sort of fellow who would get to fighting over one cave versus another, both of them large and hand-some; but distinctions must be preserved.'

'Stuff,' Temeraire said. 'It sounds to me like you have become so lazy, having all your meals given to you and nothing to do, that you do not even want to put yourself to the trouble of properly bullying other people. Or maybe,' he added, having made up his mind to be really insulting, 'you are just a coward, and thought I was the same. Well, I am not, and I am not going to give you my cave, either, no matter what you do.'

Requiescat did not rise to the remarks, but only shook his head dolefully. 'There, I am not a clever chap, so I have made a mull of explaining, and now your back is put up. I suppose we will have to get the council together, or you will never believe me. It is a bother, but it is your right, after all.' He heaved himself back to his feet and added, infuriatingly, 'You may keep the place until then; it will take me a day or so to get word to everyone,' before he padded out again, leaving Temeraire quivering with rage.

'His cave is the nicest,' Perscitia said anxiously, later, 'at least, we have certainly always thought so. I am sure you would like it, and maybe you could make it even more pleasant than this? Why don't you go and see it before quarrelling?'

'I do not care if it is Ali Baba's cave, and full of gold and lamps,' Temeraire said, not even trying to master his temper. It felt better to be angry than miserable, and he was glad of having something else to think about instead of that which he could do nothing to repair. 'It is a question of principle. I am not going to be bullied, as though I were not up to fighting him. If I made the other cave nice, he would only try and take it back, I am sure. Or some other dragon would try and push me out. Who are this council?'

'It is all the biggest dragons,' Perscitia said, 'and a Longwing, although Gentius does not bother to come out much anymore.'

'All of them his friends, I suppose,' Temeraire said.

'Oh no; no one much likes Requiescat.' Moncey said, perched on the lip of Temeraire's cave. 'He eats so much, and will never take less, even if it's short commons all around. But he is the biggest, and there should not be fighting, so the general rule is that caves go by who is strongest if there is any quarrel. No one is allowed to take a place out of his class, or others will get jealous and squabble.'

'You see, it is just as I told you: all unfairness,' Perscitia said bitterly, 'as if the only quality of any importance were one's weight, or how good one is at scratching and biting and kicking up a fuss; never any consideration for really remarkable qualities.'

'I grant it has some practical sense as a way to choose caves,' Temeraire said, 'but it is nonsense that after I have taken one— One that he might have had at any time before I came, and did not want —he should be able to snatch it from me after I have gone to so much trouble to make it

27

nice. And he is not stronger than me, either, if he does weigh more. I should like to know if he has sunk a frigate, alone, with a Fleur-de-Nuit on his back? And as for distinction, my ancestors were scholars in China while his were starving in pits.'

'Be that as it may, he knows all the council, and you don't,' Moncey said, practically. 'You are hardly going to fight a dozen heavyweights at once, and beg pardon, but no one looking at you would say, "right-o, there is a match for old Requiescat." Not that you are little, but you are a bit skinny-looking.'

'I am *not*. Am I?' Temeraire said, craning his head anxiously to look back at himself. He did not have spines along his back the way Maximus or Requiescat did, but was rather sleek; perhaps a bit long for his weight, by British standards. 'But anyway, he is not a fire-breather, or an acid-spitter.'

'Are you?' Moncey inquired.

'No,' Temeraire said, 'but I have the divine wind. Laurence says that is even better.' However, it belatedly occurred to him that perhaps Laurence might have been speaking partially; certainly Moncey and Perscitia looked blank, and it was difficult to explain just how it operated. 'I roar, in a particular sort of way—I have to breathe quite deeply, and there is a clenching feeling, along the throat, and then—and then it makes things break—trees, and so on,' Temeraire finished in an ashamed mutter, conscious that it sounded very dull and useless, when so described. 'It is very unpleasant to be caught in it,' he added defensively, 'at least, so I understand from how others have reacted, if they are before me when I use it.'

'How interesting,' Perscitia said, politely, 'I have often wondered what sound is, exactly; we ought to do some experiments.'

'Experiments aren't going to help you with the council,' Moncey said.

Temeraire switched his tail against his side, thinking, before saying with some distaste, 'No, I see that: it is all politics. It is plain to me: I must work out what Lien would do.'

He cornered Lloyd, the next morning, and said, 'Lloyd, I am very hungry today; may I have an extra cow, to take up to my cave?'

'There, that is a little more like it,' Lloyd said approvingly; not deaf at all to a request so satisfactory to his own ideas of dragon-husbandry. He ordered it directly, and while waiting Temeraire asked, attempting a casual air, 'I do not suppose you might recall, who Gentius has sired?'

The old Longwing cracked a bleary eye, when Temeraire landed, and peered at him rather incuriously. 'Yes?' he said. His cave was not so large, but a comfortable dry hollow tucked well under the mountainside, on ground overlooking a curve of the creek; so positioned that he only had to creep downhill for a drink, and walk a short distance to a large flat rock full in the sun, where he presently lay napping.

'I beg your pardon for not coming to visit you before, sir,' Temeraire said, inclining his head, 'I have served with Excidium these last three years at Dover—Your third hatchling,' he added, when Gentius looked vague.

'Yes, Excidium, of course,' Gentius said, his tongue licking the air experimentally. Temeraire laid the cow down before him, butchered with the help of Moncey's small claws to take out the large bones. 'A small gift to show my respect,' Temeraire said, and Gentius brightened. 'Why, that is *trés gentil* of you,' he said, with atrocious pronunciation, which Temeraire remembered just in time not to correct, and took the cow into his mouth to gum at it slowly with the wobbly remainders of his teeth. 'Most kind, as my first captain liked

29

to say,' Gentius mumbled reminiscently around it. 'You might go in there and bring out her picture,' he added, 'if you are very careful with it.'

The portrait was rather odd and flat-looking, and the woman in it very plain, even before time and the elements had faded her; but it was in a really splendid golden frame, so large and thick that Temeraire could take it delicately between two talon-tips to lift it, and carry it out into the sun. 'How beautiful,' he said sincerely, holding it where Gentius could at least point his head in its direction, although his eyes were so milky with cataracts he could not have seen it as more than a blur in the golden square.

'Charming woman,' Gentius said, sadly. 'She fed me my first bite, fresh liver, when my head was no bigger than her hand. One never quite gets over the first, you know.'

'Yes,' Temeraire said, low, and looked away unhappily; at least Gentius had not had her taken from him, and put who knew where.

When he had put the portrait back with equal care, and listened to a long story about one of the wars in which Gentius had fought – something with the Prussians, where pepper guns had been invented: very unpleasant things, especially when one had not been expecting them – then Gentius was quite ready to be sympathetic, and to shake his head censoriously over Requiescat's behaviour. 'No proper manners, these days, that is what it is.'

'I am very glad to hear you say so: that is just what I thought, but as I am quite young, I did not feel sure without advice from someone wiser, like yourself,' Temeraire said, and then with sudden inspiration added, 'I suppose next he will propose that if any of us have some treasure that he likes, gold or jewels, we must give it to him: it follows quite plainly.'

That was indeed enough to rouse Gentius up, with so

handsome a treasure of his own to consider. 'I do not see that you are wrong at all,' he said, darkly. 'Of course, we cannot have Winchesters taking caves fit for Regal Coppers, there would be no end of trouble and quarrelling, and sooner or later the men will involve themselves, and make it all even worse. They somehow think Reapers of less use than Anglewings, because there are more of them and they are clannish, instead of the other way round, and they have many more such odd notions. But that is not the same as taking away a cave perfectly suitable to your weight and standing.' He paused and said delicately, 'I do not suppose you had a formation of your own?'

'No,' Temeraire said, 'at least, not officially. Arkady and the others fought under my orders, and I was wing-mates with Maximus: he is Laetificat's hatchling.'

'Laetificat, yes; fine dragon,' Gentius said. 'I served with her, you know, in '76; we had a dust-up with the colonials at Boston. They had artillery above our positions—'

Temeraire came away eventually with Gentius's firm promise to attend the council-meeting, and returned to his cave pleased with the success of his primary efforts. 'Who else is on the council?' he asked.

While Perscitia began listing off names, Reedly, a mongrel half-Winchester, courier-weight with yellow streaks, piped up from the corner, 'You ought to speak to Majestatis.'

Perscitia bristled at once. 'I see no reason why he ought do any such thing. Majestatis is a very common sort of dragon; and he is not on the council, anyway.'

'He made sure I got a share of the food, when we were all sick, and things were short,' Minnow said, on the other side. She was a muddy-coloured feral with touches of Grey Copper and Sharpspitter and even a little Garde-de-Lyon, which had given her vivid orange eyes and blue spots to set off her otherwise drab colouring.

A low murmur of general agreement went around. A crowd had gradually accumulated in Temeraire's cave to offer their advice and remarks. A good many of the smaller dragons had interested themselves in Temeraire's case: those he had sheltered and their acquaintances, and the not-insignificant number, who had some injury, real or imagined, to lay at Requiescat's door. 'And he is not on the council only because he does not care to be; he is a Parnassian.' she said to Temeraire.

'If he were a Flamme de Gloire, it would hardly signify,' Perscitia said coldly, 'as he does nothing but sleep all the time.'

Moncey nudged Temeraire with his head and murmured, 'Corrected her once, six years ago.'

'It was only an error of arithmetic!' Perscitia said heatedly. 'I should have found it out myself in a moment, I was only preoccupied by the much more important question—'

'Where does he live?' Temeraire asked, interrupting. He felt that anyone who had no have time for politics must be rather sensible.

Majestatis was indeed sleeping when Temeraire came to see him; his cave was out of the way, and not very large. But Temeraire noticed that there was a carefully placed heap of stones, along the back, which blocked one's view into the interior. If he widened his pupils as far as they would go, he thought he could make out a darker space behind them, as if there were a passageway going back deeper into the mountainside.

He coiled himself neatly and waited without fidgeting, as was polite. But at length, when Majestatis showed no signs of waking, Temeraire coughed, then coughed again a little more emphatically. Majestatis sighed and said, without opening his eyes, 'So you are not leaving, I suppose?'

'Oh,' Temeraire said, his ruff prickling, 'I thought you

were only sleeping, not ignoring me deliberately. I will go at once.'

'Well, you might as well stay *now*,' Majestatis said, lifting his head and yawning himself awake. 'I don't bother to wake up if it isn't important enough to wait for, that's all.'

'I suppose that is sensible, if you like to sleep better than to have a conversation,' Temeraire said, dubiously.

'You'll like it better in a few years yourself,' Majestatis said.

'I do not expect so,' Temeraire said. 'At least, the Analects say it is not proper for a dragon to sleep more than fourteen hours of the day, so I shan't, unless,' he added, desolately, 'I am still shut up in here, where there is nothing worth doing.'

'If you think so, what are you doing here, instead of in the coverts?' Majestatis said. He listened to the explanation with the casual sympathy of one listening to a storyteller, and passed no judgment, other than to nod equably and say, 'A bad lot for you, poor worm.'

'Why have *you* come here?' Temeraire ventured. 'You are not very old, yourself; do you really like to sleep so much? You might have a captain, and be in battles.'

Majestatis shrugged with one wing-tip, flared and folded down again. 'Had one, mislaid him.'

'Mislaid?' Temeraire said.

'Well,' Majestatis said, 'I left him in a water-trough, but I don't suppose he is still sitting there.'

He was not inclined to be very enthusiastic, even when Temeraire had explained,. He only sighed and said, 'You are young, to be making such a fuss out of it.'

'If I am,' Temeraire retorted, 'at least I am not complacent, and ready to let this sort of bullying go on, when I can do something about it; and I do not mean to be satisfied,' he added, with a pointed look at the back of Majestatis's cave, 'to arrange matters better only for myself.'

Majestatis's eyes narrowed, but he did not stir otherwise. 'It seems to me you are as likely to make it worse for everyone at least. There's no wrangling now, and no one is getting hurt.'

'No one is very comfortable, either,' Temeraire said. 'We all might have nicer places, but no one will work to improve theirs; they will not if they know it may be taken away from them, at any time, because they have made it nice. Once a cave is yours, it ought to *be yours*, like property.'

The council looked a little dubious at this argument, when Temeraire repeated it to them the next afternoon. Early that morning, the rain had been broken by a strong westerly wind sweeping the clouds scudding before it. They had gathered in a great clearing among the mountains, full of pleasant broad smooth-topped rocks, warmed by the sun. Majestatis had come after all, and Gentius, although the old dragon was mostly asleep after the effort of making the flight. He was curled up on the blackest rock, murmuring occasionally to himself. Requiescat sprawled inelegantly across half the length of the clearing, making himself look very large. Temeraire disdained the attempt and kept himself neatly coiled, with his ruff spread proudly, although he privately wished he might have had his talon-sheaths, and a head-dress such as he had seen in the markets along the old silk caravan roads; he was sure that could not fail to impress.

Ballista, a big Chequered Nettle, thumped her barbed tail on the ground several times to silence the muttering that had arisen among the council, in the middle of Temeraire's remarks. 'And if we agree that everyone may keep their own cave, when they have got it,' Temeraire went on, valiantly, in the face of so much scepticism, 'I would be very happy to share the trick of arranging them better. You all may have nicer caves, if you only take a little trouble to make them so.'

34

'Very nice I am sure if you are a yearling' one peevish older Parnassian said, 'to be fussing with rocks and twigs.'

There were several snorts of agreement; and Temeraire bristled. 'If you do not care to, and you are happy with your cave as it is, then you need not. But neither should you be able to take someone else's cave, when they have done all the work. I am certainly not going to be robbed as if I were a lump. I will smash the cave up myself and make it unpleasant before I hand it over meekly.'

'Now, now.' Ballista said. 'There is no call to go yelling about smashing things or making threats; that is quite enough of that. Now we'll hear Requiescat.'

'Hum, quarrelsome, isn't he,' Requiescat said. 'Well, you all know me chums and I don't mean to make a brag of myself, but I expect no one would say I couldn't take any cave I liked if I wanted to. I am not a squabbler, and don't like to hurt anybody; a young fellow like this is excitable enough to bite off a bigger fight than he can swallow—'

'Oh!' Temeraire said indignantly. 'You may not claim any such thing, unless you should like to prove it. I have beaten dragons nearly as big as you.'

Requiescat swung his big head around. 'Isn't it true you're bred not to fight? Persy was going about saying some such.'

Perscitia gave an angry yelp 'I never!' But was quickly stifled by the other small dragons sitting around her at Ballista's censorious glare.

'Celestials,' Temeraire said, very coolly, 'are bred to be the very best sort of dragon. In China, we are not supposed to fight unless the nation is in danger, because China has a good deal more dragons than here and we are too valuable to lose. So we only fight in emergencies, when ordinary fighting dragons are not up to the task.'

'Oh, China,' Requiescat said dismissively. 'Anyway chums, there you have it plain as day. I say I am tops, and ought to have the best cave; he says it isn't so, and he won't hand it over. Ordinarily, there'd be no ways to work this out 'cept with a tussle, and then someone gets hurt and everyone is upset. This is just the sort of thing the council was made up for, and I expect it ought to be pretty clear to all of you which of us is right, without it coming to claws.'

'I do not say I am *tops*,' Temeraire said, 'although I think it likely. I say that the cave is mine, and that it is unjust for you to take it. *That* is what the council ought to be for. Justice, not squashing everyone down, just to keep things comfortable for the biggest dragons.'

The council, being composed of the biggest dragons, did not look very enthusiastic. Ballista said, 'All right, we have heard everyone out. Now look, *Teymuhreer*,' she pronounced it quite wrongly, 'we don't want a lot of fuss and bother—'

'I do not see why not,' Temeraire said. 'What else have we to do?'

Several of the smaller dragons tittered, rustling their wings together. She cleared her throat warningly at them and continued, 'We don't want a lot of fighting, anyhow. Why don't you just go on and show us a bit of flying, so we know what you can do; then we can settle this.'

'But that is not at all the point!' Temeraire said. 'It ought not make a difference if I were as small as Moncey—' he looked, but Moncey was not among the little dragons observing, so he amended, 'or if I were as small as Minnow there. No one was using it, no one wanted the cave before I had it.'

Requiescat gave a flip of his wings. 'It was not the nicest, before,' he said, in reasonable tones.

Temeraire snorted angrily. 'Yes, yes; go on, then; unless you don't like us to see,' Ballista said impatiently. That was too much to bear. He threw himself aloft, spiralling high and fast as he could, tightening into a spring, and then dived directly into formation manoeuvres, that was what would please them, he thought bitterly. He finished the training pass and backwinged directly, flying the pattern backwards, and then hovered in mid-air before descending sharply. He was showing off, of course, but they had demanded he do so. Landing, he announced, 'I will show you the divine wind now, but you had better clear away from that rock wall, as I expect a lot of it will come down.'

There was a good deal of grumbling as the big dragons shifted themselves, with dragging tails and annoyed looks. Temeraire ignored them and breathed in deeply several times, stretching his chest wide, as he meant to do as much damage as he could. He noticed in dismay, that the crag was not loose, nor made of the same nice soft white limestone in the caves, which crumbled so conveniently. He scraped a claw down the rockface and merely left white scratches on the hard grey rock.

'Well?' Ballista said. 'We are all waiting.'

There was no helping it. Temeraire backed away from the cliff and drew a preparatory breath. Then there was a hurried rush of wings above and Moncey dropped into the clearing beside him, panting, and said, 'Call it off; it's all off,' urgently, to Ballista.

'Hey, what's this, now?' Requiescat said, frowning.

'Quiet, you fat lump,' Moncey said, narrowing a good many eyes; he was not much bigger than the Regal Copper's head. 'I'm fresh from Brecon. The Frogs have come over the Channel.'

A great confused babble arose all around, even Gentius roused with a low hiss, and while everyone spoke at once, Moncey turned to Temeraire and said, 'Listen, your Laurence, word is in they locked him up on a ship called the *Goliath*—'

'The *Goliath*!' Temeraire said. 'I know that ship. Laurence has spoken of it to me before. That is very good—That is splendid. I know just where it is, it is on blockade, and I am sure anyone at Dover can tell me exactly where—'

'Dear fellow, there's no good way to say this,' Moncey said. 'The Frogs sank her this morning, coming across. She is at the bottom of the ocean, and not a man got off her before she went down.'

Temeraire did not say anything. A terrible sensation was rising, climbing up his throat. He turned away to let it come. The roar burst out like the roll of thunder overhead, silencing every word around him, and the wall of stone cracked open before him like a pane of mirrored glass.

Chapter Three

They pulled the ship's boats into Dover harbour well past eleven o'clock at night, sweating underneath their wet clothing, hands blistered on the oars. They climbed out shivering onto the docks. Captain Puget was handed up in a litter, almost senseless with blood-loss, and Lieutenant Frye, nineteen, was the only one left to oversee. The rest of the senior officers were dead. Frye looked at Laurence with great uncertainty, then glanced around. The men offered him nothing, they were beaten with rowing and defeat. At last, Laurence quietly offered, 'The port admiral,' prompting him. Frye coloured and said to a gangly young midshipman, clearing his throat, 'Mr. Meed, you had better take the prisoner to the port admiral, and let him decide what is to be done.'

With two Marines for guards, Laurence followed Meed through the dockside streets to the port admiral's office where they found nearly more confusion than had been on the deck of the *Goliath* in her last moments. After the double broadside had un-masted her, smoke had spread everywhere, fire crawling steadily down through the ship towards the powder magazine, as cannon ran wildly back and forth on her decks.

Here the hallways were suffocating with unchecked speculation. 'Five hundred thousand men landed,' one man said in
the hallway, a ridiculous number, inflated by panic. 'Already
in London,' said another, 'and two millions in shipping seized,'
the very last of these being the only plausible suggestion. If
Bonaparte had captured one or two of the ports on the Thames
estuary and taken the merchantmen there, he might indeed
have reached something like that number. He would have
seized an enormous collection of prizes to fuel the invasion,
like coal heaped into a burning stove.

'I do not give a damn if you take him out and lynch him,
only get him out of my sight,' the port admiral said furiously, when Meed finally managed to work his way through
the press and ask him for orders. There was a vast roar
outside the windows like the wind rising in a storm, even
though the night was clear. More petitioners were shoving
frantically past them. Laurence had to catch Meed by the
arm and hold him up as they fought their way out. The boy
could scarcely have been fourteen and was a little underfed.

Set adrift, Meed looked helpless. Laurence wondered if
he would have to find his own prison, but then one young
lieutenant pushed through towards them, flung him a look
of flat contempt, and said, 'That is the traitor, is it? This
way. You dogs take a damned proper hold of him, before
he sneaks away in this press.'

He took up an old truncheon in the hallway, and swinging
it to clear the way, took them out into the street. Meed
trotted after him gratefully. The lieutenant brought them to
a run-down sponging house two streets away, with bars upon
the windows and a mastiff tied in the barren yard. It howled
unhappily, adding to the clamour of the half-rioting crowd.
A beating upon the door brought out the master of the house.
He whined objections, which the lieutenant overruled one
after another, but at last conceded.

'Better than you deserve,' he said to Laurence coldly, as he held open the door of a small and squalid attic. He was a slight young man with a struggling moustache. A solid push would have laid him out upon the unkempt floor. Laurence looked at him for a moment, and then stepped inside, stooping under the lintel. The door was shut upon him. Through the wall he heard the lieutenant ordering the two Marines to stand watch, and the owner's complaints trailing him back down the stairs.

It was bitterly cold. The irregular floor of warped and knotted boards felt strange under Laurence's feet, still expecting the listing motion of the ship. There was a handkerchief-square of a window, which at present let in only the thick smell of smoke. Shining rooftops, lit by a reddish glow, were all that he could see.

Laurence sat down on the narrow cot and looked at his hands. There would be fighting all along the coast by now. Men would have landed at Sheerness, and likely along points north, all around the mouth of the Thames. Not five hundred thousand, nothing like that, but enough perhaps. It would not take a very large company of infantry to establish a secure beachhead, then Napoleon could land men as quick as he could get them across the Channel.

This, Laurence would have said, could be not very quickly. Not in the face of the Navy. But that opinion fell before the manoeuvres he had witnessed today. Pitting great numbers of lightweights, easy to feed and quick to manoeuvre, against the British heavyweights, and using their own heavyweights against the British ships flew in the face of all common wisdom. But it bore the same tactical stamp as the whirling attack which he had witnessed at Jena, spearheaded by Lien. Laurence had no doubt her advice had also served Napoleon in this latest adventure.

Laurence had reported on the battle of Jena to the

Admiralty. It was a bitter thought to know that his treason had now undermined that intelligence, and likely discredited all his reports. He thought Jane at least would still have kept it under consideration. Even if she had not forgiven him, she knew him well enough to know that his treason had begun and ended with delivering the cure. But from what he had seen of the battle, the British dragons were still locked in the same antiquated habits of aerial war.

The noises outside the window rose and fell like the sea. Somewhere nearby glass was breaking and a woman shrieked. The red glow brightened. He lay down and tried to sleep a little, but his rest was broken repeatedly by ragged eruptions of noise, falling back into the general din by the time he jarred awake, panting and sore. In his dreams, fragmentary images of the burning ship, which became glossy, black scales beneath the flames, curling and crisping at the edges. He rose once. There was a small dirty pitcher of water, but he was not yet thirsty enough to resort to it for a drink. He splashed his face with a cupped handful. His fingers came away streaked with soot and grime. He lay down again, there was more screaming outside, and a stronger smell of smoke.

It did not so much as grow light, as simply less dark. There was a thick sooty pall over the city, and his throat ached sharply. No one came with food, and he received not a word from his guards. Laurence paced his cell restlessly. Four long strides across, three lengthwise from the bed, but he used smaller steps and made it seven. His arms, clasped behind his back, felt as though they were weighted down with roundshot. He had rowed for five hours without a pause.

That at least had been something to do, something besides this useless fretting. The city was burning, and all he could do here was burn with it, or moulder to be taken a prisoner by the French, with Napoleon's army scarcely ten miles distant. And even if he died, Temeraire might never know. He might keep himself a prisoner long for lost cause, and be taken by the French. Laurence could not trust Napoleon with Temeraire's safety, not while Lien was his ally. Her voice, and the self-interest which would prompt him to be the master of the only Celestial outside China's borders, would be more persuasive than his generosity.

The guards might be tempted to let him out by their own desire to be gone, if only Laurence could convince himself he had any right to go. But he had been court-martialled and convicted, and justly so, with all due process of law. Though he would gladly have foregone the dragging out of evidence, he had been condemned already by his own voice. The panel of officers had listened with blank faces, tight with disgust. All were Navy officers, no aviator had been allowed to serve. Too many had been pulled into the vile business, implicated and smeared in any way they could be. Ferris, was singled out because Laurence must have confided in his first lieutenant. 'And it must present a curious appearance to the court,' the prosecutor had said, sneering, while Ferris sat drawn and pale and wretched and did not look at Laurence, 'that he did not raise the alarm for an hour after the accused and his beast were known to be missing, and did not at once open the letter which was left behind—'

Chenery too had been named, and only because he had also been in London covert at the time. Berkley and Little and Sutton, were all brought in to give evidence, and if Harcourt and Jane had not been mentioned, it was only because the Admiralty did not know how to do so without embarrassing themselves more than their targets. 'I did not know a damned thing about the business, and I am sure nor did anyone else. Anyone who knows Laurence will tell you he would not have breathed a word of it to anyone,' Chenery had said defiantly. 'But I do say that sending over the sick beast was a blackguardly thing for the Admiralty to have done, and if you want to hang me for saying so, you are welcome.'

They had not hanged Chenery, thank God, for lack of evidence and for need of his dragon, but Ferris, a lieutenant with no such protection, had been broken out of the service. Every effort Laurence had made to insist that the guilt was his alone had been ignored. A fine officer had been lost to the service, his career and his life spoilt. Laurence had met his mother and his brothers. They were an old family and proud. But Ferris had been away from home from the age of seven, so they did not have that intimate knowledge, which should make them confident of his innocence, and replace the affectionate support from his fellow-officers now denied to him. To witness his misery and know himself culpable hurt Laurence worse than his own conviction had done.

That had never been in any doubt. There had been no defence to make, and no comfort but the arid certainty that he had done as he ought. That he could have done nothing else. It offered scarce comfort, but saved him from the pain of regret. He could not regret what he had done, he could not have let ten thousand dragons, most of them wholly uninvolved in the war, be murdered for his nation's advantage. When he had said as much, and freely confessed that he had disobeyed his orders, assaulted a Marine, stolen the cure, and given aid and comfort to the enemy, there was nothing else to say. The only charge he contested, was that he had stolen Temeraire, too. 'He is neither the King's possession nor a dumb beast. His choice was his own and it was freely made,' Laurence had said, but he had been ignored, of course. He had scarcely been taken from the room before he was brought back in again to hear his sentence of death pronounced.

And then it had been quietly postponed. He had been hurried under guard, from the chamber and into a stifling, black-draped carriage. After a long rattling journey ending at Sheerness, he had been put aboard the *Lucinda* and then transferred to *Goliath*. He had been confined to the brig, an oubliette meant only to keep him breathing. It was a living death, worse than the hanging he was promised in future.

But that was not his choice to make. He had made one choice, and sacrificed all the others. His life was no longer his own, even if the court chose to leave it to him a little while longer. To flee now would be no more honourable than to have fled straight to China, or to have accepted Napoleon's solicitations. He could not go. He had no other way of believing himself loyal, he could make no other reparation. He might look at the door, but he could not open it.

A brief glaze of rain washed the window and thinned the smoke outside. He went to stand by the glass, though he could not see anything but a grey dimness. The sun, if it had come up, stayed hidden.

The doorknob rattled and the door opened. Laurence turned and stared at the man on the other side. His lean, travel-leathered face and oriental features were familiar but unexpected. 'I hope I find you in good health,' Tharkay said. 'Will you come with me? I believe there is still a danger of fire.'

The guards had vanished. The house was entirely deserted, but for a couple of men who had wandered in drunk off the street and were sleeping in the front hall. Laurence stepped over their legs and out into the morning. A thin pallid haze of smoke and false dawn lay over the docks, drifting out to sea. Glass, broken slate and charred wood littered the street, with other unspeakable trash. Sweepers lugubriously pushed their brooms down the middle of the lane, doing little to help.

Tharkay led Laurence down a side alley where the dead body of a horse, stripped of saddle and bridle, blocked the way. A young kestrel with long trailing jesses was perched on its side, occasionally tearing at the flesh and uttering satisfied cries. Tharkay held out his hand and whistled, and the kestrel came back to him, to be hooded and secured upon his shoulder.

'I am three weeks back from the Pamirs,' Tharkay said. 'I brought another dozen feral beasts for your ranks. In good time, it seems. Roland sent me to bring you in.'

'But how came you here?' Laurence said, while they picked their way onward through the unfashionable back streets. The town already looked as though it had been sacked. Windows and doors still intact, were shut tight, some boarded, giving the house-fronts an unfriendly air. 'How did you know I was in the town—'

'The town was not the difficulty. The wreckers off the coast knew which way the *Goliath*'s boats had gone,' Tharkay said. 'I was here before you were, I imagine. Finding out where you had been stowed was more difficult. I foolishly went to the trouble of obtaining these, first,' showing Laurence a folded packet of papers, 'from the port admiral, in the assumption he would know the whereabouts of the prisoner he was assigning to me. But he left me in the hall for over two hours, and quarrelled with me for another. Only when I had his signature did he at last confess to having not the slightest knowledge where you might be.'

They came to a clearing, a courier-covert, where little Gherni waited for them fidgeting anxiously. She hissed at Tharkay urgently. He answered her in the same tangled dragon-language, which Laurence could not understand, and then clambered up her scanty rigging to her back, pointing out the couple of hand-holds Laurence should use to get himself aboard.

'We may have some difficulty on our journey,' Tharkay said. 'Almost all of Bonaparte's men are stationed on the coast, but his dragons are going deep inland. Fifty thousand men, I believe,' he answered, when Laurence asked how they faced, 'and as many as two hundred beasts, if one cares to believe the figure. The Corps has fallen back with the rest of the army, to Rainham. I imagine to await Bonaparte's pleasure, as for why they are being so courteous, you would have to ask the generals.'

'I thank you for coming,' Laurence said. Tharkay had risked a great deal, with half of Bonaparte's army between him and the coast. 'You have taken service, then?' he asked, looking at Tharkay's coat. He wore gold bars: a captain's rank. In the army it was not uncommon for a man to be commissioned only when he was needed, but it was a rare phenomenon in the Corps, where the type of dragon dictated rank. But with Tharkay was one of the few who could speak with the feral dragons of the Pamirs it was no surprise the Corps had wanted him. It was more of one that he had accepted a commission.

'For now.' Tharkay shrugged.

'No one could accuse you of making a self-interested choice,' Laurence said grimly, with the smell of the burning city in his nostrils.

'One of its advantages,' Tharkay said. 'Any fool could throw in his lot with a victor.'

Laurence did not ask why he had been sent. Fifty thousand men landed was answer enough. Temeraire must be wanted, and Laurence the only, however undesirable, means to obtain his services. It was a pragmatic and temporary choice, nothing to give him hope of forgiveness either personal or legal. Tharkay volunteered no more, Gherni was already springing aloft, and the wind blew all possible words away.

The sky held the peculiar crispness of late autumn, blue, clear and cloudless, beautiful flying weather. They had scarcely been half an hour aloft when Gherni suddenly plunged beneath them, and trembling went to ground in a wooded clearing of pines. Laurence had seen nothing, but he and Tharkay pushed forward to the edge of the woods and peered out from the shade. Two shapes leapt from the ground, and approached. The two big grey-and-brown dragons, glided with lazy assurance, and well they might. Grand Chevaliers were the largest of the French heavy-weights, and only a little smaller than Regal Coppers. Each had what looked close to a dozen stupefied cows dangling in their belly-netting, occasionally uttering groggy and perplexed moans, and pawing ineffectually at the air with their hooves.

The pair went by calling to each other cheerfully in French too colloquial and rapid for Laurence to follow, their crews laughing. Their shadows passed like scudding clouds. Gherni held very still beneath the branches. Her eyes were the only part of her which moved, tracking the great dragons' passage overhead.

She could not be persuaded back aloft, afterwards, but curled up as deeply as she could, and proposed that they should bring her something to eat instead. She would not go up again until it was dark. That the French Fleur de Nuits would be out then, was not an argument Laurence wished to attempt, for fear of her refusing to go on at all. Tharkay only shrugged, examined his pistols, and put himself on a track towards the nearby farmhouses. 'Perhaps the Chevaliers have not eaten all the cattle.'

There were no cows left visible, nor sheep, nor people. Only a scattering of unhappy chickens, upon which Tharkay methodically loosed the kestrel, taking one after another. They would not make much dinner for Gherni, but they were better than nothing. then they discovered a small pig in the stable, rooting in the straw, oblivious both to the fate it had earlier escaped and the one now descending upon it.

Gherni was neither picky nor patient enough to demand her pork cooked, and they roasted the chickens for themselves over a small, well-banked fire, feeding the kestrel on the sweetbreads, and waving their hands through the smoke to thin it out. Without salt the meat had little flavour, but did well enough to fill their stomachs. They gnawed down to the bones, rubbed their greasy hands clean with grass, and buried the remnants.

And then they had only to wait for the sun to go down. It was scarcely noon, and the ground cold and hard to sit upon, the wind blowing a steady chill into fingers and feet, despite their stamping. But Laurence could stand when he chose, and go to the edge of the copse and feel the wind blowing into his face, and see the placid well-ruled fields in their orderly brown ranks and tall white birch-trees raising their limbs high against the unbroken sky.

Tharkay came and stood beside him. There was no alteration in his looks or manner. If he was silent, he had been silent before. To be able to stand here for a moment, not as a traitor, but only himself, unchanged, in the company of another, was to Laurence as liberating as the absence of locks and barred doors. He had suffered wide disapproval before without intolerable pain, when he knew himself in the right. He had not known it could be so heavy.

Tharkay said, 'I might never have found you, of course.'

It was an offer, and Laurence was ashamed to be tempted; tempted so strongly that he could not immediately make his refusal, not with freedom open before him and the stench of smoke and the ship's bilges still thick in the back of his throat.

'My idea of duty is not yours,' Tharkay said. 'But I can think of no reason why you should owe a pointless death to any man.'

'Honour is sufficient purpose,' Laurence said, low.

'Very well,' Tharkay said, 'if your death would preserve it better than your life. But yet the world is not shared between Britain and Napoleon, and you do not need to die. You and Temeraire would be welcome in other parts of the world. You may recall there is some semblance of civilization,' he added dryly, 'in a few places, beyond the borders of England.'

'I do not—' Laurence said, struggling, 'I will not pretend that I do not consider it, for Temeraire's sake if not my own. But to fly would be to make myself truly a traitor.'

'Laurence,' Tharkay said, after a pause, 'you *are* a traitor.' It was a blow to hear him say so, in his cool blunt way. The lack of passion in his words only made them seem less accusation than statement of fact. 'Allowing them to put you to death for it may be your form of apology, but it does not make you less guilty.'

Laurence did not know how to answer. Of course Tharkay was right. It was useless to cry that he loved his country, and had betrayed her only *in extremis*, as the lesser of two hideous evils. He had betrayed her, and the cause mattered not. So perhaps he now condemned Temeraire to lonely servitude, and himself to life-long imprisonment, for nothing. Perhaps all that could be lost, had been lost. And yet he could not answer.

They stood silently for a long time. At last, Tharkay shook his head and put his hand on Laurence's shoulder. 'It is getting dark.'

'Yes, I sent for him,' Jane said flatly. 'And you may leave off your coughing and your insinuations, if I wanted a man between my legs that badly, there is a camp full of handsome young fellows outside, and I dare say I could find one out to oblige me without going to such trouble.'

Having momentarily appalled her audience of generals and ministers into silence, she rode on, 'If the French took him prisoner, they would have two Celestials; and even if the two are too close related to breed direct, they will cross-breed them—perhaps to Grand Chevaliers, if you like to imagine that—and breed the offspring back to fix the traits. In one generation they will have a breed of their own, and we nothing. We haven't a single egg out of Temeraire yet. Put Laurence in a gaol-wagon and bring him along under guard, if you insist, but if you have any sense you will make use of him, and the beast.'

The atmosphere in the tent was not a convivial one. Conversation circled endlessly around the disaster of the landing and Laurence had already gathered enough to realise that Jane had not been in command of the aerial defence, after all. Sanderson had been made admiral at Dover, over her head.

For what reason, Laurence scarcely needed to wonder. They had never liked making her commander, but having been forced to do it by necessity, they would likely have gone on rather than admit a mistake. Had they not wanted vengeance, had they not thought her complicit in Laurence's treason.

As for Sanderson, Laurence knew little about the man. He was handler to a Parnassian and commanded a large independent formation at Dover. They had served together, but not closely. Thoroughly experienced but no brilliant officer, Sanderson's attention was badly divided. Though his Artemisia had been dosed with the cure several times, she still fared poorly from the after-effects of the epidemic. It had nearly killed him too. He was not a year short of sixty, and had scarcely slept or eaten while his dragon ailed.

He now sat in a corner of the tent and dabbing an oozing cut over his eye with a folded bandage. He said nothing while the generals shouted at Jane instead. He looked grey and faded under the bright bloody streak across his forehead.

'Splendid, so you would put a known traitor and his uncontrollable beast into the middle of our lines,' one member of the Navy Board said. 'You may as well rig up a telegraph and signal our plans to Bonaparte at once.'

'Bonaparte can't damned well have an easier time of it than he has already, unless you run up a white flag,' Jane snapped. 'He has a hundred dragons more than he ought to, by any counting. You Admiralty gentlemen swear up and down that we would know he'd stripped Prussia and Italy to the bone, so I suppose he is pulling them out of the trees, and as we can't do the same, we must have every last beast we can scrounge. Six beasts too injured to fight in the next month, four of our newest ferals slunk off, and you want to let a Celestial moulder. It's pure idiocy.'

'Why precisely are we listening to this haranguing fish-wife?' someone said.

'To be more precise,' Jane said, 'you are not listening to me. But you had better start. Begging your pardon Sanderson, you are a damned fine formation-leader, but you weren't the man for this.'

'No, not at all, Roland,' Sanderson said, dully, and patted the cloth to his forehead again.

'We are listening to her,' another general from the back, said impatiently; he was a lean sharp-faced man with a decided aquiline nose, and wore the Order of the Bath, 'because you could not scrape up a competent man for the job. We are not going to beat Bonaparte with yesterday's mess.'

'Portland—' another began.

'Stop bleating the man's name like a talisman,' the general

returned. 'If it is not Nelson with you, it is Portland. Gibraltar is as bad as Denmark, neither of them can be here in under a month. Until then, get out of her way.'

'General Wellesley, you cannot seriously support the suggestion—' another minister said, gesturing to Laurence.

'I am capable of deciding to what I will support, without consultation. Thank you,' Wellesley said. He looked Laurence up and down with a cold dismissive eye. 'He's a sentimentalist, isn't he—surrendered himself? Damned romantic. What difference does it make? Hang him after.'

Jane took him to her tent. 'No, you had better stay, Frette,' she said, speaking to her aide-de-camp, who had risen from a camp-table as she ducked inside. 'I will not make hay for any more rumours.'

She poured herself a glass of wine, and drank it with her back to Laurence. He could not quarrel with her decision, but he wished that they had been alone. He felt it impossible to speak as he wished before anyone else. Then she put down the glass and sat down behind her desk. 'Tomorrow you will go by courier to Pen Y Fan,' she said tiredly, without looking at him. 'That is where they have been keeping Temeraire. Will you bring him back?'

'Yes, of course,' Laurence said.

'They will very likely hang you after, unless you manage to do something heroic,' Jane said.

'If I wished to avoid justice, I might have stayed in France,' Laurence said. 'Jane—'

'Admiral Roland, if you please,' she said, sharply. After a moment's silence, she added, 'I cannot blame you, Laurence. Christ knows it was ugly. But if I am to do any good here, I cannot be fighting their damned Lordships as well as Napoleon's dragons. Frette will take you to the officers' tent to eat, and then find you somewhere to sleep. You will go tomorrow, and when you come back you will be flying in formation, under Admiral Sanderson. That will be all.'

She gave a jerk of her head, and Frette held open the tent flap clearing his throat. Laurence could only bow, and withdraw slowly, wishing he had not seen her drop her forehead to her clenched fist, and the grimness around her mouth.

He felt a dreadful sense of awkwardness when entered the large mess tent in Frette's company. He saw none of his nearest acquaintance, and was glad to postpone that evil, but several remarks were made by little known captains. He pretended not to hear, the discomfort and downcast faces of those who would not snub him, but still did not choose to meet his eyes, was worse.

He had been braced for this, so was unprepared when his hand was seized, and aggressively pumped by a gentleman he had only seen perhaps twice before, across the officers' common room at Dover. Captain Hesterfield loudly said, 'May I shake your hand, sir?' too late for the request to be refused, and then nearly bodily dragged Laurence over to his table in the corner, and presented him to his companions.

There were six officers at the small and huddled table. Two of them were Prussians, one of whom, Von Pfeil, Laurence recognized from the siege of Danzig, and another who introduced himself as cousin to Captain Dyhern, with whom they had fought at the Battle of Jena. They were now refugees, having chosen exile and service in Britain over the parole Napoleon had offered to Prussian officers.

Another stranger, Captain Prewitt, had been recalled to England a few months before, out of desperation. His Winchester had escaped the epidemic, as they were ordinarily assigned to Halifax covert. He had been stationed on a lonely circuit out in Quebec to put him out of the way of anyone hearing his radical political views, as he freely acknowledged.

'Or perhaps it was my poetry,' Prewitt said, laughing at himself, 'but my pride can better stand condemnation of my politics than of my art, so I choose to take it so. And this is Captain Latour,' a French Royalist turned British officer. Hesterfield and the two others, Reynolds and Gounod, were Prewitt's political sympathizers, if a little quieter than he on the subject, and Laurence gradually realized the little group not supporters of his act, but were divided from the rest of the company precisely because they quarrelled over its morality.

'Murder, murder most foul, there is no other word,' Reynolds declared, covering Laurence's hand with his own, pinning it to the table by the wrist, and looking at him with the focused, earnest expression of the profoundly drunk. Laurence did not know what to say. He had agreed, and had laid down his life to prevent it, but he did not care to be congratulated for it, by a stranger.

'Treason is another word,' another officer said, at the nearest populated table, making no pretence about eavesdropping. A half-empty bottle of whiskey stood before him.

'Hear, hear,' another man said.

There were too many bottles in the room, and too many angry and disappointed men. It was an invitation for a scene. Laurence disengaged his hand. He would have liked to excuse himself and shift tables, but Frette had abandoned him to Prewitt and his willing company, and Laurence could not imagine imposing himself on anyone else in the room. 'I beg you gentlemen not to speak of it,' he said quietly, to the table. But to no avail. Reynolds was already arguing with the whiskey-drinker, and their voices were rising.

Laurence set his jaw, and tried not to listen. 'And I say,' the whiskey-drinker was saying, 'that he is a traitor who ought to be drug outside, strung up, and drawn and quartered after, and you with him, if you say otherwise—'

'Medieval sentiment—' They were both standing now,

Reynolds shaking off Gounod's half-hearted restraining hand to get up. Their voices were loud enough to drown all nearby conversation.

Laurence rose, and catching Reynolds by the shoulder firmly, pressed him back towards his chair. 'Sir, you do me no kindness by this. Leave off,' he said, low and sharply.

'That's right, let him teach you how to be a coward,' the other man said.

Laurence stiffened. He could not resent insults he had earned, he had sacrificed the right to defend himself against traitor, but coward was a slap he could not gladly swallow. But he could not make the challenge. He had caused enough harm. He could not—would not, do more. He closed his mouth on the bitterness in the back of his throat, and did not turn to look the man in the face, though he now stood so close his liquored breath came hot and strongly over Laurence's shoulder.

'Call him a coward, when you would've sat and done nothing,' Reynolds flung back. He shook off Laurence's hand, or tried. 'I suppose your dragon would enjoy you being happy to see ten thousand of them put down, poisoned or good as, like dogs—'

'*One* at least ought to be poisoned,' the other man said, and Laurence let go of Reynolds, turned, and knocked the officer down.

The man was drunk and unsteady, and as he went down pulled the table and the bottle over with him. Cheap liquor bubbled out over the ground as it rolled away. For a moment no one spoke, and then chairs went back across the tent, as if nothing more had been wanted than a pretext.

The quarrel at once devolved into a confusing melee, with nothing no sides. Laurence even saw two men from the same table wrestling in a corner. But a few men singled him out, one a captain he knew by face from Dover, if not immediately by name. He had fresh streaks of black dragon-blood on his clothing. His name was Geoffrey Windle, Laurence remembered incongruously, as they grappled, just before Windle struck him full on the jaw.

The impact rocked him back on his heels; his teeth snapped together, and he felt the startling pain of a bitten cheek. Gripping a tent-pole for purchase, Laurence managed to seize a chair and pull it around between them as Windle lunged at him again; the man tripped over it and went into the pole with his full weight, which was considerable: he had some three stone over Laurence. The canvas roof above them sagged precipitously.

Two more men came at Laurence, faces ugly with anger. They caught him by the arms and rushed him against the nearest table. They were drunk enough to be belligerent, but not enough to be clumsy. He still wore his buckled shoes and laddered stockings, and lacked good purchase on the ground, and the weight of his boots to kick out with. They pinned him down, and one of them held out a blade, a dull eating-knife, still slick with grease from his dinner. Laurence set his heel down against the surface of the table and heaved, managing to get his shoulders loose for a moment, twisting away from the short furious stabbing, so the blade only tore into his ragged coat.

The tent pole creaked and gave way. Canvas fell upon them in a sudden catastrophic rush. Laurence had freed his arms, only to be imprisoned in the smothering folds. They were heavy, and he had an effort to lift it enough from his face to breathe. He rolled off the table, and then felt hands gripping his arm again, pulling at him. Laurence struck out blindly at the new attacker, and they struggled upon the ground until the other man managed to drag the edge of the canvas off their heads and heave them into the open air. It was Granby.

'Oh, Lord,' Granby said. Laurence turned and saw that

half the tent had crumpled in on the heaving mass beneath. Those sober enough to have avoided the fighting were carrying out the lanterns from the other side. Others doused the collapsed canvas with water; smoke trickled out from beneath.

'You'll do a damned sight better out of the way,' Granby said, when Laurence would have gone to help, and drew him along one of the camp paths, narrow and stumbling-dark, towards the dragon clearings.

They walked in silence over the uneven ground. Laurence tried to slow his short, clenched breathing without success. He felt inexpressibly naïve. He had not even thought to fear such a possibility, until he heard it in the mouth of a drunkard. But when they did hang him, knowing it would lose them Temeraire's use,—what might those men do, those men who had meant to infect all the world's dragons with consumption and condemn them to an agonizing death. They would see Temeraire dead, rather than of use to anyone they were disposed to see as an enemy: France, or China, or any other nation. They would not scruple at any sort of treachery necessary to achieve his destruction. To them Temeraire was only an inconvenient animal.

'I suppose,' Granby said, abruptly, out of the dark, 'that he insisted on it? Your carrying the stuff to France, I mean.'

'He did,' Laurence said, after a moment, but he did not mean to hide behind Temeraire's wings. 'I am ashamed to say, he was forced to, but only at first. I would not have you believe I was taken against my will.'

'No,' Granby said, 'no, I only meant, you shouldn't have thought of it at all, on your own.'

The observation felt true, and uncomfortably so, though Laurence supposed Granby had meant it as consolation. He felt a sharp sudden stab of loneliness. He wanted very badly to see Temeraire. Laurence had slept his last night beneath his sheltering wing nearly four months ago, in the northern mountains. Their treason committed, they had snatched a few hours of freedom before they made the fatal flight across the Channel. Since then there had been only a succession of prisons, more or less brutal, for them both. Temeraire had spent months alone, friendless and unhappy, in breeding grounds full of feral beasts and veterans, with no order or discipline to keep them from fighting.

They passed the clearings one by one, the millhouse rumble of sleeping dragons to either side, their dinners finished and their crews toiling on the harnesses by lantern-light, the faint clanking of hammers tapped away and the acrid smoky stink of harness oil carried on the breeze. They had a long walk out in the dark after the last clearing, up a steep slope to the crown of a hill overlooking all the camp, where Iskierka lay sleeping in a thick spiny coil, steam issuing with her every breath, and the feral dragons scattered around her.

She cracked an eye open as they came in and inquired drowsily, 'Is it a battle time yet?'

'No, love, back to sleep,' Granby said, and she sighed and shut her eye. But she had drawn the attention of the men, they looked from Laurence to Granby, and then they looked back down again, saying nothing.

'Perhaps I had best not stay,' Laurence said. He knew some of the faces, men from his own crew, even some of his former officers. He was glad they had found places here.

'Stuff,' Granby said. 'I am not so damned craven, and anyway,' he added, more despondently, when he had led Laurence into his own tent, pitched in the comfortable current of heat which Iskierka gave off, 'I cannot be much farther in the soup than I am already, after yesterday. She's spoilt, there is no other word for it. Wouldn't keep in formation, wouldn't obey signals, took the ferals with her—' He shrugged, and taking a bottle from the floor poured them each a glass, which he drank with an unaccustomed enthusiasm.

'It's not so bad, on patrol,' Granby said, after wiping his mouth. 'She doesn't need any coaxing to look out the enemy, and she'll take directions to make it easier. But in a fleet action—I don't mean she was useless,' he added, with a defensive note. 'They did for a first-rate and three frigates, and chased off a dozen French beasts. But she hasn't a shred of discipline. Pretended not to hear me, left the right wing of the Corps wide open, and two beasts badly hurt for it. I would be broken for it, if they could afford to give her up.'

He was pacing the small confines of his tent, still holding the empty glass, and talking swiftly, almost nervously. More to be saying something, to fill the air between them, than to impart these particular words. 'This is the sort of thing that rots the Corps,' he said. 'I never thought I would be a bad officer, someone who ruins his dragon, the kind of fool, kept on only because his beast won't serve otherwise. The Army— the Navy—they sneer at us for that, as much as for anything else we do, but there at least they are right to sneer. So our admirals have to dance to the Navy's tune, and meanwhile the youngsters see it, too, and you can't ask them to be better, when they see a fellow let off anything, anything at all—'

He pulled himself up abruptly, realizing too late that his words were applicable to more of his audience than himself, and looked at Laurence miserably.

'You are not wrong,' Laurence said. He had assumed the same himself, in his Navy days. He had thought the Corps full of wild, devil-may-care libertines, who delighted in disregarding law and authority as far as they dared, barely kept in check. To be used for their control over the beasts, but not respected.

'But if we have more liberty than we ought,' Laurence said, after a moment, struggling through, 'it is because our dragons haven't enough. They have no stake in victory other than our happiness. Any nation would give them their daily bread just to have peace and quiet. We are granted our license for as long as we do what we should not. So long as we use their affections to keep them obedient.'

'How else do you make them care?' Granby said. 'If we did not, the French would run right over us, and take our eggs themselves.'

'They care in China,' Laurence said, 'and in Africa. They care that their rational sense is not imposed on, nor their hearts put into opposition with their minds. If they cannot be woken to a natural affection for their country, such as we feel, it is our fault and not theirs.'

Laurence slept the night in Granby's tent, on top of a blanket. He would not take Granby's cot. It was odd to sleep warmly and wake in a sweat, then step out and see the camp below dusted overnight with snow, soiled grey tents for the moment clean white, and the ground already churning into muddy slush.

'You are back,' Iskierka said, looking at Laurence. She was wide awake, picking over the charred remnants of her breakfast, and watching the sluggish camp with a disgruntled eye. 'Where is Temeraire? He has let you get into a wretched state,' she added, with rather a smug air. Laurence could not argue, he was a pitiful sight indeed. He coat was ragged and his shoes were starting to open at the seams. The less said of his stockings the better. 'Granby,' she said, looking over his shoulder, 'you may lend Laurence your fourth-best coat, and then you may tell Temeraire,' she added to Laurence, 'that I am very sorry he cannot give you nicer things.'

However, Granby was wearing his fourth-best coat, as the other three were wholly unsuitable for actual fighting. They were ostentatiously adorned with the fruits of Iskierka's determined prize-hunting. It would not in any case have been a very successful loan, as Laurence had some four inches in the shoulders, which Granby had instead in height. But Granby sent word out, and shortly a young runner returned carrying a folded coat, and a spare pair of boots.

'Why, Sipho,' Laurence said. 'I am glad to find you well; and your brother, also, I hope?' He had worried what might have become of the two boys, brought from Africa, who had helped them there. He had made them his own runners by way of providing for them, but had then found himself unable to be of further assistance.

'Yes, sir,' Sipho said in perfect English, though less than a year before the child had never heard a word of it. 'He is with Arkady, and Captain Berkley says, you are welcome to these, and to come and say hello to Maximus would you, if you are not too damned stiff-necked. He said to say just that,' he added earnestly.

'You aren't the only one who owes them,' Berkley said, in his blunt way, when Laurence had come and thanked him for assuming responsibility for the boys. 'You needn't worry about them being cast off anyway, we need them. They can jaw with those damned ferals better than any man jack of us. That older boy talks their jabber quicker than he does English. You'd better worry about them getting knocked on the head instead. I had a fight on my hands to make the Admiralty let me keep this one grounded for now. They would have put him up as an ensign, if you like, not nine years of age. Demane they would have no matter what I said, but that is just as well. He fights,' he added succinctly, 'so he may as well do it against the Frogs, where it don't get him in hot water.'

Maximus was much recovered, from the last time Laurence had seen him. Three months of steady feeding on shore had brought him nearly up to his former fighting weight, and he put his head down and said in a conspiratorial whisper, 'Tell Temeraire that Lily and I have not forgotten our promise, and we are ready to fight with him whenever he should ask. We will not let them hang you, not at all.'

Laurence stared up at the immense Regal Copper. All his crew looked deeply distressed, as well they might, the outlaw remark being perfectly audible several clearings over. Berkley only snorted. 'There has been plenty of talk like that, and louder,' he said. 'I expect that is why you have been kept stuffed between decks in a ship instead of a in a decent prison on land. No, don't beg my pardon. It was sure as sixpence you and that mad beast of yours would make a spectacle of yourselves sooner or later. Bring him back, do for a dozen Frogs, and save us all the bother of the execution.'

With this sanguine if unlikely recommendation, Laurence reported to the courier-clearing with his orders, looking a little less shabby. Berkley was a thickset man, and if the borrowed coat was too large, at least he could get it on. And the borrowed boots were entirely serviceable, with a little padding of straw at the toes. His repaired appearance got him no better treatment, however. There were a dozen beasts waiting for messages and orders, and when Laurence had presented himself, the courier-master said, 'If you will be so good as to wait,' and left him outside the clearing. Laurence was near enough to see the master talking with his officers. None of the courier captains looked very inclined to take him up. He was left standing an hour, while four messages came in and were sent out, before another Winchester landed bringing fresh orders from the Admiralty, and at last the courier-master came and said, 'Very well; we have a man to take you.'

'Morning, sir,' the captain said, touching his hat, as Laurence came over. It was Hollin, his former ground-crew master. 'Elsie, will you give the captain a leg up? There is a strap there, sir, handy for you.'

'Thank you, Hollin,' Laurence said, grateful for the steady, matter-of-factness, and climbed up to her back. 'We are for Pen Y Fan.'

'Right you are, sir, we know the way,' Hollin said. 'Do you need a bite to sup, Elsie, before we go?'

'No,' she said, raising her head dripping from the water-trough. 'They always have lovely cows there, I will wait.'

They did not speak very much during the flight. Winchesters were so small and quick one felt always on the point of flying off from the force of the wind steadily testing the limits of the carabiner straps. Laurence's hands, already blistered, grew bruised where he held on to the leather harness. They raced past blurred fields of brown stalks and snow. The thin cold air chapped at their faces and leaked into the neck of Laurence's coat, and through his thread-bare shirt. He did not mind, he wished they might go quicker still. He resented now every mile remaining.

Goodrich Castle swelled up before them, on its hill, and Hollin put out the signal-flags as they flashed by: *courier, with orders*, and the fort's signal-gun fired in acknowledg-ment, already falling behind them.

The mountains were growing closer, and closer, and as the sun began to set Elsie came over the final sharp ridge and over the broad blood-stained feeding grounds, and the cliffs full of dragon-holes. She landed. The cattle pen was empty, its wide door standing open. There were no lights and no sound. There was not a dragon anywhere to be seen.

Chapter Four

Overnight, icicles had grown upon the overhang of the cave, a row of glittering teeth, and now as the sun struck they steadily dripped themselves away upon the stone, an uneven pattering without rhythm or sense. Temeraire opened his eyes once in a while, dully to watch them shrink; then he closed his eyes and put his head down. No one had proposed his removal, or disturbed him.

A scrabbling of claws made him look up; a small dragon had landed on the ledge, and Lloyd was sliding down from its back. 'Come now then,' Lloyd said, tramping in, his boots ringing and smearing field-muck on the clean stone. 'Come now, old boy, why such a fuss, today? We have a lovely visitor waiting. A nice fat bullock will set you up—'

Temeraire had never wanted to kill anyone, except of course anyone who tried to hurt Laurence; he liked to fight well enough, as it was exciting, but he had never thought that he would like to kill anyone just for himself. Only, in this moment it seemed to him he would much rather that than have Lloyd before him, speaking so, when Laurence was dead.

'Be silent,' he said, and when Lloyd continued without a pause.

'—the very best put aside for you special, tonight—'

Temeraire stretched out his neck and put his head directly before Lloyd and said, low, 'My captain is dead.'

That at least meant something to Lloyd: he went white, stopped talking and held himself very still; Temeraire watched him closely. It was almost disappointing. If only Lloyd would say something else dreadful, or do something foul as he always did; if only—but Laurence would not like it— Laurence would not have liked it—Temeraire took a long hissing breath, and drew his head back, curling in upon himself again, and Lloyd sagged in relief.

'Why there's been some mistake,' he said, after a moment, his voice only a few shades less hearty. 'I've heard nothing of the sort, old boy, word would've been sent me—'

His words made Temeraire angry all over again, but differently now: the sharp strange feeling was dulled, and he felt quite tired, wishing only for Lloyd to be gone.

'I dare say you would tell me he was alive, even if he had been hanged at Tyburn,' he said, bitterly, 'as long as it made me eat, and mate, and listen to you. Well, I will not. I have borne it; I would have borne anything, only to keep Laurence alive, but I will bear it no longer. I will eat when I like, and not otherwise, and I will not mate with anyone unless I choose to.' He looked at the little dragon who had brought Lloyd and said, 'Now take him away, if you please; and tell the others that I do not want him brought again without asking first.'

The little dragon bobbed his head nervously and picked up the startled and protesting Lloyd to carry him down again. Temeraire closed his eyes and coiled himself again; the drip of the icicles his only company.

A few hours later, Perscitia and Moncey landed on the cave ledge with a studied air of insouciance, carrying two fresh-killed cows. They brought them inside, and laid them in front of him. 'I am not hungry,' Temeraire said sharply.

'Oh, we only told Lloyd they was for you so he would let us have extra,' Moncey said cheerfully. 'You don't mind if we eat them here?' and he tore into the first one. Temeraire's tail twitched, entirely without volition, at the hot juicy smell of the blood, and when Perscitia nudged the second cow towards him, he took it in his jaws without really meaning to. In a few swallows it was gone, and what they had left of the first followed swiftly.

He flew down for another, and even a fourth; he did not have to think or feel while he ate. A small flock of the more diminutive dragons clustered together on the edge of the feeding grounds watching him anxiously, and when he looked for yet another cow, a couple of them rose up to herd one towards him. But none of them spoke to Temeraire. When he had finished, he flew for a long distance along the river and settled down to drink only where he might be quite alone again. He felt sore in all his joints, as if he had flown hard in sleeting weather for a long, long time.

He washed, as well as he could manage alone, and went back to his cave to think. Perscitia came up to see him, to present an interesting mathematical problem, but he only glanced at it and said, 'No. Help me find Moncey; I want to know what has been happening with the war.'

'Why, I don't know,' Moncey said, surprised, when they had tracked him down, lazing in a meadow on the mountain-side with some of the other Winchesters and small ferals. They had been playing a bit of a game, where they tossed branches upon the ground and tried to pick up as many as they could without dropping any. 'It's nothing to do with us, you know, not here. The Frenchy dragons and their captains are all kept over in Scotland, further up. There won't be any fighting round here.'

'It is to do with us, too,' Temeraire said. 'This is our

territory, all of ours; and the French are trying to take it away. That has as much to do with us as it would if they were trying to take your cave, and more, because they are trying to take everything else along with your cave.'

The little dragons put down their sticks and came closer to listen, with some interest. 'But what do you want to do?' Moncey said.

Numerous official couriers were crossing the countryside in every direction, at all speed, and the afternoon was not entirely spent before Moncey and the other Winchesters were able to return, full of as much news as Temeraire could wish for. If the numbers reported were a little inconsistent, it did not matter very much; Napoleon had landed a great many men, all near London, and there had not yet been any great battle to throw him off.

'He is all over the coast, and the fellows say there is this Marshal Davout fellow poking about in Kent, to the south of London, and another one Lefèbvre, who is already somewhere along this way,' Moncey said, pointing out the countryside west of the capital, and nearest Wales.

'Oh, I know that one, he was at the siege of Danzig,' Temeraire said. 'I do not think he was so very clever, he did not make a big push to have us out, not until Lien came and took charge of everything. Where is our army?'

'All fallen back about London,' Minnow said. 'Everyone says there is going to be a big battle there, in a couple of weeks perhaps.'

'Then there is not a moment to lose,' Temeraire said.

They passed the word for a council meeting, and everyone came promptly: the other big dragons considerably more respectful now, even if Ballista still was patronizing, 'You are upset, of course, and no wonder; but I am sure if you tell them you would like another captain—'

'*No*,' Temeraire said, the resonance making his whole

body tremble, and looked away, while everyone fell quiet. After a moment he was able to continue. 'I am not going to take another captain,' he said, 'and a stranger; I do not need a handler as if I were one of Lloyd's cows. I can fight on my own, and so can any of you.'

'But what is there to fight for?' Requiescat said. 'If the French win, they aren't going to give us any bother, it will only mean someone else taking eggs; they'll be just as careful.'

There was a murmur of agreement, and Moncey added, a little plaintively, 'And I thought you were always on about how unfair the Admiralty are, not letting us have any liberty.'

'I do not mean to speak for the Government,' Temeraire said. 'But this country is our territory as much as it is any man's; it belongs to us all together, and if we simply sit here eating cows while Napoleon tries to take it away, we have no right to complain of anything.'

'Well, what is there to complain of, then?' Requiescat said. 'We have everything as we like it.'

'So you will quarrel over a wet unpleasant cave, but you will not fight to sleep in a pavilion, which is never wet or cold, even in winter?' Temeraire said, scornfully. 'You only think you have things as you like them to be, because you have never seen anything better, and that is because you have spent all of your lives penned up here or in coverts.'

When he had described pavilions for them a little more, and the dragon-city in Africa, he added, 'And in Yutien, there were dragons who were employed as merchants. All of them had heaps of jewels – only tin and glass, Laurence said, but they were very pretty anyway; and in Africa they had gold enough to put it on all of their crew members.' There were not many dragons present who did not sigh at least a little; those who wore their small treasures looked at them, and many of the unadorned looked at them, wistfully.

'It all sounds a lot of gimcrackery to me,' Requiescat said.

'Then *you* may stay here and have my cave, which is not a quarter as nice as a pavilion,' Temeraire said coolly, 'and when we have beaten Napoleon and taken many prizes, you shan't have a share; Moncey will have more gold than you.'

'Prizes!' Gentius said, rousing unexpectedly. 'I helped in taking a prize once. My captain had a fourteenth share. That is how she bought the picture.'

Everyone knew of Gentius's painting, and an impressed murmur went around: this example proved better than hypothetical jewels in a country which none of them had seen.

'Now, now, settle down,' Ballista said, thumping her tail, but with a considerably more lenient air. 'Look here, I suppose no one much wants the French to beat us, we have all had a go with them before, if we were ever in service. But the corps don't want us unless we take harness and captains, and we cannot just wander into battles: we will get circled and shot up. That is no joke, even for us big ones.'

'If we fight thoughtlessly and singularly, we will,' Temeraire said, 'but there is no reason we must do that, and we cannot be boarded if we have no harness, or—or anyone to capture. We will form our own army, and we will work out tactics for ourselves, not stuff men have invented without bothering to ask us even though they cannot fly themselves. It stands to reason that we can do better than *them*, if we try.'

'Hm, well,' Ballista said to his convincing argument, and the general murmur of agreement found it so too.

'All right, all right,' Requiescat said. 'Very nice storytelling, but it is all a hum. Treasure and battles are well and good, but what d'you mean to do for dinner?'

The next morning, they landed together on the grounds at the feeding time. The cows in their pen were bellowing invitingly, and their delicious grassy scent made Temeraire's tongue want to lick the air. But the other dragons all kept the line with him: no one even turned their nose toward the running cattle. The herdsmen prodded the cows forward with no results, and then looked at each other and back at Lloyd, in confusion.

Lloyd began pacing up and down the line of dragons looking up at them all in bafflement, saying entreatingly to one after another in turn, 'Go on, then, eat something.' Temeraire waited until Lloyd came up to him, then bent his head down and said, 'Lloyd, where do the cows come from?'

Lloyd stared at him. 'Go on, eat something, old boy,' he repeated feebly, so it came out as a question more than a command.

'Stop that; my name is Temeraire, or you may call me sir,' Temeraire said, 'since that is how to speak to someone politely.'

'Oh, ah,' Lloyd said, not very sensibly.

'You have heard that the French have invaded?' Temeraire enquired.

'Oh!' Lloyd said, in tones of relief. 'None of you need worry anything about that. Why, they shan't come anywhere near here, or interfere with your cows. You shall all be fed, the cows will come here every day, there's no call to save them, old boy—'

Temeraire raised his head and gave a small roar, only to quiet him; snow tumbled down the slope on the other side of the feeding grounds, but it was not very much, a foot perhaps, scarcely deep enough to dust his talons. 'You will say *sir*,' he told Lloyd, lowering his head to fix the groundsman securely with one eye.

'Sir,' Lloyd said, faintly.

Satisfied, Temeraire sat back on his haunches and explained. 'We are not staying here,' he said, 'so you see, it is no help to tell us that the cows will always be here. We are, all of us, going to fight Napoleon and we need to take the cows with us.'

Lloyd did not seem to understand him at first; it required the better part of an hour to work it into his head, that they were all leaving the grounds and did not mean to come back. When it did, he became desperate, and began to beg and plead with them in a very shocking way, which made Temeraire feel wretchedly embarrassed: Lloyd was so very small, and it felt like bullying to say no to him.

'That is quite enough,' Temeraire said at last, forcing himself to be firm. 'Lloyd, we are not going to hurt you or take away your food or your property, so you have no right to carry on at us in this way, only because we do not like to stay.'

'How you talk; I'll be dismissed from my post for certain, and that's the least of it,' Lloyd said, almost in tears. 'It's as much as my life is worth, if I let you all go out wandering wild, pillaging farmers' livestock every which way—'

'But we are not going pillaging, at all,' Temeraire said. 'That is why I am asking you where the cows come from. If the Government would feed them to us here, they are ours, and there is no reason we cannot take them and eat them somewhere else.'

'But they come from all over,' Lloyd said, and gesturing to his herdsmen added, 'the drovers bring a string every week from a different farm. It is as much as all of Wales can do, to feed you lot; there's not one place.'

'Oh,' Temeraire said, and scratched his head; he had envisioned a very large pen, somewhere over the mountains perhaps, full of cows waiting to be taken out and carried along. 'Well,' he decided, 'then you all will have to help: you will go to the farms and fetch the cows and bring them along to us. That way,' he added, with a burst of fresh inspiration, 'no one can complain to you, or sack you, because you will not have let us go off at all.'

This solution did not immediately promote itself to the herdsmen, who began to protest: some of them had families, and none of them wished to go to war. 'No, that is all stuff and nonsense,' Temeraire said. 'It is your duty to fight the French as much as it is ours; more, because it is your Government, and it would press you if you were needed. I have been to sea with many pressed men; I know it is not very nice,' he added, although he did not entirely see why they did not like to go; anywhere was better than this loathsome place, and at least they would be *doing* something, rather than sitting about, 'but if Napoleon wins, that also will not be very nice, and anyway, I dare say the Government will stop your wages if they learn that you are sitting here with no dragons about. And if you come, we will give you a share of the prizes we take.'

Prizes proved to be a magical word with men as well as dragons, as did the general conviction, arrived at through a deal of quiet muttering, that if they did *not* go with the dragons, they should certainly be blamed for the desertion; but no one could complain they had not done their duty if they followed the beasts. Or at least, it would be more difficult to find them.

'We might be ready soon as next week,' Lloyd said, with one last gasping attempt. 'If you'd all just have a bite to eat, and a bit of sleep first—'

'We are leaving *now*,' Temeraire said firmly, and rising up on his haunches called out, 'Advance guard, aloft; and you may take your breakfast with you.'

Moncey and the small dragons gleefully leapt onto the herd, first for once, and went eating as they flew; it was perhaps a little messy, but much quicker to eat as one went. Minnow swallowed the head of her cow, and waved a wing-tip. 'We will see you at the rendezvous,' she called down. 'Come on then pips, off we go,' she said to the other courier-weights and they all stormed away rapidly northwards and east, along the planned route.

'Now can we eat?' Requiescat said, watching after them plaintively.

'Yes, you may all eat, but have half now and take the rest to eat along the way, otherwise you will fly slowly, and be hungry again anyway at the end of it,' Temeraire said. 'Lloyd, we are going to Abergavenny, or outside it, anyway; do you know where that is?'

'We can't drive the herd all that way by tomorrow!' Lloyd said.

'Then you will have to bring them as close as you can and we will manage somehow,' Temeraire said; he was done listening to difficulties. 'I have seen Napoleon's army fight, and within a week they will be in London, so we must be, also.'

'We are a hundred fifty miles from London,' Lloyd protested.

'All the more reason to travel fast,' Temeraire said, and flung himself into the air.

Chapter Five

Bewildered, Laurence stood in the empty grounds and called Temeraire's name a few times. There was no answer but the mumbled echoes that the cliffs gave back and the momentary attention of a small red squirrel, which paused to look at him before continuing on its way. Elsie landed again, behind him. 'Not a wing in the sky, sir,' Hollin said.

Elsie carried them up to a cave, reaching deep into the mountain face. Though the light was failing rapidly, Laurence could trace with his fingers the letters of Temeraire's name, carved deeply into the rock. so he had at least been here, and was well enough to leave this mark. They managed to fashion a torch to inspect it, but the cave was too tidy, inside, to guess when his habitation had ended: no bones or other remnants of food.

It had been only two days since the French landing, but many dragons lived in the breeding grounds; if the herdsmen had abandoned their posts and the regular delivery of cattle interrupted, the provisions would quickly have been spent. The dragons must surely have scattered from hunger, and likely in all the directions of the rose.

'Well, let us not borrow trouble,' Hollin said, consolingly.

'He is a clever fellow, and it cannot have been so long since they left. There are some fresh bones down by the pen, from only this morning by the look of them.'

Laurence shook his head. 'I hope he would not have been so foolish, as to stay to the last,' he answered, low. 'So many foraging dragons will undoubtedly be consuming all of the local supply, and he must have more food than a smaller beast.'

'I am a smaller beast,' Elsie said, a little anxiously, 'but I must have something to eat too, and there is nothing here.'

They went to Llechrhyd, the nearest settlement they could find, and bought her a sheep from a small cottager, who told them that the village, by some lucky chance, had not been raided. 'Flew off east, all of them, this morning,' the old woman told Laurence, while Elsie discreetly ate her dinner behind the stable, 'like a plague of crows. It was dark for half an hour, with all them passing over and us sure they would fall on our heads in a moment; more than that I can't say.'

'Hollin,' Laurence said, when he had turned away disheartened, 'I cannot tell you what your duty is; we have no very good intelligence, I am afraid, and if he is flying to feed himself, we cannot well imagine where he may have gone.'

'Well, sir,' Hollin said, 'they said to bring you back with him, so I suppose those are my orders until I hear otherwise. Anyways, I dare say we will find him tomorrow, first thing or as good as. It's not as though he's so easy to miss.'

But this course did not reckon with the confusion of dozens of beasts flung out upon the countryside at once. Certainly, dragons had been seen everywhere – dreadful marauding beasts – and no one knew what things were coming to when they were just allowed to go flying around loose. But as to one particular dragon, black with a ruff, no one had anything to say.

One farmer thirty miles on, belligerent enough to be brave, had not hidden in his cellar during the visitation, and swore that a giant dragon had eaten four of his cows, informing him they were being confiscated for the war effort and he should be repaid by the Government. He even showed them where the dragon had scratched a mark in an old oak tree for his reimbursement, and for a moment Laurence entertained hope. But it was not a Chinese mark, only an X clumsily carved through the bark, with four scratches below. 'Red and yellow, like fire,' the farmer's oldest boy had said, peering at them from over the windowsill of the house, despite his mother's restraining hand, which sank them completely.

In Monmouthshire, ten dragons had stopped to drink at the lake in the grounds of a stately house, the housekeeper told them, anxiously, and had also eaten some of the deer: ten neat Xs were marked in the ground by the lakeshore. 'I am sure I could not tell you if they were black or red or spotted green and yellow, it was all I could do to keep breathing, and with half my staff fainted dead away,' she said. 'And then one of the creatures came to the door and asked us through it if we had any curtains. Red ones,' she added. 'We threw outside all those from the ballroom, and then they took them and went away.'

Laurence was baffled: curtains? He would have understood better if they had demanded the silver plate. But at least they were moving in a group, and in the earnest excuses offered for the pillaging, he thought he saw Temeraire's influence, if not his presence: it was so near a mimic to the Chinese mode, where dragons purchased goods by making their mark for the supplier.

In the late evening they discovered another farmer with a collection of marks, who rather astonishingly was not unhappy. The dragons had eaten four of his cows yesterday, he agreed, but that very morning some men had passed through with a string of cattle and given him replacements, which he pointed out in their field: four handsome beef cattle, better in all honesty than the scrawnier animals in the farmer's own herd.

The next day, seven dragons had been seen in Pen-y-Clawdd, four had landed by the river in Llandogo, and perhaps one of them had been black—yes, certainly one had been black. Then a dozen had been seen—no, two dozen—no, a hundred—all numbers shouted by the crowd in the common room of an inn, growing steadily more implausible. Laurence gave them no credit at all.

A few miles further along, Elsie landed them in a torn-up meadow, with a neatly dug necessary pit on the low side away from the water, filled-in but still fragrant, with signs of occupation by at least some number of dragons. 'We must be getting right close, then,' Hollin said, encouragingly, but the next day, no one had so much as seen a wing-tip, though Elsie went miles around in widening rings to make inquiries, for hours and hours. The dragons had, one and all, vanished into the air.

'We will be getting close to the French tomorrow, so beginning today we will fly when it is dark,' Temeraire said, 'and try and be as quiet as we can; so pass the word to everyone, not to fly somewhere if you see lights; or if you smell cows, because they will bellow and run and make a fuss.'

The others nodded, and Temeraire rose up on his haunches to inspect their own pen of cattle. He missed Gong Su. It was not that cooked food was so much more pleasant, he did not care about the taste at all at present, but Gong Su could stretch a single cow among five hungry dragons. If only there were a quantity of rice, or something else like to cook with it.

The further they travelled from Wales, the more complicated everything became. Lloyd said that it was expensive to bring the cows so far, because they must be fed along the road, and they could not be brought very quickly, because they would sicken and stop being fat and good to eat. That Majestatis had suggested the notion of borrowing cows in advance, and using the later ones to repay, had helped a great deal; but if they were always flying about snatching cows from the nearby farms, the French were sure to hear about it: Marshal Lefèbvre's forces were busy snatching cows themselves.

'Maybe we oughtn't be having the cows driven to us,' Moncey said. 'We could always go and fetch them for ourselves, and then come back.'

'That is no good at all,' Perscitia said severely. 'The longer we must fly to get to the supply, the more food we must eat to reach it and come back, which is a waste, and also it means more time flying back and forth, instead of fighting.'

'Supply lines,' Gentius said, dolefully, shaking his head. 'War is all about supply lines; my third captain told me.'

He had insisted on coming along, although he could not really see well enough to fly anymore, and tired easily; but he had grown light enough that he could be carried along by any of the heavyweights, and it was very satisfying to everyone to think they had a Longwing with them.

Aside from the difficulty about the food, Temeraire was pleased with their progress. He and Perscitia had devised several manoeuvres, which even Ballista had allowed to be clever; and Moncey and the others had brought them a good deal of news about the French, although they could only sneak so close before it became too likely they should be caught. Temeraire was trying to think how they might better find a way to spy.

They had worked out how to organize their camp so it did not take over a great deal of room, by letting the smaller dragons sleep on top of the big, which was warmer anyway;

and after the first awkward day they had learned to dig their necessary-pit far away from their water. That had been very unpleasant, and five of the dragons had become quite sick from being so thirsty they had drunk anyway, despite the smell.

A few others had grown bored and gone off on their own, all of them ferals who had never served, but some of those had come back when they had not been able to find easy food on their own, which brought them straight back to the question of supply.

'We can go and fetch a great many cattle here, if they are drugged with laudanum,' Temeraire said, 'but it seems to me, that if the French are going about taking cows anyway, we would do better to eat their food first, instead of our own, and let them have the bother of gathering it; and that way we may fight and eat together.'

They all agreed it made a sensible strategy, and for Temeraire it was nearly more justification than cause: he wanted badly to fight. The urge to violence, the hunger for some explosive action, was always stirring in him now, craving release, and often Perscitia and Moncey eyed him anxiously. Sometimes Temeraire would even rouse up, not from sleep but from some halfway condition, and find himself deserted: the others all flown away some distance, crouched down low and watching him.

'It isn't healthy, how he pens it up,' Gentius said loudly after their meeting, not seeing Temeraire close enough to overhear. 'You fellows don't know what it's like, having a really fine captain and losing her: it is worse than having all your treasure stolen. That is why he goes so queer now and again. A proper battle, that is what he needs, a bit of blood,' and Temeraire wanted it very much. He did not like the sensation of being a passenger in his own life, unable to feel as he chose; if a battle would repair it, he was almost tempted to go seek one out at once.

But he had brought everyone else along, and he could not abandon them to their own devices now or drag them into a mindless squabble, even if he would have liked one. Instead he brooded on strategy, and when the urge grew too difficult to bear, he went away and curled himself tightly, with his head against his flank beneath the dark huddle of his wing, and murmured to himself from the *Principia Mathematica*. Laurence had read it to him so often that he had it all by heart, and if he spoke low, and flattened his voice, he might almost imagine he heard Laurence instead, reading to him in the rain, safe and sheltered beside him.

The very next morning, Minnow and Reedly came into camp flying so quick they had to skip-hop a few paces along the ground to stop, full of news: 'Pigs,' Reedly said, panting, 'so many of them, a whole pen, back of their army, and some of 'em are big as ponies!'

'Pigs,' Gentius said thoughtfully, cracking an eye. 'Pigs are good eating, all the way through.'

'Pigs are easy to keep,' Lloyd put in. 'We drive 'em into the forest and they will feed themselves; you can go in and take one when you want, or round 'em up to drive them along.'

'And there are only a couple of old Chevaliers to guard them,' Minnow said. 'They are big, but lazy, and they were fast asleep when we saw them.'

'Very good,' Temeraire said, attempting to sound cool and serene, although his tail wanted to thump the ground. 'Lloyd, you and your men will go with Moncey and the Winchesters. You will wait until we have attacked, and drawn everyone off, and then you will go and take the pigs and bring them along here.

'Now,' he said, turning, and swept a patch of earth smooth with the tip of his tail. 'Minnow, show me what the camp looks like.'

They set off a couple of hours before evening: Minnow and Reedly were very sure there was no Fleur de Nuit with the company, and so they would attack at night, when everyone would be asleep and most surprised, and have the most difficulty in chasing after them when the pigs had been seized. The little dragons would come behind, that much was decided; and Temeraire, after some thinking, put one of their Chequered Nettles, Armatius, in front, carrying Gentius upon his back. Ballista and Majestatis went on either side of him and Requiescat came behind them, and to either side of him a couple of Yellow Reapers carrying their flags.

They were not very elegant, only some velvet curtains tied on to saplings, but every real army had flags, and red was an auspicious colour. Streaming out, they made a fine show, especially when carried by the Yellow Reapers to either side of Requiescat's orange and red. Everyone brightened as they billowed out; the Reapers were especially pleased, and held themselves proudly. Even Requiescat turned his head as they flew and said, 'Well, those are something like, anyway,' to Temeraire, who only inclined his head, stiffly; he did not by then trust himself to speak.

They came near the camp with the sun already down behind them, and small cooking-fires alight among the tents. 'Gentius,' Temeraire said, 'when I roar, you will go in first, only show them your wings, spit somewhere near the guns, and then fly back to Armatius and go back to camp. You cannot see well enough to be spitting once we have flown in, but they will not know that, and I dare say it will alarm them greatly.'

'Ha ha!' Gentius said, 'Fighting again, at my age; I feel like a hatchling,' and he fluttered out his wings a little, making ready.

Temeraire broke away and flew on ahead towards the camp, climbing as he did, then hovered directly above it; the moon had not yet risen, and he did not think they would notice him. It was very peculiar to be so close to the enemy but not yet fighting, waiting to start a battle when *he* chose. It was not wholly comfortable. It had always seemed so very plain to him, and quite natural, when one should dart in and begin; but that was when he only needed to think of himself. Now there were so many others to consider, and the enemy too. Perhaps, it occurred to him suddenly, there were a great many other French dragons nearby, who they had not seen or heard of, and who might appear out of nowhere and turn the tide. Then they would surely lose, and it would be all his fault; he would have lost the day.

The prospect was alarming as no ordinary fighting would have been, and Temeraire almost thought that perhaps he would go back, and ask the others what they thought. He looked back northwest: he could just make them out, a great mass of shadows darker than the trees and the fields below. They were coming on as slowly as they could, wing-beats lazy so they drifted low and then swooped back up, describing great arcs instead of flying straight, all of them waiting for his signal. If only he might have a little advice . . .

But he was quite alone. He trembled, but there was no use being cowardly, there was no one to help him, and he must decide. Below, the two Chevaliers slept just one hill beyond the low rough earthwork barricade, where sentries strolled along the line, casually. In the camp, fires were scattered about, and some horses; the wind drifted a little, bringing some eddy with it, and one of the horses raised its head and whickered uneasily; another pawed at the ground and tossed its head.

'C'est rien, c'est rien,' a man said, eating his supper near them.

Temeraire drew his lungs full, thought of Laurence, and roared out his challenge.

He kept roaring for a long time. The Chevaliers jerked up in their clearing at once, their wings opening even before their eyes had, and began roaring a furious answer, their heads twisting this way and that as they searched the sky for him. Men came racing from the tents about them. Temeraire saw a captain with flashes of gold on his shoulder, being put up; they sprang into the air half-crewed, men on the ground still leapt for the harness as they rose.

'J'y suis!' Temeraire called out, propelling himself with great backward thrusts away from the camp, and roared again. 'Ici, me voici!' The French dragons wheeled in mid-air and came barrelling straight towards him, teeth bared; he hovered and waited and then dropped himself straight out of the way, his wings folded tight while they shot by, white flashes of rifle-fire sparking along their backs; then behind them, Gentius came soaring gracefully down over the camp on his enormous wings, and spat acid over ten cannon in a row.

Bells of alarum were clanging madly now, torches lit, men rushing out to form into rows as the handful of horses screamed and struggled against their handlers. Temeraire could not help but feel a wild surge of excitement, almost overpowering, as Requiescat, Ballista and Majestatis came thundering down through the camp, their claws and tails dragging through tents and pickets and fires alike, scattering them; and the red banners glowing in the fires that bloomed at once.

He dived down and joined their long straight row, stretching his ruff wide. They tore across the full length of the camp without pause, and then whipped aloft trailing canvas and rope, and anything else they had snagged upon their claws. Once they had gone high enough not to be shot, they pulled it all off and let it drop down upon the camp.

Perscitia had suggested the notion, as they had no bombs,

84

'Especially if you can get some tents pulled up, and drop them on the pepper guns,' she had said, and it answered remarkably well: most of the tents bundled up as they dropped, but one luckily unfurled and floated down in a heap on top of a company of infantry trying to aim the long-barrelled pepper guns, their bayonets poking out of it, making them only worse entangled.

'Oh!' Temeraire said exultantly. 'Oh, it is working! Perscitia, look—' but she was nowhere near to be seen, and he could not spend time finding her. The Chevaliers had wheeled about, but they were holding off—the sizzling crisp of Gentius's acid was sharp in the air for anyone to smell, and though it was dark, the fires leaping up from the camp glowed brightly enough to make it plain that there were four heavy-weights lined up opposite them. Quickly Temeraire turned and roared out, 'Chalcedony! Go around and at them!'

'What?' Chalcedony called back, circling in mid-air to try and keep his place; he and the other Yellow Reapers and middle-weights waited in a great mass for their turn to have a go at the camp.

'The Chevaliers! All of you circle about and come at them from behind, make them come towards us,' Temeraire called back, impatiently.

'Oh!' Chalcedony said, and the Reapers jumped at it, streamed out in a flock and whipped around the Chevaliers.

'Second line!' Temeraire cried, and the Anglewings and Grey Coppers all darted down in a pair of short rows, making another pass through the camp, crosswise to the strike that the heavyweights had made. They were all middle and light-weights, but so especially quick and skilful they were hard to hit even under the best of circumstances, and since the soldiers had all been aiming their guns up at the heavy-weights, in wholly the wrong direction, the circumstances were not at all the best; for the French anyway.

But many of the Anglewings were vain of their flying, and instead of going straight through the camp, Velocitas and Palliatia and a few of the others, were stopping abruptly mid-flight, cornering neat as a box and darting back the way they had come a little, then reversing again; or doing complicated interweaving tricks of flying. It was all just showing-away, and Temeraire frowned at it because they were taking a great deal longer than they ought, and would likely get shot. And anyway, it was meant to be the heavy-weights' turn to go again.

But he supposed that was selfish, they would have some splendid fighting with the Chevaliers instead; but when he looked, the Chevaliers were not coming towards them, they were too busy trying to defend themselves. The Reapers were darting at them in pairs, one from either flank, and as soon as the Chevalier turned to meet that attack, another pair would go at them from another direction. The Reapers came at them from below, so the men aboard the Chevaliers could not shoot them very easily. 'Oh,' Temeraire said, disgruntled; it was being very neatly done, but that was not what he had wanted, at all.

At least the Grey Coppers were behaving in a more practical way. While the Anglewings made their fuss, the lightweights were snatching up anything that came handy, tent-poles or young trees that came away from the ground, and whacking away at the camp with them, knocking down people and tents and spreading the fires even further.

'There goes a gun,' Majestatis said laconically, pointing with his long talons: the French had managed to pull one of their cannon around the right way, despite the confusion, and a dozen men aiming pepper guns were standing with it.

'Come away!' Temeraire called down hurriedly. 'Velocitas! Palliatia—Oh, they are not listening!' and they paid for it: the cannon fired, canister shot; the pepper guns spat, and a general shriek went up from the Anglewings as the balls scattered over them. 'Quick, Majestatis, we are fastest—'

'Hey, I ain't going to just sit here,' Requiescat said, but Temeraire was already diving, roaring.

'The gun for me,' Majestatis called as they plummeted, and he managed to bang over the hot cannon as he shot past, his wickedly long claws slashing ruin among the artillerymen.

Temeraire went for the Anglewings, bulling them along and up again, and nudging a shoulder under Velocitas, who had been worst hit by a pepper ball right in the face. His golden-yellow head was speckled black and red, and his eyes and nostrils were already swollen up so dreadfully that he could not see, streams of mucus dripped away from his face and he was moaning wretchedly.

And then Requiescat came down behind them going too fast for his weight and bowled through everyone, crashing through the camp with his wings spread trying to slow himself, and knocking soldiers and dragons every which way as he drove a massive furrow down the middle of the camp-ground with his talons and his tail.

'Aloft!' Temeraire called furiously, squirming himself free of several tents and shaking off a couple of soldiers who had been thrown on his leg. 'Everyone aloft, at once!' He punctuated the order with a roar, a proper one, which he aimed towards the caissons of ammunition stacked neatly by the guns. The pyramids of roundshot trembled and collapsed, balls rolling everywhere, crushing men's legs. The dragons all leapt aloft in the fresh confusion.

'Look, look,' cried Fricatio, one of the Grey Coppers, as he climbed up, 'look, I caught a horse,' waving it in his talons.

'This is no time to be eating!' Temeraire said, but it reminded him of their real purpose, and he flew a little higher to see. Sure enough there were a great many shadows moving about near the pigs, and the gate of the pen was swinging wide open. 'We have the pigs!' he cried, and everyone cheered noisily, and Temeraire added, 'Now we can go!'

'Why?' Majestatis said.

'What?' Temeraire said.

'Why ought we go?' Majestatis said, and pointed down: the soldiers were now fleeing in a body eastwards, entirely routed, only stopping long enough to heave the wounded upon wagons and drag them away. Far aloft, the Chevaliers were turning tail and going too, and the camp in all its flames was left deserted, to its conquerors.

'Well,' Temeraire said, peering down the slightly charred barrel, 'it is very nice, but I am not sure what we can do with it.'

'Drop it on their heads, next battle?' Moncey suggested.

'Listen to you talk; we shan't waste a real cannon like that,' Gentius said. 'What we need is some men to fire it for us. A proper artillery company. And we need some proper surgeons, too,' he added, 'for us and for 'em,' meaning the prisoners, most of them wounded who had been left behind on the field. There were not very many; by the time the dragons had managed to put out the fires, nearly all the casualties had died.

Lloyd and the men had helped the survivors away, and put up a tent for them, but that still left all the dead men lying about. The battle had been very satisfying, if not quite as long or as ordered as one might have wished. Temeraire was not sorry to have killed the soldiers, it was just as well they had, since otherwise they would have had to fight them again; and after all they had invaded. But he was sorry they were dead, and it made one rather sad to look at them.

Most of the ferals had not understood the difficulty, and a couple were even for eating them. Temeraire had flattened his ruff in horror as everyone else hissed disapprovingly, so the suggestion was quickly withdrawn. 'Yes, that is enough of *that* kind of talk,' Gentius said. 'But we can't leave them lying about, either. That just isn't fitting; they were good enemies.'

So a couple of the Reapers had dug a grave, perhaps a little deep – some twenty feet – and the couriers had collected up the dead and put them inside. After they had filled the hole, Chalcedony had respectfully stuck one of the least-charred French flags upright into the mound, and they had all bowed their heads solemnly for a moment; then they had eaten some pigs.

They had then begun the careful work of picking through the remains of the camp. Most things had been burnt-up, but for the metal pots, buckles and cannon-shot, and most excitingly, a great solid lump of gold – a heap of sovereigns melted all together – which had been found in the charred remains of a chest. Reedly had nosed it out onto the ground in front of them, and many heads had craned to look at it in rapt admiration; it shone brilliantly in the morning sun.

'Well, how is it to be shared out?' Requiescat had asked, eyeing it covetously.

'We must put it aside somewhere safe,' Temeraire said, 'and when the war is over, we shall take all the treasure we have won, like this, and have some splendid pavilions built all over the country, which we can all use whenever we like, which will be better than for each of us to have only enough of a share to buy a piece of a pavilion. And what is left over, we shall use to get medals, for everyone, and everyone will have a medal to suit their size.'

All approved of this arrangement, and a few dragons were detailed off – after complicated negotiations, which resulted in an escort of Reedly, Chalcedony, another Yellow Reaper *and* an Anglewing, when Reedly could easily have carried it alone – to accompany the chunk of gold to a place of safety back in the breeding grounds. The rest of them had fallen back to searching the camp with even more enthusiasm than before. Then they had uncovered the cannon.

Most of the guns had been ruined; those whose housings were not burnt or acid-eaten had been spiked by their crews before being abandoned. One however, had escaped destruction under the protective weight of a smothering tent. It was a little pitted, and its wheels were perhaps a bit singed along the edge, but it was a real great gun, a good twelve-pounder, and they had plenty of balls for it. There was even a store of gunpowder left, as the wagon full of powder had been kept some distance away from the rest of the camp.

'But how are the men to know what is to be done with it, if they are not already soldiers?' Temeraire said. He had seen the guns fired many times, aboard ship, but he did not recall perfectly just how it was managed. 'Perhaps Perscitia can work out—' he looked, and realized that she was not poking through the camp with the others, but was sitting near the water-hole curled up in a lump.

'Are you hurt?' he inquired, having gone over to her.

'Of course I am not hurt,' she said, waspishly.

'Why are you sitting over here then, instead of coming to see; we have found some gold already, and maybe there is more—'

'Well, it is not as though I will have a share,' she said. 'I did not do any fighting.'

'Everyone had a chance,' Temeraire said, injured; he did not feel he had been unfair. Naturally the heavyweights ought to go first, if they could do the worst . . .

Perscitia looked away, and hunched her wings more snugly. 'You may go away, if all you mean is to sneer and be unpleasant. I am sure it is no business of anyone's if I did not care to fight.'

'I am not sneering, at all, and you may stop being so quarrelsome!' Temeraire said. 'I did not notice that you did not fight.'

She fidgeted a little, and muttered by way of apology, 'Others did,' glancing towards the other dragons.

'But why did you not, if you mind so much now?' Temeraire asked. 'You might have, any time you liked.'

'I did not like to,' she said, defiantly, 'So there, and you may call me a coward if you want; I am sure I do not care.'

'Oh,' Temeraire said, and sat back on his haunches. He was not quite sure what to say. 'I am very sorry?' he offered, uncertainly. He supposed it must be very unpleasant to be a coward. But he had always thought cowards were wretched creatures, who would likely do something unpleasant such as steal your things, even if they knew they could not win fighting for them, and that was not what Perscitia was like, at all. 'You are never shy of quarrelling with anyone.'

'That is not the same,' she said. 'One does not get shot for quarrelling, or have a wing torn up, or a cannonball in the chest—I saw a dragon take a cannonball once, it was dreadful.'

'Of course,' Temeraire said, 'but one must simply be quick enough, and then you can dodge them.'

'That is nonsense,' she said. 'A musket-ball can go much quicker than any dragon, so it is all decided by chance, before you ever think of evasion, or even notice that someone is shooting at you. If you are very quick, of course, then you can very often be gone before they have even fired,' she added, 'so your chances *are* better, but they are best if you do not go anywhere in front of a gun at all—And I am not very quick.'

Temeraire rubbed the side of a talon against his forehead, pondering. 'In China,' he said, 'only some kinds of dragons fight; a great many of them are scholars, and would not know what to do in a battle at all. No-one thinks any less of them, or calls them cowards; I suppose that is what you are.'

She lifted her head, and Temeraire added, 'Anyway, we are all perfectly happy to fight, so there is no sense in your doing it too, when you dislike it so.'

'Well, I think just the same,' she said, brightening, 'only I do not like anyone to say I did not do my part, and there is no part other than fighting.'

'We must work out how to use the gun,' Temeraire said. 'That would be very useful, and perhaps you can think of something we might do with it, to help us while fighting? That is surely a fair share, as no-one else knows how to do it.'

This solution suited her so well that by the end of the day, Perscitia had a dozen men working busily as a gun-crew. They had come to them, along with another thirty, from the local militia, who had rather nervously come to the battlefield in the morning bearing muskets, to see what had happened during the night. Reassured by the gaily-fluttering flags, they had come near enough to be pressed into service with cheerful ruthlessness by Lloyd and his fellows, tired of being hands for near sixty dragons as well as their herdsmen.

The militiamen were abjured not to be such lumps when they cringed from Perscitia in fear, and were lectured with great pomp by Lloyd on the need to stop Bonaparte, before they surrendered to her tender mercies. They spent the day working through the mechanics of the gun-firing, the swab-bing, the wadding—all the steps Perscitia had pieced together by interrogating the men, on how their muskets were fired, and then every dragon who had ever been in service on board a ship or in a fleet action, and might have seen the great guns go.

It had been a little difficult: everyone remembered the sequence a little differently, and for a moment they were at a standstill, until she hit upon the notion of making a tally, of which order everyone recalled, and then taking the most popular. By evening they had successfully launched their first round-shot across the camp with a bang, to the great startlement of all the other dragons napping full of pork and satisfaction.

'If we could only work out a way for it to slide properly, there is no reason you might not take it aloft,' she said wistfully that evening, coming to join the discussion with her old sense of assurance restored. She would happily have kept working, but her men having grown sufficiently used to her—their remnants of fear had at last been outweighed by their fatigue—had rebelled and demanded a chance to sleep and eat. 'At least, maybe Requiescat might, and it could perhaps be set off upon his back; but the recoil, that is the difficulty.'

'What to do next, *that* is the difficulty,' Temeraire said, and bent his head over the information which Moncey had brought and sketched out into maps, wondering how they might learn what the French would do next, and how soon he might bring them to another battle.

Chapter Six

'Sir,' Hollin said, 'I don't like to make you think of it, but with him loose this long, gone this far off from the grounds, it stands to reason he isn't flying wild—He has gone to look for you.'

'I know,' Laurence said.

If Temeraire had gone to Dover, he had flown straight into the arms of Napoleon's invading army. And Laurence could not follow: Jane's very justification for retrieving him from prison had been to keep him out of French hands. Already he was four days overdue in camp, or generously three, and their absence would reflect on her just when she most needed all forces of persuasion aligned in her favour to prepare for Napoleon's inevitable march on London.

He knew what duty demanded he do: return, report his failure, and wait until some word at last came in of Temeraire's fate; to sit in gaol endlessly, with no notion of what had happened to Temeraire. Laurence did not know how he would bear it. But there was no other alternative. Already he had likely injured Hollin's career, if prior association with him had not been tarnish enough; just as he had injured Jane, and Ferris, and so many others. As if he had not already done enough harm.

'We might go another day,' Hollin suggested. 'Work our way back towards London, sir, asking along the way, and maybe see what anyone has heard about the French. It stands to reason the generals will want to know that anyway, sir.'

Laurence knew he ought to refuse. It was a generosity offered from friendship, not Hollin's real and considered judgment. 'Thank you, Hollin; if you think it justified,' he said at last, the internal struggle lost, or at least some ground yielded. 'But we shall go straight towards the camp,' he added, to win back a little of it, and tried to persuade himself that perhaps Temeraire had heard, somehow, of the main body of the army, and gone there. They might find him waiting in Rainham—but no, that passed the limits of optimism. Temeraire would not wait anywhere, if he knew where Laurence was, and likely even if he had not the least idea. He had crossed half of Africa without the slightest notion and had found Laurence in the middle of an unfamiliar continent; so he would certainly not be discouraged by the need to search all of Britain if need be, even in the middle of a war; and as like as not get himself hurt thereby.

They flew much-interrupted, stopping at any farm with a herd of moderate size, and at any town with a clearing large enough for a courier; but they received no news, or at least none that they had wanted. 'Lost twenty of my sheep, but not to any dragons; to the French, damn their eyes,' one angry herdsman informed them.

'They are so close?' Laurence said, in dismay. They were several hours west of London as the dragon flew, further than he would have imagined the French had come.

The man spat. 'Came through here yesterday, pillaging buggers; begging your pardon sir, but it is enough to make a saint swear. Three of my best ewes gone into their bellies, and a stud all because of that lunk-head boy of mine didn't get them into the hills in time. But there, who thought they would be here so soon?'

The mayor of Twickenham confirmed the French presence. 'We have heard from Richmond that they were dropped in dragon-back,' he said, 'they have been all up and down the countryside thieving. Our lads are gone to fight them north of here. There has been a militia mustered up 'round Richmond and there are, I believe, some dragons with them there, sir. A courier came here to fetch out our boys, as they had heard nothing yet of what to do. But of any loose dragons not a thing have I heard. We will be sure to keep our cattle under cover, though; you may be most sure of that.'

He gave them dinner, very kindly, and waved away Hollin's offer of payment, accepting an amount only for the goat which went to feed Elsie. The mayor's wife and oldest girl, a few years out of the schoolroom, ate with them, and Laurence was occasionally recalled to his manners enough to make some little conversation, but he was too burdened to be fit company. The fresh intelligence meant they must now go back, at once; the generals must know that the French had penetrated this far.

'There were some eagles, I hear,' the young woman ventured. 'Georgie said, before he went, the boys from Ham saw two of them.'

That was bad, very bad; two French regiments, and so far from the bulk of Napoleon's army, likely meant a Marshal lay somewhere in the area. The worst of the Marshals were competent; as the hands of their chief they were dangerous as vipers. There was nothing strategic to be won here, in the west of England, but there was a great deal of food; food which would keep those French dragons in the air. 'Had they cavalry?' he asked abruptly, raising his head. 'I beg your pardon,' he added, realizing belatedly that he had interrupted a conversation, which had moved on without him; Hollin and the young lady had been talking about the places which he saw on his route.

'Oh—I am sorry, sir; no, I don't remember Georgie saying so,' she said, abashed at being addressed.

'I think they do not, Captain,' the mayor affirmed. 'They came on foot here, anyway.'

If Napoleon had thrown all of his strength into air power, Laurence was not sure what that might mean. It disregarded all established wisdom about modern warfare, which held that a properly organized force of cavalry and infantry together, supported by pepper guns and artillery, could repel virtually any dragon attack. But no one had ever heard of a dragon attack using more than fifty dragons before Napoleon's first attempt at crossing the Channel in the year five. Laurence remembered their astonishment at his managing to bring together a force of a hundred beasts.

He went outside after the meal, and waited politely while Hollin took Miss—the name had already escaped Laurence—to see Elsie, by her nervous request. The dragon was also interested to meet her, ladies not common company for dragons but for the female captains, who rarely dressed for their natural station; and Elsie was quite willing to be petted and offered a blancmange that the young lady had made, which she politely licked up from the serving plate in a couple of swipes.

'Why, what a lovely plate,' she said after, with much more enthusiasm, and was visibly sorry to see it drawn back; it had a gaily painted border in red and blue with a few small touches of silver. 'I have never seen anything so pretty,' Elsie added, stretching her head to look at it again.

'Why, it is only an old—' the girl said, and then quickly swallowed the rest, and added, '—design, which I have painted over. I am sure you may have it, if you like it so.'

'Oh,' Elsie said, and said urgently to Hollin, 'Will you keep it for me? Perhaps it might be washed, and packed away safe?'

It took another half an hour for this to be done to her satisfaction, with much bobbing of heads and exchanges of compliments on both sides: a happy conversation which went past in a buzz of noise for Laurence, until at last he made an effort, and forced himself to say abruptly, 'Hollin, we had better be going.'

'Oh,' the girl said. 'But, shan't you wait for him?' She pointed; and they looked to see another dragon in the sky, flying in their direction.

'A fine thing,' Miller said, 'a fine thing. Expected four days ago in camp and I find you here, Captain Hollin, wandering around where you oughtn't be, and taking a convicted felon into good society.'

Hollin flushed and said sharply, 'If I have done wrong, Captain Miller, you may be sure I will explain myself to those as has the right to ask me to account for it. We have been looking for the dragon we was sent to fetch, seeing as how those fellows in the breeding ground have forgot their duty and gone, and the beasts all scattered.'

'What?' Miller said, forgetting to be pompous in alarm. 'All of them gone, out of the grounds? Where have they got to, what have they been eating—'

Miller's courier beast, Devastatio, was markedly smaller than Elsie, who was big for a Winchester. Hollin had known better than most new young courier-captains how to see to the proper feeding of a dragon, and he had already been on friendly terms with most of the herdsmen around the bigger coverts, a further advantage. Devastatio had landed showily, strutting the last few strides into the clearing, and having realized too late that he was outweighed, was now trying his best to puff out his chest, and surreptitiously climb a hillock. Elsie eyed him puzzled, and then offered, 'Would you like to see my plate?'

'Gentlemen,' Laurence said sharply, seeing Miller dragging Hollin through all the narrative of their search. 'We have no time for this. The French have been sighted nearby, and we must bring the intelligence to camp at once.'

'We already know about the French being here, there has been some fighting,' Miller said. 'Some bright militia-officer has raised the countryside and beat them properly over at Wembley, and again at Harlesden this morning. That is why we are here: I am carrying a colonel's commission for him.'

'Oh!' the young lady said, having hung back a little from their conversation. 'Have they been beaten, at Harlesden? Georgie will have been there—I must go and tell mother—' She half-turned, then turned back and curtseyed, and then hesitantly raised her hand a little. Hollin, stepping towards, her brought it to his lips, also a little hesitantly, and said, 'Your servant, Miss Jemson, and I hope my rounds might bring me again—'

'I hope so, too,' she said, pink, and having dared so far, turned and fled.

'Sir, if the news is in, and Miller will tell them where we are, we might keep looking—' Hollin said, turning back, his own cheeks a little ruddy.

'Oh, no; no, thank you, there'll be none of that,' Miller said. 'Your orders are not to go wandering over all Creation, they are to get the dragon and come back; and well, if you haven't got the dragon, you can only do what is left, and that is to come back. If they want you to keep looking, they will tell you so. We will fly in company, like we ought when there is news like this to be bringing back, in case one of us is brought down. A hundred dragons out wild, eating people as like as cows? I don't know what you was thinking

100

not to return at once, except to save the neck of one as don't deserve—'

'Captain Miller—' Hollin said.

'Enough,' Laurence said. 'I do not intend to be the subject of a quarrel in circumstances such as these. Captain Hollin, we had some rational hope of finding Temeraire quickly, having arrived so shortly after the dispersal of the breeding grounds; but now we can have none. I am most sensible of your generosity, but will not trespass upon it further. Let us go at once.'

He had steeled himself to it, and now wanted nothing more than to have it over. The quicker he returned, the less damage would be done by his having kept them away so long, selfishly, further contrary to his duty; success only could have made it forgivable. Even then he ought to have been reproached. Granby had been right, all along. His discipline had been wholly corrupted, Laurence saw now. Perhaps the effects were all the worse because he had not been brought up properly within the Corps, and had let the sudden liberty of the service, looser by necessity than the Navy, go to his head completely and become license.

He swung himself up and over onto Elsie, after Hollin had climbed up, and silently strapped himself in, heavy with self-reproach. He gave no attention to their surroundings, or the journey, and let the cold wind in their faces make him dull. Devastatio flung himself ahead far of Elsie; further self-puffery, which he was able to manage as she was burdened by two instead of one. It was all that saved them: because of the distance, the Petit Chevalier could not come at them together, and so he bore down on Devastatio alone in the lead.

The little Winchester squalled and tumbled straight down, blood streaming from his wing and side where he had been savagely clawed. He managed to right himself with great hissing gulps of breath, puffing out his sides until his fall slowed enough for him to gain purchase, but he was not flying properly, only able to limp half-skewed to the ground. Satisfied that he had been grounded, and might be retrieved at leisure, the Petit Chevalier wheeled about, and turned his attention to Elsie.

The name of the French breed was appropriate only by comparison to the Grand Chevalier; the heavyweight heading towards them was some eighteen tons, his claws already stained with Devastatio's blood, and he roared threateningly as he drew closer. Elsie gave a small desperate gasp and dived out of his way. She twisted nearly upside down to evade the attack, sending Laurence and Hollin to dangle from their straps, and then shot forward with all her might past the great dragon's belly as rifle-shot from the bell-men whistled like wasps past their heads.

But she was too weighted down to reach her full speed. The Petit Chevalier doubled back on himself and set in steady pursuit: over distance his strength would tell, and he would have them if she could not escape before then. He was fast enough to keep her in his sights for an hour, Laurence judged, looking down over Elsie's side to watch the dragon's shadow flashing by over the ground.

It came chasing after Elsie's smaller shadow like a racing cloud, pouring up and down the curves of the hills, darkening slopes and sending deer bounding away through the trees. The outline of the dragon remained steady as the ground rolled away beneath them with blazing speed, at least twenty knots with the wind howling and tearing at their clothing no matter how low they crouched against Elsie's neck.

The Petit Chevalier roared behind them. Laurence could not lift his head up into the wind to look back, but they were over a broad stretch of farmland, fields laid out in neat snow-powdered squares bordered by roads, so the dragon-shapes made perfect silhouettes upon white, and as Elsie's first desperate sprinting failed, the distance between the two shadows began slowly and inexorably to narrow.

And then, sliding into place behind the Petit Chevalier's shape, a third shadow joined the line: beginning first as a small speck and rapidly growing, larger and larger, until at last it swallowed the other, and with a dreadful shattering roar a tremendous Regal Copper thundered down from above. The enormous red and gold beast pounced directly upon the Petit Chevalier, serving him with the very same trick he had used on Devastatio, and without any restraint bowled him over and down.

The two heavyweights tumbled, head over heels, snarling and snapping wildly; a couple of men went flying from the French dragon's back, and munitions, bombs and rifles tumbled loose towards the countryside. Laurence had no idea how the Regal Copper's crew were managing, and then he realized that the dragon wore no harness at all.

Elsie was panting as she slowed, curving in a wide arc so they could look back at the titanic struggle. 'Oh, I am glad,' Elsie said, gulping air between words. 'I am not—quite sure I could have run away from that big French one.'

'I hope we do not need to run away from that other fellow,' Hollin said, a sentiment that Laurence shared: the Regal Copper outweighed the other dragon by at least another seven or eight tons. He had now hooked his claws into the Chevalier's shoulders and was scratching at him with his hind legs, shaking him all the time so the riflemen could not find their feet well enough to fire at him properly; the handful of wild shots which they managed did not trouble him greatly.

It was a savage style of fighting, and if cruder than formation flying, on the level of such an individual contest the unexpected ferocity told worse than discipline. The Chevalier squalled frantically at last, and with a great convulsive heave managed to tear himself free, leaving great torn gashes in his flesh, three furrows along each shoulder almost like bars of rank. He bolted headlong away, leaving the Regal Copper in possession of the field.

The victorious beast spread his wings, glowing vividly red with the sun behind them, and roared triumphantly after the Petit Chevalier, a deep bellowing noise like thunder; then the Regal Copper turned to look at them and spoke, in tones of great disapproval, 'Well, and what are you about? I don't think much of your sense, taking on a fellow that size.'

'Pray,' Elsie said timidly, 'we didn't mean to, only he came on us all of a sudden; and Devastatio is hurt.'

'Oh, there is another of you?' The Regal turned and scanned the ground. They had drifted some way off in the fighting, and Devastatio had tried to drag himself under some trees, for concealment, but Regal Coppers had only tolerable eyesight from a sufficient distance, and after a bit of scanning about he said, 'Ha, there he is,' and flew over to the hiding place, landing with a tremendous thump. 'You lot were all told this morning not to come round here,' the big dragon said severely, nosing over Devastatio's wounds. 'I said those big Frenchies were going to be going up and down carrying soldiers about all this way, didn't I? This is going to be nasty healing.'

'We were told nothing of the sort!' Miller said, having to lean rather frantically away to keep from being squashed by the prodding.

The Regal jerked his head back in surprise, and then put it further back, squinting at them rather uselessly. 'Is that a man? Why, you are under harness,' he said, exclaiming, and turned to squint at Elsie too. 'Both of you!'

'Of course they are,' Miller said, and added, with what Laurence had to admit was marked courage, if not much sense of gratitude, 'Why are you flying about wild like this? Why have you departed from the breeding grounds?'

'Hum,' the Regal Copper said. 'I am no good hand at explaining things, so I suppose you had better come along with me and talk to the commander.'

'What do you mean, commander—' Miller said, bewildered. '—are you fighting with the militia?'

'Yes, all those fellows are with us,' the Regal Copper said. 'Come on then, up you get,' he added, to Devastatio. The Winchester sniffed a little, still licking at his wounds, but obeyed, climbing awkwardly up onto the enormous dragon's back. The Regal Copper went up with a tremendous propelling leap, took on a little height, and ponderously began to flap away, with Elsie darting after him anxiously.

The flight was short, despite his slow pace, and astonishingly he landed them just outside the edges of a vast and neatly organized camp. Laurence caught a glimpse of many dragons lying about in the clearing as they descended, and also a large pen full of enormous black pigs.

The Regal padded along a broad cleared lane through the trees towards the heart of the camp, only to pull up short when a little Winchester, also without any harness, popped up on the border and said loudly, 'Stop and give the watch-word!'

'It's me, isn't it?' the Regal Copper said. 'And these two are with me, so they are all right, too.'

'That don't matter,' the Winchester said, stubbornly. 'Everyone must give the watch-word, or else I am to yell, but,' he said hastily, as the Regal Copper lowered his head, snorting, 'I suppose that don't mean you,' and hopped aside.

Laurence was startled to find a commander who had so little prejudice against unharnessed dragons that he had somehow conceived both to recruit them and make use of them in such a fashion. He wondered if the man could have some experience of the Corps, if he had a relation, or had perhaps lived near a covert. The system made for a good solution twice over: both to keep the dragons from roving wild across the countryside, pillaging, and to strengthen his own militia force greatly. It did puzzle Laurence to see a dragon on watch duty; but perhaps it would serve all the better to put off any spies.

Miller's expression, from where he sat perched on the Regal beside Devastatio, stroking the injured dragon, suggested he was less impressed than scandalized to see such beasts without harnesses, and serving in such a role.

For his part, the Regal did not seem to think much of it either. 'I am sure I don't know what the world is coming to,' he said, shaking his head as he padded along. 'It is all well and good to be talking on about pavilions and such,' and Laurence's heart leapt, even before the Regal brought them into the clearing at the centre of the camp and said, 'Temeraire, there are some fellows here to see you.' Laurence flung loose his carabiner straps and leaped down from Elsie's back, to see the great black head swinging around towards him.

'It is very good to have an eagle,' Temeraire said. It was a particularly bright gold now that they had washed all the mud from it. Everyone had been ready to help, and the standard with it was very handsome too now that the men had brushed it clean. It would be quite a wrench to sell it, he felt, and the way everyone else looked at it he knew they felt the same. 'But we must not begin to expect that we will have things all our own way. There have not been very many French dragons to fight yet, because they are all busy carrying the men about, but sooner or later we will have to manage them.'

'I have some notions which we might like to try,' Perscitia said, 'when we have more to fight—'

'Temeraire,' Requiescat said, coming into the clearing behind him; Temeraire looked around and saw an injured

Winchester on his back, and another trotting along behind him, carrying his old ground-crew master.

Requiescat continued to talk, and Perscitia was going on about pepper, but Temeraire did not understand either of them; their words did not seem to want to make sense. Laurence was coming towards him; but Laurence was dead. Then he was saying, 'Temeraire, thank Heavens; I have been trying to find you these last four days.'

'But you are dead.' Temeraire said, uneasily. He had never seen a ghost, and though he had often thought it would be very interesting to, this was not, at all; it was dreadful, to see Laurence just as in life, to want to reach out and gather him in, and keep him safe, knowing he could not.

But Laurence simply said, 'Of course I am not dead, my dear; I am here,' and Temeraire bent down his head, peered very closely and put out his tongue experimentally to sniff at him; and then at last he cautiously, so cautiously, put out his forehand to curl about Laurence and lift him, and oh, he was quite solid. He was there, and he was not dead at all. Temeraire gave a low joyful cry and curled around his captain tightly and said, 'Oh, Laurence; I shall never let anyone take you from me again.'

PART II

Chapter Seven

'No; they nearly drowned you, and not even on purpose but only through carelessness. I am not letting them have you back,' Temeraire said. 'Besides, I cannot go; I cannot just leave everyone here.'

'You are more desperately needed with the main force,' Laurence said, trying to explain, but the obstinate gleam in Temeraire's eye was discouraging. 'We must speak to the commander.'

'I am the commander,' Temeraire said.

Laurence stared up at his earnest expression from within the protective wall of dragon encircling him, and then pulling himself up onto the ridge of Temeraire's forearm looked around the clearing. There was not a senior officer to be seen, anywhere, and none of the dragons – many of them regarding him with equal curiosity – were harnessed. Besides the enormous Regal, lay an old Longwing, with milky orange eyes half-lidded sleepily, and a big Chequered Nettle, a Parnassian, and a scattering of smaller dragons all around.

Beyond them Laurence could see a camp full of dragons: Yellow Reapers by the dozen sleeping nearly in a single heap, and smaller courier beasts and lightweights sprawled upon them. There were a handful of men dealing with the pigs and a few cattle, penned up to one side, but they wore rough clothing, obviously not officers of the Corps. There were some few hundred redcoats mostly grouped by the guns, and some volunteers in private coats, but that was all. 'The militia,' Laurence said, slowly.

'Yes, Lloyd and some of our herdsmen told us where to fetch them,' Temeraire said. 'They are very good fellows, once they settled down at least, and began to believe we were not going to eat them. We needed them to fire our guns.'

'Good God,' Laurence said, comprehensively; he could well imagine how the Lords of the Admiralty might react to the intelligence that the well-formed militia which they confidently expected, with a clever young officer at its head, was in fact rather an experimental and wholly independent legion of unharnessed dragons, without great sympathy for their Lordships, and under the command of the most recalcitrant dragon in all of Britain.

'Well,' Temeraire said, when he had listened to Laurence's awkward attempt to explain the orders which had brought them, and the Admiralty's misunderstanding, 'it does not seem at all complicated to me; they did not say that you were only to give the commission, if the commander were a man?' he asked, lowering his head towards Miller.

'Why, not—no—' Miller said, staring, 'but—'

'Then it is perfectly plain,' Temeraire said, riding over him. 'I shall write and say I am happy to accept my commission, and apologize that my duty to the regiment prevents my returning with Laurence at present. They cannot complain of that. Anyway, we must send at once to warn them: Napoleon will be attacking London in two days.'

A more sensational means of diverting their attention he could hardly have conjured. Laurence did not know what to think at first; Temeraire had perhaps a dragon's idea of distances, and did not fully appreciate the difficulties inherent in moving so many men and horses, along with their supply, from a landing site on a hostile shore to assault-readiness. It had been only a week. Without opposition, in that time Bonaparte might have marched his men in a long string to the city, but as an army, ready to fight, no. Laurence relied on it; fervently wished to rely on it. But he recalled too vividly the thunder of the guns at Warsaw, a month and more before the French ought to have been there, and doubted uneasily. 'Can you be certain?'

'We have been watching Marshal Lefèbvre's corps,' Temeraire said. 'They received orders this morning and set off directly; and they have been moving soldiers about all of today, towards London. Requiescat saw them.'

'Requiescat?' Laurence said.

'You have met him, he brought you here,' Temeraire said.

'He cannot have gotten very close, unnoticed,' Laurence said: a Regal Copper was an odd choice of spy.

'Oh, he did not try to sneak,' Temeraire said. 'No one very much likes to start a quarrel with him, you see, so he could get quite close before they were ready to fight. And when the French could see no one was with him, they simply supposed he was run away from the breeding grounds, and only looking for other dragons to have some company. So they were very eager to tempt him to stay, and even put out cows for him in their camp. It was much easier than feeding him ourselves, and he was able to see everything they were doing.'

'Which is, hieing themselves off towards the city,' Requiescat put in. 'They was all looking for us before then, as we had blacked their eye a couple of times, but soon as the orders came in, off they went; and they sent all the cattle on ahead,' he finished, in gloomy tones.

'Blacked their eye,' Miller said, with a snort. 'Yes, damned likely.'

'Like enough,' Hollin said, and pointed: an eagle standard jutted from the ground, the *13éme* regiment blazoned on the banner. 'I'll take the news, sir,' Hollin added, looking at Laurence. 'Me and Elsie can make the dash quick, on our own, and let them know—'

'Damn nonsense,' Miller cut in. 'The news you ought to be taking is that there are sixty dragons that need rounding up, and herding back to the breeding grounds—' He stopped abruptly, as Temeraire took a step towards him and lowered his head very close.

'We are not going to be herded anywhere,' he said, dangerously, 'by Napoleon or by your admirals; and if you like to ask the other dragons of the Corps to try it, I expect they will soon see how very foolish it is to try, and if not, I will explain it to them; I dare say they will join us instead.'

Laurence had a fair notion of which dragons would be perfectly prepared to join Temeraire under such circumstances. That would bring their tally to two Longwings, even if one of them was surely past his real fighting days, and two Regal Coppers to join with the five other heavyweights Laurence could see, and a full complement of middleweights and couriers. It would make Temeraire's army very nearly the equal of the Corps in strength, at least those forces presently in England and under harness.

If he were not fully aware of these prospects, Miller was wise enough to blanch at the suggestion and to be quelled at least a little. He settled for writing a letter, in a quiet corner, while Temeraire dictated his own:

Gentlemen,
   I am very happy to accept your commission, and we should like to be the eighty-first regiment, if that number

is not presently taken. We do not need any rifles, and
we have got plenty of powder and shot for our cannons,

Laurence wrote with a vivid awareness of the reaction this should produce.

but we are always in need of more cows and pigs and
sheep; goats would also do, if they are good deal easier
to come by. Lloyd and our herdsmen have done very
well, and I should like to commend them to your atten-
tion, but there are a lot of us, and some more herdsmen
would be very useful.

'Pepper, put in pepper,' another dragon said, craning her head. She was a middleweight, yellowish striped with grey; some kind of cross-breed. 'And canvas, we must have a lot of canvas—'

'Oh, very well then, pepper,' Temeraire said, and continued his list of requests adding,

I should very much like Keynes to come here, and also
Gong Su, and Emily Roland, who has my talon sheaths,
and the rest of my crew; and also we need some surgeons
for the wounded men. Dorset had better come too, and
some other dragon-surgeons.
  You had all better not stay where you are at present

'Temeraire, you cannot write so to your superior officers,' Laurence said, breaking off. He had forgone any attempt to explain that the commission would certainly be revoked instantly and had swallowed many protests already on the language of the letter, in favour of getting its urgent news sent quickly. Jane would understand it, at least; but there were limits.

'But they really had better not,' Temeraire said, surprised. 'They have not enough soldiers, not anywhere near, because they are moving too slowly.'

Laurence persuaded him at last to soften the language:

Napoleon will be attacking you on Saturday, with nearly all of his army; the French are going very quickly because they are all being carried about by dragons, and the reinforcements from Wales will not reach you in time. Our couriers have seen them on the road and they are only travelling fifteen miles in a day.

'But what if they do not realize that it means they ought to retreat?' Temeraire objected.

'They will understand, I assure you,' Laurence said; he did not bother to say that they would very likely not believe it, and that nothing would come of Temeraire's advice.

In this at least he was thoroughly wrong: a great deal came of it, if nothing very desirable. Laurence awoke the next morning, on his dragon-arm pallet, to a furious yelling outside the sheltering membrane of Temeraire's wing. He was not allowed to get to his feet for he was snatched up at once and put on Temeraire's back, near the breastplate-chain. Temeraire pushed himself up to his feet, just as a couple of courier-weights came bounding in urgently from the camp boundary-line, half-flying and half-leaping, and gasped out, 'Temeraire, she hasn't the watch-word, but—'

'I do not need any silly watch-word,' Iskierka said, padding into the clearing She coiled herself back on her hindquarters and snorted a thin stream of fire for emphasis, and the whole mess of the Turkestan ferals came tumbling along behind her.

'What do *you* want?' Temeraire said, very ungraciously. He did not see why Iskierka had to come, showing away and making a great noise.

116

'To fight,' Iskierka said, as if the answer were obvious. 'We are supposed to be in a war, but there has not been any fighting for four days, and I have not even been let to go flying anywhere and,' she hissed smoke again, 'they came and lectured my Granby, when I went out for just a bit of hunting.'

'Well, there is about to be a great deal of fighting back there,' Temeraire said, 'so you ought to return now.'

'No there is not,' Iskierka said, 'at least, they are not getting ready for any fighting; they said it would be another week before there is a battle. But we heard that you had had two battles already, and then your letter came saying that there was going to be some more, so we have come to have a share of the fighting also. And,' she added, 'when we have finished and beat Napoleon, I have decided that you may give me an egg.'

'Oh!' Temeraire said, swelling with indignation, 'how very kind! I am to be honoured, I suppose.'

'Well, I am much richer than you are,' she said, 'and also I can breathe fire, so you ought to be.'

'I would not give you an egg,' Temeraire said, 'if you were the very last dragon in the world, but me; I should rather have none at all.'

'You haven't,' Iskierka said. 'No one has gotten an egg by you yet, so you see, I am very generous even to try.'

This was not comfortable news, and Temeraire drew back a little, startled. He had not been very enthusiastic about all the breeding, but one could not help but feel satisfied at being wanted, and think how many eggs there should be. He did not understand why there should be *none*. It did not sound very well; not that it made him wish any more to give Iskierka one.

She, meanwhile, preened herself smugly, stretching out her coils in a messy way so everyone would notice her

117

more. She had a lot of gaudy stuff attached to her harness: chains that were probably not real gold at all, and which held chips of what were certainly nothing more than coloured glass; and Temeraire could not help but be conscious of Granby's attire, as he spoke with Laurence and Tharkay near the standard in low voices. He wore a very fine green velvet coat, trimmed all over in golden braid, with not one but two swords at his waist, one of them short, but both brilliantly ornamented at the hilt, and housed in fine shining leather sheaths; even if he did not look very happy at present. Laurence was in a shabby coat, which did not suit him at all.

The others were eyeing her with admiration—Arkady and the other ferals too, all of whom had bright stuff hooked haphazardly onto their harness, making them look rather like slovenly pirates, Temeraire thought; and Arkady, Temeraire realized in outrage, Arkady had Demane on his back! Demane who was of *his* crew, so he said reproachfully to the boy, 'What are you doing with him?'

'He does not know what the other soldiers are saying with the flags,' Demane said, looking up, 'so I tell him, and then we decide whether to listen. The flags are wrong sometimes,' he added.

They had not brought along anyone else from his crew, or any food, or anything useful at all. They had no notion of how they were to be fed or where they were to sleep, and did not respect the order of the camp at all. Wringe, who was rather big for a feral, a good-sized middleweight, tried to shove a Yellow Reaper out of his place, and so of course all the Reapers jumped up and hissed at her, and then Arkady and the others joined in hissing back, and Temeraire had to roar to get all their attention and push them apart.

'You are new, so you must clear your own places,' he said sternly.

'Oh, that is easy,' Iskierka said, and hissed a command at Arkady, who quickly chivvied his gang to one side. She then blasted out fire across a swath of ground at the edge of their clearing, dry leaves crisped and tree-bark popped off trunks with sounds like gunfire. One old dead pine caught like a torch and went into a perfect crackling blaze, as everyone else squawked and jumped to their feet.

'That is enough!' Temeraire said. 'You may not go about setting fires in camp; we have powder all about, and you will have us all blown up. Now put out those trees, and clear it properly, by pulling them out.'

The ferals, in a rather surly way, obeyed and smothered the flames with soil; but Iskierka did nothing but sit down, yawn and observe, while everyone in the camp watched her, more impressed than otherwise. It was not at all satisfactory, and when he said as much to Perscitia, she added insult to injury by having no sympathy, and saying instead, 'A fire-breather will be very useful,' and then showing him several manoeuvres, which she had sketched out to make use of Iskierka especially.

'They didn't believe a word of it,' Granby said to Laurence though it was no surprise. He looked rather exhausted, and left sweat streaked on his forehead when he rubbed his hand against it. 'The generals did not, anyway; *she* swallowed it whole, and nothing would do but to come and fight with you, or else Temeraire would be getting all the glory, and prizes, and she wanted an eagle too. Once she has decided on something, those ferals will follow her to the end of Creation.' Arkady was still their leader, but even he had evidently taken to regarding Iskierka as a force of nature beyond ordinary leadership, especially since she had led them to seize so much treasure.

'Roland was damned understanding,' Granby added.

'She sent a courier after us with orders, and put us on detached duty, scouting, so I am not insubordinate technically. But—' He raised his hands, helplessly.

'No preparations were made for a French attack?' Laurence said, low. 'None whatsoever?'

'To be fair,' Granby said, 'there is not much they can do; they haven't the men yet. Admiral Roland tried to persuade them we ought to be ferrying in the troops, but to their minds, such action will only make a mess, and cause mutiny everywhere when the men won't go aboard.'

'They might retreat,' Tharkay said, 'rather than wait to be routed.'

'Well,' Granby said, and Laurence felt much the same; it was one thing to retreat from the coast, having failed to prevent a landing, but another matter entirely to let London be taken without a shot.

'Is there any hope that you are mistaken?' Laurence asked Temeraire, a little later, after the ferals had been settled into the camp.

'They are moving their men *somewhere*,' Temeraire said, practically, 'and I cannot think where he would move them, other than to London, where your army is. There are plenty of cows around here, so it would not be only for food. But if you like I will ask Moncey and the others to go and see if they can work out where they have gone, for certain.'

Before this plan could be wholly put into effect, however, it was rendered unnecessary: Elsie came flying desperately into camp, nearly skidding across the ground. 'Hurry, oh, hurry,' she cried, 'they are not attacking tomorrow, they are attacking tonight.'

Hollin came scrambling off her back and said, 'It is all true, sir; the scouts have seen them formed up not an hour's march away, and there are ten Fleur de Nuits arming themselves to the teeth in their camp.'

Laurence now had opportunity to see for himself how quickly an army of dragons might go, when their own camp moved. First, the herd of cattle were sent bellowing down the road in a cloud of dust, with the herdsmen beating them along, with a few aerial shepherds for encouragement. 'We will meet you at Harpenden,' Temeraire said to the chief herdsmen, 'or send you word there, of where to bring the cows, and along which road.'

'Aye, sir,' the man said, touching his forelock quite automatically, and cheerfully shouting to his men, he kicked his mule and moved along.

The handful of tents were struck and bundled up, stakes and all, into a crumpled heap upon one large cloth; cooking gear was thrown in too, the great cauldrons all filled with roundshot. The middleweight dragons seized the guns, and the militia and the remaining hands clambered up onto the smaller beasts using ropes to secure themselves. 'It needs less rope, you see,' Temeraire explained, 'for the little ones to carry, and the men say they like it better if they can sit astride, instead of being cross-legged.'

He kept a stern headmaster's eye on the operation, and from time to time darted an anxious glance at Laurence, as if to gauge his opinion; but there was nothing to complain of at all. As the dragons went aloft, they dipped down over the rear of the moving herd, and each snatched themselves some dinner, a cow or a fat pig, and flew away eating, with no evident difficulty in combining the activities, if they did spatter themselves somewhat with blood in the process.

'There, now we are ready also,' Temeraire said, and put out his hand for Laurence, to set him up aloft, and with a leap they were up: not an hour gone by, and beneath them nothing was left but the bare untidy field.

The dragons flew in no particular order but one great disorganized mass, shifting continuously; or so it first seemed to Laurence, and then he discovered that the small dragons were dropping back, now and again, to rest upon the largest. The discovery was made rather abruptly, when a small muddy-coloured feral dropped down onto Temeraire out of mid-air, and clutching on put her head out to peer at Laurence, with rather a critical expression, while she caught her breath with great gulps.

'Will Laurence, at your service,' Laurence said cautiously, after a few moments of silent staring.

'Oh, I am Minnow,' the dragon said. 'Beg pardon, only I was a bit curious, because himself was so low, over losing you, I wondered if maybe you was different from other men.'

Her tone suggested she had found nothing out of the ordinary to admire. Temeraire put his head around indignantly. 'Laurence is the very best captain there is. We have just been saving everyone, and fighting the admirals, so of course we do not have our nicest things with us presently.'

'Have you never wanted a companion?' Laurence asked the little dragon; little being a relative term of course, as her head alone likely outweighed him.

'I have chums enough,' she said, 'and as for the harness, and being told always where to go; no thank you. I expect it is better for you big fellows in service,' she added to Temeraire, 'as no one thinks that they can bull you into anything you really do not like, but I hear enough from the old couriers to know it isn't so for me. Broke-down by the time their captains go, and nothing to show for it but harness-stripes.

'There, that has set me right, off I go,' she said, and jumped off again, with no more ceremony than which she had arrived, and dashed off again out in front.

Laurence then saw the manoeuvre a common one, and responsible for the greater part of the confusion of shifting beasts. The heavyweights did not much change their positions, but made steady bulwarks in the force, timed to Requiescat's pace, as he was the slowest. The middleweights, with more energy to spare, would occasionally break off and dive low to the fields, returning, now and again, with cow or pig or sheep, which they either ate themselves or brought to the larger dragons.

'Yes, so we needn't all stop,' Temeraire said, 'and this way no-one is hungry when we arrive, not even Requiescat, even if he complains a little anyway just for show.'

'It isn't for show,' Requiescat said, swinging his head around. 'When I was in real fighting trim I was twenty-six tons. I am not back up to snuff just yet, after that nasty cold,' a rather mild way of describing the effects of the virulent epidemic, which had struck the Regal Coppers particularly hard. All of them had lost a great deal of weight, which now was slow to return; although it was difficult to imagine Requiescat much larger than he was.

They met no opposition along the way, only a few French scouts that sighted them and turned and fled at once, bearing the news away. It was too much to hope that so large a force, aloft, would go without notice; but if it made Napoleon delay his attack, it was indeed desirable that he should have the news.

Their flight bore them over Hammersmith and Kew, the snaking brown ribbon of the Thames with sparkling ice on its edges and a crust of snow, and then over the city itself.

Hollin took Elsie out in front and threw out signal-flags, then the guns spoke from below, acknowledging, and below people came running into the streets to cheer them on, a heartening noise if made faint by distance. Temeraire called ahead, 'Dirigion, Ventiosa, go on ahead so that they may see our flags,' and two Yellow Reapers darted forwards, red velvet curtains streaming from their grasp.

Another twenty minutes' flight made the army visible: a

sea of redcoats in the churned mud and snow of camp. Temeraire took on height as they came in, so he had a clear lane before him, and then drawing breath he roared. The air before them was cold and full of fragile wisps of white cloud, and these gave an ephemeral physical form to the terrible ringing of the divine wind, breaking before its force into wide striated ripples, very much like the haze of heat over ground in high summer. They melted away almost at once, but below, the dragons of the Corps raised their heads to watch them, and roared out glad greetings in answer. Temeraire, banking, took them down in a broad field on the army's left flank.

'Laurence,' Temeraire said, as they were settling, 'pray will you tell the generals that I am very happy to come and speak to them, but that they will need to clear some room at their tent if it is that large one in the middle of camp, and also they had better do something about the horses.'

'I must prepare you; they will not be in the least happy to have you come,' Laurence said, 'nor will they take any act towards easing that end.'

'Then,' Temeraire said, 'we will all go away again, and they may fight Napoleon without us. They have asked us to come, and they need our help; they may not treat us like slaves. And I dare say we will manage to feed ourselves somehow or other, even if they do not like to keep giving us cows.'

Laurence hesitated; he wished to voice some protest, and speak of duty, but justice silenced him. It was surely not Temeraire's duty, nor the duty of any of those dragons, who had never been asked for an oath, nor received any recompense for service. His own duty, he saw less clearly. If he were ordered to remain, to serve whether in the field or under sentence of death, there could be no alternative. But he feared rather that the duty demanded of him would be to persuade Temeraire to stay, against the dragon's own interests.

He was brought to the same tent, now much altered: the map tables unfolded wide and littered with markers and figures, occupied the lion's share of the floor. A steady low argument continued in a back chamber, a back chamber which had been added, through a fresh-cut flap — voices querulous and frightened, and only a few holding any note of decisiveness. Laurence could hear Jane's voice rising clear and ringing above them all. He was kept standing silently, trying not to overhear.

A group of young lean unsmiling officers worked over the tables; they looked at Laurence with cold disdain, and then paid him no attention. At length a colonel came out and said to Laurence, icily, 'I am to tell you that you will be pardoned, if you can make the dragons fight.'

That the remark gave him no pleasure was evident. 'Damned disgrace,' one of the young men in the corner muttered, without looking up.

'Bring me sixty dragons the hour before a battle and I will pardon you for treason, and murder, too,' Wellesley said, emerging from the back room. 'I don't know what sort of genius of disaster you are, Laurence, but if you can be aimed at Bonaparte instead of us, you are worth not hanging. Can you make the beasts obey?'

'Sir,' Laurence said, 'I have brought you no dragons; it would better say, the dragons brought me. They do not obey me but Temeraire—'

'And the creature obeys you, that is good enough for me,' Wellesley said. 'I am not in a mood to have my time wasted with legalities. Do your damned duty, or I *will* have you hanged, before I go and get myself shot on the field.' He snatched a paper from the table and scribbled upon it a few hurried lines, which could have been interpreted in nearly any fashion one chose, and thrust them out.

Laurence looked at the paper, life, liberty, duty all in one; and was almost grateful to Wellesley for the bribery and threats, which could only make the command easier to refuse.

'You will forgive me, sir,' he said, 'I cannot make you the promise you wish; I have not the power to make it good. If you wish to speak with the leader of the dragon-militia, that is Temeraire himself. And he will not obey, nor the beasts with him, if they are not consulted.'

'For the love of God, and Bonaparte on our doorstep,' Wellesley said. 'Do you imagine we have time to go jumping a mile across camp, to coddle dragons?'

'He needs no coddling, sir,' Laurence said, 'beyond what information you would consider appropriate for any commander of a substantial militia who arrived late, and without any prior knowledge of your plan of attack. He is more than willing to come to you, if there were space cleared for him and the horses secured against their natural instincts.'

Wellesley snorted. 'Plan of attack? He can't know any less about it than any man alive. Rowley,' he said, turning abruptly to one of the young men at the side of the tent, who jerked to attention, 'Go tie up the horses and clear room enough for him to land. How much does he need?'

He waited for no answer, but went back into the general staff meeting. 'Temeraire will require some hundred feet square to come down,' Laurence said to Rowley, going outside with him.

'What is he, clumsy as a cow?' said the young man sourly, and shouted orders for several tents and an entire picket-line of horses to be moved. 'I won't answer for your neck if he eats the General's favourite horse,' he added.

Laurence did not bother to answer these remarks, but went as quickly as he could back to the clearings, and halted: word of their arrival had travelled at speed, and a handful of his crew had come to the camp, having slipped away from their other assignments. 'Sir,' Fellowes said, glancing up from his work, and Blythe beside him with a small forge. Gangly young Allen stood up flushing, two inches taller at a glance than he had been, and touched his hat, and with them Emily Roland.

'Gentlemen,' Laurence said, torn between gratitude and dismay, for they were working not on harness and armour but on Temeraire's platinum breastplate, and Emily had brought Temeraire's jewelled talon-sheaths.

They had been given to him in China, and were remarkably beautiful, and remarkably gaudy: gold and silver engraved with elaborate Oriental designs and studded with small chips of gemstones. His breastplate, with its great pearl and sapphires, further advanced the service of vanity, with his old smaller string of gold and pearls suspended from its chain, not at all complementary. Besides this adornment, Temeraire had arranged to have himself scrubbed until he gleamed, and had even had, Laurence was sorry to see, his handful of scars painted over with a pot of the sort of glossy black used upon doors and iron railings. It was most notable upon his chest, where a barbed French ball had taken him, during an engagement at sea; the wound had been ugly, and though healed cleanly had left a puckered knot of scales.

When Laurence arrived Temeraire was engaged in examining himself, as best he could, in a large dressing-room mirror good enough only to show perhaps five feet of him at a time, and considering whether to add a spangled net of chain over his ruff.

'Iskierka offered me it,' he said, 'and while ordinarily I would not borrow anyone else's things, and pretend that they were mine, I am only thinking that, as we have not had time to make medals yet, it might stand in for them.'

'Pray let me advise you against it,' Laurence said, sadly, imagining the generals' reaction. 'Borrowed finery cannot be to anyone's taste, and if it should be lost, or damaged, you would be indebted . . .'

'Oh,' Temeraire said, 'that is very true; I suppose I had better not' and he sighed wistfully. 'Very well, Roland, take it off,' and he lowered his head reluctantly.

It did not much matter, however, in the end. Temeraire descended to a great silence, even the horses' frightened cries died away to overwhelming stillness. Rowley, still waiting outside, paled beneath his dark narrow moustache, as Temeraire neatly fitted himself into what was indeed a very cramped space for him, coiling his tail up as he landed.

'Well, is it here?' Wellesley said, coming out. He paused, looked up and up, and up, and said nothing more. A few pieces of jewellery were perhaps not much to notice, Laurence realized, when one had never seen the whole dragon before; and as a cavalry-officer, Wellesley had likely never been close to a beast over courier-weight.

'I am Colonel Temeraire, at your service,' Temeraire said, peering down with interest.

'You are, are you?' Wellesley said after another moment, recovering his voice. 'You'll do to stop a few mouths, anyway. Rowley, go tell those fellows in there to come out, so they can meet with our new colonel.'

A man came hurriedly out of the tent: no military officer, but a gentleman in a neat sombre suit of dark brown. 'General, if you will forgive me, the Ministry feels there is some danger of a precedent—if I might have a word—' He had not properly, fully, taken in Temeraire yet. While he talked he caught glimpses of black scales, the smooth horn of the talons: impressions which over the course of his sentence accumulated until at last he raised his head and fell silent.

'No, you mightn't,' Wellesley said with satisfaction, watching him choke, and pressed him unresistingly into a folding-chair. 'Have a seat, Giles. Rowley, go on and tell the rest of them to come out here at once.'

'I beg your pardon,' Temeraire said to the poor man who trembled violently as Temeraire's head lowered, 'but if you are part of the Ministry, I should like a word, myself. We would like to vote, please, and also to be paid.'

The professional soldiers were not quite so easily quelled. Jane dispelled a great deal of the effect by coming out and saying to Temeraire, 'Did you deck yourself out for Christmas? This is a war, not a Vauxhall burlesque.'

'I have put on my nicest things, to be respectful,' Temeraire said, injured.

'To show away, you mean,' Jane said, and as this mode of conversation did not result in her being eaten, or squashed, the others grew bolder. More bold than Wellesley would have liked; he had evidently hit on the notion of stifling dissent for his own proposals through intimidation by proxy, rather than possessing any real interest in Temeraire's opinion.

The threat they faced was no longer the subject of disagreement; scouts and word along the road had brought enough intelligence for that. The Fleur-de-Nuits would come, two formations' worth of them, likely near the middle of the night; and would bombard them steadily until morning when the massed French lines would fall upon them and try to drive them from their position.

Their position was indeed an enviable one: the generals had retreated from the coast to reserve for themselves the luxury of choosing the next battlefield. That Napoleon would seek to occupy London, had never been in doubt. He had occupied Vienna, though that city lacked strategic value, and marched through Berlin, only for the moral value of these victories, the personal and not the military satisfaction of standing in his enemies' palaces and feeling them his own. And London had a great many banks. Gold and silver to fuel his invasion, and the chance to split the country south from north, with the Thames as a useful vein bringing him lifeblood from the coast.

So the British army had arranged itself to one side of the best and broadest road to London, and had established barricades across all alternate roads. If these were not as advanced as one would have liked, Napoleon having moved too quickly, still they would nevertheless delay the progress of any great mass of men, and give the British time to fall upon the enemy from behind. But Napoleon did not mean to scorn the gauntlet that had been thrown down: he was coming to them along the main road.

The British had the advantage of higher ground, with several stout farmhouses and a few old stone walls and fences for barricades and fortifications, which should make them all the harder to dislodge. 'We will hold here,' Sir Hew Dalrymple said: he had the command, an older officer with a stout neck and fair hair creeping back from his temples. 'It would be folly to yield so advantageous a position—'

'And if we are *forced* to yield it?' Wellesley said, dryly; there was marshy ground on their western flank, sodden with snow; but no one would discuss this difficulty.

'He has moved quicker than we expected, but we must not let this throw us into disarray,' General Dalrymple continued. 'That is how the Prussians ran into trouble, letting him cast them into confusion, changing their minds and their ground ten times a day.'

'Sir, I beg your pardon,' Laurence said, unable to restrain himself. 'That a lack of decision plagued the Prussian army, I cannot deny; but they were out-fought, sir, on open ground—'

'With this trick of horse-blinders you have gone on about in your report,' Dalrymple said. 'You may set your mind at rest,' he added, in an ironic tone, which said without a word

130

how little he trusted Laurence's anxiety, 'we have not discounted what could be confirmed of your intelligence; our horses have their own damned hoods now, and if Bonaparte thinks he will stampede us with a few dragon-charges, he will soon learn otherwise.'

'And this time, Bonaparte has let his thirst for speed outpace his sense,' another general said. 'All the scouts agree, even the beasts,' he added coldly in Jane's direction, 'that he has not brought up all of his army yet. He has some thirty thousand men, not fifty; so we are not far short of him even without our levies and reinforcements.'

'You will be a damn sight shorter by morning,' she answered, 'if you mean to lie here and be bombarded. And my scouts too have made thirty thousand, but that does not mean there are not more to come.'

'You have caterwauled without pause on how we *must* have these sixty more dragons,' another officer, a colonel, said belligerently, 'and how we must swallow treason and tolerate unhandled beasts to have them, and now you talk as though we have nothing to do but sit and bear it while the French drop roundshot on our heads. If they are of no use here, they are of no use to us at all.'

'We have seen a great many of the French along our way from Wales,' Temeraire said, putting in his own oar, 'and of course we can stop the Fleur-de-Nuits, if we can only see them, but at night that is difficult.'

'Difficult? So is winning battles difficult,' General Dalrymple said, scowling without looking up. He beckoned to his aide and thrust a map at Laurence. 'You will take the beasts here, a mile out past camp,' he said, 'and hold the Fleur-de-Nuits there, until morning—'

'*That* is very silly; the Fleur-de-Nuits will go right around us if we are a mile out,' Temeraire said.

'A couple of rounds against Lefèbvre's rear-guard, and

now you try to tell us our business,' Dalrymple said to Laurence. 'By God, I have half a mind to—You will obey orders, damn you. You will do as you are told and be grateful for the chance—'

'If I had done as I was told,' Temeraire said, 'you would have sixty less dragons, and Lefèbvre would have a good deal more food, and tomorrow Napoleon would likely beat all of you for good. So that is a very stupid thing to say. Whyever ought I do as I am told?'

'If you do not, we will hang—' the belligerent officer began, and Jane said, 'Maclaine!' too late; Temeraire growled, deep in his throat, and lowered his head with his ruff up.

He had briefly become simply another voice in their deliberations, if a queer, more resonant one speaking from aloft. But what contempt the little familiarity had produced, vanished in the face of that growl, the great glossy head with the eyes half a foot across and glittering yellow like lamps, and the jaw full of serrated teeth – the very smallest of which was the size of a man's hand. It was a palpable reminder that they were in the presence of a creature who could have, with a stroke, killed them all with very little effort. To Laurence, Temeraire could never seem viscerally a threat; but he had handled the dragon from hatchling to maturity, and remembered him as a creature scarcely larger than a dog.

'Laurence has taken oaths and feels duty to you; he would even let you hang him, although I do not understand why,' Temeraire said after a moment, low and angrily. 'And I cannot make him come away with me against his will, because that would also be wrong. But I will *not* allow him to be parted from me again, and if you do hang him, I will take my friends and go; but not back to China. I will go to Napoleon, and I will tell him he may have my territory, if only he destroys you all, and I will give him any help he wants of me to do it. Now, threaten me again, if you like.'

132

Laurence stood wretchedly by, helpless. He ought to have expected it. Lien had done as much over the death of her companion, Prince Yongxing; she had put herself freely into Bonaparte's hands, despite having nothing but contempt for him and all of the West at the time, and even though Napoleon, the master of Europe, might very well turn his eyes against her own nation, someday. And what small sense of loyalty Temeraire might have begun to feel towards Britain had been thoroughly undone, first by the Admiralty's plan to infect and kill all the dragons of the West, by reserving the cure for British use; and then by their later imprisonment of, and the pronounced death-sentence on Laurence, which had been used as a bludgeon against him: and now used once too often.

To think his execution would not leave Temeraire free to make his own way back to China, but a devoted enemy of Britain, was a fresh agony. Laurence had no doubt that such a threat would only make the generals despise him and the dragon all the more, and see in it his own scheme for preserving his neck by blackmail. They might choose not to provoke Temeraire now while Napoleon had men on British soil, but that, he hoped profoundly, was only a temporary state, after that . . .

Laurence did not discount Temeraire's achievement, as Dalrymple did. Without experience or training for the task, or anything but will, he had persuaded sixty lazy, well-fed dragons to go to war with him; and had already won two victories against the French army. That Lefèbvre was not the best of the marshals, that he had no great number of dragons with him, that Temeraire had only engaged with small companies, meant very little next to the greater success of keeping his force together and well-fed. These men might short-sightedly think themselves happy to be rid of Temeraire and any dragons recalcitrant enough to follow him; and if they did not, they would more than likely take his outburst as still more cause to try some low scheme of murder against him.

'Temeraire,' he said into the lingering silence, 'Temeraire, you cannot say such things; you are a serving-officer now; these are your superiors; you may not make threats, or growl at their orders. You must withdraw the remarks.'

'I did not growl at their orders,' Temeraire said after a moment, still angry, but he drew away his head a little, and all around the circle chests rose with postponed breath. 'I did not growl at the *orders*, and will not, no matter how stupid they are. But as for hanging . . . If anyone should try to take you from me again, I shall growl at *them*, and worse, and it is no use telling me I ought not.'

'As one might expect—' Maclaine began, a little faintly, only to be interrupted by Wellesley.

'Damn you, Maclaine, stop baiting the damned bear to see it dance.' Wellesley seized the moment and addressed the others, still silent and shaken. 'This is all nonsense. I do not believe for a minute that Bonaparte has come up with a man less than all of his army, whatever phantasy the scouts have brought you. We can get forty thousand men at Weedon, with their guns and supply, and if we give Bonaparte one of his precious pitched battles without every last one of them, then we are a pack of fools.'

'Then what do you propose we do?' Dalrymple snapped. 'Stand aside and wave him on to London?'

'London was lost three days gone,' Wellesley said, 'if not two weeks, when Nelson was sent to Copenhagen with twenty ships, and Bonaparte saw his main chance. The sooner we swallow it, the better. Get the army on the road tonight, at once. They have been lying about with nothing to do but get drunk, gamble and whore for a week, they can give up a little sleep.'

Cries of protest began rising; accusations of defeatism and

surrender. Wellesley raised his voice and kept going, 'Waste munitions and men and beasts to hold a lost position?—We ought to be hanged for traitors if we do it. To Scotland—To Scotland and the mountains, damn you all! He can't hold the country and keep the Channel open. Let him have England for a month, let him spend men and dragons trying to hold it, and march for Loch Laggan. We will have a hundred thousand men by Christmas, and will come down on him when *we* choose, not when Bonaparte—'

'And let him milk London dry, and wreck the country in the meantime?' one man shouted.

'Send men on to London to warn the tradesmen and the bankers out of the city with whatever they can manage,' Wellesley said. 'Half of them have gone running to Edinburgh already, after the King; let the rest of them go too.'

'If they choose to,' someone said, 'instead of stay and shake Bonaparte's hand as he comes in.'

'If they mean to stay, they'll stay,' Jane said. 'You won't make 'em less eager by letting Bonaparte beat you beforehand. Scotland is the first damned sense anyone has made. We needed these sixty beasts, Maclaine, but you cannot throw sixty dragons like roundshot and hope they land somewhere useful. In a week I will have worked out a way to use them, and by Christmas I will know how to do it properly. Tomorrow we can do no more than cut them loose on his flank and let them do as they like.'

'But that sounds perfectly agreeable to me,' Temeraire interrupted. 'I do not see at all why we ought not beat Napoleon tomorrow, even if he outnumbers us; it seems quite cowardly to run away from him.'

Laurence heard this speech, which he was sure could have no salutary effect, with a sinking sensation. If he did not much like the idea of retreat, he had yet to hear a plan of battle, which offered him any reason to be confident that the British were prepared to meet Bonaparte; and he was not heartened, to see that those officers advocating battle the loudest were, by and large, those in finer clothes, and fatter than field rations could keep a man.

'O, you wretched bloodthirsty creature,' Jane said, 'as if it were not bad enough dealing with all the thrusting chests already, now you must do it too; we need more sense, not less.'

'I am not thrusting out my chest at all,' Temeraire protested, pulling himself rather concave instead, 'and I am being very sensible, because if you *did* run away, it would not do any good, at least not if you go by foot as you have been. He will just go after you. He can catch you up in a trice: they go fifty miles in a day.'

'Nonsense,' someone said.

'It is not nonsense,' Temeraire said. 'Yesterday we saw Lefèbvre's company, eight thousand men, near Swindon, and then we flew over them at Borden on our way here this morning; so he *can* do it.'

There was a moment of perfect silence, on all sides: it was one thing to argue over retreat, but another entirely to hear that the enemy could not be escaped. After a moment, Jane said, 'Well, he can beat us by numbers, but we have a round two dozen heavyweights now, and he hasn't more than ten, aside from his Fleurs. I will take it upon myself to beat his speed, if you will only let me—'

'—put redcoats on dragons, yes, yes, as you keep saying,' she was interrupted, by another colonel. 'I should like to see it.'

'You can come to our camp if you would,' Temeraire offered. 'We have been carrying along a lot of them; although,' he added severely, 'if you wanted us all to carry, you ought to have spent a little time making carrying-harnesses, which I know Laurence told you of. It would be a good deal more convenient than rope, and we could manage a greater load; but perhaps if they do not mind being bundled up into sacks made out of tents, or belly-netting—'

'I should damned well say they will mind,' one general said.

'Are they soldiers or aren't they?' Wellesley snapped. 'Shoot the first insubordinate bastard to refuse and the rest of them will go quietly enough.'

But it was too far; he and Jane were both shouted down. 'Enough of this craven counsel,' General Dalrymple said. 'We stand, and we fight. General Wellesley, you will take the right flank tomorrow and hold the line at the farmhouse. General Burrard, you will take the left, and plan on pinching him just when he has worn himself out trying to fight uphill against the main body of our force.'

Wellesley stiffened at the assignment. It was something of a slap, to be set in the position where less manoeuvring would be required, and less initiative. He made no outward protest, but his fingers on the hilt of his sword drummed.

'And as for you, Roland,' Dalrymple added, 'if the damned beasts will not fight the Fleur-de-Nuits—'

'I did not say that at all!' Temeraire said, bristling. 'We will fight anyone, I only said we cannot stop them if you send us out of camp to do it. The Fleur-de-Nuit can see at night, and we cannot; it stands to reason that they can go right around us, above or below. We cannot stop them just by lining up somewhere in their road and hoping.'

'You can hear them, can't you?' Dalrymple demanded, exasperated enough by repeated interruption to address Temeraire directly, for once.

'A Fleur-de-Nuit sounds just like a Yellow Reaper to us, flying,' Temeraire said. 'They beat at the same pace.'

Laurence blinked; he had never noticed such a thing before, nor considered it a difficulty, and by the expressions upon the faces of the other officers, neither had any of them. Even Jane looked surprised by the intelligence, and she was an aviator of thirty years' experience and more.

'And anyway,' Temeraire added, 'one cannot tell where a sound is coming from, not when one is aloft and moving, and there are a great many other dragons about all beating in circles. If the Fleur-de-Nuits should go past us one at a time, we would likely never notice them at all, and then we would come back and you would complain that we had not done anything. If you want us to stop them, you may say so, and then let *us* work out, how it is to be done.'

Chapter Eight

Temeraire could not call it a satisfactory conversation, although he congratulated himself on putting an end to the threats against Laurence. The generals were not very clever at all, and whatever Laurence might say about superior officers, it seemed to Temeraire that if they were superior, then they ought to give him better orders than those he could work out for himself, not worse. Some of them had even wanted to run away, only because they did not have as many people as the French.

'But, at least I have spoken to a fellow from the Ministry, and told him that we require voting and pay, and he did not refuse; which I think is encouraging,' he told the others, 'and they have been sensible enough to let us manage the Fleur-de-Nuits how we like: only, now we must work out how.'

'If we fight them here at the camp,' Perscitia said thoughtfully, the tip of her tail flicking urgently back and forth, 'then they must come to us to do any good, and there would be enough light from the fires to see them at least a little, and we can fight them off straightaway.'

'They need not fight you at all, if you are above the camp,' Laurence said. 'They need only dart in and drop their bombs

139

and fly away again. They are sure to hit something of value, without needing to be particular about their targets.'

'Perhaps we should make a ring about the camp,' Temeraire said, 'and then if we heavyweights fly patterns back and forth, they could not come in without our noticing them, and we could catch them and teach them a good lesson; they would not long keep at it.'

'Yes,' Admiral Roland said, 'and tomorrow we will have not one of you fit to fly. Napoleon will have bought a cheap advantage at the price of sending out ten dragons who are no good in the day any road. No, we can't spend so much of your strength. Tonight every last heavyweight must eat and get at once to sleep; you have already been flying more than you ought to the day before a battle.'

Unfortunately the good sense of this rather dull objection, which Temeraire would have liked to dismiss, was making itself felt in a palpable way: Requiescat was snoring noisily in his corner, even though he was supposed to be attending their conference. Even Temeraire could not deny that his mind drifted to his dinner more often than was fitting, with a battle ahead. He sighed, and acknowledged the justice of it.

'But the little dragons cannot fight so many big, without any of us,' he said. 'And we will need them too, tomorrow. Otherwise Napoleon will send his little ones against us, and even though most of us have no crew to be captured, they will still tangle us.'

Admiral Roland rubbed her cheek with her knuckles and then she said, 'Well, since we can't spare the strength to keep them from the camp, we had better keep the camp from them.'

It was a little while before they could begin to put the plan in motion. Admiral Roland had some arguing to do first, but at last the fires were being put out, all across the camp, and the men were taking down their tents, whilst grumbling against the cold.

'This is boring,' Iskierka said to Temeraire, dissatisfied, as they sat waiting as a large square of forest just beside the camp was marked out for them by middle-weights. 'It is not at all as good as fighting, and I do not want to sleep.'

'Well, you must sleep, or else you cannot fight tomorrow,' Temeraire said, although privately he felt rather much the same. 'Now hurry, we do not have a good deal of time; the sun is already going down, and they will be sure to realize something is wrong, if it gets dark and they can see everything is ablaze.'

'Yesterday you did not want me setting trees on fire,' she said still grumbling, but then leapt aloft and strafed across the marked square with her flame, until the trees began to catch. The middle-weights had pulled up a good broad line of trees all around, and then clawed up the ground, to create a fire-break. It made a fine blaze, pleasantly warm—

'Temeraire,' Laurence said, gently touching his neck, and Temeraire jerked his head up; it had been very comfortable to doze.

'I am awake. Is it our turn yet?' He leapt aloft, and studied the still-blazing trees critically. He could not just cry away at them, for if they fell athwart the fire-break, they would ignite the rest of the trees, so he flew in a careful perimeter about them, and roared into the square. The fire-weakened trees crashed and fell in the most satisfying way, sparks flying up in great glowing orange clouds like small fireworks.

'Well, I suppose it is a little easier to knock them down after they have been burnt someways,' he admitted to Laurence, 'not that I could not have managed it alone.'

'You must also reserve your strength,' Laurence said. 'Another pass, and that will do it, I think; a few trees left standing will do no harm. The signal, Mr. Allen,' Laurence

141

added, and when Temeraire had given the field another circle, the middleweights came in, dropping their loads of mud scooped up easily from the riverbed of the Thames using wagon as shovels, onto the remaining flames.

What was left would not have been of much use for a real place camp: the field was a wet and smoky mess covered with heaps of debris and the cracked stumps of trees poked inconveniently out of the ground at odd intervals. No dragon could have comfortably stretched out within it, not without a great deal more work to clear it out. There were still a few small fires crackling, around which the men dug rings to keep them from spreading, and after a little shovelling, a handful of tents were put up. From aloft the scene would look convincing enough, especially with the stuffed redcoats, coats and breeches filled with straw, which Admiral Roland's men had arranged about some of the fires.

'I like those,' Perscitia said, eyeing the figures, and paced back a few steps to examine them more critically. 'One must be quite close to notice, and I dare say if one were moving quickly, it would be quite impossible.'

'I hope it will do for the Fleurs, any road,' Admiral Roland said. 'And now, the lot of you to the herds, and then to sleep. Laurence, do you want your officers?'

'I would not have them removed from other posts, if they have been placed,' Laurence said, 'but I defer to your judgment, Admiral.' Temeraire tipped his head and put his ear toward Laurence, puzzled a little to hear his tone, which seemed to him a little odd.

'Are you not happy?' Temeraire asked anxiously, while he waited for his dinner; the herdsmen at the pen were conferring about the rations, throwing occasional anxious glances towards the sixty dragons patiently arranged outside the fence. Laurence had been so very quiet, since the conference. 'We are together again, and we will soon beat Napoleon;

142

I am sure the generals cannot help but see, when that is done, that we have done everything correctly. I see now,' he added, 'why they were ready to be so wicked. They are just so very afraid of losing. And I cannot really blame them for being afraid, because they do not seem to be very clever; but they should at least be clever enough to see that they ought to let us manage things, since they are not very good at it themselves.'

'I would not for the world diminish your spirits,' Laurence said, after a moment. 'I am very glad indeed to be with you again, and for the prospect of action; but I will counsel you against that degree of overconfidence, which only lends itself to disappointment. That,' he added, lower, 'was perhaps, as much as anything, the cause of the Prussian loss.'

'Well, they were very slow,' Temeraire said. 'And it seems to me that so are these fellows, but at least now that cannot matter, since we are to fight here. We do not need to hurry anywhere. But whyever is it taking so long?' He stretched his head out over the fence. 'What is the difficulty?'

They did not have enough to go round: there were less than eighty cows in the pen, and all the harnessed dragons to be fed also. 'Then you must make soup, and roast and crack the bones to make it tastier, and so we can eat those more easily; you might put some grain in it too, and some vegetables,' Temeraire added, to the rather perplexed looking herdsmen. 'Laurence, where has Gong Su gone to?'

'I do not know,' Laurence said. 'He was privately hired, not an official member of the crew, and my affairs have been in no kind of order. I have not been able to carry on any sort of correspondence, nor meet my obligations. I expect he must have sought other employment. I hope he was successful.'

'I did not think all my crew would be taken away in this fashion,' Temeraire said, feeling rather displeased, 'or I would have brought everyone with us to France; except then I suppose they would all have been called traitors too, and perhaps some of them would not have liked to go.'

'No,' Laurence said. 'But I thank you for the reminder; I must make arrangements, while I can. I must make inquiries after Gong Su, and make good my other debts.'

'There will be a great deal of time, after tomorrow,' Temeraire pointed out.

Laurence paused and then said, 'Best to clear away such things before a battle, my dear.'

The soup that the herdsmen managed, at length, to make was not very good: the meat and vegetables sunken congealed lumps at the bottom, squashy and flavourless, but they were all hungry enough to eat it. Only Gentius was pleased. He ate twice his usual amount, and pronounced it excellent, truly excellent; he would have managed another serving if there were any left.

'Not much like proper food,' Requiescat said unenthusiastically.

'Well, tomorrow when we have won, we will go and get our own herd. And perhaps by then, Laurence will have found of Gong Su again,' Temeraire said. 'He will make us a feast to celebrate, something very nice, perhaps a dish they cook in the Imperial Palace.'

'I will be happy enough with a proper cow, fresh,' Requiescat said, and then sat up abruptly, throwing back his shoulders, as with a great thump Maximus came down in the clearing before them and rattled all the trees nearby.

'Hm,' Maximus said, and drew himself up on his haunches too.

'You are here!' Temeraire cried, joyfully. 'Is Lily with you also? Are you well?'

'Right as rain,' Maximus said absently, without looking

away from Requiescat. Both heavyweights were prickling their spines and staring at one another directly in the eyes.

'Where is—Maximus?' Temeraire said, puzzled. 'What are you doing?'

'Laurence!' a voice yelled faintly from outside the camp, and Laurence looked up from where he was sitting and writing. 'Laurence, get that damned lump of mine out of that camp, you have another Regal there!'

'Oh,' said Temeraire, and roared loudly, over their heads; Maximus and Requiescat both jerked violently and turned to look at him instead, blinking. 'There, now do not start that behaviour again, we have a battle tomorrow,' Temeraire said, 'and you had better stop Berkley from running so fast, or he will have an apoplexy,' he added.

Maximus turned his head and said, 'You do not have to run, what is there to be running for?' as Berkley came staggering into the clearing. Laurence went to lend him an arm over to the fallen tree that Temeraire had pulled down for him to sit on.

Berkley stared from Maximus to Requiescat and back again, very suspiciously, while he gulped for breath. 'Pray do not worry, I will not let them fight,' Temeraire said. 'I would have thought you had more sense,' he added to the dragons severely.

'I was not going to fight,' Maximus said unconvincingly. 'Only I have never seen anyone big as me before, except when I was still growing.'

'The girls are bigger,' Requiescat said, with a reminiscent tone. 'But that is different.'

'I do not see why,' Temeraire said, 'and it is not as though Grand Chevalier are much smaller.' He did not think himself much smaller, either, but thought that perhaps to say so would be rather puffing himself up.

'Don't much like them either,' Requiescat said.

145

Maximus nodded vigorously in agreement. "I knew you must be back, as soon as they brought us this mess for dinner.' He nudged Temeraire's shoulder with his head, in a friendly way. Temeraire wobbled, but managed with some effort to keep his balance.

'Tomorrow there will be plenty, and anyway, even if there were not, I dare say you could fly in opposite directions and find something, without having to quarrel over it,' Temeraire said. 'But where is Lily?'

'She is in Scotland,' Maximus said. 'Catherine has had her egg, so she cannot fly to the fight.'

'I suppose I did not tell you before: it was a boy,' Berkley said to Laurence, gloomily, 'so no use to us; and ten pounds, damn him. Nearly killed her.'

'The egg is very noisy,' Maximus added.

'I hope they both do well now?' Laurence said.

'She can write and say so, which I expect means that she is only half-dead,' Berkley said, heaving himself to his feet. 'Have you finished your damned card-calling?' he said to Maximus. 'If this fine scheme of Roland's is going to do any good, you cannot be hopping all over the camp now it is getting dark. And you may carry me this time, instead of taking yourself off without a word.'

'I only wanted to come see Temeraire a moment,' Maximus said, putting out one great curved claw for Berkley to climb onto. 'And now we have, we may go.'

'We shall see each other tomorrow in the fighting, anyway,' Temeraire said, with satisfaction, and curled himself up to sleep with a sense of great contentment.

He was jarred rudely awake an hour later by the queer muffled booming of falling bombs, and the popping voices of the pepper-guns answering them.

He put his head up, but he could not see anything more than the occasional white blooming of powder-flash from the ground, where the artillerymen were firing and the great yellow bursts of flame as the bombs struck and burst. When there was no firing going on, he could only make out the faintest shadows of the handful of lightweights circling. They were mostly mongrels with better night-vision than most, Minnow and some other of the ferals, who had been organized into shifts to give some semblance of resistance to enhance the ruse.

'You ought to go back to sleep,' Laurence said, rousing, and Temeraire lowered his head to nose at him carefully. How good it was not to be alone, and to know Laurence was with him and safe; it would have been better still if only they might have gone fighting together.

'I will, in a moment,' Temeraire said, privately hoping that the Fleurs would realize the trick at any moment, and they might have to go and join in. But the French dragons were flying too high, and the fires on the ground and the explosions of their own bombs dazzled their sensitive eyes too badly, particularly with the flash powder being shot in their faces whenever the fighting detachment, including Arkady and some of his ferals with their small crews, could manage.

He sighed and put his head down again, twitching as yet another of the bombs went off.

Silence woke Laurence a little while before dawn: the bombardment had stopped. He rolled off Temeraire's arm and went to wash his face, breaking the crust of ice in the bowl and scrubbing as best as he could: there was no soap. Smoke still rose from the decoy field, but the sky above was empty and lightening quickly. The French would be on the move by now; an hour, perhaps and they would see them.

A bell began ringing, distantly, a frantic note in its voice; others picked up the alarm, coming nearer and nearer, sounding all over the camp, and Temeraire put his head up and said exultantly, 'It is time to fight.'

He put Laurence aboard into an odd harness arrangement, with only a few straps that Fellowes and Blythe had managed for him, Allen and Roland to latch onto. There would be no one more going up with them. He had considered sending Roland back to whatever post she had abandoned, from concern that her action might reflect upon Jane. But he did not know where she had been serving, and when he had inquired, Roland had put out her chin and said only, 'I should prefer to stay, sir.' She just shook her head when he asked her if she had been signal-ensign. 'Fifth look-out, sir; I shan't be missed.'

Of course, Emily had no need to worry about her future, which was quite settled: on her mother's retirement she would inherit Excidium, a promotion guaranteed. Blythe and Fellowes were ground-crew masters and could always be sure of a place. Allen, however . . .

'No, sir, well,' Allen said, stumbling over his words, 'that is, they hadn't given me a place again, sir, aloft. I was with the clerks, so, it doesn't much matter for me.'

A desk was, Laurence privately and sadly felt, a better place for him: Allen was hopelessly clumsy, and more than once had nearly accomplished his own end. But Laurence would not tell any man, who wished to be with them, to stay behind the lines.

The crew stumbled from their small cold shelter, little more than a few branches laid down on the earth next Temeraire's side, to keep them from lying in the wet. Laurence reached a hand down to help them up where before many dozens would have been.

'I am coming too,' another thickly accented voice said. Laurence looked over and saw Demane standing beside him, having climbed up Temeraire's other side. The boy was bristling with arms: two small-swords, two pistols, two knives, all with mismatched hilts, and a sack of small bombs slung over his shoulder, which he now strung onto the harness without waiting for permission. 'No, you sit there,' he told Allen, pointing further back along Temeraire's shoulder to the look-out's place. So great was his air of decision that Allen meekly obeyed; though he had three years and a foot in height over the younger boy.

'Are you not assigned to Arkady?' Laurence asked.

'We are of your crew,' the boy said, meaning himself and his brother, Sipho, who Laurence now spied down in the clearing helping Fellowes and Blythe to arrange their meagre supply of tools in case Temeraire should need to come back in for repairs. 'Both of us, together. You said.'

'That is quite right,' Temeraire said, looking around, 'and I am sure Arkady does not need him; *he* was allowed to fight last night and will no doubt be sleeping late. I daresay we will have won by the time he wakes up.'

So they were four aboard, where thirty were common and hundreds had been managed, all of them latched to the one thick band: it circled Temeraire's neck, and was joined by securing straps to bands about his shoulders, so it would not slide about. When they had all hooked on their carabiners, Temeraire sat up, and Laurence could see past the trees to where a cloud of French dragons moved like bees, back and forth along the road, setting down great numbers of men and guns.

He had seen these manoeuvres before, at the battle of Jena, and he was heartened a little to see that the British army was not idling by; guns were being hastily advanced to fire upon the French positions before they could be secured. The guns moved slowly however; the men struggled to drag them forward through the mud, and already the French were answering nearly as vigorously.

149

'They are beginning without us,' Temeraire said, and his roar roused all the dragons at once. 'The enemy are here; are you all quite ready?' he asked them.

'No, wait, I have had an idea,' the blue-green dragon said, the one called Perscitia, and leapt into the air. In a moment she had returned, with something in her talons, which she laid down upon the ground: it was a heap of the sodden and ragged straw figures from their decoy clearing; some were still smoking and charred. 'Tie them on to us,' she said, to the group of militiamen, rubbing their eyes, who had been sleeping beside her. 'Tie them on with rope.'

'They are quite wet,' Temeraire said, sniffing at the figures. 'I do not see the use of that.'

'They will think you harnessed!' Perscitia said. 'Oh, and the paint, where is that black paint? Bring it at once too, and make straps for them—'

'We have no time,' Temeraire protested.

'Their dragons are not fighting yet,' Perscitia said. 'Very well, very well, we will do it only to the heavyweights! Do you not see,' she snapped, 'they will jump over to try and board you, and then there will be nothing for them to latch onto, and you will have them off in a trice.'

'Ha,' Jane said with satisfaction, when she had landed with Excidium only a little while later, and had the plan explained to her while the men finished painting Requiescat with the false harness-stripes. 'Yes, very clever. They will smoke it soon enough, but while the trick lasts, they will be jumping over to board you big ones by the dozen. All right, gentlemen,' she looked over at Temeraire, 'here are your orders, then: you unharnessed fellows will go in first, and at close-quarters. If you can draw their boarding-parties they will be undermanned when we come in. We have the advantage in weight; he has only eight heavyweight beasts brought up from the coast, as yet. I dare say he has had to send the rest back, for lack of food.'

'And when you have come in?' Temeraire asked.

'Then I cut you loose against the flanks of their infantry,' Jane said. 'If we are fighting aloft together we will only get ourselves into a tangle, but you cannot do anything but good against them closer to the ground, so long as you keep out of the line of fire of our artillery.'

'And keep out of range of our acid, too,' Excidium added, and leaped into the air.

'We have acid ourselves,' Gentius muttered, from where he perched aboard the big Chequered Nettle, Armatius.

Temeraire turned his head and asked, 'Are you all quite secure?'

Laurence checked his borrowed cutlass and pistols one last time. 'We are,' he answered, and they sprung aloft with a great surging rush of wind.

Bonaparte's Armée de l'Air was easily seduced into trying the strategy, which had served them so well at Jena: the cloud of smaller dragons rushing the heavyweights loaded with men. Laurence looked away; thirty Frenchmen had flung themselves with enthusiasm and courage onto Requiescat's back, to face the large company they expected, and a shrug of the great Regal Copper's shoulders had thrown them off, grasping with futility; a few of them cried out as they fell, dreadfully, until the noise ended below.

'Ow!' Temeraire said, suddenly jerking, and Laurence looked back to see that he too, had been boarded; but one of the men, an ensign, had saved himself by stabbing a knife into flesh and clinging on to the hilt. 'Ow, ow!' Temeraire added, as the French officer drew another blade, and began crawling grimly upwards stab by stab.

Laurence tightened his hands uselessly, on the harness;

151

if there was nothing for the man to cling to, there was also nothing for them to use, to climb back and fight him off, and the Frenchman was placed near Temeraire's back haunches where he could not reach with his claws. Laurence realized, that with a few more of his laborious steps, the Frenchman would be well placed to try and stab at Temeraire's spine. 'Take hold of the harness,' Laurence instructed his small crew, and called forward, 'Temeraire! We are well secured, turn over and shake him off—'

The world spun sickeningly, and for all his effort Laurence's hands pulled loose from the harness, which left him dangling by his carabiner straps as they turned, once and twice spiralling, and then righted again; all of them a little green from the close and rapid turn, and the two knife-hilts jutting alone from Temeraire's back, the small cuts trickling a little blood down his side.

'That has torn it, sir,' Emily said, pointing; and Laurence nodded. The French had noticed their lack of success, and the loss of men: they were no longer trying to board, but had turned a steady rifle-fire upon the beasts instead. It happened quicker than he might have hoped, but their attempts had at least borne some fruit: many of the French middleweights and lightweights, who had so daringly ventured close to the decoyed British heavyweights, had paid dearly. Blood ran freely down many a side, black and steaming in the cold air.

'Throw out a signal, Mr. Allen: we are made,' Laurence said, and leaned forward. 'Temeraire, you had better pull away now and go for their flank. They have a weakness, there on their right; do you see it?'

'No,' Temeraire said, rather reluctantly detaching himself from the Pêcheur-Couronné he was presently mauling, who had with more valour than sense made a direct run at him. But the movement of men below caught his interest. 'Wait,

I do; where that ditch is in their way, and they are having to go around—'

'Yes,' Laurence said. The French lines were compressed awkwardly where the men were crowding to advance, and they made an ideal target for an aerial strike, which should drive a hole not easily repaired into Napoleon's flank. 'Quickly, before they have got past—'

'*Alors, vous penserait mieux, avant que vous m'attaquer-ais,*' Temeraire said to the smaller beast, before he let it flee with a final shake. Turning towards his fellows, he gave a roar unlike any Laurence had ever heard from him: an odd inflected sound, rising and falling in an eerie, musical way. It pulled the attention of the other unharnessed beasts quickly, and they peeled away from their individual battles with the French beasts, as the formal ranks of the Aerial Corps charged forward to take their place.

As Temeraire banked away, Laurence turned in his straps to watch: the ranks of the Corps were coming on, not in their usual arrowhead formations, but drawn out into a single thin line of lightweights, courier beasts and middle-weights. At intervals flew small clusters of harnessed dragons: two middleweights in front with a heavyweight behind, like knots on a string. Maximus made one of them: red-gold and roaring behind Messoria and Immortalis.

As the two forces met, the middleweights clawed their way into the cloud of French lightweights, opening room for the heavyweights to bull through behind them; the lighter British dragons also engaged, but only a little, slashing and continuing on so the whole line advanced together through the French ranks, scattering them above and below.

It was as neat an answer to the harrying French strategy as any that could be imagined, and now the heavyweights swept through with their tremendous loads of munitions: dropping bombs and spikes like black iron rain upon the

French infantry and their gun emplacements. Laurence could see Excidium, those vast purple-and-orange wings spread wide as the Longwing darted low with a protective guard of two heavyweights, and another on his flank who must have been Mortiferus, with a more yellow cast to his wing-tips. Their acid caught the morning sun and sparkled as it descended; a hot grey cloud of smoke and agony rose in its wake.

The gap in the French defences did not last for long. The French dragons regrouped and flung all of their heavy-weights after the Longwings: three Petit Chevaliers, a couple of Defendeur-Braves, and a marbled orange-yellow Chanson-de-Guerre. Together they massed some hundred tons and more, and descending with ferocity they could not be turned aside. Excidium and Mortiferus were forced back up into the safety of the British line, as the other British heavyweights turned to cover their escape, and the quick skirmishing cloud of the French harried them back away from the field.

Laurence was only vaguely aware of the last of this, Temeraire had stooped down upon the infantry, shockingly low, and now the unharnessed dragons were wreaking ruth-less havoc on the awkwardly placed French infantry, who could not easily get their guns up to shoot, compressed as their column was by the uneven ground. The great Chequered Nettle, Ballista, even landed for a moment, and laid waste with her massive barbed tail in great sweeps.

Temeraire was so close to the ground himself that Laurence was able to draw his pistols and shoot four men from his back; Demane and Emily accounted for another two apiece, and Allen another. It was more difficult to miss than to hit at first, so packed were the French ranks. Then Laurence and his small crew stood in their straps and drew their swords as a few of the soldiers leaped aboard daringly.

'Hi! Look there, the eagle, the eagle!' Moncey yelled in great excitement, darting around.

But a young lieutenant shouted, '*À moi! Vive l'Empereur!*' and seizing the standard he leaped into the ditch, quickly followed by the remnant of the company. All of the men knelt, heedless of the wet, and together they became a bristling mass of bayonets and rifle-fire spitting at the dragons from below.

'Well, that is bad luck,' Temeraire said, as they were forced to lift away for a respite; but Laurence could not agree: they had wrecked the advance on the French right flank with too little cost to call it anything but the very best of luck. Some of the dragons had taken fire, and a handful were turning tail for the camp with shots to their wings or heads. One small Yellow Reaper being helped away by his fellows had a long dreadful bayonet-slash across his belly, which had lain him open to the ribs. But they were still more than forty in number, after casualties and those who had been up at night fighting, and in a few hours the latter would return to the field.

The opening gambits had been made; no decisive stroke had yet fallen. The aerial combat settled into the steadier, grinding work of attrition. 'You must send some of your fellows to rest,' Laurence said to Temeraire when they had been aloft for an hour, fighting nearly without a pause and in a tiring style. The French had not made any more convenient mistakes, so it was quick darting strikes, whenever an opening could be seized, to get past the pepper guns and the rifles and do a little damage. 'You cannot get worn down. The French dragons will take advantage as soon as they see you slowing. You see they are already departing the field in shifts.'

'I suppose,' Temeraire said, rather disconsolately, 'only it is difficult enough already with all of us here, to manage to do any good. We have not seized a single eagle, or even taken a gun; only that one Majestatis broke, just now,' he added, 'but that is not as good.'

'You are doing better than that; you have worn down their right flank, and the advantage to our own infantry will tell more and more over the course of the day,' Laurence said. 'You cannot expect a quick victory. Remember how long the battle lasted, at Jena?'

It was still a struggle to make him rest; he would not do so until Laurence at last resorted to pointing out, 'If you do not, then you will only get more tired; and if Lien should come in at the last moment—'

'Oh!' Temeraire said, 'That would be just like her; I suppose I must. Ballista!' he called, 'you must take charge, so I can go and rest, in case Lien comes sneaking in later. I wonder where she is hiding,' he added, rather darkly, and craned his head to scan the rear of the French lines, hidden around a curve of the river.

The sky was brilliantly clear, and the sunlight though not warming was bright. Lien's red eyes and fragile white skin were vulnerable to such conditions, and it was most likely, Laurence suspected, that she would make no appearance, save in desperation. But if his suggestion was a deception, it had sufficient good effect to make its own excuse. Temeraire grew rather drooping as they flew back to the clearings, and he fell with ravenous hunger on the dead horse, which was laid out waiting for him still in its cavalry saddle.

He shut his eyes and was asleep at once, after. Laurence climbed down to stretch his legs, and to let Fellowes and Blythe make their survey of the abbreviated harness while he made his own, walking up and down Temeraire's sides to see what injuries had been made. Emily was carefully removing the two knives, slowly, as fresh blood trickled. The handful of stab wounds had crusted over, at least, but there were half a dozen musket-shot wounds, balls in the meat of Temeraire's flanks. Near one of them, Laurence was alarmed to notice, was a puckered mark he had not before noticed: a ball had gone in not long ago, and not yet been removed.

'Sipho,' Laurence said, 'go and find Mr. Keynes; you know him? Good. Find him, or Dorset, and bring them at once, with their kit.' He dragged over a barrel and climbed up to lay his hand on the old wound. It felt a little hot and swollen, but perhaps it might only be the heat of battle, radiating from all Temeraire's muscles as he lay.

'Infection,' Dorset pronounced with certainty, as soon as he had peered at it through his spectacles, and touched it with his fingertips. 'My lancet, if you please, and have the tongs ready,' he said to Sipho, and then he slashed deep through the pucker, past the layer of scales and fat. A gush of white and yellow pus came running out with a dreadful sour stench that made Laurence turn his head away. Dorset did not pause for an instant, but seized the tongs and drove them in deep. He pulled away and brought out the musket-ball, black and shining with fluid, as Temeraire roared awake with a bellow that shook the trees and knocked Dorset, Sipho and Laurence flat as he flinched.

'It is all over,' Dorset said in answer to his shocked protesting, 'and now you know why we take them out at once. It would have been more unpleasant if you were awake.'

'I do not see how,' Temeraire said, rather bitterly, 'and at least I would have been warned.'

'And would have jerked twenty feet, before I could have the ball out,' Dorset returned unrepentant. 'Enough complaining; now I must have the others.'

'But I must go back to fighting,' Temeraire said hurriedly, trying to escape; but to no avail, and he put his head down, ruff flattened back, and muttered unhappily as Dorset went after the other balls, which were at least less deep.

'It will be done soon,' Laurence said, stroking his head. Demane came out of the woods carrying a small deer, slung over his shoulders, which Temeraire picked and nibbled on for consolation.

Excidium set down beside them with a rustling like heavy silk, as his great wings folded shut. His crew swarmed down in a rush to treat his wounds: only a few scattered claw-marks and one musket-ball, whose removal he bore with perfect stoicism. Temeraire's complaints – as Dorset seared his cleaned wounds – promptly fell silent.

'Here you are, then,' Jane said, coming over and spying Emily, who looked a little hangdog as she was caught liter-ally red-handed: holding the blood-wet instruments for Dorset as he worked. 'And has Sanderson given you leave from your post?'

'Artemisia can only fly an hour at a time, anyhow,' Emily said, but there was rather a mulish gleam in her eye. Laurence did not imagine she had liked her mother's previous demo-tion, nor serving with her usurper.

'Admiral,' Temeraire said, 'have you any more orders for us? I am sure we could be of great use aloft with you; and it is not much fun poking at the infantry,' he added, his studied formality failing him.

'You do very well where you are,' Jane said. 'This is no time to be going off half-cocked, old fellow. I will even go so far as to say I think we are very nicely placed. He is making us work for every inch, but we are getting them, and soon we will have them up against the trees. Closer run than I would like, but Dalrymple was right after all, and I was wrong; it was a good chance to take.'

'I was sure it would go well,' Temeraire said, 'but I would like at least one more eagle before we make him run away again.'

'*If* we take him,' Jane said, and reached to scratch

Temeraire's harness, against such tempting of fate, 'I hope to get more than his eagles; we will get him. Yes, he is here,' she added, when Laurence could not help but ask. 'He is beyond the curve with his Old Guard and his pet Celestial; a splendid creature, from what I have been able to see of her.'

'I knew she would be hiding from the battle,' Temeraire said, darkly.

'Keeping them in reserve, and her, too,' Jane said, 'but that will not be enough. We have our own reserve: Iskierka will be waking up any moment now, and the others who were out tonight.'

'She fought last night?' Laurence said.

'Yes,' Jane said. 'Can't get her off the field once she is on it, not until the enemy has quitted; so I had Granby rouse her when it began to get a little light, and chase off the last of the Fleurs. Then she was tired enough to sleep again for a while. She will wake up full of vim, and just what we need. Bonaparte has let Prussia go to his head, I suppose, and thought he could beat us with less than his full strength.'

'I have just been thinking,' Temeraire said, after a moment, 'where do you suppose his Grand Chevaliers are? And Marshal Davout? I have not seen his standards anywhere, on the field.'

'Returned to France, I imagine, or still on the coast ferrying,' Laurence said. 'And Davout—'

'Portugal, last report,' Jane said.

'Well,' Temeraire said, 'we saw two just west of here. We stole their pigs, but they had plenty of food besides that. And Davout cannot be in Portugal at all; we saw him north of London, two days ago.'

'What?' Jane said; but did not wait for an answer as she was ran to Excidium at once, shouting orders, and leaping for the harness and her speaking-trumpet. Excidium went up even while her ensigns latched her on. 'Alarm!' Laurence heard her shouting, 'sound alarm, enemy to the north,' and flags flashed on every dragon as their crews caught the signal from Excidium's back.

Temeraire sat up. 'Whatever is she so worried for?' he said, looking at Laurence rather indignantly, but Laurence had a dreadful, a sinking sensation. 'Aloft,' he said, 'come; we must go aloft as far as you can.'

When Temeraire had climbed high enough to make trees and hills and farmhouses blur into the wide gentle curve of the earth, he paused, hovering, and in subdued voice said, 'Yes; I see them.'

Davout was coming, directly for their rear, with thirty dragons and at least twenty thousand men.

Chapter Nine

Another hour, and there would have been nothing to do but stand and be pounded to pieces from either side; but the little warning was enough to try and disengage, at least, and Dalrymple at once issued the order for the retreat. Wellesley fought a brilliant rear-guard action, bloody and terrible, stretching his men to hold the full breadth of Napoleon's line while the rest of them withdrew behind that shield.

But the retreat became rout by the end: ten thousand men were left floundering in the marsh to be taken prisoner, and the rest to straggle ignominiously away north through the countryside with no more than their muskets and their boots, and often lacking those. The dragons carried the guns dispiritedly. Occasionally Temeraire would look back over his shoulder at the battlefield they had fled and the dragons in the distance, chasing, with a quivering ruff. He did not propose that they turn, but simply looked away again, put his head down, dogged, and kept flying.

Bonaparte's harrying pursuit at last fell away near evening: the French dragons, having laboured all day in battle or in carrying Davout's men, had reached their limits. One by one, they began to sink further behind until they must have been called off and could just be seen turning away in the gloaming.

Laurence put his hand on Temeraire's neck. 'We have slipped the trap,' he said quietly. 'You have bought us that, at least.'

'I still think we ought to go back,' Iskierka grumbled as she flew beside them. She had been very angry to awaken only to be told that she would not have to fight after all, and Temeraire had only just managed to half-persuade, half-bully her into flying along with the rest. 'I am hungry, and I do not like carrying this cannon; it makes my shoulders ache.'

'We are all hungry,' Temeraire said, in a temper, 'so pray stop complaining; you are very tiresome.'

'I am not!' she said, 'And only because *you* do not want to fight, and would rather run away—'

'That is enough,' Excidium said to her sternly, as he descended. 'We will go back when we are ready; when we have more men and guns, and can be sure to win. That is strategy,' he added, 'and you are old enough to understand it.'

Iskierka subsided, still muttering, as the older dragon flew on ahead.

Somewhere far behind them, the remnants of the infantry and cavalry marched on, towards reinforcements and supplies at the well-defended central depot in Weedon Bec. The dragons however flew straight on through the night and the next day, putting an impractical distance between them and pursuit, and ensuring the safety of the artillery. There was not much for them to eat: the farmers hid their cattle, and they could not easily stop to hunt during the day. 'The Quality must sacrifice their game,' Jane decided, and divided them into small companies, each ordered to make camp on any estate large enough to have a deer park.

They would be in Nottinghamshire before nightfall, and Wollaton Hall had a herd of four hundred or more. 'I could send you elsewhere,' Jane said, but Laurence shook his head. He had little wish to be at home under present circumstances: as a condemned traitor, carrying the worst sort of news, and bringing twenty hungry dragons to tear up the estate. But it could not be helped. It would be much worse if he took himself to some other house nearby, without paying his formal respects, and let some other group of dragons use the grounds; it would be cowardly. If Lord Allendale chose to forbid him the house when he came, that was his father's privilege; his own duty was to endure the rebuke he had earned.

They landed a few hours later, the dragons setting down their burdens with deep and grateful sighs. It was no easy task even for a heavyweight to carry two sixteen-pounders a distance of over thirty miles, and Maximus and Requiescat had been loaded down with four apiece. Temeraire sighed and stretched himself out upon the cool ground like a long black snake.

Laurence slid down from Temeraire's back, weary and sore from the long hours dragonback. 'Will you speak to them up at the house?' Jane asked him, 'or will I send Frette?'

'No. I will go,' Laurence said, and touching his hat turned away.

'Pray give my best regards to your mother,' Temeraire said, rousing a little, when Laurence rubbed his muzzle in farewell.

He walked slowly and with reluctance to the house; the windows were mostly dark, only a few link lights burned near the door. There were a couple of footmen outside gripping muskets, nervously. 'It is all right, Jones,' Laurence said, when he came close enough to recognize their faces. 'It is only me. Is Lord Allendale at home?'

'Oh—Yes, sir, but,' Jones said, looking at him wide-eyed, and then the door opened. For a moment Laurence thought it was his father, but it was his eldest brother George, in dressing gown and slippers over his nightshirt, with a valet fussing a coat on over his shoulders.

'For Heaven's sake, Will,' George said, coming down the stairs. He was Laurence's senior by six years, and nearly as much time had gone by since Laurence had last seen him. He had grown stouter, but his exasperated tone remained unchanged. 'That will be all,' he added abruptly to the footmen, 'you may go back inside.' He said nothing more until the door had shut behind them, and then turning back to Laurence he hissed, 'What in God's name are you doing here? And coming to the front door—You might have a little discretion, at least. Have you—Are you . . . hungry? Do you need—'

He floundered, and Laurence flushed in sudden understanding, 'I have not fled gaol and come to the door to beg, sir; I am paroled, to fight the invasion.'

'Paroled?' George said. 'Paroled for the invasion, and yet you are here in the middle of Nottinghamshire! Whosoever is likely to believe such a story, I ask you?'

'Good God, I am not lying to you, brother' Laurence said impatiently. 'I am not going to explain this twice over. Will my father see me?'

'No; and I shall not tell him you were here,' George said. 'He is sick, Will: three stones down since August, and the doctors have said he must keep quiet. Do you understand? Perfectly quiet; if we want him to see another year. He cannot even oversee the estate manager anymore; why do you think I am here? And no wonder, with the worry he has had. If you need money, or someplace to sleep—'

'I am not here for myself,' Laurence broke in at last, feeling stiff and strange; the idea of his father ill, reduced, seemed unreal. 'I am here with the Corps. We must requisition the deer to feed the dragons. There are nine at present,' he added, 'but there will be more before morning; I did not want you to be alarmed.'

'Nine—' George looked towards the deer park, and saw the lights casting the shadows of many dragons. 'Then, you are not lying,' he said slowly. 'What has happened?'

The news could hardly be concealed. 'Trounced us, outside London,' Laurence said. 'The army is strung out from here to Weedon, and he took ten thousand prisoner. We are falling back to Scotland.'

'My God,' George said, and they stood in silence for a moment. 'Are you staying by the wood?' When Laurence had nodded, George said, 'Well—you may take whatever you need of the deer, of course; they are the King's. There are the stables for your men, too, and the farmhouse. I will send food down to you all from the kitchens, and your commander, we can give him a bed—' It was a long delaying tactic, but at last he came to it and finished, awkwardly, 'I am still not going to have you in, Will; I am sorry.'

'No,' Laurence said. 'No, of course.' He might have insisted, for himself or his fellows: it was their right as officers to be quartered in the house when there was room. Jane might, if she chose; But he could not bear to force his way in.

'Will you tell me—Will he come through here?' George asked him, quietly. 'Ought I to send Elizabeth, Mother and the children away, to Northumbria perhaps?'

'I imagine he could send men to take the cattle for his beasts,' Laurence said, 'but if he marches, he will march up the coast; he cannot leave our outposts behind his flank.' He drew his hand across his forehead, tiredly. 'I am sorry, I cannot be confident of such counsel, but I think there are few places much safer, unless you send them to Liverpool and by ship to Halifax.'

George nodded, then turned and went up the steps. He hesitated at the door, as if he might speak again; but in the end said nothing. He went back inside, and the door was shut behind him.

Laurence walked back from the house alone, his feet sure on the familiar lanes despite the dark. He heard no sound but the occasional sighing of the wind, shaking the few dried leaves left on autumn branches like rattles, and drifting the smell of the dragons and smoke near. The ground-crews of the harnessed dragons were making a little camp, not entirely comfortless; fire was easy enough to come by when Granby needed only ask Iskierka to oblige them. The other captains stood by it, warming their hands and talking in low voices, tracing the course they should take in the morning.

Some of the dragons who had guarded the rear of the retreat were still arriving, and others were already deep into their dinners, as the lean bodies of deer were stretched out limp upon the ground. Iskierka was doing the hunting, to the satisfaction of all except the smaller creatures of the forest, who fled out into the open with the panicked deer when she belched a roaring tongue of flame over the timber: mice, rabbits and sparrows, and even a few poachers from the village escaped with their snares.

'Wellesley will pick up ten thousand men at Manchester,' Jane was saying, 'and twenty at Ripon, and so on, making his way to Scotland. It will be a precious slow trip, but we needn't expect our friend to come after us again so soon.'

'But can we keep the beasts fed along the way?' a woman's voice asked from above, as another Longwing settled. 'Mort, be a love and set me down.'

Laurence had never met Captain St. Germain before; she had long been assigned to Gibraltar. Mortiferus put her down beside the fire. She was a very tall and fat woman with delicate features, a mop of fair hair curling in wisps about her face and pale-lashed blue eyes; in complete effect rather like a Rubens.

'The country gentlemen may find venison thin on the ground for a few winters, but we will manage somehow,' Jane said. She looked around at a small shriek; the servants from the house had come down the lane with lanterns and baskets of food, and one of the maids had fainted, upon seeing the dragons. 'Why, I call that handsome, Laurence; I hope you have given them our thanks,' she said, and waved her men forward to go take the food off their hands.

Laurence felt rather that he might blush for this family's lack of hospitality, to have left them out in the cold with the great house standing there on the hill, with so many windows staring out empty. But he was, evidently, the only one so conscious: the other aviators walked up the hill wearing expressions of pleased surprise, to meet the baskets full of cold meat and bread, fresh-boiled eggs, and many pots of hot tea. One servant had come down the hill carrying an enormous steaming platter that smelled pungently of Oriental spices, and even before he had stepped into the fire-light, and Laurence saw his face, Temeraire had raised his head and said joyfully, 'Gong Su, you are here!'

The cook came forward and bowed repeatedly to Temeraire, and as an afterthought to Laurence also, beaming as he relinquished the platter down to the aviators. 'I am glad to find you well; but how came you here?' Laurence asked.

'Lady Allendale's generosity,' Gong Su said, and turned to Temeraire, explaining in Chinese that Lady Allendale had written to the Corps, and obtained the names of Laurence's followers, to see them taken care of; she had given Gong Su a place.

'And he says that he will come with us again,' Temeraire added with satisfaction, 'so we may have properly cooked

167

food. He also says that if we will stop eating the deer now, he will stew them for us, with some grain.' At this announcement, several of the dragons drew their deer all the closer and began to eat as quickly as they could.

A fuss was still being made on the path; the maid was now enjoying her hysterics sufficiently to resist being helped away by a couple of the footmen. 'That is quite enough, Martha. Peyle, take her back to the house and give her some hartshorn,' Lady Allendale said, putting an end to the noise. She continued on steadily, well-wrapped in furs and trailed by an unhappy footman with a lantern, who lagged behind as they came closer to the clearing.

Lady Allendale paused, near the edge; she had last seen Temeraire some ten weeks after his hatching, well before he had reached his full growth or even sprouted his ruff. To encounter one half-grown beast in broad daylight was a rather different experience than being faced with a dozen of them, including heavyweights and the alarming orange-eyed Longwings, covered to their jowls in blood and magnified by the flickering play of the fire upon their scaled hides.

Laurence was already on his feet; the other officers hastily stood as she came timidly to their circle. 'I am very happy to see you again, my Lady. Thank you for keeping Gong Su safe for me.' Temeraire said, adding in an undertone to Laurence, 'that is correct, is it not?'

'Quite correct,' Lady Allendale said. Coming forward with an unhappy smile, she gave Laurence her hands; he bent and kissed her offered cheek. It was paler than it had been, the skin a little dry and papery, and more lined; her hair was quite silver now. She did maintain her smile long, but let it fade, and took his arm, for once she truly needed to, to take a tour around the camp. 'I hope you are all comfortable; we should be happy to make up beds, inside, for you gentlemen. I am sure room can be found.'

No one answered immediately, and so Jane had to say, 'We do very well here, ma'am, although I thank you for the hospitality; we sleep with our dragons when we are on the march. Frette, can you manage a chair,' she added, and Lady Allendale looked at her and then at Laurence, with a bewildered expression.

There was no help for it, of course, and he said, 'Mother, may I present Admiral Roland, of Excidium; Lady Allendale.'

Jane bowed and offered her hand to shake, Lady Allendale recovered herself enough to accept it with cordiality, and also the folding camp chair which Frette brought from out of Jane's tent and set near the fire, beside another for Jane.

Captain St. Germain was walking up and down the camp, stretching her legs, and had not yet noticed the visitor. 'Thankee, Frette, I had rather stand; we will be sitting all day tomorrow,' she declined when he offered her a chair too. She pulled up short upon seeing Lady Allendale. There followed a little awkward silence. Lady Allendale gazed with fascination at Jane and St. Germain, and indeed all of the camp, with far more attention than she had ever paid before to the aviators. She was no fool; Laurence saw her marking out the handful of other female officers: another on Jane's crew, a lieutenant on Berkley's and a few midshipmen and ensigns scattered about.

No one offered any explanation, and of course she did not ask, but politely asked, 'You are bound for Scotland, then,'.

'Aye, ma'am,' Jane said, 'I hope we do not put you out,' which proved an admirable beginning to a brief exchange of wine and small conversation, which might be easily brought to a close with no offence on either side.

But Temeraire was now unoccupied, waiting for his dinner to be cooked, and he put in, anxiously, 'Perhaps you had better come with us, and not stay here. I have just thought of it; Napoleon may come here before we have had a chance to beat him properly.'

'You cannot be carrying civilians about where ever you like,' Jane said to him, repressively. 'A nice job we would do of keeping anyone safe, when it is our duty to go look him out. He may come marching through here by bad luck, but we are sure to meet him sooner or late.'

'Yes, but when we meet him, we can fight him,' Temeraire said, 'and be sure of keeping our friends safe.'

'I am very grateful for your concern,' Lady Allendale said gently, 'but we will not go, I think; it would be quite unforgivable to leave our servants and the tenants alone to manage in such circumstances: that is *our* duty.'

This quite changed the conversation. She then inquired of Jane, whether her own family was somewhere safe. 'I haven't any one to worry for, but my Emily, and of course I am lucky enough to have her in eyeshot at present,' Jane said, nodding at where her daughter was helping to put up the camp.

Emily had then come over to be introduced, and having made her bow added earnestly, 'And thank you very much, my Lady, for the present; I am much obliged to you.'

Laurence knew his mother well enough to see, as most strangers would not have, that she was puzzled before sudden understanding dawned. 'You like the garnets, then?' she said, and leaned forward to search Emily's face with a very different sort of interest; and Laurence felt his heart sink.

In London, the past year, his father had drawn entirely the wrong conclusion from Emily's inclusion in Temeraire's crew and about Laurence's evident responsibilities towards her; and he had passed his conclusion along to his wife in terms not sufficiently guarded as to prevent her becoming very interested in Emily's welfare.

'Oh yes,' Emily said, 'and I have been able to wear them twice, to the theatre in Dover.'

'Are you—Are you in service, then?' Lady Allendale asked, willing to play inquisitor where she felt she had a right.

Emily nodded, unaware of any undercurrent, and said, proudly, 'I am lately made ensign, my Lady.'

'There, enough puffery; Dorset is looking for you,' Jane said, more discreet, and Emily bobbed once more and dashed away.

Lady Allendale watched her run back to her duties. The surgeon was working over the dragons. Temeraire was not the only one of the unharnessed beasts who had been carrying a musket-ball for too long. Fortunately, Dorset laboured downwind at present, and worked on Ballista's far side, so the gruesome operation was not in open view. Emily vanished around her flank, and Lady Allendale turned back and ventured, 'She is very young,' to Jane, with not a little anxiety.

'Oh, she has been in harness since before she could walk,' Jane said. 'We start them young, ma'am, so they don't have much to be trained out of; and she must be up to snuff to take Excidium when I get too long in the tooth to be scrambling about aloft.'

'Well, I see where you come by it,' Jane said to Laurence, later. Most of the dragons and the aviators were asleep, and the fire crackling covered their low conversation, a conversation made easier by several glasses of the wine which had been sent down for their supper, 'all that noblesse oblige. But it is not stiffness. I like her. That is prodigious kind of her, to have taken an interest in Emily; does she think her your by-blow?'

So Laurence, who had been hoping devoutly that Jane had noticed nothing out of the ordinary, had to admit the wretched muddle. Jane laughed heartily, as he had feared she would; but under the circumstances he found that he could not be sorry to have given her a cause for unfeigned pleasure, even one he found embarrassing. 'Whyever did you not set her right?' she said, amused. 'No, never mind. I expect she has not said a word about it openly, which you could answer, and I know you would not breach the subject if hot pokers were put to you. It must be very inconvenient, talking of anything awkward in your family.'

She fell silent then; it evoked too well their own awkward circumstances, and she looked down at her cup and rolled it between her palms. 'I do beg your pardon,'

Laurence said, after a moment, 'With all my heart.'

'Yes,' Jane said, 'but you beg it for the wrong things. Charging off alone, without a word, and that appalling letter you left for me, all 'I could not love thee dear, so much,' as though you owed me apology as your lover and not as your commander. I blushed to show it to anyone, but of course it had to be handed over. For a week, I could cheerfully have run you through myself; sitting in rooms with them reading out bits of it in their insinuating tones, and putting Sanderson over me, damn them.'

'Jane,' he said, 'Jane, you must see, I could tell no one; to have put you in such a position—'

'The position, in which you put me, regardless?' Jane said. 'They could not have suspected me more if I had truly possessed all of the guilty knowledge in the world.'

'If I had spoken, you should have been obliged to stop me,' Laurence said.

'And a good thing too if I had,' Jane said. 'One private note to some Frenchman with a little rank, and they would have had the mushroom in hand within a month. Do you think every servant at Loch Laggan is incorruptible, knowing that Bonaparte would pay a million francs for the damned things?' He recoiled inwardly, and she saw it. 'No, of course it would not have suited you to have done the whole thing quietly, you and your damned honour.'

172

'It would not have been any less treason,' Laurence said.

'No, but as you were bent on that in any case, it would have meant a good deal less pain,' Jane said, and then she rubbed the back of her hand across her forehead. 'No, never mind. I do not mean it. I do not suppose there was any decent way to go about it: all decency was already gone. But damn you anyway, Laurence.'

He felt the justice of her rebuke, and bowed his head over his hands. After a moment she added, 'And to crown the whole, you come back and try to make a martyr of yourself, so that anyone who cares a farthing for your life must watch you hanged. That is, if they do not decide to make a spectacle of it and draw and quarter you in the fine old style. I suppose you would go to it like Harrison, *as cheerful as any man could do in that condition.* Well, I should not be damned cheerful, and neither should anyone else who loved you, and some of them can knock down half of London Town if they should choose.'

'I should certainly choose,' Temeraire said, and thought that he would make a point of speaking again to the Ministry gentleman, or perhaps to one of those generals, to make it perfectly plain. 'Pray do not worry, Laurence,' he added, 'I am sure they will not be so foolish.'

'Men can be very foolish indeed,' Laurence said. 'But I must, I do, beg you not to enter into a resolution, which should prevent my being able to face death with equanimity. You should make me a coward, if I must fear that my death should turn you against my country.'

'But I do not at all want you to face death with equanimity,' Temeraire said, 'if by that you mean letting them hang you, instead of making a fuss. If that causes you unhappiness, well, I should be unhappy if you were killed. It was dreadful, so dreadful, when I thought that you were gone.

173

I did not feel as though I knew myself anymore. I even wanted to kill poor Lloyd, for no reason at all, and I do not ever wish to feel so again.'

Laurence said, 'Temeraire, you must know that you shall, inevitably; I have two score years or three perhaps at most, and you ten, to look forward to.'

Temeraire flattened his ruff, unhappily, not wishing even to speak of the matter. 'But that at least, will not be anyone's fault; no one will have *taken* you.' The distinction was very plain in his mind. Anyway, he did not mean to think about something so far away. He might perhaps think of some way to prevent it, by then; if dragons lived for two hundred years, he did not see why people might not, also.

He turned his head gladly as Moncey came down beside him. 'Temeraire, they are hungry over by Nottingham Castle: there were not enough deer for everyone.'

'They may come here and share our breakfast,' Temeraire said, indicating the great pit where Gong Su had made them a great thickened wheat porridge flavoured with venison, greens and preserved lemons. It had been ingeniously water-proofed by a thick lining of canvas, and heated by stones which Iskierka had fired and dropped in. 'And from now on we will all go on shares; you must all admit,' he said to the others, 'that it is perfectly nice.'

'Nothing as good as a fresh hot buck all to oneself,' Requiescat said, grumbling.

'Well,' Temeraire said, 'if you prefer, you may take a single buck or a cow to yourself instead of three days of soup or porridge, because that is how far they may be stretched, Gong Su says.'

He was very happy to turn to mundane affairs, and pretend that he and Laurence had finished their conversation, although it made him feel a little ashamed. He knew Laurence would not interrupt him: Laurence did not think much of officers who had conversations or pleased themselves while their duty waited. So it was a good excuse, and as long as Temeraire made himself busy, he could be sure not to return to the difficult and unhappy subject.

He was quite resolved that he was not going to let Laurence be killed, no matter what. Laurence would certainly not be happy after being killed, so it did not seem to Temeraire much consolation that he should be a little happier beforehand. He was now very sure that the only certain way of protecting Laurence, was to make it plain to their Lordships that something dreadful would happen to them, if they dared to hurt him, so Temeraire had no intention of withdrawing his threat. But he could not help but peer cautiously sidelong to where Laurence now spoke with Admiral Roland: he looked tired, and although he would never let his shoulders slump, there was some quality of unhappiness in the way he stood, and Temeraire's conscience smarted.

At least Laurence was dressed respectably now. Temeraire felt that there, at least, he had done his duty a little better. He had whispered a quiet word to Lady Allendale, last night, and she had sent down some clothes from the house: a warm thick cloak, and some of Laurence's old things, which had been given to her to keep when Laurence had been imprisoned. It was not quite how Temeraire would have liked to see him dressed, but at least he had his sword again and better boots, and a coat that fitted.

Palliatia landed with four more Yellow Reapers and a couple of Grey Coppers, all hungry, and punished him by making his subterfuge quite real. They fell upon the porridge, and were noisy and quarrelsome while eating. When it was all gone Palliatia said belligerently, 'And where will we eat tomorrow? No treasure and no food either; what of all your fine promises now?'

He was rather taken aback to be so challenged, and said,

'You needn't snap at me, because we have lost a battle. If Napoleon were so easy to beat, he would not have any treasure worth taking. So you must expect some difficulties; and I call it poor-spirited to begin to complain only because you were not clever enough to find enough dinner last night.'

'Oh, but you did not talk of difficulties before,' she said, 'and you did not seem to think so much of Napoleon either. If he has so much treasure, then it stands to reason he must be *very* difficult to beat, and perhaps we are not going to win at all.'

'And if we do,' a Grey Copper named Rictus said pointedly, raising his head out of the porridge-pit, 'I suspect there will be no pavilions, or treasure for us, or leastways not for those of us who haven't got our captains again, and a place in the Corps waiting for us any time we like. No, it'll be back to the breeding grounds with us, and if we are only to end up as we began I don't see why we are going about getting ourselves shot and clawed, and flying across all creation hungry.'

There was a low scattered murmur of agreement, and worse, several other dragons raised their heads, to see how he would answer. Temeraire sat up angrily. 'I am not a sneak, and if you like to call me one, you may say so at once, and plainly, instead of creeping about implying it.'

'Well then, what *do* you mean to do, when we have won?' Ballista said, having listened in so far. 'Rictus isn't wrong to worry: you are not unharnessed anymore, even if you haven't much of a crew to speak of.'

Temeraire flattened his ruff at this last remark. After all, he had Gong Su back now, and Dorset, even if Dorset was not quite so desirable as Keynes, and there were of course Emily, Demane and Sipho, and Fellowes and Blythe, and even Allen, so he had a perfectly respectable number. 'You had a crew before, and might have one again; so might any of us,' he pointed out, 'so the question is not whether one is in harness, but whether one may choose to be, or not; and if it is only a choice between being in harness or being in the breeding grounds, then that is not enough of a choice at all.'

'Yes, but—' Ballista said, and then paused until Majestatis, lying next to her, said bluntly, 'Look, old worm, we are all doing what you say, but what if they should offer you something you want, if only you keep us quiet and fighting with the rest of the harnessed fellows? We all know they want to hang your captain—What if they should offer you his life?'

Temeraire paused in his turn. 'Well, I am not going to let them hang Laurence no matter what,' he said, with a hasty glance to be sure he had not been overheard, 'but I do see what you mean: they might offer me a very large pavilion, or a great deal of gold.' He rubbed a talon back and forth over his forehead, thoughtfully. 'It would not be fair,' he said at last, 'if I took anything for myself alone, when I should be getting it, not for my own work but for all of ours: we are sharing. So perhaps,' he added, 'one of you had better come along, when I go and talk to the generals again. One of the little ones, who can go all about and let everyone else know what it is they will give us.'

'I will come along,' Minnow said. 'I have never been harnessed, and I don't look to be ever, so no one can say I am inclined to go soft on them. Anyway I would like to see a general, I never have.'

Temeraire stretched his head over to ask Laurence and Admiral Roland who was presently in command, and where the generals might be; which he thought quite a straightforward question. 'Well, it isn't,' Admiral Roland answered him. 'It is still Dalrymple for the moment, I suppose. But he is likely to be replaced as soon as we get to Scotland and the Government have a chance to take him out of harm's way:

our harm, that is. If there is a lick of sense among them it shall be Wellesley in his place, but we ought not put our hopes so high.'

'But then who am I to talk to?' Temeraire. 'I do not like to say so, but the others are not quite happy. After all our hard work, we have lost, and have got no treasure, and they would like to know what use it is to keep on. Not,' he added hastily, in case Laurence or Admiral Roland should think that he was a poor officer, 'that we have no discipline, but after all, they are not harnessed, so they wonder why they are risking so much.'

Laurence was silent for a moment, and then he said, 'We may as well speak to Wellesley. It cannot much matter who we make arrangements with, if the war is lost.'

Admiral Roland nodded and said, 'Now we have got the guns out of the way, I meant to send some of us back anyway, to cover the infantry when they come out of Weedon. It is too close to London, and Bonaparte has too many dragons by half. I think I have worked out where he is getting them from,' she added. 'He is using unharnessed beasts, too, pulled out of his own breeding grounds. I dare say that Celestial of his can talk them out of their caves as well as Temeraire can ours.'

'I do not imagine she needed go to any special effort,' Temeraire said, with feeling, 'when Napoleon is doing everything nice, and giving his dragons pavilions and treasure, too, I expect: I am sure no one is complaining to *her*.'

Admiral Roland snorted. 'Well, whether she has had much work or not, I am confident that this is how he has laid hands on a hundred spare dragons in so little time; he hasn't taken a single beast off his eastern borders at all. And that means he can afford to spend a few dozen of them to harry our foot, on the march.'

Laurence nodded, and Temeraire saw the danger plainly:

with the infantry walking to Scotland, they would be an easy target on the road for aerial assault; and going at their creeping pace of twenty miles a day they would be in striking range of dragons headquartered at London for at least a week.

'The unharnessed beasts are less easily taken by boarding, if Bonaparte should manage to put together some clever little strike,' she went on, 'so it would be just as well to make Temeraire's regiment the guard, and let him hash this out with Wellesley before we have a mutiny on our hands. I haven't the right to promise them anything, and you may be sure that even if I did their Lordships wouldn't abide by it. And if you do secure them any pay,' she added dryly, 'pray be sure it comes to the harnessed dragons, too. I am sure Excidium would not refuse a little treasure of his own.'

'It seems a great bother to me, to be flying back,' Armatius grumbled, when Temeraire had brought back the news. The big Chequered Nettle did not much like carrying Gentius around, but he was the least manoeuvrable of the heavyweights, bar Requiescat, so it fell to him nearly all the time.

'At least you do not need to carry a gun in this direction' Temeraire said, 'and flying slower we will be able to find more food. Anyway, we are going to go arrange for our pay, which is like treasure that is given to you every month without your having to work for it, so you cannot complain.'

The harnessed dragons sharing the park with them were disgruntled at not being allowed to come along. 'Well, I *am* going back with you,' Iskierka announced, and would not be dissuaded, no matter what Granby said. To Temeraire's deep disgust Admiral Roland finally said, 'No, it is just as well, Granby, she will only fuss, lying about in Scotland or going on patrol.'

But despite this setback, it was satisfying to be flying south again, even though they were not to stay, because it felt to

Temeraire a little as though they were reclaiming their territory; or at least refusing to acknowledge it was not theirs anymore. He still did not like to fall back all the way to Scotland, no matter how much more secure it was. They should certainly not have run there directly from the battlefield, with the French dragons on their heels all the way; but perhaps now they would even have a little fighting, if the French tried to attack the infantry on the march.

Weedon was visible aloft from a long way away: the walls of the depot were built of thick grey blocks of granite, with tall narrow turrets at each corner reaching far into the air, and bristling with pepper guns. Around the walls, enormous stands of long halberds and arrow-head spears had been planted on the ground in lines, so a great company of men might sleep safe from aerial assault, and the remnants of the infantry and cavalry were bivouacked among them. It did not look at all comfortable to attack, and due to the defences, Temeraire had to lead everyone else to land on the far side of the camp.

Wellesley came the long distance out to speak to them with no good grace, especially as he had to walk most of the way. 'What the devil are you doing here? You ought to be nearly to Scotland by now, and half my cavalry are in fits.'

'We are here to protect you,' Temeraire said, injured, 'and also to talk to you about pay, and our rights, since we did not win treasure.'

'Why, damn you, you can wait to bring the lawyers into it until after we have run the French out,' Wellesley said. 'Good God, you may be sure Bonaparte does not have to argue his way through every battle.'

'If you would like to be compared to him,' Temeraire said, 'then Bonaparte has also made a marketplace in Paris, for

180

his dragons, and has built them pavilions, and he is not penning them up in breeding grounds either, if they do not like to be there—'

Laurence laid a hand on Temeraire's leg, and Temeraire swallowed his remaining remarks; it was difficult to remember that one must be respectful to a senior officer, when the senior officer was so unpleasant in return, and to have to think carefully about what one said, instead of laying everything out plainly, even if it was perfectly obvious and fair.

'Sir,' Laurence said, 'we have been ordered to cover your retreat,' and handed Wellesley Admiral Roland's note: a brief scrawl in her bad handwriting, which Temeraire could not quite read from overhead.

Wellesley scowled through the explanation, and then he crumpled the note and pitched it away; one of his aides hastily retrieved it out of the mud behind his back, to be sure it did not lie about to be picked up. 'That woman is to be relied upon more than half the general staff; it is a damned embarrassment. So this Chinese beast is managing Bonaparte's dragons for him? How did he get the creature to obey him in the first place? He was not there for her hatching.'

'She is snobbish, so I suppose she liked that he is an emperor,' Temeraire said, 'and that he should make it easy for her to be nasty to me: she is a very unpleasant sort of dragon.'

'I think perhaps you dislike her too greatly to be just, Temeraire,' Laurence said, and to Wellesley, 'Sir, she had lately lost her companion before coming to France, and being bereft was perhaps more vulnerable to a kindness which ordinarily pride would have armoured her against. But Bonaparte has not won her by any trick, only a high degree of real affection, and certainly all the outward shows of respect; and he has materially altered the conditions for dragons under his rule, for the better.'

'So anyone can manage a dragon, then, if you bribe the creature properly, and cosset it like a woman,' Wellesley said.

Temeraire laid back his ruff. He did not think he had been unjust to Lien; but he did see that Laurence's explanation was the more important one, for their case; and Lien was not helping Napoleon just because he had given her a few presents. Not that Temeraire would have said no to a diamond as handsome as the one she had been wearing at the battle of Jena; but that was *after* she had decided to help. 'It is not bribery or cosseting, if you pay someone what they deserve, and if they do not like to help you otherwise.'

'It is a good four hundred pounds to feed a beast your size for a year,' Wellesley said. 'Do you expect more?'

'Then give *me* the four hundred pounds,' Temeraire said, 'and I will undertake to feed myself, and put aside the rest, as I like.'

'Hah,' Wellesley said, 'and when you gamble it away, and are starving, and you steal a cow to eat, then what is to be done with you?'

'Of course I would not gamble with treasure,' Temeraire said repressively. 'If I wanted to take someone else's treasure, I would fight them; and if I did not want to fight them, then I would not want to take it with a game anyway, because if I did win, then of course they would want to fight to get it back afterwards.'

'And I suppose every other dragon has as much sense?' Wellesley said.

'If you prefer, sir,' Laurence said, 'you may pay them their board and a wage above it; the form matters little. The question at hand is, whether you will agree that they have a right to pay, and to all the same rights and liberties under which any man serves.'

'Why the devil ask me?' Wellesley said. 'Go speak to Dalrymple. I have no authority to make commitments on behalf of the Government.'

Laurence said, 'Sir, you are likely to be appointed to the command; we both know that their Lordships are not likely to overrule whatever commitments you feel necessary to make in order to secure so critical a victory, nor even question them greatly, if those commitments should deliver a substantial force of dragons, which might otherwise have no inclination to remain and to serve.'

Wellesley tapped his boot again, and said nothing for a moment, looking at Laurence. 'I give you my word it will be considered, shall we say,' he offered, 'and I can promise your beast the four hundred pounds per annum directly, as he is so sure he may be trusted. And we need hear nothing more of your own, difficulties.'

'Hah,' Minnow said, putting her head over Temeraire's shoulder. 'Just so: they *are* offering you something, only for you and your captain!'

Wellesley started back. He had not noticed Minnow sitting quietly on Temeraire's back, listening in.

'Yes, but I am not going to take it,' Temeraire said, and lowered his head more closely, so Wellesley had to look at him directly. 'I do not choose to wait, and rely on uncertain generosity. I know perfectly well how generous their Lordships can be. If you would like our help now, then you may say now how much it is worth to you. And if that is not as much as *I* think it worth, I will tell the others so, and I expect they will leave. I myself will stay for Laurence, but I will not keep the others for my sake. And it is not very handsome of you to propose anything so insulting, either,' he added reproachfully, lifting his head back away, 'when you know I cannot fight you over it, because you are too small.'

183

'Do you know, you are the most damned peculiar pair of traitors I have ever heard of,' Wellesley said to Laurence. 'Are you trying to get yourself into Martyrs of the Christian Faith?'

Temeraire snorted angrily. Laurence had read him sections of that book; it was all about people who had died in especially unpleasant ways. But Laurence only said, 'Sir, there are abundant proofs for any man, that a nation which gives its dragons liberty and brings them into the life of the state, winning their loyalty directly and not by intermediaries, profits to so great an extent that no enemy can hope to mount an aerial force to compete with them without following the same course. If you do not care to learn from the example of China—'

One of the young officers on Wellesley's staff, who had walked out with him, made a rude noise. 'You need not sniff, either,' Temeraire said. 'China may not have as many guns, but there are thousands of dragons in their army.'

'Thousands indeed,' Wellesley said, sceptically.

'Six thousand, two hundred and eighty-eight, my mother told me,' Temeraire said. No one said anything for a moment, and he supposed that perhaps it seemed odd to be so precise, so he explained, 'Because that is a lucky number. Of course they have many more dragons who can fight, but those dragons are not officially in the army.'

'And,' Laurence said to Wellesley, 'if the population of France is not so great as that of China, should they achieve even the same proportion of dragons to men and arable land, using the same techniques of husbandry which you may be sure Lien has conveyed to Bonaparte, their nation will shortly be equipped to field a military force of a thousand. Would you care to face that in five years, with the Corps at its present rate of growth?'

'Damn you, I am in no mood to be lectured at with figures,

as though I were in a boardroom in Whitehall,' Wellesley said. 'Very well. Your beasts will have their keep, and above that the same wages as any other man in service under the Navy Board—'

'A shilling a day will keep a seaman's wife and children, and let him carouse on shore a little when he comes into port, but it will not do as much for a dragon.' Laurence said.

'And we don't want little coins that we must keep track of, either, and cannot hold onto,' Minnow put in. 'A proper mess that would be.'

Temeraire nodded. 'No, and what we really want is to be able to go where we like. *That* is what I want promised, also. If we may go where we like, and do any work that is offered to us, then even should the Government offer us unfair wages, we can work for someone else instead. And the same for harnessed dragons too,' he added.

'Any work that is offered to you?' Wellesley said. 'By all means. As for going where you like—'

He and Laurence wrangled a long time, in low voices, over sums and coverts, and how much ought to be paid to a heavyweight, over a courier, and so on. Temeraire listened carefully, but he did not know all the places that Laurence named, where coverts ought to be, and also he was not quite certain about the money. His breastplate, he knew, was worth nearly ten thousand pounds, but shillings and pence were new. They were interrupted at last only by the arrival of a breathless courier from the main camp, to inform them that the last stragglers from the battlefield had regrouped, and were ready to begin the march to the north.

'I have no more time for this,' Wellesley said. 'Twenty coverts, on the Bath Road and the Great North Road, where they can go to sleep and be fed. As for pavilions, they can build the damn things themselves with their own shillings;

set themselves up like admirals, if they like. And after this, they had damned well better keep in line.'

'Sir,' Laurence said, and made a bow to Wellesley's back; the general had already turned and walked away.

Laurence found himself the focus of a large and interested audience of dragons, all pressing in and jostling for room to hear him, as soon as he had begun to try and explain the system of coinage to Temeraire and Minnow.

'So ten pounds will buy one cow?' Minnow said intently, 'and a pound and a shilling is a bit of gold?'

'If it is twenty shillings to a pound, and twenty-four shillings a day, then that is nearly four hundred pounds a year for a heavyweight—' Temeraire said thoughtfully, performing the calculations in his head, which produced a buzz of satisfaction among the other dragons.

'But where is it?' Iskierka demanded. 'I did not come back just to hear numbers; what sort of treasure is it?'

Temeraire snapped at her a little. 'It is reliable treasure,' he said. 'Not all of us want to be always running around picking quarrels and making difficulties, like you, grabbing more and more. This is for everyone who does their duty every day, like proper soldiers, and it is fair.'

The other dragons were generally of his mind, even if Iskierka continued to sulk, and agreed they were satisfied with their lot. But Laurence felt not a little disgusted for having stooped to such back-room negotiations, at such a moment. Manoeuvring for personal interest, while Bonaparte marched into London and the French followed on their heels, felt like treason to him. 'We must see to your dinners,' he said, more out of an urgent wish to put an end to the gloating noise. 'The army will march at first light, and we must be ready.'

*　　*　　*

186

In the morning, before the dragons had breakfasted and gone aloft, the first regiments were out on the road, their pace sluggish enough that Requiescat remarked, near dinner-time, 'Now, this is what I call a pleasant flight, no fussing or hurry.' Temeraire only sighed.

'We might offer to carry them, at least a little way, for as many as could climb aboard us?' he suggested to Laurence. 'I am sure they could go faster.'

'Not without orders,' Laurence said. He could well imagine Wellesley's reaction, or Dalrymple's, if the dragons should begin to fly towards the ranks, and likely panic some of the men and cavalry-beasts into running, after all the difficulty in forming them back into their regiments.

'It is only so dull. We could fly to tonight's rendezvous and back again three times over, before they have got there,' Temeraire said, 'and some of us more than that. What if Requiescat and a few of the others should stay pacing them, and we go ahead—Or perhaps,' he added, ruff coming up with enthusiasm, 'we might go back, and see if we cannot pay Napoleon back a little, for everything he has done.' He peered back over his shoulder, to see how this was received.

'It is not your place to propose such a thing, anymore,' Laurence said. 'You have accepted a commission; you are obliged to preserve discipline, not to undermine it—' Hearing himself thus condemned from his own mouth, Laurence stopped; he realised he did not know how to speak to Temeraire of duty, without being a hypocrite.

'I suppose,' Temeraire said, regretfully. 'It is not always pleasant to be an officer. And I am sure Iskierka will complain, all night, and say more cutting things about going slowly, and running away, and not getting treasure.' He snorted, and looked, and then said doubtfully, 'Where *is* Iskierka?'

She had been flying sullenly to their rear all the morning, amusing herself by making occasional wild darts into the heavy clouds above, where her flames made gold and crimson and purple flashes through the white and grey. But Laurence did not remember her doing it the last two hours and more. Arkady was gone also, with a handful of the other ferals; and when questioned, Wringe had a guilty twist to her neck, even while she professed her surprise and confusion.

Temeraire did not miss it. 'But how am I to make Wringe tell me where they have gone?' he asked Laurence, and batted her talons away from a bleating sheep. He had brought them down in a broad meadow, to better interrogate the remaining ferals. The other dragons made busy driving the luckless resident herd towards them, so they should make a meal while they worked out what Iskierka and the others had done. 'No, you may not eat; not until you have told me. They have made a great deal of trouble for all of us.'

'I call that hard,' Requiescat said, mumbling around a sheep. 'It isn't as though we will not outstrip those redcoats, and nobody minds a snack either.'

'You may find it less pleasant when we have had to fly thirty miles back to catch Iskierka, and then sixty on to the rendezvous,' Laurence said grimly. It was the very best outcome they could hope for.

'Hum,' Requiescat said, licking his chops thoughtfully, 'that's so, but I don't see why we have to go finding her at all. She and those fellows know where the rendezvous is as well as anyone, and they have some men and their compasses with them, if they should get themselves lost like hatchlings. We can just go on and let them catch us up.'

'They must know we would miss them, after they have been gone so long,' Temeraire said, 'so I expect that they have got themselves into a fight, and are probably all dying somewhere full of French bullets.' He did not sound as though he would be very sorry if that proved to be the case.

Wringe squirmed as Temeraire pointedly translated this

for her, but remained silent. 'Temeraire,' Laurence said, low, 'this is not only foolishness on her part; this is a challenge to your authority.'

'Oh!' Temeraire said, and having told Wringe as much, he added, 'so now you *will* tell me, or else,' and when she continued mute, he drew a great expanding breath and roared out, over her head.

'*Payom zhe reng!*' Wringe said, flattening herself to the ground, as everyone jumped. A gentle pattering like rain came from the trees: old acorns shaken loose into the dead leaves, and among them a few small birds stone dead. Gong Su promptly went in after them while Wringe muttered her confession: the miscreants had gone back towards London with a notion of taking some of Napoleon's army by surprise, and winning either treasure or accolades. There had been no very well-formed goal; they had gone looking for a fight as much as for any practical reward.

'We ought to go on and leave them to catch up,' Temeraire said, panting a little, still ruffled and angry, 'just as Requiescat says. Except then I dare say she will come back with two eagles or something like, and there will be no living with her at all.'

Laurence did not like to ill-wish aloud, but if Iskierka had so over-ridden Granby as to make herself a deserter, she was unlikely to be guided in any other respect of sense either, and he thought Temeraire's earlier expectation was the more likely.

But Temeraire brightened after a moment and added, 'Anyway, I do not suppose anyone can blame us for going after her, to fetch her back, Laurence? After all, she is very important; or so everyone says.'

The roads beneath them were empty as they flew warily back towards London. The haze of dust, which the British soldiers raised had already settled, and there was no sign of

French pursuit. No one was to be seen out of doors, but farmers and herdsmen: cattle and crops cared nothing for Napoleon or politics, and implacably demanded the same attention in war and peace. But even these few men kept their heads low, and hurried through their work; so by late afternoon the countryside seemed nearly deserted, with the sun yearning impatiently to its rest.

'We ought to see her miles off, if she is showing away as she always does,' Temeraire was saying ungraciously, as they flew, and then he pricked up his ruff: a small speck in the distance had emerged from the clouds and begun to resolve itself into wings.

It was Gherni: a very battered Gherni, panting with the speed of her flight, her face mazed with a trickle of blood she ineffectually tried to rub off against her shoulder, now and again. Tharkay was with her, and he leapt down to Temeraire's back from hers mid-flight, like a boarder, but tethered by a long double strap of thick leather. He unclipped it from his own waist as soon as he had landed and latched on to Temeraire's harness. Gherni caught up the snapping-free loose end, which jangled loudly with small clapper bells, and wrapped it around her own forearm a few times.

'What is that?' Temeraire said, with interest, craning his head to see.

'I had it made in Istanbul, my last journey,' Tharkay said, and to Laurence said, 'Iskierka has been taken.'

He led them to Arkady and the other deserters, huddled and licking their wounds in the shelter of a tall hill that shielded them from the road and cast an afternoon shadow long enough to conceal them from cursory observation from aloft. The red-patched feral roused when Temeraire came in to land, and mantled his wings defensively.

'That is enough, you shan't bristle at me,' Temeraire said. 'You knew very well you were behaving like a—' he paused, for consideration '—like a scrub, or else you shouldn't have sneaked, and if you have been served out as you deserved, it is no one's fault but your own. You had better to be sorry and promise not to do it again, rather than hiss.'

'They broke away a little before noon,' Tharkay told Laurence, as they squatted down and scraped clean a patch of ground, for him to sketch out the action. 'They had been going into the clouds all morning, and making a noise with their singing, so by the time we realized they had turned us around you were all far out of earshot. Granby's gunners shot off a few flares, but it was a hopeless effort.

'From there, two hours flying towards London without any challenge, so we were on Bonaparte's doorstep by the time we came on any other beasts; and then it was Davout's advance guard out gathering cattle: two Grand Chevaliers and another half a dozen heavyweights. Of course all of them went directly for her; I think I saw sixty men jump for her back at once. Arkady grew remarkably less deaf, after that, and we managed to get away; but the French already had Granby trussed like a chicken on one of the Chevaliers and were racing him away as fast as they could go, with Iskierka flinging herself madly after them.'

'I knew I ought never have let her have Granby,' Temeraire said stormily. 'Look how she has lost him, and not even in a real battle. We ought to get him back and leave her to them, and good riddance.'

Laurence exchanged a glance with Tharkay: it was by no means good riddance to lose their one fire-breather to the French, no matter how recalcitrant. 'Did you see where they went?' Laurence asked, low.

'Straight for London,' Tharkay said.

Chapter Ten

'I am now an officer too, though,' Temeraire said, 'so I do not see why I must wait.'

'You could be a general, and it would not make you any smaller,' Laurence said. 'A twenty-ton dragon must give over trying to sneak, and that is our only hope at all of getting Granby out.'

'But what if *you* should be captured,' Temeraire said, 'and then I would be just as wretched as Iskierka: it is my duty to keep you safe.'

They had very nearly fought this battle before, in Istanbul, and so his protests were an expression of unhappiness rather than fresh and determined objections. 'We have not time to quarrel; Granby's liberty if not his very life may depend on quick action,' Laurence said gently, and Temeraire sank to his belly with his ruff pinned back, threshing the matted straw of the meadow uneasily with his claws and raking up dust and furrowed earth with it.

Laurence was grateful for familiar conversation, if a little guilty, for it allowed him to practice a degree of deceit: he knew that under ordinary circumstances, he would not go, however much he might wish to. If he were captured,

Temeraire would become a prisoner, and in their already dire straits the risk should not be run, not for so slim a chance as they faced to free Granby and Iskierka.

But circumstances were not ordinary. Laurence was a man already dead by law. He could not value his own life very high; and so as long as he were killed instead of captured in the attempt, which he had some right to hope he might be, Temeraire would not be lost to Britain: he had made the agreement with Wellesley, and now was bound directly.

And there was no one else to go, anyway. Iskierka had been the only one of their motley company to possess a proper crew, and they had been captured with her: lieutenants, midwingmen, even her ground-crew. All that were left were Laurence's small handful of crew; the only senior officers Dunne and Wickley, former midwingmen of Laurence's crew who had acquired enough of the ferals' language to become useful translators. A handful of other officers had been similarly placed with the ferals for their gift with languages more than any other quality. Most of them were young, nearer fourteen than twenty, and not to be sent on an expedition with odds little better than a throw of a dice.

Tharkay shook his head at the lot of them, and said to Laurence, 'Better if we go alone.'

Tharkay had taken a commission with the Corps, at least for the moment; but this was not something which service could demand. 'You are not obliged—' Laurence began.

'No,' Tharkay agreed civilly, with one raised brow, and Laurence bowed and left it there.

Laurence exchanged his bottle-green coat for Blythe's leather smock, its pockets large enough to conceal a multitude of sins. He carried two pistols, a good knife and one of Blythe's hammers. Tharkay gave him a handful of mud for his face, and rubbed more onto his hands and beneath his nails.

Dunne watched their preparations at a distance, with occasional glances at the other officers; but he did not say anything. It was not cowardice. He had made sufficient proof of his courage, in previous service, that Laurence did not doubt it now. Dunne's reluctance had a source less palatable: it was plain that he did not wish to serve with Laurence again. There could be no harm to Dunne's career from such cooperation, though there might indeed be some if he chose not to go and Laurence did not return, so his objection was simply one of principle.

Laurence bent his head over the fresh loading of his pistols, and did not witness more of Dunne's struggle; the sense of disapproval did not weigh upon him so greatly, now. He felt himself a righted ship, heaved off her beam-ends and into a dangerous course, which was at least for the immediate distance, clear, even if there was a lee-shore off his bows and impenetrable murk ahead. He might be dashed on rocks, if the wind turned against him, but for the moment he knew what must be done, and he was free to do it.

They were ready in less than ten minutes, and would have gone at once, but Gong Su came and offered them a makeshift plate of bark with two small skewers upon it: tiny hearts and livers, still steaming from a makeshift butchering, and raw. Laurence regarded it with dismay. 'A little of the divine wind inside,' Gong Su explained: they had come from the birds, which Temeraire had slain. 'That makes good fortune.'

Laurence was not superstitious, but he ate; they could hardly refuse any advantage whatsoever. Tharkay took his own dose, pulled up the hood of his cloak over his face, and they went out to the road.

'They may have already sent Granby to France, of course,' Tharkay said to him in Chinese, while they sat in the back of a drover's cart.

'I hope not risk the Navy,' Laurence said, fumbling in his

turn through the difficult language, which he knew he made nearly unintelligible, despite Temeraire's many despairing attempts to correct his pronunciation. It gave them some privacy from the hungry curiosity of the drover, who for a couple of quiet shillings had agreed to take them along to market with the cattle he hoped to sell before they should be confiscated.

Tharkay nodded. If Napoleon were sure enough of his grip on London, he might choose to keep his valuable captive penned rather than risk Granby's death in a crossing under fire, and the resulting frenzy of a Kazilik unleashed upon his forces. They could hope for at least a brief delay if the question were considered, during which Granby would be held near-by. They had to hope: otherwise there was no chance at all.

The last two crawling miles to the city were infuriating, when they had flown fifty that morning in much less time, and the outskirts of London sounded already like a province of France. Tens of thousands of soldiers were busy making encampments, calling to each other and to the dragons who were helping them dig ditches, move stones and even widen roads, and local merchants more industrious than patriotic ran up and down the lanes of the camp, plying food and more commonly drink in far reaching voices and awkward, badly-accented French: 'Une frank, monser' and 's'il voo plait,' but they were already improving.

'He is not shy of making permanent alterations,' Tharkay said, indicating the buildings that were being raised: large stones were being laid into the ground and pressed down by dragons, to make a raised platform once mortar had been poured over and between them, and logs sunk at the corners. There were no walls to the shelters, but as they came closer to the city Laurence saw one already finished and in use: dragons slept on three sides, and soldiers were crammed into the sheltered space between them. The men would sleep warm despite the coming winter; warmer than the British soldiers. The work bore all the hallmarks of long occupation; Napoleon was not planning any immediate campaign, Laurence realized grimly, but rather to entrench himself.

Driven on by the drover's boys, the lowing cows plodded along after the cart, the sour grassy smell and the dust of the road rising up thick around them. Their shillings and tried patience bought them an easy entry into the city: the French sergeant on duty brightened at the sight of the cattle and waved them in with only a cursory question or two for the farmer, swiftly pointing them towards Smithfield and the slaughterhouses. Laurence and Tharkay stayed in the cart until it had turned into the maze of streets, and the herd and the boys had slipped momentarily out of sight, then quick and unannounced they slipped into a narrow alleyway between two houses.

They went to Whitechapel. A few coins at a pub bought Laurence a healthy dose of gossip and rumour, most of it worthless and irrelevant, but for the information that Bonaparte was staying in Kensington Palace, and that his unnatural white beast, with its horrid red, eyes was lying in Hyde Park like some overgrown eel.

Tharkay had better fortune at the docks, among the polyglot mass of men with no allegiance to anyone but the sea, and those who would pay them. Prisoners were being kept at Newgate, but there had been no new arrivals. They had also, without prompting, mentioned Iskierka. She had been seen eating two cows in Hyde Park, and had also set the entire city ablaze, if some of the reports were to be believed; but one street-sweeper swore that no British aviators or crew had been brought to Newgate that day.

'In consolation,' Tharkay said, 'neither have they been

shipped to the coast. No large dragons have left, either, since she came in, and he has certainly not sent anyone by boat.'

'He might have Granby in Kensington Palace,' Laurence said after a moment.

'It would be very convenient for us, certainly,' Tharkay said, dryly.

'It sounds like folly, I know,' Laurence said, 'but if I may be pardoned for forming an opinion on the grounds of one meeting, I would say that Bonaparte is unreasonably fond of seduction, to the point that he likes to believe he has a chance of persuasion where rationally there is none. He will never miss a chance for a grand gesture, if he thinks he might coax Granby into service.'

Tharkay listened and shrugged. 'We may as well take the chance; the trail is cold otherwise.'

It was dark by the time they reached the outskirts of Mayfair. Here and there the life of the city continued, in a muted tone; ale-houses spilt warmth and the smell of fresh beer onto the dirty cobbles, and firelight gleamed from behind the closed shutters of those who had not fled the city, whether from unwillingness or from inability. In the fashionable section, Laurence took the lead from Tharkay. These streets he knew well, going past his father's house and those of his friends and political acquaintances, some of them men Laurence had known in the Navy, all of them shuttered and dark. Laurence did not hesitate: he had expected silence, abandoned houses, and perhaps even wreckage and looting. He moved on steadily and did not look to see what damage might have been done, until he came into Dover Street, and was at last surprised: to find it crammed with carriages. Ten linkmen stood at the door of one great town houses; fine young ladies with their chaperones, British gentlemen and French officers flooded the steps as a great bustling noise of music and laughter and dish-clattering spilled down on them.

He stopped in the street, appalled, and had to be drawn back from the lights by Tharkay. 'We will not get past that soon,' Tharkay said. Laurence, choked with anger, did not immediately answer. He had never been a visitor to the house, but thought it had been let to a Radical member from Liverpool, a man who might have voted with his father on occasion. He mastered himself and drew Tharkay a few doors along to another house still occupied, but quietly so: a few subdued lights gleamed from between shutters, not a party to welcome the conquerors. Waiting by the gate they might pass for footmen or grooms, and be dismissed as such by the guests and their servants; with any luck the owner and his family were already abed.

They stood nearly an hour, stamping a little to warm their feet, and drawing back against the sides of the house now and then as another carriage reached the door to disgorge its passengers. Every minute brought fresh cause for indignation: the smell of hot roast beef, a burst of singing in French, a lady waltzing with a French officer past the open balcony doors. The carriages thinned out only a little over the course of their wait: a sad crush, with the King fled to Scotland and thousands of British soldiers dead or held prisoner.

Then a troop of horses came down the street: Old Guard, in their tall hats and pomp, shouting to clear the way. They muscled the remaining carriage-horses aside showing cool indifference to the protests of their drivers, to make room for a great coach to come rolling along through the crush. An eagle had been painted in gold upon the door. It drew up before the house, and through the ranks of guards lined up the stairs, Laurence just saw Napoleon emerge from the carriage and mount the steps to the house. He wore trousers and hessian boots, and a long leather coat more suited to mid-air than a drawing room, though it was splendid with gold braid and buttons, and dyed richly black. Another man was beside him, one of the Marshals: Murat, Laurence thought, the Emperor's brother-in-law. They went up the stairs together, and applause welcomed them inside.

'Disgusting,' a man muttered quietly, nearby, and Laurence started and looked around. While he had been watching the spectacle, two gentlemen had descended from a carriage at the very door of the house where he stood. They were presently between him and Tharkay, who had drawn back a little into the shadow of the house. 'Do you know, I heard Lady Hamilton was going to attend?'

'Her and half the women of quality left in the city,' the second gentleman answered him, a voice vaguely familiar. 'You there,' the man raised his tone to address Laurence, 'what do you mean, loitering on the street gawking as though you were at a play? They don't need any damn encouragement,' and Laurence, with a sinking sense of disaster, recognized him as Bertram Woolvey, the son of a friend of Lord Allendale's.

Woolvey had married Edith Galman, if any better cause were needed for the lack of love between him and Laurence, and they had never been friends even before that event. Woolvey was a gamester and a spendthrift, with the one saving grace that he could afford to be, and their circles had always been most different. Laurence knew nothing good of him besides his choice of wife.

Woolvey now stepped closer, frowning at the lack of an answer. Laurence was out of the circle of street light, his face obscured by the mud he had applied, but at a moment he could be recognized, and bring it all to an end: the slightest outcry would alert at least ten men from the guards outside the party, whether Woolvey meant to draw them down on him or not.

Laurence took two quick steps to Woolvey's side and

gripped him by the arm, covering his mouth with another hand. 'Say nothing,' he hissed quietly, to Woolvey's staring eyes. 'Do you understand? Say nothing; nod if you understand me.'

Woolvey's companion said, 'What are you,' and stopped. Tharkay had caught him from behind and clapped a hand over his mouth also.

Woolvey nodded, and when Laurence took away his hand said at once, 'William Laurence? What the devil are you—' and had to have his mouth covered again.

The door of the house opened, and a footman peered out, puzzled. 'Into the house,' Laurence said. 'Quickly, for God's sake,' and half pushed Woolvey up the steps, before they drew attention. The footman backed in at a loss before their awkward rush, Tharkay and Woolvey's companion – a gentleman Laurence vaguely recognized as a Mr. Sutton-Leeds – followed directly on Laurence's heels.

Tharkay let go of Sutton-Leeds as soon as they were inside, and snatched the door away to shut it again. 'What on earth,' the man said, 'is it thieves?' more incredulous than alarmed.

'No, stay there, and for God's sake do not stir up the house any further,' Laurence said sharply to the footman who was edging towards the bell-pull. 'Enough of a muddle as it—' and stopped.

Edith was on the stairs, in a dressing gown and cap, saying, 'Bertram, may I beg you to be as quiet as you can? James is only just asleep—'

There was a moment of uncomfortable silence, until Woolvey broke it by saying pompously, 'I think you had better explain yourself, Laurence. What you mean by this invasion of my house?'

'Nothing more,' Laurence said, after a moment, 'than to keep you from drawing the attention of the French on the stoop: we may not be discovered.' His hand was closed hard upon the pistol at his waist, for no good reason. *The fool, the damned fool, keeping his wife and child in the middle of an occupying army.* Laurence had no right and knew it, but he could not help but ask, 'Why in God's name have you not left the city?'

'Measles,' Edith said, from the stairs. Her face was composed, but her hand gripped tightly on the railing. 'The doctor said the baby should not be moved.' She paused and added quietly, 'The French have not troubled us: one officer came to question, but they have been perfectly civil.'

'Not that we are sympathizers, and if you mean to suggest—Wait,' Woolvey said, 'haven't I heard—Were you not—' He stopped, and was plainly stuck for an explanation. Laurence had not the slightest desire to aid him.

'I must beg your pardon, I do not know what you have heard,' Laurence said eventually. 'I am most earnestly sorry to have troubled you, but we are on an urgent errand, and it is not of a nature to be discussed in your front hall.'

'Then come into the sitting room, and discuss it there,' Sutton-Leeds said, more than a little drunk, if not to the point of slurring. 'Secret mission; splendid. I have been aching to do something against these damned Frogs, prancing through the city as though they owned it.'

Woolvey appeared slightly more sober, or perhaps it was belligerence, and he seconded this demand, but with suspicion added, 'And I tell you, Laurence, I expect some better answers. No, you shan't go, unless you do want me to set up a shout. You cannot accost a man in the street during times like these and then claim it is all about secret missions and go bounding away, with this Chinaman in tow.'

'I beg your pardon,' Tharkay said, in his most frigidly aristocratic accent, and drew their stares. 'I do not believe we have been introduced, gentlemen.'

'What the devil are you doing made up like a Chinaman,

then?' Sutton-Leeds said, peering at Tharkay's face, as if he expected to find some artifice responsible for his features.

Given this brief distraction, Laurence caught Woolvey's arm and said low and sharply, 'Do not be a damned fool. If they take us in your house, they will take you for a spy, do you understand, and if they care to be thorough your wife also. Forget we were ever here and pay your servants to do the same: every moment we stay here, we put you all in danger, to no purpose.'

Woolvey wrenched himself free and returned, as coldly, 'That you take *me* for a fool, I very well know, but I am not so simple as to take the word of a convicted traitor— Yes, I *have* heard—And one skulking loose in the streets, the day after Bonaparte marches in.'

'Then I am lying and a turncoat for the French,' Laurence said impatiently, 'and if you interfere with me I might have you all arrested: either way you had better let me go.'

'I am no coward, sir,' Woolvey said. 'If you are on some black business for that Corsican, I will stop you even if I have to blow a hole through you to do it, yes, and go to prison for it too, damn you.'

'Gentlemen,' Edith said, breaking the charged atmosphere, 'I beg you all go into the sitting room before you wake the entire house,' and there was nothing to be done for it.

Sutton-Leeds was disposed of by means of a substantial glass of brandy, which left him snoring in an armchair. The credit was Edith's: they had scarcely entered the room before she had come down again, hastily dressed, and taken the decanter around at once. But though Woolvey accepted a glass, he simply looked at it, set it down, and said, 'I will have coffee, my dear, if you please,' with determined mien, and waited with his arms folded across his chest.

Laurence looked at the clock: it was nearly eleven.

Bonaparte's engagement at the party, with so many of his entourage surely gave them their best chance of success, and every minute was now doubly precious.

Tharkay caught his eye, and said low, 'He has horses,' with a jerk of his head at Woolvey: a suggestion Laurence did not like in the least. He saw no better alternative however, despite his intense reluctance to put his life, all their lives, in Woolvey's hands; and he did not trust the discretion of Woolvey's servants.

They remained standing in silence, except for the continuing low snuffles of Sutton-Leeds' snoring. A maid brought the coffee service, and took a long while arranging it on the table, covertly glancing up at them all. They made an absurd gathering: Woolvey in his evening-dress; Edith in a soft high-waisted morning gown of sprigged muslin, without stays. Tharkay and himself, in their rough workman's clothes, all smudged with dirt and stinking, no doubt, of cattle and the docks.

'Thank you, Martha,' Edith said at last, 'I will pour,' and bent over the table when the maid had gone. She gave handed cups to Woolvey and Laurence; hesitated a moment, and then finally poured another for Tharkay.

Tharkay smiled with a faint twist at her doubtful gesture towards him. 'Thank you,' he said, and drank the coffee quickly. Setting down the cup he went to the door and opened it again. The maid and footman caught lingering outside made quick shift to vanish. Tharkay glanced back at Laurence and at the clock, meaningfully, then slipped into the hall, closing the door behind him: no one would be able to eavesdrop now.

Laurence put down his cup of excellently strong coffee, and looked at the window casement, framed with thick curtains of pale blue velvet, with elegant gold tasselled cords. He had the unreasonable desire to smother Woolvey with one of them, and leave him trussed on the floor while they fled; but of course he would begin to shout at once, and Laurence could not put Edith in such a position.

'Well?' Woolvey said. 'I am not going to be put off, Laurence, and if you keep me waiting any longer I'll have my footmen put you in the cellar, and there let you sit until morning.'

Laurence pressed his lips together on the instinctive answers he wished to make. He was aware he was being unjust. Woolvey had no more reason to love him than the reverse, and no reason to believe him either. 'We do not have until morning,' he said, at last, shortly. 'Earlier today a British officer was captured, a dragon captain—'

'What of it? I hear ten thousand men were captured yesterday.' Woolvey spoke bitterly and with real feeling: one sentiment Laurence could at least share.

'It means that his beast is also taken prisoner,' Laurence said. 'He is hostage for her good behaviour; and his beast is our fire-breather—Our only fire-breather.'

'Oh,' Edith said, suddenly. 'I saw her this afternoon. She came down in Hyde Park.'

Laurence nodded. 'And there is some little chance that he is held at the palace itself,' he said. 'Do you now understand our urgency? While Bonaparte—'

'I am not a simpleton, sir,' Woolvey said, interrupting, 'but why send only you and this havey-cavey fellow—'

'One good man is better than a dozen of lesser ability in such an expedition,' Laurence said. 'We were the only ones close enough to make the attempt. No, enough questions,' he added sharply. 'I am not going to waste time answering every objection you can dredge up. If you mean to continue this blundering interference, when you have no understanding of the situation, you may be damned: we will take our chances in the street with Bonaparte's guardsmen.'

Woolvey looked still undecided. 'Will,' Edith said, quietly, and they both looked at her, 'will you swear on the Bible that you are telling the truth?'

This gesture did not entirely satisfy Woolvey, but Edith took him by the arm and said, 'Dearest, I have known Will since we were children. While I can believe he would easily manage to get himself convicted of treason, I do not think that he would lie under oath.'

Sullenly Woolvey said, 'Still; it is all a dashed rum affair if you ask me.' He drew away from her and poured himself a second cup of coffee. He was so irritable and tense that he splashed it across the china and the polished wood; he did not bother to put in the cream but drank it straight from the cup, a few swallows only, and set it down again with a clatter. 'So what is it, do you mean to rescue him?' he said abruptly, with a fresh note of something even more dangerous than suspicion: enthusiasm.

'If we can,' Laurence said, and forced himself to ask, 'If you can spare us your carriage-horses?'

'No,' Woolvey said after a moment. 'No, *I* will take you, in the carriage. Lord Holland's servants know me, and his grounds march with the palace gardens. It is not a mile from his house. If you really mean to get yourselves into the palace, and this is not all some fantasy, I will see you get there. And if it is all a pack of nonsense, and you have some other mischief in mind, I dare say the coachman, footmen and I can just as well put paid to your notion.'

Edith flinched. 'Woolvey, do not be absurd,' Laurence said. 'You have not been brought up for this sort of work.'

'Driving you an easy couple of miles, to the house of a gentleman of my acquaintance, and taking a stroll through his park?' Woolvey shot back, sarcastic. 'I dare say I will manage somehow.'

'And then?' Laurence said. 'When we have gone into the

206

house and taken Granby out, and a hue and cry is raised after us?'

'I am certain I know Kensington park a damned sight better than you,' Woolvey said, 'so as for getting out, I have a better chance than you. What is your next objection? I am ready to be as patient as you care to be, Laurence, but *you* are the one insisting on haste.'

Woolvey went upstairs to change his clothes, having first taken the precaution of calling down two footmen to watch Laurence and Tharkay while the coach was pulled around. 'Can you not persuade him?' Laurence asked Edith, low, in a corner: she had her arms folded about her waist, and her hands gripped her elbows.

'What would you have me say?' she returned. 'I will not counsel my husband to be a coward. Will this not be of assistance to you?' He could not deny it, and she shook her head and looked away, her lips pressed tight. Laurence could not work on her any further. 'I had thought I was done with these fears,' she added, low and unhappily, but he knew how little her personal feelings would be permitted to sway her judgment: as little as he would have allowed himself.

He moved away from her, as Woolvey came down the stairs and went to bid her farewell. The two of them stood talking quietly, hands clasped, and then he bent his head to hers.

Tharkay was watching the scene with a dry interest. 'I beg your pardon for embroiling us so,' Laurence said.

'In a practical sense, we could ask for nothing better,' Tharkay said. 'We are not likely to be stopped in a blazoned carriage, in open view of everyone. Noticed, certainly, and he may find his neck in a noose for it afterwards, but that is his concern, and those who would weep for him.' He looked at Laurence. 'Although those may be of interest to you also.'

Laurence was sorry to be so transparent, and sorrier still to be shut up in a carriage with Woolvey during the half an hour drive to Holland House. There was no conversation of any kind; there was nothing that could be said between them, the rejected suitor and the husband. Laurence was silenced further by an inchoate sensation, which had no place in the present circumstances and yet insisted on making itself felt.

He had never thought very much of Woolvey; he had dismissed the man as a spendthrift idler, but in fairness, Woolvey had never been given impetus for his own improvement. With nothing to do but spend money, he might easily have developed a vicious character, a gamester or a selfish coward. But he had chosen instead to establish himself respectably, and with a wife no man could blush for; and no coward would act as he had tonight. If he were a little dull and mulish in his cups, and angry for his country's humiliation, that was not the worst thing that could be said of a man.

And Edith had looked very well. Not happy, no one could be happy with an army at the door and a quarrel in the entrance hall; but that she was contented with the lot she had chosen was plain. She did not regret.

Laurence wholeheartedly wished her happy, and his feeling held no envious quality. But it was uncomfortable to think Woolvey had brought it about, when, Laurence was painfully aware, *he* had not. He had kept Edith on the shelf with expectation when she might have had more advantageous offers. He did not care to remember their last interview: all selfish petulance on his side, even the gall even to make her an offer, which could only be unwelcome after he had pledged himself to the Corps. He looked at Woolvey, who was staring out of the carriage window. What had Edith to regret? Nothing: she had better congratulate herself on a lucky escape.

The coach drew to a halt. Holland House was dark. The horses stamped uneasily, their warm breath steaming in the air while a footman came rubbing sleep from his eyes to hold their heads. 'Yes, I know the family are away,' Woolvey was saying, already climbing out as another man opened the door for him. 'Be so good as to stable my horses and bring Gavins out, I want a word with him.'

He gave only airy excuses for his presence in the city, and for his late visit: the baby ill and squalling, the wife impatient, '—and I thought to myself, what I need is a walk in the fresh air, and a look at the stars—Too many lights in Mayfair—I am sure Lord Holland would not mind—'

It was a bizarre proposal, at midnight, with an army in the streets and two men in rough clothing behind him, but Gavins only bowed: familiar with the odd starts of gentlemen in their cups, and too well-trained to show it, if he were puzzled. 'I must advise you, sir, not to go too close to the east end of the park, if you should walk beyond the gardens,' he said. 'I am afraid we have several dragons sleeping there.'

'Oh,' Woolvey said, and when they had been let into the park, whispered, 'What are we to do about the beasts?'

'Walk by them,' Tharkay said, blowing out the lantern they had been given.

'There is no need for you to come any further,' Laurence said. 'You have done us a great service already, Woolvey—'

'I am not afraid,' Woolvey returned, angrily, and strode on ahead.

Tharkay shook his head, and when Laurence looked at him said quietly, 'It must be difficult to follow an officer of public repute, in the affections of a woman who loves courage.'

It had not occurred to Laurence, that Woolvey meant this display for Edith's benefit, or that he felt any sense of competition with him. 'My reputation is hardly one any sensible man would covet.'

'It does not name you a coward,' Tharkay said. 'Whatever has Bertram Woolvey done?'

The grounds near the house were wooded; cedars stood fragrant amid the silent denuded oaks and plane trees, all crusted with frost. These yielded to broad, hard-frozen meadows; their boot heels crushed the grass like sand underfoot. If their desire to observe the stars had been truth, they would have been served well: the night was clear and cold and still; the wind had died, and there was no moon.

The dragon interlopers were snoring peacefully, if a noise like mill wheels grinding could be described so; it was audible for a quarter of a mile. It did not hold the same hollow-chested resonance of the voices of the great combat-weight beasts, and there were few men about, and no fires: it looked to be a company of courier dragons with their solitary captains sleeping huddled against their sides.

Laurence thought himself well used to the company of dragons by now, he had not minded the streets of Peking, or the pavilions where the great beasts slept in vast coiled heaps; but in the near absence of light, the persistent low growling noise was magnified, and he could not wholly repress the shudder which climbed his back as they walked from one stand of trees to another, carefully crossing the meadows where the dragons slept.

His intellect might know these were thinking creatures, who would much rather capture than kill him, but his belly did not. It knew only that near-by lay a dozen beasts, which in the ordinary course of animal life would have made an easy meal of him.

Laurence calmed himself, in cool reasoning terms, before every outline became a dragon, and every grumble of rustling leaves a prelude to attack. They had yet to keep moving on steadily, through pitch impenetrable enough that Laurence put out his hand before his face, to keep from running into any branches.

Woolvey's breath rasped loudly ahead of him, short ragged breaths, and his occasional stumble. Tharkay had taken the lead, but Woolvey kept moving. Laurence paced breath to footsteps and doggedly followed: as near to blind as he ever hoped to be.

A flicker, some vague impression of movement, made his head snap sideways, and he stopped for a moment, trying to make it out. It was a hopeless attempt, he could see little more than a dark snaking blot reaching into the sky.

He quickened a few steps to stop Woolvey, and gave a soft hiss to make Tharkay turn. Crouching, they waited, listening. The dragon heaved a great yawning sigh and murmured something in French. Then with a quick flurrying leap, a leathery flap of wings, it was aloft. They did not move while it was overhead, and stayed a while longer, meek as rabbits, before they could make themselves resume.

It seemed a very long time before they came at last to another broad stand of trees. The ground underfoot abruptly became the loose crunch of finely gravelled road: they had reached the end of the estate. Across the road, the broad hedge of the palace garden rose before them. Lights distantly visible at either end of the lane, gleamed as small as fireflies: the guards on watch. But there were none directly ahead, the patrol idled near their sheltered posts.

Tharkay motioned Laurence to wait with Woolvey, and after a moment came back to silently guide them to a place he had found by the hedge: a low rock near the wall, with a thick elm branch above. He had already rigged a cord to hang down. Laurence nodded, and taking off the thick leather apron threw it over the top of the hedge. The scramble was as quiet as he could make it. Woolvey came after him, with some delay, panting heavily and in disarray: the fine buckskin of his breeches, was torn and bloodied. Tharkay last, silent and quick.

The great palace lay across a narrow lawn before them. Its windows were lit, and shadows passed back and forth before the lights. Another half a dozen dragons stood in their way; not sleeping beasts, either, but couriers wide awake and waiting for messages.

'The stables,' Woolvey whispered, pointing: the dragons had been positioned as far from the low outbuilding as could be managed. 'There is a door, on the side, and from there we can cross a narrow gap to the servants' entrance into to the kitchens.'

The horses whickered at them uneasily, and stamped, watching their movements with liquid terrified eyes; but this was not unusual behaviour with the dragons at their door: no one stirred or came to look in at them. Tharkay paused at the far door, his fingertips resting against the wood. They could hear voices outside, surly and English voices. Through a crack Laurence peered at a pair of workmen, who were trundling manure to the midden without any semblance of pleasure.

'Hst,' he said, softly, when they came close, and the men jerked. 'Steady now, men, and quiet, if you love your country.'

'Aye, sir, only say the word,' one whispered back, with an automatic touch of his forelock. He was badly wall-eyed, and had ink stained forearms: a sure mark of the sea. He scowled at the lanky young fellow with him, whose ready protest had subsided into silent fidgets and darting glances at them.

'Is there a prisoner kept here?' Laurence asked. 'He would have been brought today: a man not thirty years of age, dark-haired—'

'Aye, sir,' the seaman said, 'brought him in with a guard like he was the King, and to the finest bedroom but the one old Boney copped for himself, if you please. There was a right noise about it. And that beast of his out front wailing fit to end the world. We thought she would have us all on fire; she said she would. She has only gone quiet this last hour.'

Laurence risked it. A quick dash to the corner of the house was enough to confirm Iskierka's presence. She was coiled in what had been a small garden adorned with statuary, and which was now a heap of rubble. She no longer wailed, but gnawed sullenly upon the remnants of a cow, with steam issuing from her spines, and she was not alone. Lien was sitting beside her, saying, 'You must know that he cannot be given back to you, unless he gives his parole and swears never to take up arms against the Emperor again. There is no sense in your lying here and being uncomfortable. Come away to the park, and you may have something more to eat.'

'I am not going away anywhere without my Granby,' Iskierka said, 'and he will never do any such thing. As soon as I have him back I will kill you, and your emperor, and *all* of you, only see if I do not. Here, you may keep your nasty cows,' and she threw the mauled remainders of her dinner in Lien's direction.

The white Celestial flattened her ruff in displeasure for just a moment, and then nudged a mound of earth over the carcass with one talon, careful never to touch the offal. 'I am sorry that you insist on being so disagreeable. There is no reason we should be enemies. After all, you are not a British dragon. You are a Turkish dragon, and the Sultan is our ally, not Britain's.'

'I do not give a fig for the Sultan. I am Granby's dragon, and Granby is British.' Iskierka said, 'And anyway, I have

213

stolen thirty thousand pounds of your shipping, so of course we are enemies.'

'You may have another ten thousand, if you would come and fight for us, instead,' Lien said.

'Ha,' Iskierka said disdainfully, 'I will have another thirty thousand instead, and take the prizes myself; and I think you are a spineless coward, too.'

The nearest troop of guard, and the couple of courier beasts prudently stayed back, with a nervous eye upon Iskierka, and so a clear path lay open from the house towards her. 'If we can get hold of Granby,' Laurence said quietly to Tharkay, once he had crept back to the stable door, 'and get him out to the open, even an upper window might do, anywhere she might reach us—'

'As soon as we are seen looking like ragpickers, it will send up a howl,' Woolvey said.

'Begging your pardon,' the seaman said, 'but there is six of them cavalry-officers sleeping over the stable, in their clothes.'

They set the nervous stable boy at the door, with Woolvey to watch him. 'Name's Darby, sir, but Janus they call me,' the seaman said, 'on account of a surgeon we shipped on the *Sophie*, a learned bloke and no doubt, saying I saw both ways like some old Roman cut-up by that name; and there I would be still, but my girl in the city losit her mum, and took sick, and her with three, four mouths to feed,' he added vaguely. Likely it had been not one girl but several.

'Very good, Janus,' Laurence said, and gave him a pistol. They put out the lantern swinging by the door, and at a nod from Tharkay the three of them went up the ladder into the loft, swift on bare feet.

The men lay asleep, half sunk into broken-open bales of hay, with their sabres and pistols beside them. One after another Laurence woke them, placing a folded pad of leather over their mouths. Janus pinned their heels and Tharkay held a pistol steady in each face as they were turned over and trussed quickly with straps, and heaved up onto the stack of bales.

The fourth man opened his eyes too soon, and managed to drum his heels as they reached for him. The other two roused sluggishly and groped for their missing swords and pistols, which Tharkay had already collected, three of them thrust into his waistband in piratical fashion. It was a short but brutal struggle, even numbers and with the necessity for silence driving them: Laurence went for his knife and grimly thrust it into the unarmed man's throat as the Frenchman tried to wrestle himself up from the ground. The man sank back limply, staring blindly at the ceiling, blood spilling from his neck to soak into the straw. Laurence took up a sword and killed another, quickly, while Janus held him. Tharkay dispatched the last.

The horses below were stamping again, whickering at the smell of blood. 'Are you all right?' Woolvey whispered, putting his head up into the loft, and stopped with his mouth open.

'Yes,' Laurence said shortly, his heart still hammering. 'Go below, and keep that fellow at the door.'

Woolvey made no protest but obeyed in silence, vanishing again below. The trussed men fought and kicked as they were turned over and stripped of their coats and cuirasses, and one of them made a low moan behind the gag as his eyes fell on the dead men. Friends, or brothers, perhaps; Laurence closed his mind to the thought.

Or he tried to: Woolvey's shocked expression lingered. The hard use, the necessary brutality of the service, were not of the same world as his England, as home; and it was that division which allowed a man the chance to be a gentleman and a practical soldier both. But now he was home, and in the stables of Kensington Palace with his palms wet with blood, on a spy's errand. Yet it was as necessary as any military action. But let it only take place in Paris, or Istanbul, or China, and let Woolvey read of it in the papers and applaud; for it did not belong here, a black rotten canker taken root in the stable attic, above the peaceful gardens.

They scavenged the four uniforms not overly stained with blood, and Laurence threw a stable-blanket over the men now stripped and bound again, against the chill. The coat, warm from a dead man's body, sat uneasily on his shoulders as he climbed down the ladder and handed the last coat to Woolvey.

'We will bind you also,' Laurence said to the boy, 'unless you will come with us, to the rescue and to the dragon?' but the boy shook his head vigorously, and preferred to be bound.

'Perhaps half an hour now,' Tharkay said, meaning how long it might be for, before their discovery: Laurence himself thought it likelier to be a quarter.

'We go in quickly, then,' he said. 'No running, but move with purpose: do you know where he is, Janus?'

'Well, sir,' Janus said, shrugging awkwardly inside his makeshift uniform, and looking a poorer match for it than Tharkay, 'the maids will sometimes take a fellow up to the better rooms, and I don't mean to say I haven't had an invitation or two; but which will be his room, I am sure I don't know.'

'There will be no difficulty there,' Laurence said. 'It will be the only door that is guarded.'

He went first, with Woolvey beside him. A quick glance would at their faces and perhaps most would miss the others. Tharkay held a handkerchief to his face, as if to catch a sneeze, for some more concealment. They climbed the back staircase, and at Janus's whisper turned off the landing into the hallway.

Some eight or nine men stood talking in the hall near one of the rooms to the rear of the house. Undoubtedly there would be more guards within. Laurence did not pause, but kept walking steadily towards them. The men were not wary at their posts but lounging freely. Some sat on the floor, engrossed in a game of cards, as others crouched to observe their play Only a few men were standing. A maid came down the hall loaded down with washing, and as she began to pick her way through the knot of soldiers, had a moment's awkward struggle to win past one over-enthusiastic sergeant, who caught at her waist.

'Keep your hands off,' she said coldly, and jerked expertly free with a twist of her hips, while the other officers roared with laughter at their fellow's expense. She won past them at last, cheeks flushed with colour and her eyes downcast. Laurence was nearly even with her now and as they passed one another he seized one of her sheets and snapped it open over the entire company.

A confused babble of shouting arose at once. They rushed the swathed men, toppling those who had been standing. The door to the room opened and another man looked out. Tharkay shot him, and kicked the door wide. Granby, warned by the commotion, took the opening at once and came rushing out of the room sporting a bruised cheek and a bandaged arm. 'Thank God. Give me a pistol,' he said, and threw off the sling.

'The window,' Laurence said, and turning at the report of a shot, received Woolvey into his arms. There was a startled look on Woolvey's face, and a great stain spreading through his shirt, just visible beneath the swallow-wing lapels of his coat. Another shot was fired and another, and bullets tore wildly through the sheet, small fires catching the linen in their wake. The maid had fled down the hall screaming.

'Iskierka!' Granby was shouting. He had dashed into the room across the way and was leaning out the window.

A look was enough to be sure. The light had already faded from Woolvey's eyes. 'Laurence,' Tharkay said, and shot the first French officer struggling free of the tangled sheet.

'Damn you,' Laurence said, not very certain if he meant Woolvey, or the man who had shot him, or indeed himself. Stooping, he worked the wedding-ring from Woolvey's hand, and went after Tharkay into the bedroom. They shut the door and barricaded it with a wardrobe. It would hold only for a moment, but they needed no longer, Iskierka's talons were already tearing at the window, scrabbling away glass, masonry and brick in great shattering blocks.

Chapter Eleven

It was not at all pleasant to wait, and wait, and keep waiting. Temeraire paced, and then went aloft to look in case there should be any sign, and then came back down and paced a little more.

'There is no one coming, is there?' Perscitia asked, a little anxiously, worried in another direction entirely. 'No French dragons? Perhaps you should stop going up so much. Someone might see you, and,' she added quickly, 'if we had to move, it would make it hard for Laurence to find us again, on his way back.'

Temeraire tried to settle. He could not help but see the sense in this remark, but he shook his head at her offer of a haunch of cow. The smaller dragons had gone out quietly hunting for all of them, but he did not have much appetite.

'It was not very fair of those dragons,' Arkady said, 'all coming on at us at once like that. If you ask me, they are all cowards. We should go fly in and get Iskierka out ourselves.' He had recovered his spirits and was eating a sheep, which his fellow, Lester had fetched for him, with great cheer.

'We will do no such thing,' Temeraire said. 'There are

four times as many of them as there are of us, with guns and soldiers, so they will only have us down. Anyway that would not help us get Granby back, they will just shoot him,' and maybe Laurence too, he thought anxiously. It was all the more unpleasant to have Arkady make such a reckless suggestion, when it was exactly what Temeraire wished to do himself.

'What are we going to do, then,' Arkady returned, 'if they do not come back?'

'If they do not come back,' Temeraire said, and paused, 'then we will think of something,' he finished lamely, not liking to imagine the prospect. He had already thought Laurence dead once, and it had been just as dreadful as if he really had been dead. It made one unsure of the distinction between the events imagined and real, and therefore, Temeraire felt that any speculation on the subject, of any sort, was perhaps a little risky. Laurence thought such concerns to be foolishly superstitious, Temeraire knew, but to him it was a danger not worth courting.

'What is he saying, the rascal?' Gentius asked, scowling at Arkady, in great disapproval. He was not very happy with the extra flying, which he had to endure on Armatius' back, or the uncomfortable state of their camp. 'I hope he is properly ashamed of himself.'

'No,' Temeraire said, 'he is not, not at all; and he is making foolish suggestions, too.'

'Well, pay no attention to him,' Gentius said. 'Now,' and he lowered his voice, 'I don't like to make you worry, Temeraire, but have you thought about what we will do, if they don't come back right off?'

Temeraire flattened his ruff and, unable to repress the desire, went aloft to look again. It was beginning to grow dark across the eastern edge of the sky, a watery moon near the west horizon ready to set, and a few plumes of dust here and there from herds of cattle. Not a sign of Laurence though, or of Iskierka. He looked back the other way and saw a Winchester in harness flying towards them.

Elsie landed panting. 'Oh, we thought we would never find you. What are you doing here? Scotland is not this way, you are going back towards London.'

'We are not lost!' Temeraire said, rather coldly. He did not much like Elsie, Hollin had been a very good ground-crew chief. Fellowes did his best, but he was not quite as attentive to the way the harness lay against one's hide, or as prompt in getting it off in the evenings. Not that Temeraire had much of a harness at present, but it was the principle of the thing. Fellowes was also a little dull, if one were alone in the evening, and wanted a little conversation. In short, Hollin had been his first and Temeraire had not ceased to regret the loss. 'We have not gone the wrong way,' he repeated. 'We are waiting for Laurence and Tharkay to rescue Granby: Iskierka has had herself captured.'

'Oh, Lord,' Hollin said, sliding down from Elsie's back. He had a satchel over his shoulder. 'When did they go?'

'Hours ago,' Temeraire said, despondently, 'though Laurence said, they would most likely need a day to reach the city on foot, and that if they could locate Granby, they would not try and get him out until it was dark, and nearly everyone asleep. So they are not late, at all; they are in good time.'

Hollin rubbed a hand over his mouth and said, 'I have a dispatch—'

'How large is it?' Temeraire inquired, and Hollin took out a folded snippet of paper from his satchel, handsomely sealed with red wax, and too small for Temeraire to read from. 'You will have to read it to me out loud,' Temeraire said.

'I am not sure I ought to,' Hollin said, apologetically. 'It says it is for Captain Laurence, you see here.'

'I am sure Laurence would want us to know if it is anything important,' Temeraire said. 'Anyway, if contains our orders, then I suppose that whomever addressed it must not quite understand that I am colonel of the regiment, and they have simply made a mistake.'

Hollin hesitated and, looked around the clearing at the other men. None of them ranked higher than lieutenant.

'Stop looking at them,' Perscitia said irritably. 'It stands to reason that it is orders for us. And since we cannot carry them out without knowing what they are, you had better tell us, or go back and see what this Wellesley fellow wants you to do. But if you ask me, he will only be annoyed that you have wasted so much time going back and forth.'

Hollin shrugged helplessly, and her argument carried the day. He broke the seal and read aloud, 'You are requested and required to proceed, without the loss of a moment, to Tuxford, and resume your duties guarding the withdrawal, instead of—' He paused in his reading, and then clearing his throat finished, '—instead of whatever damned fool start you have got into your heads now. Be assured that if you have forgotten the end of our last conversation, I have not, and if you want pay for your damned beasts, you will keep them at their work.'

'I do not see why everyone assumes that we are just dashing off madly, without thinking where we are going,' Temeraire said, exasperated. 'Of course we would be doing that if Iskierka had not got herself captured, but she has, so Laurence has had to go and rescue her. We cannot go right away, because they are not back yet.'

'Some of us might go back and join them?' Perscitia suggested, rather hopefully.

'No, we are staying together from now on,' Temeraire said, 'and Arkady and Iskierka and all of the other ferals will always fly out in front where we can see them, as they cannot be trusted to behave properly,' and he translated this for Arkady's benefit.

'Bah,' Arkady said, with a dismissive sniff, 'you would have done the same, if you were not trying to play at being a human, flapping along as slow as if we had to creep on the ground like them. They have nothing to complain of, we did not leave them in any danger. We would have seen if this Napoleon's army were chasing you, and there has not been any sign of them.'

'I would have done no such thing,' Temeraire returned smartly, 'because I would have had better sense than to go wandering off for no good reason, with no particular notion of what to do, just to please myself—'

'We had very good reason,' Arkady said, 'we went to bring back the food that the French were stealing—'

'You did no such thing!' Temeraire said outraged. 'Wringe told us, you went to get prizes for yourselves and that you did not mean to share with anyone at all.'

Arkady had just enough grace to look uncomfortable for a moment, but no more than that. 'Well, it was Iskierka's idea,' he said, with a flip of his tail, and Temeraire snorted in disdain.

'But anyway,' Temeraire said, turning back to Hollin, 'that much is true. We have not seen Napoleon's army on any of the roads today, and we would have, if they were in pursuit. So they needn't worry—' He trailed off; Wellesley might not need to worry, but Temeraire realized that he himself had every cause. Napoleon's army must be somewhere, and if it were not on the road to London, it was most likely in London, with Laurence and Granby.

Of course he could do nothing but fret. Even if they had set off right away, there had been little chance of reaching London before it was quite dark, and he did not need Perscitia's anxious whispered hints to realize that it was madness to fly into a French camp at night when they had Fleur-de-Nuits about. 'But in the morning—' he said, and then put down his head without finishing. There would still be guns in the morning, and thousands of men, and who knew how many dragons. It would still be quite useless.

'Perhaps he will be back before morning,' Perscitia said in a tone so gloomy it left Temeraire in no doubt of her scepticism.

'Well,' he said to Hollin, 'you had better go back and tell Wellesley that we will come as soon as I have Laurence back, and that he should not worry about the men, unless of course Napoleon has flown all his soldiers ahead to attack him,' he added hopefully: perhaps that was what had happened.

'We should have seen them going by, if that is what they were doing,' Perscitia pointed out depressingly.

After Hollin left, the hours dragged. Temeraire slept fitfully and uneasily, rousing at every rustle or whisper to peer into the darkness, and before dawn he was awake for good and uncomfortable. He had an unpleasant sharp ache in the underside of his jaw and all along his neck to his breast-bone, where the knotted scar bothered him. He tried to crane his head down to rub his nose against it, but could not quite manage it. His neck felt very strange when he tried, and crackled as he stretched. He could not make his foreleg bend to it either, and at last he sighed and lay himself back down upon the cold ground, thinking wistfully of the warm stone at Loch Laggan, and of the pavilions in China.

There was a faint orange glow of approaching sunrise to the west; but then he raised his head again realizing that it was quite impossible. 'Oh, oh!' he cried, 'wake up, everyone!' and flung himself aloft as Iskierka blazed towards them, turning now and again to fire flames into the face of her pursuit. Seven or eight dragons were trying to get near enough to board her again, and there were a handful of struggling men on her back already. 'Laurence!' Temeraire cried, straining his eyes to make him out among the dim figures.

She shot by overhead but her pursuers backwinged as Temeraire rose into their path, scrambling to avoid running into him. Temeraire opened his jaws and roared furious thunder on them; a Pêcheur-Rayé in point-blank range took the brunt of the attack. The French dragon wavered for a moment in mid-air, his eyes now blood-shot and strange, as a great gush of blood poured from of his nostrils. He sank from the sky, and his wings broke beneath him like kites as he smashed into the ground.

Majestatis appeared beside him and then Ballista. The other French dragons, all middleweights, turned tail and fled. Temeraire hovered for a moment longer, panting with frustrated energy and confusion. Requiescat was rising too, complaining, 'What is all the noise for? It is too dark to fight.'

'We do not have to fight,' Temeraire said. 'They have all run away.'

'Oh, the cowards!' Iskierka cried, circling back. 'They did not mind fighting so much when *they* outnumbered *me*.' She turned her head to glare hotly at the French boarders upon her back. 'Granby, you are well? Are you sure I should not just kill these men?'

'No, they have surrendered, and now they are our prisoners,' Granby said. 'There is head-money for prisoners,' he added, wearily.

'I would rather kill them than have the money,' Iskierka said. 'They hurt you.'

'*You* have hurt him,' Temeraire said, angrily, 'and after I gave him to you, too,' and he reached out to take Laurence off her back. 'Are you quite well?' he said anxiously.

'Yes,' Laurence said briefly, in the way that meant he was not well at all, but did not like to say so publicly. Temeraire sniffed at him surreptitiously; he did not think Laurence was bleeding, but it was so dark he could not be sure he was not missing some injury. 'We must away at once,' Laurence added, 'they will bring on more pursuit, and we have neglected our duty for too long. We will be missed.'

'We *have* been missed, and Wellesley sent a very rude note, too,' Temeraire said to him, turning his head back to talk when they were underway, 'which was not very sensible, but we have worked out that the army has gone back to London. How did you get Granby away?'

'We had help,' Laurence said. He was looking at something very small in his hand, which glittered a little in the early dawn light.

'Is that a prize?' Temeraire asked in interest, cocking his head to look at it.

'No,' Laurence said.

The flight to rejoin the army was long, but at least uneventful. Iskierka gave them no further trouble. If she was not chastened, she was at least solicitous of Granby, and willing to do nearly anything just to please him. Temeraire had rearranged the order of flight, in any case, so she was directly under their eyes.

The ring was like a coal in the small breast pocket inside Laurence's coat, heavy beyond its weight. Woolvey's blood had dried cold and stiff on his stolen shirt. Laurence tried not to think of Edith, and how she would learn the news, or what her fate would be, widowed and alone with a small child in the occupied city.

'He was a brave fellow, sir,' Janus ventured. The old sailor had climbed over to Temeraire for the trip. 'Bad luck we had, there.'

Laurence only nodded. He could not go back, his duty lay ahead.

They caught up with Wellesley's corps that afternoon, and kept pace with them for the rest of the long way to Long Eaton, as a bitter wind blew southwards: just a taste of the weather they would have in Scotland. They shuffled more quickly as they came at last to the cold comfort waiting for them. The ground was frozen solid as stone, and covered with drifting flurries of snow, but the wagons rolled easier, as the muddy road had frozen into uneven ridges.

'I don't see why we must stay up here,' Requiescat said, gliding into another slow circle. 'There is a nice clearing below us. We could see just as well from there if anyone attacked, which they won't, as we would have seen them sometime during the last hundred miles.'

'We may not land until the infantry are settled,' Temeraire said, but then turned his head back and murmured, 'Laurence, why can we not?'

'They have less comfort marching than do we aloft,' Laurence said tiredly, 'and will sleep in worse. The least we can do is protect them until they have established their guard-posts, and lit their fires. If you went to your leisure while they struggled, it would only arouse envy and discontent.'

Temeraire said, 'Well, I can hover, but it is not very easy for the others to stay up. We had better go down there and help them. We could pull up trees for them, for firewood—'

Laurence opened his mouth to say that it would undoubtedly throw the soldiers into a panic, but looking down at their slow and weary ranks, he did not think they had the energy to run. 'The smaller dragons, perhaps, might begin.'

Temeraire turned and spoke to the ferals. Gherni led a handful of the smallest down to pull old dead trees from the forest. They shook needles, soil and squirrels out of the logs as they lifted them up, and carried them by twos and threes to the camp. The men were breaking up the ground for ditches and did not at first notice the activity at their backs, and then only flinched as the first logs were put down. They stared up at the dragons clutching their shovels and pickaxes in their hands. Lester, who had just landed, stared back at them curiously, and then poked his head over to look at the ground and ask them something in his own tongue.

'He wants to know why they are digging,' Temeraire said, and, 'No, no—' he called, and then went down himself to stop Lester from picking one of them up, with the plan of shaking him for answers, as if this would enable the man to speak the dragon tongue.

'It is for a midden, stop being so foolish,' he informed Lester, and then turned his head back to Laurence, 'I suppose we may help them with this also? I can do what Lien did at Danzig.'

Lien had used the divine wind at Danzig to help the French dig their siege-trenches, breaking up the frozen ground to make it easier for them to move. But it took several attempts, and the ruin of some fifty trees brought down by excess, for Temeraire to manage the same effect. 'It is not,' he panted, having taken a moment to breathe, 'quite as easy as it looks. I see how it ought to be easier to roar just a little, than all-out; but it is not. I do not understand why. Not,' he added hastily, 'that I cannot do it perfectly well. If Lien can do it, so can I.'

'Since you are having trouble, I will help, too,' Iskierka announced, landing beside them, and before anyone could stop her, she had put her head down and blasted flame out onto the icy ground.

A great cloud of steam arose from the centre of her strike, but for the most part the flames licked and billowed over the hard surface. Thankfully the ditch-diggers had established themselves at a safe distance, and were watching rather nervously with their officers, unsinged. But the fire had caught in the heap of trees that Temeraire had knocked down.

'Now see what you have done,' Temeraire said. 'Quickly,' he called up, 'fetch earth to put out the fires.'

'Wait,' Perscitia said, landing. 'If we lay the logs where you mean to dig the ditches, they will melt the ground, and the men can get warm too, while they wait.'

'See, it has all worked out for the best,' Iskierka said to Temeraire, brazenly adding, 'I meant it so.'

He flattened his ruff and said, 'Then you may help put the logs in place, since you have so very cleverly set them on fire *before* they were lined up properly.'

Laurence dismounted as they worked, and went to speak to the sergeant and his men to explain the scheme. 'They won't come this way?' was all the man wanted to know, wiping a nervous dirty hand over his blond moustaches, and leaving them streaked and muddy.

'If they do, they will do you no harm.' Laurence said, with no more patience, 'They are saving you an afternoon of hard labour after marching. When the fire in the logs has died down, you will find the ground much easier to dig, and you may chop up the remaining wood for tinder and sleep warmer tonight than any of you hoped.'

Wellesley rode up on his dark horse, wrestling to keep it under control, the animal skittish and shy of flames and dragons both. 'What the devil are you doing?' He did not wait for an answer, but threw an eye over the works and snorted. 'Clever as foxes, I see. Well, don't stand there, man,' he said to the sergeant. 'Go and clear the rest of that brush. Goren, we'll have the wounded over here, nearest the fires. At least they can't get up and run away from the dragons like ninnies, half of 'em haven't legs anymore. And as for you and that beast of yours,' he added to Laurence, grimly, 'finish here and be at the clearings within the hour. I have words for you I don't care to have interrupted.'

The horse and the general wheeled away and Laurence went back to Temeraire, who was pushing the last few logs into place with a broken-off branch, to save his talons from singeing. Demane had vanished, as he was wont to do given five minutes upon the ground. 'Roland, go and fetch him out,' Laurence said, and waited tapping his thigh until she came out of the woods some ten minutes later, half-dragging Demane. He held a string of rabbits and squirrels gathered from the wreckage the dragons had made, and looked surly to have been interrupted.

'Go set up a tent in camp, if you can,' Laurence said, 'and then see what you can do in the way of forage for the dragons. Janus, I am sure you can be of use to Mr. Fellowes, or Mr. Dorset.'

'Aye, sir,' Janus said.

'*You* may keep working here until it is done,' Temeraire said to Iskierka, rather smugly, 'since it was all your notion,' and carried Laurence over to the clearings, where Ballista was already improving their comfort by smashing up shrubs and thornbrake with her barbed tail. Perscitia had managed to establish a remarkably lively bonfire, by setting several of the fallen trees into a tent-pole shape, and using the crushed and pounded wreckage for tinder. She was now, however, eyeing the towering blaze a little nervously. It had grown a good deal higher than her head.

'A handsome signal,' Wellesley said sarcastically, when he came. 'It is kind of you to spare Bonaparte the trouble of having to find us in the dark.'

'You have a dozen fires lit just over the hill in the other part of camp, so I do not think it makes much difference that this one is a little bigger,' Perscitia said, defensively. 'And,' she added with sudden inspiration, 'this is so bright the Fleur-de-Nuits cannot come near us. And it will hurt their eyes too much to see anything else around.'

Wellesley only snorted at this justification, and turned to Laurence. 'And I suppose you have another clever explanation you would like to feed me—'

'Sir,' Granby said, breaking in, 'the fault was mine, for letting Iskierka run away with me—'

'I imagine there is no shortage of blame to parcel out among you,' Wellesley said cuttingly.

'It is not Granby's fault at all!' Iskierka said, overhearing. 'He did not like to go, and I am sorry now to have disobeyed him, but I do not see why we must flap along after you like chickens, with no one to fight all day. If we are supposed to protect you, we would do much better if we were to find someone who meant to attack you, and simply kill them before they did. What I did was perfectly sensible, really, and it was just bad luck we got captured. And since it has all come right in the end, you haven't any cause to yell.'

'Yes, I begin to see that your captain might be wholly innocent,' Wellesley said, eyeing her. 'Granby, is it?'

'Yes, sir,' Granby said, miserably.

'The next time this creature disobeys you, you will cut her loose,' Wellesley said. 'You and your crew will be re-assigned. As for her, I do not care if she goes in the breeding grounds or flies across the sea; if she won't follow orders, she is useless, and worse than useless when she induces others to risk good beasts after bad.'

'Oh!' Iskierka said, jetting a hissing cloud of steam. 'Oh, I am *not* useless! I have taken more prizes than anybody. I can beat anyone who tries to fight me—'

'Brawling does not impress me,' Wellesley said. 'We are here to win a war, not a single battle or a private mill; and any one dragon, like any one man, is expendable. The nation has managed without a Celestial or a fire-breather this long, and we will manage again without you if we must. If you are spoiling for a fight, you will have one when we are ready to give it to the French, until then, you are going to behave, or you can give up your captain and get you gone. We will find other work for him.'

'Granby, you would never,' she appealed, and poor Granby stood white and wretched and looked at Wellesley. Then he said, low, 'Dear one, I am an officer of the King.'

Laurence looked away. He did not know if he could have passed a similar test. Temeraire was not wilful, in the same fashion, his disobedience had been more deliberate and graver than Iskierka's, but that was an excuse. If Wellesley, or any superior, ordered him to leave Temeraire, a simple plain order to go to another duty, and not as simple punishment . . .

Iskierka made a dreadful keening noise in her throat, and hissed out a whistling of steam so thick it clouded the ground around her feet. Then she leapt across the clearing and huddled herself into a heap of coils. Arkady sprang to her side and began speaking to her hurriedly in the dragon-tongue.

'I would not care if she did go away with them,' Temeraire said, listening, 'and if you ask me, it serves her just right. I should be very happy to have you back, Granby,' he added.

'I beg your pardon,' Granby said, looking wretched, and ran across the clearing after her.

'You have damned little right to criticize,' Wellesley said to Temeraire.

'I am not always running off to please myself!' Temeraire said. 'I have never disobeyed, except when someone tried to take Laurence from me, or hurt him first; and when the Government tried to murder all the dragons in the world.'

'So you have only been insubordinate or treasonous a dozen times, is that all?' Wellesley said dryly. 'No, save your breath and the rest of your excuses. Carry on this way again, under my command, and I will treat the promises I have

232

made you as cavalierly as you do *your* duty. Do you understand me? Both of you,' he added, 'as I see I cannot lay the guilt on your handler's shoulders alone; but I will be damned if I will try to apportion the guilt.'

'Yes, sir,' Laurence said quietly.

'But we have not done anything wrong today. That was all because Iskierka ran off,' Temeraire protested. 'It is not my fault, or Laurence's.'

'It damned well is, if you are her commanding officer,' Wellesley said. 'Do not let me hear you blame one of your subordinates again.'

'Oh,' said Temeraire, quelled, and looked a little ashamed.

'Now,' said Wellesley, 'if you have finished with this back-talking: since you have spent half the day flying hither and yon, I mean to at least profit by it. Where is Davout bivouacked, and how many soldiers does he have on the road in reach of us?'

'But I told Hollin to tell you,' Temeraire said. 'They have all gone back to London.'

'There were thirty thousand men behind us yesterday morning,' Wellesley said. 'I don't care if Bonaparte is chasing them with whips from morning to night and using dragons for supply, they cannot have reached the city in a day. You must have seen some sign, pickets or fires—'

'Sir,' Laurence said, 'there was no sign. No sign reported by the beasts which flew off earlier, or from when we pursued them. We saw Davout's regiments making camp around London, and Murat was in the city also.'

'And I have already told you all,' Temeraire said, 'they can go fifty miles in a day, we have seen them do it, so—'

'It is one thing to move a brigade or two by dragonback,' Wellesley said impatiently, 'and quite another to move an army. You cannot put more than two hundred men even on the largest beasts.'

'That is not how they do it,' Perscitia put in, unexpectedly. The other dragons had been listening in on the interview with interest. 'They do not just take a hundred men and fly with them straight, all day. They take a hundred men and carry them as far as they can in an hour, and put them down, and those men start marching from there. And then the dragons go back and get the next hundred men, who you see have been marching all this time, so they are not as far off, and the dragons take *them* forward for—'

'Wait, they fly back?' Requiescat asked, and with much irritation Perscitia had to interrupt her explanation to claw a picture into the soil, to illustrate how the companies would each in turn leapfrog over those in front of them, each receiving two hours of the dragons' time.

'And so on, until they have carried everyone a little way, and given them all a rest.' Perscitia said, 'So the men can walk thirty miles instead of twenty, and the dragons fly everyone twenty miles on top of that, so the whole company can move fifty miles, together.'

She finished triumphantly, and Requiescat said, 'Well, it seems like a lot of bother to me, just for an extra twenty miles. Even I can make that in an hour or two,' and Perscitia huffed in indignation.

Wellesley had a better appreciation of her explanation, however, and studied the diagram with fierce intent. 'So this is what Roland has been going on about, then?' He looked at Laurence and said sharply, 'And can your beasts manage the same?'

'If the men would go aboard,' Laurence answered him.

'They will go aboard if I have to shoot them,' Wellesley said.

For all his harsh words, however, the next morning he took the Coldstream Guards apart, and addressed them personally. The seven Yellow Reapers and three Grey Coppers were lined up some distance behind him, facing away so their jaws and teeth could not be seen. They had been rigged out with rope and sackcloth, and his aides were climbing over the new harnesses to no purpose but pure drama, as the rigging had already been thoroughly tried by the dragons themselves tugging on it.

'Men,' Wellesley said, 'it is a damned sorry state of affairs we are in. That Corsican upstart sleeps in the King's bed, while his bully-boys steal cattle and wreck the harvest. It is more than any red-blooded Englishman can bear, and we are not going to bear it for much longer.'

'That's right,' a couple of men called back; a 'hear, hear' among mutterings of agreement.

'Every one of you knows they cannot out-fight us, and now we have learned they cannot out-walk you, either. It is just one of Boney's tricks. Those damned lazy Frenchmen are being carted around on dragonback. That is how they have been getting the jump on us,' Wellesley said, jerking his head back towards the dragons. 'I say it is time we put a stop to it, and your colonel here has solicited for you the honour of going first.

'It is no treat to go aloft, so I rely on you all to set an example for the rest of the Corps. When your sergeants give the word, you are to go aboard the dragons, one to a company, one column to a side, filling the rigging from front to back. The first company aboard in good order will have the honour of carrying the flag when we give Boney his well-deserved drubbing, and find an extra ration of rum in camp tonight.

'And I hope there is no man here more faint of heart than a Frenchman,' he added, 'but if anyone here is too craven to go aloft for an hour, he may say so now, and be excused.' He nodded to the colonel of the regiment, turned and walked over to the dragons, to make a show of speaking with Rowley.

No-one spoke, and the men filed in perfect order aboard the beasts. The rest of the army had been roused to watch the dragons lifting off. After a little prodding from the sergeants, the men aboard jeered cheerfully at the regiments marching below they sailed away.

The first few days were confusion. It was difficult to match the supply to the men at the end of each day, and more than one set of rations went astray. At first they did not manage to go more than ten miles beyond their usual distance, and the brigades on the road became a wretched muddle, with some regiments on each other's heels, and others separated by miles. The dragons were also not very pleased, either. 'One of them poked at me with a bayonet,' Chalcedony complained, indignantly, 'and when I turned around and told him to stop, he shrieked at me. He is lucky I did not toss him off.'

But a semblance of order was gradually imposed on proceedings, and in the end, the march, which ought to have taken a long slow month, was completed in two weeks. The advantage of air transport was proved all the more as they came through the mountains. The dragons carried the men over the worst stretches, where snow and ice had made the road impassable. Winter was now upon them in earnest, and they flew deeper into it as they went north, until the Cairngorm range became visible one clear morning, and with them Loch Laggan, and its citadel, which looked down upon the frozen black waters.

'Oh, at last,' Temeraire said, with relief, peering down at the courtyard with its heated stones dark and bare of snow.

But Laurence was looking at something else. There was a dragon already in the courtyard. A Papillon Noir gorgeously ornamented with iridescent stripes of blue and green, curled comfortably upon the stones with a flag of parley and a tricolour upon its shoulders.

Chapter Twelve

It was a great relief to at last off load his last shipment of men and supply. Temeraire understood the necessity of moving as quickly as Napoleon, and if he had been disposed to doubt it at first, Perscitia's calculations had showed plainly how quickly the difference of thirty miles a day, added up to make significant difference. But it was so very tedious going back and forth on these short hopping flights. An hour in the air, then letting men off, and then flying directly back to have another load put on. It was impossible to fly quickly or freely with men clinging to the makeshift rigging, and then there was all the unpleasantness of their dirt. His own crew were well able to handle such matters without spattering him, even little Roland, and since the passengers were only an hour or two aboard at most, Temeraire felt it was not too much to ask that they show some restraint. But some of them simply could not manage it, and if he dived a little to catch a better air-current, or twisted to keep on an updraft, he was sure to be soiled. It would take a week of bathing before he felt at all clean again.

But the lake was frozen solid, so for the moment he had to be content with rolling in the thick snow on one of the neighbouring hills until he was wet and cold all over. The encampment had been going up all day as they delivered men by air. By now the officers were coming up the hill in clusters to eat in the citadel, leaving their horses stabled away at the foot. Loch Laggan had an ample herd, and having eaten, the unharnessed dragons began to negotiate the complex aerial manoeuvres to settle in their respective landing-places on the hill, courtyard, or further out in the clearings.

'Do you suppose,' Temeraire said to Laurence, as he set himself gladly onto the baking-hot stones, 'do you suppose that Celeritas will have forgiven me, for lying?' He raised his head over the squirming mass of dragons, mostly middleweights trying to fit themselves around him, Requiescat, Ballista, and Armatius, who had smugly claimed a place, with the other heavyweights thanks to Gentius drowsing upon his back. The lightweights and couriers were perched on the walls and battlements, waiting for the middleweights to give up before they began their own squabble over who would have a place.

Majestatis had ignored the struggle, and taken a place on the other side of the courtyard wall, to the south. Temeraire could hear Perscitia arguing with him indignantly. 'You ought to go take a place in the courtyard,' she said.

'I am very comfortable here,' Majestatis returned placidly.

'You would be *more* comfortable in the courtyard,' Perscitia said, 'and you can have a place there if you only push a little. You do not need this one.'

'But I like this one, and I did not have to push to have it,' he said. 'The ground is warm.'

She gave a sulky hiss. 'I dare say you do not even know why.'

'The hot water for the baths runs under this part of the hillside, too,' Majestatis said.

238

There was a brief silence. 'Yes,' Perscitia said, 'it must, because this is the lower side of the slope, and it must drain away somewhere, but how did you know that?'

'There is steam coming out of that crack in the ground there.'

'Oh,' she muttered.

'I am going to sleep now,' Majestatis informed her. 'I don't mind if you want to share.'

'I do not *want* to share,' Perscitia said, but a low deep rumbling breath was the only reply, and after another fit of grumbling she reconciled herself. Both of their snores were audible before the rest of the quarrelling had resolved itself into a settled order for the courtyard.

But there was no sign of Celeritas. The old training-master did not sleep in the courtyard, but in a private mountainside cave. But he might come out to see them all, Temeraire thought, with some anxiety. He had not been happy about lying to Celeritas when they had come to steal the mushrooms, and he had never had the chance to apologize properly. He was quite sure Celeritas would have understood and approved of the mission. At least he was as sure as he could be, because anyone could take an odd start. But Celeritas might still be angry over being tricked into letting them in, unchallenged.

'He is not here anymore,' a Winchester said; he was not anyone Temeraire knew. A small bright-eyed courier-beast, in harness, he perched upon the wall behind them, out of the way of the confusion. 'I think he has gone to the breeding grounds in Ireland.'

'But whyever would Celeritas go to the breeding grounds?' Temeraire protested. The little Winchester only fluttered out his wings in a shrug. 'It is very boring in the breeding grounds,' Temeraire said to Laurence. 'I do not understand why he should have left his post here.'

Laurence did not say anything for a moment, and then he said, oddly without conviction, 'Perhaps he grew tired of the work.'

He said nothing else, nothing more reassuring, and Temeraire looked at him sidelong. Laurence was sitting upon one of the low benches by the wall, looking again at the gold ring which he had brought back from London. He had not said where it had come from, and Temeraire felt a little shy of pressing him. Laurence seemed so very unhappy and Temeraire did not understand why. They were together, not pent up anywhere, and soon they would have a splendid battle to take back their territory; and then the Government would pay them money. So there was nothing to be sorry about, except perhaps that they had retreated in the first place, but the rest would make up for that.

Temeraire sighed, and warned the squabbling Reapers, 'You had better leave some room. Maximus will be here soon, with the rest of the Corps. Should Lily not be here already?'

Laurence raised his head. 'They all should,' he said. 'They were ahead of us.'

He went into the citadel to try and gain information from the other officers. Meanwhile, Chalcedony, Gladius and Cantarella finally won out over the other Reapers and settled themselves down, so the Grey Coppers, Winchesters and ferals could now squeeze themselves in among the rest. Moncey and Minnow had settled themselves on Temeraire's back, and he felt quite ready for a proper drowse.

Then the Papillon Noir raised his head and said, 'How pleasant it is here! It is almost as nice as the pavilions the Emperor has built for us in Paris.' He spoke in English, with a curious accent, and many of the other dragons raised their heads in interest. 'Those are much larger, of course,' the Papillon continued, 'so no one has to sleep outside if they do not want to; and there is a charming little stream which runs past them, so if one wants a drink, one only has to stretch out one's neck. But these are just as warm if it is not raining, or snowing.' A little drifting snow began to fall in that moment, slicking the stone.

'I expect,' Temeraire said, rather coolly, 'that he is imitating the pavilions from China, which are very splendid.'

'Yes, exactly,' the Papillon said enthusiastically, 'although Madame Lien says, he has made them even nicer. And we each have a box at the pavilions, where we can put our treasure, and the palace guard keeps watch over it when we are not there.'

'Hum, and I suppose they don't take it,' Gentius said, sceptically, cracking one luridly orange eye.

'No, never,' the Papillon said. 'I have three gold chains and a ruby there, and they are always just as I have left them. The guards will even polish them for me, if I ask them.'

Everyone was wide-awake by *three gold chains and a ruby*. 'I have earned them,' the Papillon said, seeing that he had his audience, 'by helping to build roads, and for some fighting, and I have been promoted to captain, see,' and showed off a handsome badge pinned to his harness: a round disk of some shining metal. 'So anyone, who wishes to serve the Emperor can,' he added, significantly.

Temeraire laid back his ruff. 'Certainly, if they do not mind helping someone who goes about stealing other people's territory, when he already has plenty of his own, and kills heaps of men and dragons to do it,' he said coldly. 'Anyway, we are also receiving pay, and *I* have been made colonel.'

'I congratulate you!' the Papillon said. 'How much have you been paid so far?' And when Temeraire had made an awkward, sputtering explanation, the Papillon went on, 'Well,

241

I am sure the emperor would pay you right away, and give you even higher rank.'

There was a low thoughtful murmur going around. Temeraire put his head sidelong to nudge Roland, who was begrudgingly attending lessons with Demane and Sipho. It was from less of her own volition than at Sipho's insistence, he was beginning to outstrip her as well as his older brother. Roland had never been very interested in studying. 'You had better go and tell Laurence, that the French dragon is making all sorts of promises, which I am sure are lies, if we would agree to serve Napoleon. And pray make him come and put a stop to it,' he finished plaintively. He did not know how to answer the French dragon, who after all was offering just what he had asked for; except that he did not want it from Napoleon, who had invaded England and made so much trouble for everyone, and who let Lien do as she liked.

'Oh, I will go at once,' Roland said, with relief, and left. Demane said, 'I will go too,' and went after her.

'But who is going to check my work?' Sipho called after them unhappily.

Laurence had not gone further than the great hall of the citadel. Officers stood in scattered groups, talking in low voices that blended with echoes within the great vaulted ceiling into hollow unintelligible murmur. He hesitated in the entryway for a moment. There were few faces he knew, and fewer still he chose to impose himself upon. Then he saw Riley in a corner of the room.

Riley wore a look half-dazed with exhaustion, and he said wholly tactlessly, 'Hello, Laurence, I thought you were in prison,' in a tone more puzzled than condemnatory, 'I have a son,' he added.

'Give you joy,' Laurence said, and shook his hand, ignoring

the rest of the remark. Riley gave no sign he noticed the omission. 'Is Catherine well?'

'I haven't the faintest notion,' Riley said. 'The lot of them took off like a shot for the coast three days ago, and she insisted she could not be spared, if you will credit it. Thank God we had already found a wet-nurse from the village, or I dare say she would have gone anyway, and let the child starve. Do you know, they must be fed every two hours?'

He did not know why the dragons had gone or where; what little attention he had to spare from the new child was devoted to the *Allegiance*. He had left her in dry-dock in Plymouth, recovering from their voyage to Africa, and with Bonaparte and his army now between him and the port, he fretted about her fate. 'I am sure the Navy will keep him out of Plymouth,' he said, 'I am sure of it. But if he should somehow get a hold on the whole south, then—'

'Sir,' Emily said, and Laurence looked down, she was panting at his elbow, Demane beside her. 'Sir, Temeraire sent me—Very well, us—to tell you, that French dragon in the courtyard is preaching sedition, and trying to bribe everyone to go over to the Emperor, with pavilions and jewels and such. He can speak English.'

'Where is the envoy?' Laurence asked Riley. 'Do you know who they have sent?'

'Talleyrand,' Riley said.

The conference was being held upstairs, in the little-used library. Wellesley had gone to join the discussion, directly on their arrival, and he was, Laurence thought, their best hope. But guards and aides barred the room, among them ten Frenchmen in long coats made of leather with heavy gloves in their belts. Laurence did not know how they might get word inside, until he caught sight of Rowley and called to him.

Rowley's personal disdain had not subsided, but he had

just seen a month shortened to two weeks, and though unsmiling he heard Laurence out, and said shortly, 'Very well, come with me,' and took him into the room by the side door.

Talleyrand had not come alone. He sat on one side of a long table, laid on for the occasion, with a Marshal sitting beside him. It was Murat, Bonaparte's brother-in-law. They made an odd pair. Talleyrand, brushing long aristocratic face through his thinning fair hair seemed washed out and pale next to Murat, who had thick curly hair and bright blue eyes in a face ruddy with weather and work. He also possessed a powerful frame, every inch the soldier. Murat's clothing was absurdly splendid. He wore a coat of black leather with gold embroidery and gold buttons, over a snowy white stock and shirt, with gloves of black leather and gold on the table beside him. Talleyrand was more quietly elegant.

Opposite them sat half a dozen ministers, in nothing like the same state, all of them marked with the long and hasty retreat from London, and the discomfort they must have felt at being sequestered in a military camp. Perceval, the Prime Minister, looked particularly drawn and unhappy. His ministry was shaky and doubtful to begin with, a collection of lesser evils and men he had cajoled into their posts. His predecessor Lord Portland's government had collapsed under the weight of the disaster in Africa, and the old man had refused to try and build another. Canning, the last Foreign Secretary, had tried for the post himself, and upon failing, had both refused to join the new ministry himself, and blocked the Secretary of War, Lord Castlereagh, from joining it: all circumstances that forced Perceval to make do with Lord Bathurst and Lord Liverpool. They were good men, but these were times in which the most gifted were needed, and though Lord Bathurst had been sympathetic to the abolition cause, Laurence could not help but acknowledge that he was not the ideal to man face across from Talleyrand the negotiating table.

Lord Mulgrave, the First Lord of the Admiralty, had preserved his post. Dalrymple, the old fat soldier, sat with him: neither looked to be a match for the Marshal. The weight of power and composure sat on one side of the table: the refinement and sophistication of the *Ancien Regime* married to the brutal strength of the Empire. Only Wellesley, sitting at the other end beside Lord Liverpool, did not look defeated. He instead waited in a glittering temper: his jaw set coldly.

Rowley bent to whisper in his ear, and Wellesley looked at Laurence and then leaned forward and interrupted the conversation going on in French, 'What the devil is this? You come here under a flag of truce, and meanwhile your dragon is in the courtyard trying to bribe our beasts with trinkets?'

Murat exclaimed at the accusation, and said, 'I am sure there has been some misunderstanding. Liberté has much enthusiasm, but he would never mean to offend—'

'I am sure General Wellesley does not mean any insult.' Lord Eldon jumped in with apologies. 'Surely Your Highness' Bonaparte was fond of making his family princes, 'must be familiar with the frank address of soldiers—'

Talleyrand watched the discussion with half-lidded eyes, which flicked to Laurence for a moment. He leaned back for a whispered consultation one of his aides. Then, when the first exchange had died down, he intervened, 'Perhaps Marshal Murat and I will go and have words with Liberté, to ensure there is no more confusion. We have been speaking long, and a little rest would do well for all of us.' He pushed himself to his feet, bringing the rest out of their chairs, and leant towards Perceval, 'I hope we will have an opportunity to speak again this evening?'

Bowing first to Murat, he let the Marshal leave the room. Limping out after him, he paused at the door to turn to Laurence and say, in a clear voice, 'Allow me to express again the thanks of His Imperial Majesty's government, Monsieur Laurence. And to once again assure you that Emperor has not forgotten her debt of gratitude.'

The graceful words cut him worse than knives. His pain was incidental, of that Laurence was bitterly sure. Talleyrand had aimed the remark at ministers, to discredit any report Laurence might have brought. 'Your government, Monsieur,' Laurence said, 'owes me nothing. I did not act for their sake.'

Talleyrand only smiled gently and half-bowed again before he left the room.

'By God, the impudence,' Wellesley said savagely, scarcely waiting until the door had shut, and in no low voice. 'That arrogant pig— Son of an innkeeper and a whore, and married to another; *that*, to be king of Britain—'

'They have made no such suggestion,' Lord Eldon began. He was Lord Chancellor, having risen to the peerage as a notable lawyer, and thence to the Tory government for his steadfast opposition to Catholic emancipation.

'Do you imagine that upstart parvenu's circle being content with mealy-mouthed governorship?' Wellesley said. 'Give him six months, and it will be King Murat, as soon as he has taken the Army and the Navy to pieces.'

'No, the terms are unacceptable,' Perceval said, without great conviction. 'But these are only a beginning position—'

'They are an insult from first to last,' Wellesley said, 'and ought to be rejected out of hand.'

'One of his proposals, at least,' another minister interjected, 'gentlemen, I beg we consider its merits, and may I urge that a swift decision be taken to Their Majesties in Halifax, with all haste and all necessary considerations for their security?'

'Defeatist nonsense,' Wellesley snapped. 'Bonaparte is not coming anywhere near Scotland before spring, no matter what we do.'

'Our scouts have reported his soldiers all over the north of England.'

'Foraging,' Wellesley said, 'in small parties. We have two dozen outposts and garrisoned castles between London and Edinburgh, and he cannot march his army past them.'

'Surely the risk ought not to be run. Bonaparte went from Berlin to Warsaw on the eve of winter—'

'Because half the garrison commanders threw up their arms and surrendered at nothing more than a fanfare at their gates. I have more faith in our officers than that.'

'The King is not a young man,' Perceval said, breaking into the increasing heat of Wellesley's exchange with the minister, 'nor in the best of health—'

'No one proposes that he should expose himself upon the battlefield,' Wellesley said, 'but he can still address the troops.'

Perceval paused, and heavily, quietly said, 'The King is not well.'

No one spoke for a moment, then someone said to Wellesley. 'If the Prince of Wales stays, or Prince William, and the King goes?'

Wellesley shrugged it away, a tight angry motion. 'If you are determined to send him away, send him. But if you mean to give away his throne, too, why not make a parcel of it, with whatever else these snakes are asking for? Perhaps we should let them preach sedition to the troops directly?'

'Come, General Wellesley, this is surely overreaction—'

'If you believe for an instant they did not know perfectly well what the beast was about—'

'I hope we are not going to be distracted by some notion that Talleyrand, if not Bonaparte himself, concocted a plan of subterfuge to be carried out by a dragon,' Eldon said. 'I have heard the idle chatter about the beasts, but let us not read conscious and deliberate intent from it.'

'Sir,' Laurence said, and bore the looks which he received for having the temerity to interject, 'perhaps you are not aware that dragons learn their tongue in the shell, and do not ordinarily acquire another. It cannot be mere coincidence that they have brought a beast who can speak English, and easily communicate with our own.'

'So feed them twice over and drive any seditious thoughts from their heads, if indeed any managed to find their way in,' Eldon said. 'What else could Bonaparte possibly offer the creatures anyway.'

'Respect, if nothing else,' Laurence said. 'The neglect and disdain with which they have been treated has left them open to the meanest approach, the least offer of courtesy and reward—'

'That is enough from you, Laurence,' Lord Mulgrave said icily. 'You have done more good for Bonaparte than Talleyrand and Murat could achieve here, if we gave them every opportunity in the world.'

Laurence flinched, and hoped he did not show it. Mulgrave had approved the plan to send the sick dragon to France. He had chaired the inquiry where Laurence had learned of it by accident and Mulgrave had chosen the men for his court-martial, and overseen it personally, with resentful venom.

'A man may be a wild enthusiast without being a traitor,' Mulgrave said, 'but you are both. Even if you have been allowed to live a little longer, by counsel other than mine, you are the last man on whom anyone sensible would rely.'

Wellesley said sharply, '*This* is their intended distraction, gentleman; and I dare say Talleyrand would congratulate himself on its success. Sir,' he said to Perceval, 'throw him out, I beg of you, and Murat with him. Every minute that flag of parley sits before the eyes of the army, you cut a little

248

more of the heart out of my men. We ought to be speaking of the counterattack, not debating terms of surrender. That is what these are, however you like to dress them up.'

'General Wellesley, you and General Dalrymple will forgive my bluntness,' Lord Liverpool said, breaking in, 'but as unpleasant as these terms are, we may well find them preferable to the ones he offers us in March. I hope my remarks are not taken as judgement upon the Army, but it is a plain fact that Bonaparte has beaten every force that took the field against him, the Russians, the Austrians, the Prussians, the Turks, and us. We should perhaps agree to whatever he wants, while the Army and the Navy are preserved a little while, and the King safe; anything to get him out of London and back to Paris. Then we can manage Murat—'

'Are you—' Wellesley cut himself off, and began again in a flat tone, 'We can end this with a single victory while Bonaparte is in England; not only the invasion, but the entire war, this conflict of ten years and more. The last thing we want is to see him go; the only damned thing to be thankful for is that he has put himself within our reach. In a month we will have fifty thousand men here, and at Edinburgh another sixty. We have a hundred and fifty fighting beasts, on our own ground; in a month—'

'Half the Grande Armée is sitting on the coast of France waiting for their turn to come over for a share,' Eldon said. 'In a month, Bonaparte will have two hundred thousand men, or more.'

'No, he will not.' The door banged, and Jane Roland came in, stripping off her gauntlets. Blood streaked her face and hair, and stained her coat. 'What?' she said to their startled questions, and looked at herself in the glass on the wall. 'Oh, I look a fright. No, it isn't any of mine; I suppose it is that poor damned Frenchman's. I broke a sword on the fellow.'

She took the glass of brandy offered her anyway, and drank it straight. 'Thank you, sir,' she said, setting it down, 'that puts life in one's breast. I beg your pardon, gentlemen, for coming in my muck. I am fresh from the coast. He tried another landing at Folkestone, but he did not have as much luck as he would have liked. We have countered his harpooning trick. Our smiths have made us some sharp wire, and working in twos, the couriers can cut the ropes in a trice. Here are the dispatches,' she added, as Frette trotted in behind her and laid packets down on the table in front of Mr. Perceval, 'from Admiral Collingwood: of ships of the line, he has taken six, sunk four and burnt two; and not a thousand men landed out of sixty.'

The noise her intelligence produced was extraordinary both in volume and in the change of tone; out of proportion perhaps for a victory that only left them no worse off, than they had been before. But even a small taste was sweet to those who had been long deprived. Eldon was silenced, and Wellesley sprang up to shake her hand.

'So he cannot bring over any more—How many men does he have, now?' Perceval said, urgently.

'He can still bring them by air, at night,' Jane put in. 'We will patrol, and so will the Navy, but we won't catch every Fleur-de-Nuit that slips over the Channel. They can carry as many as two hundred.'

'He may send ten of them every night,' Wellesley said. 'He cannot meet our forces before we are ready to meet him. Sir—, gentlemen,' he said, turning to sweep his eye over all of the table, 'no war was won at the conference table, but many have been lost there. Do not let me see a room of cowards before me, but one of Britons. Give me your confidence and a hundred thousand men, for I do not fear Bonaparte.'

There was a pause; several men looked at Dalrymple. 'Perhaps, a joint command—' one man started.

'No,' Wellesley said, cutting him off short. 'If you have no faith in me, choose another man.'

The silence fell again; only a moment's hesitation, but Wellesley had timed his challenge well, the glow of victory and success, lingered still, and carried the day. Perceval stood and put his hands flat on the table. 'So be it. Lord Bathurst, you will inform our guests the parley is at an end. General Wellesley, you have command, and may God be with you.'

Not a minute later, Wellesley was halfway down the corridor outside, 'A wretched waste of time and spirit, but at least it is over with, and no irreparable harm done. Roland, I need a hundred dragons, for transport—'

'I can't hand you off a hundred beasts when I have five hundred miles of coastline to watch,' Jane said, matching his stride.

'I have another thirty thousand men to get here, and forty to Edinburgh,' Wellesley snapped.

'Tell me where the men are to be found and where you want them landed, and I will contrive,' she said, 'with what dragons are on patrol, in flying distance.'

'Well enough.' He gave her a curt nod. 'Rowley, get her the list of garrisons,' he said, over his shoulder. 'Tell me, what sort of supply do you imagine Bonaparte needs?'

'For the beasts? A hundred bullocks a day,' Jane said. 'More if he is heavy on fighting-weight beasts, and they are working for their supper. He is managing it, though; has foragers out, of course, and we have fewer dragons south of the mountains to eat up the supply.'

He nodded. 'Very good. I must get to Edinburgh, and get the rest of this army into order—'

'Wellesley,' Jane said, 'before you go, you will pardon me for saying: I can put the army wherever you need it, but I can't make Bonaparte come and meet you there. He is pretty well dug in at London, now, and come spring we are going to begin to have some trouble with supply ourselves. Scotland's herds can't support this number of dragons forever. We will be eating into the breeding stock.'

He shot her a hard look. 'You will oblige me,' he said, 'by not mentioning that particular difficulty in front of their Lordships. Damn, but I miss Castlereagh!'

She snorted. 'I don't need a lecture on managing politicos who don't know a damned thing about my business.'

'No, I imagine not,' Wellesley said, grudgingly. 'Well, bring me the army, and let me worry how to get him out of London.'

Returning to the courtyard, Laurence found Temeraire in glad convocation with Maximus and Lily, also freshly returned from the coast. The two had unceremoniously displaced several disgruntled Yellow Reapers and a much offended Ballista to claim places on the warm stones beside him.

'Yes, the egg is hatched,' Lily was saying, 'but it is not much use to anyone. It only lies there and squalls all day, and I do not like the way it smells. Not,' she added loyally, 'that any of that is Catherine's fault, I am sure that awful sailor is to blame. I ought never to have let him marry her, and now she cannot even make him divorce her.'

Harcourt was standing by them, with Berkley, but Laurence did not hesitate to approach. He was too weary and too soiled to dread another awkward meeting. Catherine did not say anything, however, but gave him a handshake, which she would have liked to make heartier than her strength could presently manage. She looked fragile as an eggshell and nearly as white, so her pale red hair stood luridly against her skin and the blue rings beneath her eyes. She still carried the little thickness she had gained in her pregnancy, but her arms were thin of muscle and of strength, too. She ought to have been resting.

She caught his eye, and said sharply, 'Pray, no lectures; Lily cannot be spared at a time like this. He tried to land another sixty thousand men, did you hear?'

'I did, and I congratulate you on the victory,' Laurence said. He did not have a right to speak, in any case, as Riley did. 'And on your son,' he added.

'Oh, yes,' she said, despondently. 'Thank you.'

The French embassy was leaving. A small sheltering tent in domed shape was put up on the Papillon Noir's back, and Talleyrand was handed into it, clambering cautiously and slowly into his place. Murat sprang up like an aviator born to the life, and latched himself on at the neck. The Papillon made a great show of shaking out his dappled iridescent wings and showing off a small but flashy medallion on his breast to the other dragons, as he was boarded. He called cheerfully, 'Goodbye! I hope you come and visit me, any time you like, in London or in Paris!' before he leapt aloft.

Arkady made a rude noise after him, and nosed his own dinner-plate medal, which Jane had awarded him a year ago as an incentive to patrol. 'Yes, and good riddance,' Temeraire said, staring after the vanishing French dragon with a cold eye. 'I am sure it is all a hum, and he hasn't any rubies or gold chains at all.'

Laurence was as glad to see them gone, but they left behind a long shadow, which would not be lifted save by a victory that seemed at the moment distant and unlikely. The terms Bonaparte had offered now would be generous by comparison, if he managed to maintain his occupation until the spring. One by one the outposts throughout England would be starved out, or pounded into surrender; then he would turn the besieging troops upon the port cities, and begin to cut off supply for the Navy. Meanwhile his dragons would be eating up British cattle, while their own beasts began to go hungry, and the melting snows would open up all the mountain passes for his infantry. He had only to enjoy the comforts of London, and wait.

'We are going out again on patrol tonight, along the North Sea,' Maximus said to Temeraire. 'Are you with us, this next run?'

'Patrolling,' Temeraire said, with a sigh, 'but yes, of course we shall go together; shall we not, Laurence? It is better than ferrying.'

'You may have other duties, to your regiment,' Laurence said.

It was no easy matter to organize the whole company of unharnessed dragons into patrols. Temeraire insisted the Yellow Reapers should be allowed to all go together, as they seemed to prefer it, even though by general rule they would have been balanced out in mixed groups. Arkady's ferals, on the other hand, he divided up among many bands, even though they could not speak a word to the other dragons. 'Yes, but they do not need to speak out loud to understand enough for patrols,' Temeraire said, 'and otherwise they will fly off adventuring, especially,' he added darkly, 'if Iskierka is let anywhere near them.'

'She is a good deal improved, though,' Granby said to Laurence and Tharkay, over dinner one night, while they were all encamped near Newcastle. Temeraire and Iskierka were squabbling at volume a little way back from the fire, and Arkady was throwing in his occasional piece. 'She makes just as much noise,' Granby added hurriedly, 'but she has turned perfectly obliging: has flown all the patrols as neat as a pattern-card, and no haring off after prizes at all, or a word of complaint. I would gladly be captured five times over for as much.'

Laurence looked down at the fire. He felt the price of Granby's capture too strongly. He had heard nothing of Edith's fate, though he had begged Jane to make inquiry of the intelligence officers. Spy reports came in the dozen each day from London, but the arrest, or God forbid, the execution, of a solitary British gentlewoman might be too insignificant to mention in the greater scheme of things.

Tharkay said to Granby, 'I would not diminish your satisfaction for the world, but "perfectly obliging" raises caution. I would feel more secure with a smaller improvement. No creature in the habit of freedom is easily persuaded to adopt discipline,' he added, offering a gobbet of meat to the kestrel, who observed their roasting rabbit with a cocked and eager eye.

'I am disciplined,' Iskierka said, overhearing. 'I will not run off at all; and I am very happy to carry more,' she defended, meaning cattle. They were each carrying half a load of supply along with their crew: Jane's compromise between transport and patrol. Even a party of middleweight dragons could move half a load with a full company with their officers without weighting the dragons too much to fight. Their own party was presently advancing along the North Sea coast, and gathering what supply they could find. Iskierka was already responsible for the transport of a dozen large black hogs, presently penned outside the camp and squealing occasionally through their drunken haze. They had been dosed with the easiest drug to supply, strong liquor, and smelled powerfully of spirits.

'If you ask me, it is only an act,' Temeraire said, disdainfully, 'because you are trying to show Granby he ought not leave you. You know perfectly well we haven't any more.'

Deer could not be successfully transported, panicking themselves to death before they could even be drugged, and fish did not keep, they were only good for feeding the dragons on the wing. Already cattle had begun to grow scarce along the coast, and the more time they spent inland searching, the more risk of leaving an opening in their patrol where a

255

substantial number of soldiers could be brought over. Bonaparte had dragons loaded down with men flying along the Channel, daily, waiting for just such a chance.

Tharkay said, 'We will find more tomorrow,' with a puzzling degree of confidence. The next evening he took Arkady into the lead and flew directly to an estate with several handsome dairy farms, which yielded two dozen bullocks. Tharkay watched the stupefied animals being loaded onto the dragons with an odd, wry expression, which made Laurence wonder how he had known. They were just over the border into Scotland. Laurence knew Tharkay had been embroiled in a law-suit here, although he had none of the details; and if Tharkay did not choose to volunteer them, respect dictated they could not be pursued.

The cattle completed their supply tally, but only just, and they found nothing more on their patrol, or on the flight to deliver their supplies to Loch Laggan. The farmers had grown adept at hiding their diminishing herds.

'Damn the lot of them and Boney too,' Jane snapped, when Laurence gave her the news, and rubbed the back of her hand across her forehead. 'Tell him he has one week less than I said,' she told the aide hovering at her desk. The young man, an army officer, was at once more nervous and impatient, shifting his weight side to side. 'And no, he may not have twenty, he may have ten, and not all of those heavy-weights, either. Wellesley wants you,' she added to Laurence, and tossed him a wax-sealed packet from among those upon her desk, 'and as many as I can spare, in Edinburgh.'

Laurence broke the seal and unfolded the orders, a single sheet, a few lines only, hastily and informally written, with no signature: *Bring that fire-breathing monster, and however many more Roland will give you – the best fighters you have, and the more vicious the better.*

He read it over slowly, and then folded it back up again;

vicious was a cold indigestible presentiment. Jane, he thought, had not seen the contents; she would object as strongly as he would. He looked up. She had scarcely interrupted her work. 'Frette, have Rightley take himself and ten middle-weights to Inverness, and send a note to that damned colonel saying that if he does not get his men on board tomorrow night when the beasts land, I will have him court-martialled the next morning. We have no time to waste on this nonsense,' she said, handing off three orders at once. 'Laurence, you may choose your beasts, anyone you like; formations make no nevermind.'

He could not burden her. 'We may have ten?' Laurence said. 'Wellesley wants Iskierka,' he added.

'Yes,' Jane said, distracted, 'you may as well take her. Lord knows it is a waste to keep her patrolling if there is skirmishing to be had. Oh, and here,' she added, giving him a letter dug out from beneath many others on her over-burdened desk, 'you may read that here, although I cannot let you take it.'

A hand had written, broadly and with many misspellings and stray capitals:

> *The Lady In Question is watchd, but, not yet Molestd;*
> *I have Contrivved, to Whisper in a few ears, that her*
> *Husb'd was a Nown Enthusiast and she Married Late*
> *in Desp'ration. May she one day Forgive This Slur*
> *aganst her, and upon the name of a Hero of His*
> *Country! I hope the Danger, of Arrest, is Passd. This*
> *is All I can convay Reliably, as she refuses to Receve*
> *Me as a Caller, but Gossip says she is Much Grieved*
> *and the Child continues Sick.*
>
> *To-Morrow I am invitd to Dinner with Marshl*
> *Davout, but do not Expect Much as he is Close-Mouthd*
> *unlike M. Murat.*

The letter had no signature. He read the section over twice, and gave it back again. 'Thank you,' he said only, and bowing left. He did not trust himself to say anything more.

Temeraire was very pleased to be singled out for a particular assignment, and even more to be escape patrolling and ferrying men about, however important it might be. The only difficulty was in deciding who should be chosen to come along. 'Wellesley wants the best fighters you have, and the most enthusiastic,' Laurence said, which was fair, anyway, as those had the most right to be doing something more exciting than carrying the infantry. But there were more than ten deserving, and it was really only eight, because of course he would go himself, and so would Iskierka, even though she did not merit the privilege at all.

Temeraire found her showy fire-breathing rather ordinary. Anyone could set things on fire, if only they had a little bit to start with. Temeraire sighed, but she was not of much use here, she had already been let off carrying people, because it was difficult for many soldiers to sit upon her spikes, jetting off steam as they did. So he had to put up with her. Then, Maximus and Lily had to be asked, of course, although to Temeraire's startled dismay, Laurence tried to speak against the choice.

'But it would be very unhandsome of me not to invite them for some real fighting, when I may,' Temeraire protested, looking over his shoulder, lest Maximus and Lily should overhear, and be offended. Fortunately, Maximus slept solidly, snoring under a blanket of nine Winchesters and little ferals, and Lily was presently encamped outside the far wall of the citadel just below Captain Harcourt's window, jealously: Catherine was gone inside to see to the baby.

'Harcourt is not well,' Laurence said.

'Yes,' Temeraire said, 'Lily thinks so too, but that is as

much a reason to ask her as any. She is quite sure Catherine would do better to go south, and have some real fighting, than continue flying back and forth in the wet. She takes cold so easily now, and ought not to be so long aloft.'

'Berkley don't take cold easily, because he is so fat,' Maximus said sleepily, cracking open an eye, 'but I would also like to go and fight.'

So that was settled, but for the rest, Temeraire scratched his head a little. 'Gentius may as well come with us, without counting against our tally.' he said at last, 'It is not as though he can carry anyone or even patrol. He is only staying here in Loch Laggan and sleeping, so we shall have Armatius to carry him. That would do very well for heavyweights. I do not think I ought to take Majestatis or Ballista, for they are so very handy at managing the others, nor Requiescat, because no one who is under a heavyweight will argue with him, even if he must be told what orders to give.'

He was a little puzzled how to leave them behind without giving offence, until he hit on the notion of giving them rank instead. 'You do not suppose Wellesley can mind?' he asked Laurence.

'It is a capital scheme,' Admiral Roland said in amusement, when Laurence had consulted her. 'Your militia had better be shifted under command of the Corps in any case, so we will make you a commodore instead of a colonel, and your officers shall be captains; although it will be damned difficult to manage epaulets for them.'

'Oh, epaulets,' Temeraire said, eagerly. The party of seamstresses who had been recruited from the local villages around Loch Laggan to help sew carrying-harnesses, for the transport of the soldiers, were now induced to make up rosettes out of some of the leftover silk and leather. The results were not much like real epaulets, nearer instead to enormous mopheads made up of the brightest colours, with a little gold cloth at their knotted centres, and a great many ties to attach them to a harness. But no one minded, in the least.

'I call that handsome,' Requiescat said, admiring the bright green knot upon his shoulder from every direction, even craning his head almost upside down. Even Majestatis did not manage his usual degree of amused disdain and kept glancing sidelong at his own: it was red, to go well against his cream-and-black. It looked almost as fine, Temeraire thought, as his own pale blue matched set. He of course had needed two.

'Yes, and if anyone should be particularly clever at helping you to manage, you may make them lieutenants, and they may have a smaller one,' Temeraire said. 'So that is all settled,' he added to Laurence. 'And for the rest, let us take some Yellow Reapers, and Messoria and Immortalis, of course, because they are our wing-mates, and that will do very well, because I also want Perscitia. She is very clever, and,' he confided, 'if I leave her here she will offend someone. Anyway, we may need her to manage some artillery.'

The Reapers quarrelled amongst themselves, and finally decided that Chalcedony and Gladius should come. Cantarella, staying behind, would take charge of the rest, and have an epaulet. Moncey got one for command of the couriers; it was nearly as large as his head but pleased him very well and Minnow also.

So there was no quarrelling or ill-feeling in the end, which Temeraire felt was a credit to his arrangements. 'We are a very handsome company, are we not?' Temeraire asked Laurence, hoping to find him satisfied. 'It is a pity about Iskierka, but no one could quarrel with *our* choices, I am sure.'

'Yes,' Laurence said.

'I have been thinking,' Temeraire said, with a sidelong look; he hoped he would not seem selfish, 'how well it might be, if we got back the rest of our crew. Not that we are not perfectly comfortable as we are,' he added, 'but a few more bellmen to manage some bombs . . . and it might be convenient to have Winston back, to help Fellowes—'

'Those who wished to return have done so,' Laurence said. 'I cannot demand any man serve with a traitor.'

'Oh,' Temeraire said, 'But—' and stopped. It had not occurred to him that the crew had *chosen* not to come back, that they might want rather to be elsewhere, on another dragon with another captain. It seemed very strange to him, when he was now a commodore, and must surely have been more impressive. He wondered if perhaps Laurence was mistaken, or if he was simply shy of asking for them. Perhaps they did not even know that he and Laurence were free. 'But surely Martin, at least, or Ferris, would come?' he said.

Laurence was very still for a moment, and then he said, 'Ferris has been dismissed from the service.' The admirals imagined that Ferris had been of some help, even though he had done nothing whatsoever.

'But then where is he?' Temeraire asked. If Ferris were not with some other dragon, it stood to reason he would rather be with them. But Laurence said with finality, 'Any communication from me must be wholly unwelcome.'

Temeraire did not press him further, but privately he thought that perhaps *he* would write to Ferris, if he could get Emily or Sipho, perhaps, to take down a letter and find out Ferris's direction . . .

Then a dragon he knew a little from Dover, Orchestia, landed in the courtyard. She was back from a patrol, and his own midwingman, Martin, was with her crew, his bright yellow hair standing out against his green coat.

'Mr. Martin,' Temeraire called out, seeing him go by, thinking perhaps to ask him over and see if he knew that

Temeraire had been made commodore; and inquire whether he was quite sure he would not prefer to go with them.

Martin started a little, at being called, and looked over; but then he turned his back and walked on into the citadel with the rest of Orchestia's crew without a word, or even a gesture.

'Temeraire,' Laurence said, 'you will oblige me very greatly if you will make no such gesture again.'

'No, I will not,' Temeraire said, much subdued. It was not only that Martin had ignored them, though he had done it so very openly, as though he wanted everyone else to know he meant to do it, there was something particularly unpleasant to it. One may at times not feel like conversing, of course, but he had been showing-away how little he wanted to with them. 'But surely,' Temeraire said to Laurence, slowly, 'does that not mean he disapproves of what we did, that we took over the cure? He would not have wished to see all those dragons dead—'

'Between the two evils, he might have found that the lesser than treason,' Laurence said, without lifting his head from the book he was reading.

'Oh! then I am not sorry to lose him,' Temeraire said defiantly. 'He may stay with Orchestia; if she wants him.'

He felt rather wounded, though, for all his bravado, and had not yet understood the worst. He did not realize the full implication of what they had done to poor Ferris until that very afternoon. They were assembled and ready to fly. Temeraire's harness was rigged out and his epaulets shone bright in the thin wintry sunshine. A runner approached to let them know they might go to Edinburgh, and he said, 'Mr. Laurence, your orders, sir, from the Admiral,' handing over the packet.

'Yes,' Laurence said, and did not correct the boy. He simply took the papers and put them in his coat pocket; and for the first time Temeraire realized, looking closely, that Laurence was not wearing the gold bars upon his shoulders, which the other captains wore.

Temeraire did not want to ask; he did not want to hear the answer, but he could not help it. 'Yes,' Laurence said, 'I have been struck from the service, too. It does not matter now,' he added after a moment, when of course it mattered, as much as anything. 'We must away.'

Laurence stood by the parapet, looking out to sea, from the upper courtyard of Edinburgh Castle; Temeraire lay somewhere in the dark covert below, resting in the darkness beside the illuminated city that stretched around the castle and down to the river Forth. Ships rose and fell in the harbour uneasily as he watched, and the wind blew sharp needles of frozen rain into his face. In the far distance he could see a handful of lights moving: too high for ships, too bright for stars, a few dragons on patrol.

'Another three hundred thousand of them buggers are lying along the coast from Calais to Boulogne, just waiting for their chance,' a Marine sergeant said to his fellow soldier as the two of them came by on their round.

They had not yet seen Laurence. Wellesley and his staff were inside the tower chambers. He had been left outside until called for, despite the night cold and wet, the stones slick with ice, and room enough in the antechamber for him to wait inside: a deliberate slight. The damp penetrated his cloak and his leather coat effortlessly. But he had chosen to stand at the limit of the parapet, out of the lantern-light, so he could see further out. It was a romantic impulse; he could not see anything of real significance at this hour.

'He'll squeeze over another thousand tonight,' the sergeant went on. 'Every dark night, those fucking Fleur-de-Nuits carry them. The Navy shot one down two days ago, though,' he added, with vindictive satisfaction. 'Dropped down into the ocean like a stone, and two hundred Frogs on its back, I hear; but more often than not they can't be seen.'

'I heard as he burned Weedon to the ground,' the young soldier beside him ventured. 'I heard he set his dragons on it, sent the whole place up.'

'Fucking Jacobin buggers,' the sergeant said gloomily. 'Begging your pardon, sir,' he said, seeing Laurence and touching his hat.

He nodded to them, and they fell silent, taking their post. A door opened in the side of the tower and raised voices came drifting out while it sighed gently shut again. Laurence looked over, but it was not Wellesley or one of his aides, it was an old man in nightshirt and bed slippers, muttering to himself as he came into the rain. His hair was grey and thinned out, matted and without a wig, and he walked with the uneasy hitch of rheumatism as he groped his way towards the chapel across the courtyard.

'Is it the vicar?' the young Marine whispered.

'At this hour?' the sergeant said, doubtfully, and they both looked at Laurence.

Laurence crossed the courtyard to go to his side The old man did not seem steady on the wet icy stones, and he was talking to himself: a stream of low unintelligible speech, which remained incomprehensible even as Laurence drew close enough to make out the words. 'Horses,' the old man said, 'horses and mules, and three weeks' grain, and Copenhagen; the fleet in Copenhagen. Thirty-three pounds.'

He did not seem to notice Laurence's approach at all, until Laurence said, 'Sir, should you not go back inside?'

'I will not,' the old man said, querulously. 'Is that you, Murat? Is that you?' He peered at Laurence's face, touched his coat, and evidently satisfied, nodded. 'You are not

Napoleon, you are Murat. Are you here to kill me? Give me your arm,' he said, abruptly peremptory, and taking a grip on Laurence's arm, leaned on him heavily. He had fixed his gaze on the chapel, and started determinedly to limp on towards it. 'They all mean to kill me,' he told Laurence, confidentially. 'They are in there talking of it now. My son is with them.' He sounded neither indignant nor afraid, rather as though he were sharing a piece of interesting gossip.

Laurence looked back at the tower and then at the old man again, at his profile; then recognition came. 'Sire,' Laurence said, low and wretchedly, 'may I not help you inside? You ought not to be out in this weather.' He pulled the ties of his own cloak, and shrugging it off managed to put it over the King's shoulders.

'I will go to Windsor,' the King said. 'Napoleon is not there. Why may I not go to Windsor?' He continued his unsteady progress towards the chapel, and Laurence had no choice but to pace him or let him go alone. 'He is in London, he is in London. He is not in Windsor. I need not go to Halifax. It would be cowardly to go. Do you want me to go to Halifax?' he demanded. 'My son wants me to go. He wishes me to die on the ocean.'

'I would wish to see you safe, Sire,' Laurence said, 'as I am sure would he.'

'I will not go,' the King said. 'I will die in England.'

The door was flung open again. Frightened servants hurried out with cloak and umbrella to hold over him, and coax him back within. They gave Laurence no more than a glance, and he stepped back to let them work. The King's voice rose in protest over their insistent hands, and then died away again into muttering confusion as he let himself be drawn gradually back inside.

'Poor old fellow,' the sergeant said, coming close to peer

after them, for a glimpse inside the tower. 'Gone out of his head, I suppose. Who was he?'

Laurence stood in the courtyard behind the closing door, rain running down his sleeves and his face said aloud, 'O God, I wish I had not done it.'

PART III

Chapter Thirteen

Temeraire pulled close around himself, his tail coiled snugly around his body, and tried without much success to sleep. There were a great many things he did not want to think about, but so long as he continued awake, they clamoured for his attention.

They had landed in Edinburgh covert after dark, and found it wet, bleak and muddy, and the water of the pond unfit to drink: there had been too many dragons buried there, too recently. So they were reduced to waiting their turn at thin run-off from the castle walls, which tasted unpleasantly green, and then settling themselves uncomfortably between the two burial-mounds most widely separated. They were crowded, and although there was plenty of room for one or another of them to go and sleep among the other mounds, no one at all proposed to go off alone; they preferred to huddle closely.

Laurence had left almost at once to go and speak with Wellesley, and he had been away a long time. So long, that they had finished their dinner long before his return. They had enjoyed a couple of old tough cows and three sheep, hacked up and pit-roasted with a great heap of potatoes, which Gong Su had. Happily these last took on some of the flavour of the meat and were not unappetizing at all, once they had cooked for long enough.

'I don't hold with this cookery thing much,' Maximus had said, licking his chops, having slowly and thoughtfully wrecked seventeen bushels of potatoes roasted in their skins, 'but these are not half bad; if one cannot have a nice fresh cow, that is.'

Temeraire took a long time over his meal, but as Maximus was eyeing the last pile of sheep-intestines hopefully, he was forced to finish it off hurriedly. Then he had nothing to do but lie uncomfortably in the mud, curled up small to stay warmer, and worry about Laurence.

'Of course he isn't happy,' Gentius said sleepily. 'The country overrun by all these Frogs, who would be happy? I would not think much of his sense if he were dancing a jig.'

'But that is not the same as being unhappy,' Temeraire said, 'when we are going to fight to make the French leave, and will have some battles soon.'

Gentius cocked his head ruminatively. 'Men like to be unhappy sometimes,' he offered. 'My second captain would sit under my wing with a book and weep over it, most evenings. I thought at first she must be wounded, but she told me not to fret, that she liked to do it. The next morning she would be right as rain again.' Temeraire was doubtful. He had never noticed Laurence weeping over a book, although sometimes he did not enjoy them very much.

But he did not like to press the conversation too far. To be perfectly honest, Temeraire was a little afraid that he might learn that Laurence was not so much upset as angry. He was afraid that Laurence was angry with him.

Temeraire had not understood what it would mean for Laurence to be called a traitor. Of course, the Government meant to execute him or imprison them, but Temeraire had thought, that with those two fates averted, all would be much the same. It had seemed so, at first; they flew together, and were given orders, but it was not really the same at all. Of course there had been no other alternative but to take over the cure; only, Temeraire had not known that treason meant Laurence should lose his life, and his crew, *and* his rank.

'At least,' he said, 'at least, you are still *my* captain; and while there are many captains who have some sort of dragon, I am the only dragon who is a commodore—' He had tried this argument out privately to himself, but it did not sound really consoling after all: puffing himself up, as though Laurence ought to be satisfied with Temeraire's consequence and have no care for of his own. It would add insult to injury: Laurence had lost his gold bars, too.

Temeraire raised his head out of the mud and said, 'Roland, do you know Captain Fenter's neck-chain, the gold one, with the emerald? It is not official, is it? Might anyone wear its sort?' It was a handsome piece, he and the others at Loch Laggan had remarked upon it often. The chain belonged to the captain of a smug Anglewing named Orchestia, and Temeraire thought its quality very suitable for the captain of a dragon of elevated rank, however neglectful the Corps might be of him. 'Do you suppose that Laurence could buy something like it, here in town?'

'I expect he could not afford it. The law suit, you know,' she said wisely, looking up from her boots, which she was blacking.

'What law suit?' Temeraire said, puzzled.

'Over those slaves,' she said, 'who we let loose in Africa. The slave-owners we carried back sued the captain, and I suppose he could not fight the suit very well, as he was in prison, so they have taken all his capital.'

'*Taken* it?' Temeraire kept his tail from quivering and thumping upon the ground with great difficulty. 'Surely not *all* his capital,' he said, in a strained voice.

'I heard it was ten thousand pounds, or something like,' Emily said.

'Ten thousand pounds!' Gentius exclaimed horror-struck, jerking his head from the ground. 'Ten thousand pounds! You did not say anything about *ten thousand pounds gone*. Why, that is ten of those eagles, or more!' Everyone murmured their shock; even Maximus and Lily flinched, and could not quite look at Temeraire.

Temeraire felt quite staggered, and ill. Laurence had not said anything; he had not said that all his treasure should be taken away, or so Temeraire tried to argue to himself. But it felt a very flimsy and weak excuse when he opened his mouth to make it, and he stopped without giving it voice. He had not troubled to find out. Here was he, a commodore, showing away with jewels and two epaulets, while Laurence had nothing but a plain coat growing shabbier every day.

'Ten thousand pounds,' Gentius said again, censoriously, wagging his head from side to side. 'You have certainly made a good mull of it,' and Temeraire huddled himself down further, feeling he thoroughly deserved the condemnation.

'But, if we had not taken over the cure,' he said, rather weakly, 'a great many dragons might have died, even those who had nothing at all to do with the war, or France. It cannot have been all wrong.'

'If you ask me,' Perscitia said, after a moment, 'the French ought to have given you some treasure to make up for it, seeing as you went on their account; or at least, not entirely on their account.' she amended, 'But they did well out of it, so I don't think much of them letting you come out the worse for it, when you needn't have done it at all.'

'Well,' Temeraire said, and was forced to admit that such an offer had been made, and a most handsome one. 'Only Laurence said no, because that would have been more treasonous,' he finished.

'I myself don't see how getting treasure *after* you have already done treason, could make it any worse,' Chalcedony said. 'After all, they are the enemy, and if they gave you treasure, they would have less of it, and that would be worse for them. So if you ask me, it would have made up for the treason, to take it, really,' which struck Temeraire as a very just point, and one he rather wished he had thought of at the time.

'Only, I did not realize Laurence would lose his capital,' Temeraire said unhappily, 'so I did not think the offer would be so important.'

'Well, well, you are a young fellow yet,' Gentius said, relenting a little, 'and you have time to make it up. Win battles, take some prizes while you are at it, and it will all come right in the end. The Government will see you right, if you are only heroic enough.'

'But I have been *very* heroic,' Temeraire protested, 'and they have not been fair at all. They have even tried to take Laurence away from me.'

'You aren't been the right sort of heroic,' Gentius said. 'You must win battles, that is the road. That is how my first captain was made, you know. They never used to let Longwing captains be proper captains. They called her only Miss, and put a fellow aboard who she was supposed to listen to; only he was a lummox and managed to be drunk out of his wits just when we had a battle to join, and all our formation waiting.' He snorted. 'So she said to the crew, "Gentlemen,"' here he paused, frowning, and rubbed his forelegs against one another, restlessly.

They waited, and waited, and waited. Temeraire was almost quivering with impatience. If Gentius's captain had gone from *Miss* to *Captain*, surely Laurence might have his rank repaired, in the same fashion . . .

'It is difficult to remember, the exact way she said it,' Gentius said defensively. 'They don't talk now as they used

273

to, but I think I have it. She said, "Gentlemen, seeing that our duty consisteth going to war, I should judge this situation a sad excuse for failure if we were to contrive without Captain—Captain—" bother,' Gentius muttered, interrupting himself, 'I have forgotten his name; but she said, "if we were to contrive without his company, a worse outcome upon the field than our complete absence will ensure. Therefore will I continue on, and any man who wisheth not to venture himself under my command, may remain behind."'

He triumphantly completed his recitation, but then had to wait for applause while his audience worked out just what had been said. 'But I don't understand, did you win the battle or not?' Messoria said finally, still puzzled.

'Of course we won the battle,' Gentius said irritably. 'And we did a sight better without Captain Haulding—Hah! I have remembered his name after all—I can tell you that. I was even writ up in the newspapers, and Government gave over and made her captain properly, because we had done so well,' he finished, with a meaningful nudge to Temeraire's shoulder. 'That is the road. Win battles for them, and they will come about, see if they don't.'

'That is all very well,' Iskierka remarked, "as long as they let us have some battles. There he comes now, ask him when we shall be fighting,' and she nudged Temeraire as Laurence came down the path from the castle.

But Temeraire hardly knew how to look Laurence in the face. He was bitterly conscious of his guilt, and half expected Laurence to upbraid him at once. But Laurence said only to Roland and to Demane and Sipho, 'Go and rouse the other captains at once, if you please,' and stood waiting silently until the others had been drawn from their uncomfortable bivouacs. 'Gentlemen, I have been commissioned temporarily, and given command of this expedition. You will find your written orders there, and I trust they allow no ambiguity.'

Laurence had a sheaf of papers in his hands, packets each sealed and addressed separately. He handed the orders to Sipho to carry around.

'Damned paperwork, with Bonaparte in our parlour,' Berkley muttered. 'Trust the Army for this sort of thing—'

'You will oblige me greatly, Berkley, by putting those orders somewhere they can come to no harm,' Laurence said, when Berkley would have crumpled the parchment. 'I would be happier to know that the chain of command can be made quite clear, to anyone who should inquire, in future.' All the other captains paused and looked at him, and Temeraire wondered why it should matter; the red wax seals affixed to the parchment were attractive, but they might be easily copied; and Laurence had not kept one himself.

But Laurence did not explain further. Instead he went on, 'The French are harassing our farmers, and so supplying the wants of their army using raiding bands. Our duty is to stop this predation and, so far as is practicable without undue risk to the dragons, to reduce the forces available to Napoleon.'

There was a pause, and then Granby said, 'You mean, his irregulars?'

'I do,' Laurence said.

'What does he expect us to do with the prisoners, cart them about with us in the belly-rigging?' Berkley said.

'No quarter will be given,' Laurence said. There was a heavy finality to his tone, which somehow warned off further questions. The captains said nothing. 'We will begin in Northumberland, tomorrow, and work our way south. We leave at dawn gentlemen; that is all.'

They stood a moment longer looking at their orders and at Laurence, with oddly uncertain expressions, but in the end drifted away back to their tents without quietly. Temeraire himself was at a standstill. He could not under-stand why Laurence should have taken the command. *He* was

275

already in command, and it was important, was it not, for a dragon to have the post? Laurence had said as much himself. But Temeraire did not mean to be selfish anymore, not now that he knew he had already been selfish. If Laurence wished to have the command, of course he should have it, and yet, if it mattered for politics sake, for the dragons . . .

He struggled over it, and ventured at last to ask, timidly, though he added hurriedly, 'I do not mind at all, for myself, I am very happy that you are restored, and a captain now again. Only, if it is important—'

He was coiled up with the others, but everyone else was asleep and the other men in their tents. Laurence had told Roland, Demane and Sipho to go and sleep in his tent, and had stayed out wrapped in his coat and cloak to look over the maps, which he had laid out on a small camp table. He was marking them with a small wax pencil, here and there, as Temeraire spoke.

'In the present, it is the more important that you should not be in command, nor anyone but myself,' Laurence said.

There was something odd in his voice, it was queerly flat as if he did not much care what he was saying, and he did not look up from his work. Temeraire wished it were not so dark, and that he could see Laurence's face. 'In any case,' Laurence added, 'whether the courts will believe you truly command is a proposition yet untried; and I hope you would not risk the lives and the careers of the other captains for the sake of your precedence.'

'But,' Temeraire said, 'are they not risking their lives anyway?'

'In battle only,' Laurence said, 'not afterwards.'

Temeraire did not much want to pursue; however dreadful it was to think Laurence angry with him, it would be all the worse to know it, to hear it from Laurence himself. 'Laurence,' Temeraire said anyway, bravely, 'pray explain to me; I know—I know I have let you be hurt, because I did

276

not try to understand well enough, and I do not mean to let it happen again; only I cannot help it, if I do not know.'

Laurence did look up at that, his eyes briefly catching the reflection from the castle upon the hill. 'There is nothing to help. I am in no danger.'

'If they should be, so should you,' Temeraire said.

'I cannot be condemned twice,' Laurence said. 'Pray get some rest. We have a hundred miles to fly in the morning.'

'I want him bled,' Wellesley had said, in the tower room of Edinburgh Castle, as they stood over the map of England swarming with blue markers, with the icy rain lashing at the windows. Down the hall, the muffled sound of the King's voice was rising in some complaint. To Laurence it seemed very loud. 'Every man to him is worth five to us. He must bring them across at great expense, and he must spend his dragons' strength to do it. And his men live off the land; he relies upon them raiding the countryside, feeding themselves and driving in cattle for the dragons, and keeping his supply lines meagre and short.'

'You mean you wish us to attack his irregulars,' Laurence broke in, tired of evasions.

'His supply lines, his foragers, his scouts.' Wellesley thumped the map. 'He has hundreds of small raiding parties scattered throughout the country north of London; he cannot survive long without them, and they are exposed. You will destroy every one of them you can find.

'You will not engage,' he added, 'any substantial party, other dragons in number, or artillery: I do not mean to lose any of our beasts.'

Laurence had expected something of the sort, from the tenor of Wellesley's summons, and heard it with dull acceptance. The strategy was sound, coldly speaking. If Bonaparte began to lose men quicker than he could replace them, and found his supply growing short, he would have to accept a battle on whatever terms it was offered him, or withdraw entirely.

But dragons were not usually put to such a use in civilized warfare; Wellesley knew it, and so did he. Pragmatism alone held them too valuable to risk and too expensive to supply, save against a more substantial target of strategic importance. However, it was not pragmatism but sentiment that with a single voice called the exceptions inhuman. Little aroused greater horror and more condemnation from ordinary men than the prospect of dragons set loose against them. Men had been court martial and hanged for it, even by their own side.

'Pillaging,' Wellesley added after a moment, 'of course, cannot be tolerated—'

'There will be none,' Laurence said, 'save what must be requisitioned to feed the dragons. Is there anything else?'

Wellesley looked at him narrowly. 'Will you do it?'

There was little enough Laurence could do, to repair what he had done; he could not restore the lives of the slain, or raise sunken ships from the Channel, or make recompense to all the ordinary countrymen whose livelihood and possessions had been raided away by an invading army. He could not repair his father's health, or the King's, or Edith's happiness. But he had already stained himself irrevocably with dishonour, for the sake of an enemy nation and a tyrant's greed; he could stain himself a little more for the sake of his own, and shield with his own ruined reputation those who still had one to protect.

'I do not need written orders for myself,' he had answered Wellesley. 'But I require them for those other officers of the Corps involved: you may say merely that they must follow my orders.'

Wellesley had understood very well, what Laurence offered him, and he had not refused it. The orders were written, and he had left Wellesley in his tower, and gone down and down, to the waiting covert.

It was a silent, grim camp in the morning, as they harnessed the dragons and the crews went aboard. Twice or more, Laurence thought Harcourt almost meant to speak to him, but in the end they mounted up and flew with no words exchanged. The cold wind in Laurence's face was welcome, and the steady beat of Temeraire's wings, and the silence. His small crew did not address him, and sitting forward on Temeraire's neck, they might have been alone in a wide-open sky; the rolling unmarred moors beneath them knew nothing of war or boundaries.

Wellesley's spies had reported already a dozen raiding bands or more, moving through the North Country, stealing from farms and seizing cattle. Laurence had marked them on his map, as best the reports could place them, but the enemy provided them also with a convenient beacon of smoke, easily visible ten miles off. It was a thin black coil turning lazily upwards from the roof of a great farmhouse, the fire mostly extinguished by the time they arrived. The rest of the village stood empty, when they came down, but for two men in homespun. They were villagers, not soldiers, and had been laid out in the road dead, with stab wounds flower-red upon their bellies: bayoneted.

'The villagers shan't come out while we have the dragons here,' Harcourt said. 'If we leave them outside—'

'No,' Laurence said; he did not meant to waste time on such things. He cupped his hands around his mouth and shouted, 'We are officers of the King. You will come out at once, or we will have the dragons tear down the houses until you do.'

There was no reply, no stirring. 'Temeraire,' Laurence said, and indicated a small neat cottage near the end of the village lane. 'Bring it down, if you please.'

Temeraire looked at it, and said uncertainly, 'Shall I roar?'

'However you choose,' Laurence said.

'Should I bring it down all at once?' Temeraire asked, turning his head to inspect the cottage. He darted a look

279

back at Laurence, as if trying to gauge his real intent. 'Perhaps, if I just took off this chimney—'

'Oh, you are taking too long,' Iskierka said, and promptly blasted it with fire, the dry thatched roof catching alight in a crackling instant.

It burned fiercely; the flames licking eagerly towards its neighbours. Laurence sat waiting, and after a moment a cellar door creaked open and a few men came forth, 'Put it out, for God's sake put it out,' one of them begged gasping. 'All of the village will catch—'

'Berkley, if you will be so kind,' Laurence said. Maximus took off the burning roof, and after laying it on the ground scraped some soil over it with a clumsy swipe, leaving it half-buried. Laurence looked back at the villagers, who stared up at him pale and sweating. 'Which way did the French go?'

'Towards Scarrow Hill,' the older man said, his voice still trembling. 'With all our cattle, every last one—' The faint lowing of a cow from the woods made him a liar on that point, but Laurence did not care. 'They left not an hour—'

'Very good. To quarters, gentlemen, and let the riflemen make ready,' Laurence said over his shoulder, to the other captains. 'Aloft, Temeraire, along the road.'

They caught the French fifteen minutes later, or heard them first. They were singing a bawdy snatch of *'Au près de ma blonde, qu'il fait bon, fait bon, fait bon'* as they marched through a forested section. Then they emerged out onto the road again, the cattle followed in a bellowing string, throwing their heads uneasily as they scented the dragons aloft. The men pulled irritably on the cows' tether and tried to drag them along. They did not look up.

Temeraire craned his head back and looked at Laurence. Ten dragons came on behind them. 'Mr. Allen,' Laurence said, 'signal the attack.'

Chapter Fourteen

'I do not see what is wrong with it,' Iskierka said, still nibbling upon the charred bones of her dinner. 'They are stealing the cows for their dragons, it is not our fault if their dragons are too lazy to come and get the cows themselves.'

'It is not wrong,' Temeraire said, dissatisfied, 'precisely.'

'Not very sporting, though,' Gentius said. 'They did not even have a gun.'

'The village did not have a gun, either, or even muskets,' Lily said, 'so it was not very sporting of those soldiers, in the first place.'

'Anyway,' Iskierka added, with an air of smug virtue, 'we must obey our orders.'

Temeraire did not argue. It was not that he minded for himself, anyway, although it had not been a very interesting battle: they had dived, and the soldiers had fired a few shots, but then they had all run away into the woods, if they were not dead. That had lasted scarcely five minutes, and they had nothing to show for it, except of course for the cows, but those they mostly had to give back.

He was not going to say so, of course, but he rather felt Iskierka was right. If the soldiers had not wanted to be attacked, they ought not have been about other people's territory, taking their food and much more than they could eat themselves. Only, he was a little worried, because it seemed to be the sort of thing that Laurence might have minded, and he did not seem to care.

The villagers had certainly been very grateful. 'Two months to spring. We would have starved, or near. Thank ye, sir,' the village headman said, the half-burned cottage quite forgiven, as the others came nervously out to look over their cattle and their goods, and make their own anxious courtesies.

A few young men from Maximus's ground crew had driven back those cows that had not been killed or panicked to death in the fighting. Gladius and Chalcedony had carried back the two large carts of grain, also, and the villagers had sent word back along the road, to those others pillaged, to come and share what there was left.

But Laurence did not seem pleased by their thanks; he only nodded, and said, 'Send word also that if you should see or hear of any French movements, you are to light a beacon: smoke, or a bonfire at night, and we will come for it if we see.'

Gong Su had taken the slaughtered cows, enough for all the dragons to have a little fresh roast beef, and then provided a share of soup, made with the bones and a little meat mixed with vegetables and grain, for all the crew and everyone in the village besides. The atmosphere was celebratory, and became more so when the villagers brought out a concealed store of honey wine. Temeraire even enjoyed a cupful, so he might close his jaws on it and keep the crisp fragrant smell on his tongue.

Laurence had not eaten very much, and now came away from the village and the celebration, back to Temeraire's side; but only to get out his maps again and study the roads.

Temeraire drew a deep breath, watching him, and said valiantly, 'Laurence—Laurence, I have been thinking. Perhaps you might sell my talon-sheaths. I do not mean just now,' he added, hurriedly, 'but, when the war is over—'

'Why?' Laurence said, a good deal more absently than Temeraire felt such an offer merited. 'Are you tired of them?'

'No, of course not; who could become tired of them?' Temeraire said, and then paused. He was not sure how he might explain without betraying his knowledge of the loss which Laurence had concealed, surely because it wounded him greatly. 'I only thought,' he tried, 'that perhaps you might like to have some more capital, as you have given me so much of it yourself.'

'I have no need of capital,' Laurence said, 'and you had better keep them, against future need. Though I thank you for the offer; it was handsomely made,' he added, which ought to have been a tremendous relief, but Temeraire found that it only made him more unhappy. He had tried his most desperate notion to no avail. Laurence had not seemed even a little moved by the prospect of having so splendid a treasure for his own; the gratitude had been simply formal.

He rested his head upon his forelegs and watched Laurence work a little longer. Laurence had a lamp, and in the light, he looked a little odd. He was not quite clean-shaven, Temeraire realized, and there was some dried blood upon his jaw, which he had not cleaned off. His hair was tied roughly back, and had grown long. But he did not seem to care for any of it; all his attention was for the map, and the figures he studied.

'May I not help you, Laurence?' Temeraire asked at last, rather hopelessly, for lack of any other idea.

Laurence paused over the papers then put one sheet out with the lamp upon it. 'Is it large enough for you to see? It is the tax roll for the last year. I expect the French will plunder the wealthier estates and villages first, so we will look for them there.'

'Yes, I can read it,' Temeraire said; it was only a little difficult. 'Shall I tell you all the richest ones, in order?'

As they pushed gradually southward, the raiding parties grew steadily larger and more desperate. They were no longer small bands, out to forage for themselves as much as for the beasts, but were now urgent support for dragons headquartered now at small outposts and encampments throughout the heart of England, formed to distribute the burden of their feeding. If the cattle did not arrive daily, the dragons would soon go hungry; and some number of them would have to be transferred, southwards, or even perhaps back to France.

Already the disruption of the supply was having an effect. Without the small parties bringing in regular provender, the soldiers faced more effort to keep themselves fed, as well as their dragons, and this made them all the more ruthless. Villages and farms and estates were now stripped to the bone and often torn apart in the search for hidden stores; or sometimes to no other end but wanton destruction. If any villagers sought to protect their homes and livelihoods, they were often murdered or abused, or at best left to starve with a burning house.

These brutalities soon roused the countryside from a sullen, small resistance, to open hatred. No one fled from the dragons now when they landed, they marched out their cattle to feed them instead, and daily the plumes of beacon-fires rose. The little feral dragons of the mountains, who ordinarily raided farms for their meals, had been recruited to their cause by hunger and through Temeraire's persuasion to collect far-flung intelligence. They darted from one beacon to another, where the townspeople provided them with a sheep or goat, and in return they carried the information back to Laurence's encampment. Laurence thought it likely he knew more of the movements of the French than their own generals did, and daily he sent long letters back to Jane and to Wellesley.

A little blue feral came darting into camp one evening in Cumbria, while they sat mostly dull and quiet, sharpening bayonets or drinking watered whiskey at their small fires. In an incongruously deep voice he announced, 'The French are coming this way, with guns, and twelve dragons.'

'Leave the camp,' Laurence said, standing, and put back on his sword. 'No, everything; we need the time more than the supply. Leave the fires burning. All aloft, gentlemen, at once,' he said sharply, when everyone hesitated for a moment, and spurred them into action.

'But, Laurence,' Temeraire murmured, as he climbed aboard, 'why do we not stay and fight them? It is our first chance of a real battle, and perhaps they will have eagles—'

'There is no honour to be won in battles between thieves,' Laurence said flatly, taking the maps Demane held out to him, and skimming over them. 'Divide into parties of no more than three and take separate routes, all of you; we rendezvous at Cross Fell,' he called. And one and all they lifted away.

They were too agile a band to be easily tracked or caught, with a thousand eyes in every direction looking out danger for them. Three more such attempts failed as thoroughly as the first, never finding more than their abandoned fires and cooking pits. Rewards, offered in vast sums, were scornfully ignored, and in frustration the French grew savage and turned instead to reprisals against any they suspected of providing intelligence or comfort. At Howick Hall, perhaps two weeks into their raiding, Laurence's band caught a large company, busy pillaging not only the cattle and the food, but carrying out paintings, and china plate, and great silver candelabra, also; while the house burned slowly down around them, and their officers laughed and drank wine from the cellars in the courtyard.

The dragon-shadows falling over them silenced their merriment, and two dozen muskets were raised up hurriedly. Temeraire hovering over them roared at the house, and almost the whole front wall, flickering with flame, slid down in a heap and buried half the soldiers with it, leaving the building looking like a doll-house, open for viewing, with more of the looters staring out of the exposed rooms.

Then the roof, groaning in complaint, gave way, and the great house folded in upon itself, walls crumbling into brick, slates clattering and spilling down upon the lawn. The horses and cows stampeded, and the remaining soldiers fled in the other direction, leaving a great heap of goods in an ox-cart, next to the smouldering ruins.

The village had also been struck. The men had tried to resist and had been slaughtered nearly one and all. The women and children had taken shelter in the church, which had not given them much protection: the soldiers had come in, outraged some of the young women and murdered the elderly vicar when he had feebly tried to intercede.

'We ought to hunt down the rest of them,' one young midwingman said, 'every last one,' and there was no disagreement.

Laurence felt very weary. 'Berkley,' he said, 'have your men clear the village, and let the dragons bury the dead. Sutton, Little, take the other Reapers, and bring over what you can from the house: they will need more supply, here. Or we can take you to Craster,' he offered, to the matron who had arranged the survivors into some order.

'They won't have better houses for us there,' she said.

'Whatever you can bring us, we'll thank you for, Captain, and we will manage. They didn't find all there was to find.' She did not have to say that they also had now fewer mouths to feed.

The Yellow Reapers took a while to return, and eventually came back with an air of grim satisfaction, bloodstained, carrying dead cattle and deer.

'I will venture a little further,' Laurence said. 'We will not make camp yet, we will raid further south, as far as we can fly in and out again in a day.'

'Just as well,' Little said, low. 'Let them look over their shoulders, everywhere in England,' to a murmur of agreement. The French had reconciled them all to their mission. Few of the captains now looked askance at their attacks, or argued for quarter. Laurence heard it without satisfaction.

'I am sure I can fly a little quicker, if I try,' Maximus put in. They held their conferences out in the air, so the dragons might listen in.

Some four days later, summoned by another column of smoke, they found and destroyed another raiding-party at Wollaton. Flying back from the battlefield, the corpses left behind dark and crimson on the snow, Laurence saw the blackened husks of houses he knew. Great houses were burning everywhere. They made ideal targets with their cellars full of wine and brandy and their pantries laden for winter. The Galman estate still stood, but was deserted, with ragpickers' wares strewn all over the courtyard: curtains and carpets, torn and trodden into mud, and more hanging hanged out of the shattered windows. The stables were burnt to the ground, and the old lily-pond, where he had used to walk with Edith, was choked upon the bloated corpse of a horse, torn at the haunches where dogs had got to it.

He knew he must expect to find Wollaton Hall itself

burned, and only hoped that his family had managed to flee in time. He was steeled for it, he thought; at least he could contemplate the possibility without a feeling of anything more than a calm and distant regret. Then they came over the lake, and Wollaton Hall stood, gilt and golden, upon the crest of its hill, untouched, with light in the windows and neat thin trails of smoke only from the chimneys. Deer bounded away urgently across the estate grounds.

They landed in the park, and the dragons went to hunt. Laurence climbed a ridge and stood looking at the house with a sense almost of unreality. Twilight was deepening as he watched, and in the muted light the edges of the house were blurred. 'Well, it is jolly good luck,' Harcourt said to him, uncertainly.

'You will pardon me,' he said. 'I will not be long,' and he walked across the lawn towards the house. The hedgerows were trim and the walks had been swept clear of snow. There was a murmur of noise and life, which grew louder as he came to the house until, standing in the formal gardens, he looked in through the glass at the candle-lit ballroom, full of people, standing and sitting and lying, on pallets and on camp-beds: cottagers he recognized, others from the village.

'Here now, what are you about? You may come to the front, if you're wanting something,' someone said to Laurence, making him start. A young gardener, stood before him, scowling and holding a rake as though he would be happy to undo something with it.

'I am William Laurence,' he said. 'Is Lady Allendale here?'

She came out to him wrapped in a cloak against the chill: wool only, and not her furs. 'Will, my dear,' she said, 'are you well? Have you come alone?'

'We are encamped in the park, to hunt only,' Laurence said. 'We leave again as soon as the dragons are fed. Are you well? And my father?'

'As well as anyone could expect, with all this upheaval,' she said. 'He knows a little of what has happened. He knows you are with the Corps again,' she added, anxiously.

He said nothing; there was nothing to be proud of, in the service he was providing. 'I am glad to find you unmolested,' he said after a moment, feeling strangely reluctant. 'We came over the village—I hope Lord and Lady Galman are well?'

Lady Allendale, too, hesitated. 'Yes, they stay with us.'

He paused again, and reaching into his coat brought out the ring, still in the small envelope of paper he had folded around it. 'I wish that I had not—I am sorry to bear ill tidings,' he said. 'Mr. Woolvey was killed, in London—I have kept it to send to Edith, when that might be possible. If her parents might—'

'Yes, we had word,' she said, low and unhappy, and took it from him. She curled her hand around the envelope, and her face looked drawn.

'He died well,' Laurence said, 'if that can be said; he died bravely, at least, in service to the Crown.'

She nodded, and they stood silently; a little snow was falling, white flecks settling upon her dark cloak. 'Tell me,' he said, finally.

'An officer came, and gave us the Emperor's compliments, and his assurances that we would never be harmed,' she said. 'None of the raiding parties have come here; even lately, when they are pillaging everywhere—'

'Yes,' Laurence said, stopping her. 'I understand.' Bonaparte had managed to pay him for his treason, after all.

'We can shelter a great many more,' she said quietly, after a moment. 'Our stores, also, are untouched, if there are any you would like to send to us.'

'If you can send a cart to Wollaton,' he said, 'they were struck this morning, and have wounded.'

'Yes, of course,' she said. 'Can you not stay the night?'

He only touched his hat. 'I must beg your pardon; we have some hours yet to fly tonight,' he said, bowed, and turned; the lights of the house glittered on the snow as he walked away.

Temeraire had caught three deer, despite their springiness, and felt rather pleased with the world until Laurence came back from the house, all pale, and refused his share of dinner. 'I am very happy the house is not burnt up,' Temeraire said to him anxiously, as they made ready to get underway. He wondered if something else perhaps had happened, if there was some damage which he could not see.

Laurence paused, and looked over his shoulder. Temeraire looked too, and thought the house looked very like a jewel. Its pale yellow stone glowed with warm and inviting light, streaming from the many windows in so interesting a variety of shapes; the dozens of intricate towers and ornaments all in perfect order.

'I will never come here again,' Laurence said, and pulled himself up the harness. 'Let us be away.'

Laurence was not himself at all, and Temeraire was becoming increasingly certain that they would never make matters right this way. They had taken no prizes whatsoever for all their long weeks of raiding. The French soldiers had nothing of value but the food they had stolen, not even a cannon or a flag to be proud of, and ever more suitable battle was offered, Laurence would insist on their flying away at once, to hide.

What battles they did have were over very quickly. Perscitia had devised a method of tearing up tall yew trees, with bushy tops and smooth long trunks, and dragging their crowns along the ground in a diving rush. It was most convenient: the soldiers could simply be swept away in their dozens, and the branches sheltered one from the musket-fire nicely, so there was no risk at all. The chief difficulty was to keep the men from scattering. It felt rather unpleasant and odd to be chasing one so very small, who would just as soon have run away, even if, as Messoria explained, they would only regroup and go stealing again. It was not the sort of fighting Temeraire had looked forward to, even though everyone else seemed to approve.

'Where is the rest of the army, I should damn well like to know! But at least you fellows are showing the Frogs what-for,' one stout elderly gentleman said, thumping his stick on the floor for emphasis. They had just stopped a raiding party outside a village in Derbyshire, and the children had been brought out to see their saviours. A few of the older boys, very bold, came running up to touch them. One put his hand on Temeraire's foreleg, and then stared up very large-eyed when Temeraire peered down at him in interest and said, 'Hello.'

The child ran away very quickly. 'Chinese children are braver,' Temeraire said to Laurence, 'but I am glad that these are getting a little better, and coming to see us. I suppose it is because we are being heroic?' he added; he was hopeful that even if this was not very interesting fighting, it was at least of the sort that Government would like.

'Their parents would do better to keep them locked away,' Laurence said, without much emotion. 'Will you look over the maps with me?'

So it had certainly made Laurence no happier, although Temeraire did not perfectly understand why Laurence should insist on fighting so, if he did not approve of it himself. Since they had seen Wollaton Hall, however, he seemed all the more fixed upon his course.

'I fear it is the unhealthy climate and the diet of this country,' Gong Su said. 'No one could be well, eating in such an unbalanced way.'

'But we do not have much choice over what we eat while we are at war, and I cannot do anything about the climate,' Temeraire said.

'Too bad,' Demane said, rather indistinctly. He was not enjoying his first British winter, and snuffled almost continuously into his sleeve. Sipho was not suffering, or rather not in the same manner, he was bundled into every spare piece of clothing Demane could find, and now wore three shirts, a knitted waistcoat, two light coats, a boat-cloak, a hood, and a hat crammed down upon it all; he could scarcely move from where he had been put down near the fire.

Roland was sitting with her arms curled about her knees. 'It is not right,' she said. 'I don't mean, we ought not be stopping them, but we ought to be letting them surrender when they see us, and take them prisoner; although I don't know what we should do with them after that. I wish Mother was here,' she added, desolately.

Many of the other captains were also dissatisfied; the very next day Temeraire overheard Granby speaking with Laurence, in low voices, and then Laurence said, 'Captain Granby, I hope you know that you may transfer to a new station, at any time you wish. I would not keep anyone at this task against their will.'

'Why, damn you, Laurence,' Granby said, and walked away.

'Of course Granby is not happy,' Iskierka said, yawning, when Temeraire went so far as to ask her. 'I am not happy either, this is all very boring, and we have no treasure. But it is still better than just carrying soldiers about, or patrolling. At least we are doing something. And it is orders, anyway; which you ought not question,' she added. Temeraire put back his ruff.

*   *   *

Farmers now slaughtered their own cattle if they heard the French approaching, and even poisoned their grain. Villagers in vigilante bands ambushed soldiers while they slept; and one foraging mission after another returned to French encampments empty handed, if they returned at all. A sorely pressed outpost commander at last made the mistake for which Laurence had been waiting, and sent out his dragons to hunt for themselves. The farms immediately around their position had already been depleted, and so the beasts separated to look farther afield.

'There are nine in all, two of those big grey ones, and the rest smaller, with three only a little bigger than I am,' one of their small spies informed them. 'The big ones went alone, south, and the others went towards a town north-north-east, with a red steeple, and parted there.'

Laurence nodded, and Gong Su led the feral to his reward, a portion of mutton stewed with rabbit, which the little dragon tore into ravenously: the supply of meat was growing increasingly thin throughout the countryside.

'I am sure we can beat seven dragons,' Temeraire said, his ruff already up, and his tail switching.

'We are not going to fight seven,' Laurence said. 'We are going after the Chevaliers.' He laid out his map quickly: a large estate lay some three miles south of the outpost, with a dairy.

They kept high over the cloud-cover, and emerged only just above the estate. The Petit Chevaliers were still on the ground, eating. It had most likely been a few days since their last meal, and they were trying urgently to make up for it. Two carcasses each already lay stripped to bones, and they had moved on to thirds. Their crew had dismounted and were ransacking the dairy-house with similar energy.

'Those are milk cows,' Demane said indignantly, peering down at the dragons and their repast; his own people were great herdsmen, and valued proper husbandry high.

'Signal the attack,' Laurence said, and roaring, Temeraire plummeted with the rest; the Chevaliers panicked and flung themselves aloft instinctively. One leapt up only to meet Maximus's full weight upon her back, and was driven down, bellowing dreadfully, to the ground again; a snapping crack and she went silent. Maximus staggered off and shook himself, dazed by the impact. She did not move, and her captain crying her name flung himself reckless across the field towards her.

The other Chevalier managed to beat a little further aloft, and shouldered past Chalcedony's eager but over-optimistic attempt to repeat Maximus's feat, bowling the Yellow Reaper over; but Iskierka was lunging with ferocious glee, and a torrent of flame engulfed the Chevalier's wing and neck.

'Ow!' Chalcedony said, barely dodging the edge of the flames himself. 'You needn't hit me!'

'Well, get out of the way, then!' Iskierka called over her shoulder, already pursuing the crying Petit Chevalier, whose hide and tender membrane showed the blackened marks of her flame. The dragon was trying to come back around: his captain was yet upon the ground, and despite his wounds, the dragon would not abandon him.

'*Je me rends*!' the captain cried, from the ground, through a speaking-trumpet; he was waving a white handkerchief furiously. '*Je me rends*!'

It was the only hope for his dragon. Lily was winging in from the other direction, and Temeraire hovered aloft; the Reapers had barred every point on the rose. In a moment they would bring the Petit Chevalier down.

For a moment, Laurence did not move. A heavyweight was difficult to manage. Then he said, 'Mr. Allen, signal Captain Berkley to take charge of the prisoner. Temeraire, tell that dragon to land by those trees and keep away from his captain.'

The rest of the French aviators backed away as the dragons came down, and then fled into the dairy-house and the woods behind. The dead dragon's crew dragged their captain away, the man wept openly like a child. Laurence looked down at the misery and hatred in their faces turned briefly towards him.

The other French captain submitted to being bound, and was put aboard Maximus while his dragon called to him anxiously. 'Is he fit to fly, Berkley?' Laurence asked.

'I am only a little jarred,' Maximus said, trying to nose at his own chest. Berkley's surgeon Gaiters was already palpating the massive ribs with his hands, carefully, in either direction.

'I do not believe there is a crack,' he said, 'but a few days' rest—'

Berkley snorted. 'After this? Not unless we were in Scotland. They will be out in force after us.'

'No,' Laurence said, still cold, 'they will not. They cannot afford it.'

In the morning the first reports came from their little spies. The French heavyweights were retreating south, towards London, forced back into territory more thoroughly under French control, where their hunger could be satisfied. The rest of the combat-weight beasts melted away after them, more every day as the stores depleted, until nothing remained but the small couriers. Now their infantry were exposed, unless they kept to their encampments; in which case they would starve. A few large bands ventured out with artillery, but could not find enough for all, and in desperation soon broke into smaller parties for foraging. These were at their mercy.

Blue pins marking the small French companies that daily marched across his maps, were plucked one by one and laid back in their tin, and Laurence rinsed blood mechanically off his hands at the wash-basin. Very little thought was now required, and he was glad of it, distantly.

Their own supply gave them no difficulty. If they landed near a town or a village, meat would somehow be managed for them and the dragons, even if the villagers themselves went hungry as a consequence. Occasionally the French tried again to pursue them, attempts orchestrated from further south, but warning reached them so early that they had merely to draw back a little, and let the dragons sleep, while a flock of little ferals kept watch.

It was the first week of March, and they had been raiding for nearly two months when Arkady arrived in a great flurry of noise, carrying Tharkay and with three of his ferals for escort. He at once began to parade before Temeraire and the others, telling tell them of his adventures since their last meeting. He had only been patrolling with the others, but by his account he had fought off hordes of French dragons and captured many prizes, and he bragged that they too would do well, now he had come to join them; at which Temeraire laid back his ruff in irritation.

'I have a message for you, from Wellesley,' Tharkay said to Laurence, and went inside with him. The implacable maps were laid out upon a makeshift table, a door laid over two old trestles, inside the small cottage where he had sheltered overnight. Tharkay stood in the doorway looking out while Laurence opened the letter. Their camp was a strange, silent place: no prisoners but the one solitary French captain, sitting desolately outside a hut with his hands loosely tied and bound to a stake in the ground, under the guard of a couple of Granby's bell-men. The massacred trees, which the dragons used for their sweeping, lay in a great heap at the edge of camp and the bare branches dark with dried blood. Every man went about his work silently, and without either fuss or satisfaction; they had killed fifty men that morning.

Wellesley's new orders had not much changed. He directed their efforts more particularly towards the eastern coast, and carefully avoided suggesting what those efforts should be; all was left unstated. Wellesley closed with, *and you are welcome to this jabbering creature and his fellows, if you can make better use of them.*

'Very good,' Laurence said, setting it aside. He drew out the map of the North Sea coast, to consider it. There had been some raiding near Stickney, last week, and at an outpost near Cromer, one of the places the Fleur-de-Nuits would likely be landing with fresh troops when they could get across. 'They must send out foragers there twice a week,' Laurence said to Tharkay. 'I will send you there with Berkley, which will free the rest of us to go after them at Stickney. If you begin near the outpost and circle outwards, you are likely to find the foragers soon enough; there ought to be no more than fifty men. They have stopped sending out larger bands. Berkley will approach from their forward direction, and you will cut off their avenue of retreat—'

'I beg your pardon,' Tharkay said. 'I prefer not to.'

Laurence paused; his hand arrested in mid-air above the map.

'Arkady, I am sure, will oblige,' Tharkay said, 'but someone else must captain him. I regret,' he added, with a lash of irony, 'I have not the luxury of setting aside the veneer of civilization; I must be a little more careful. A temporary viciousness may be pardonable in a gentleman, even admirable, but it would forever brand *me* as a savage. Laurence, what are you doing?'

The question was simple enough, and ought to have afforded a dozen answers. 'Killing soldiers,' Laurence said, at last, 'most of whom are starving, and vicious, so they give us still better excuse.'

It had the poor advantage of being true. Giving it voice, Laurence tasted all its ugliness on his tongue. He sat down and put a hand over his mouth, and found his face was wet. He could not speak again for a little while, struggling to master himself. At last he said to Tharkay, hoarsely, 'If you will not go, what will you do?'

He did not mean the question in the immediate sense, and Tharkay did not take it so. He shrugged in his restrained way, the movement of a hand only. 'There is work enough in the world,' he answered, 'and little enough time.'

'And no one to decide it, but yourself,' Laurence said. 'No authority but your own conscience.'

'There are authorities to choose from,' Tharkay said, 'to suit any action. I prefer to keep the choice a little closer.'

It seemed to Laurence the most miserably solitary existence imaginable; isolated by more than distance or even disdain. 'How do you bear it? The choice, and all the consequences thereof, alone?'

'Perhaps practice has reconciled me; or,' Tharkay said dryly, 'perhaps I simply have less natural inclination to hold myself responsible for the sins of the world, rather than for just my own.'

Laurence covered his face with his hands and shut his eyes against the filtered reddish light. The hayloft smell of straw and vanished horses, warm and familiar, and the sulphur tang of the dragons outside, woodsmoke and Arkady's smug prattle, broken occasionally by Temeraire's more resonant protests.

'Very well,' he said, and went out, leaving the orders upon the table.

Chapter Fifteen

'Forgive me,' Laurence said. Temeraire had settled himself for the night, curled up comfortably in an old ploughed field behind the barn, fallow now and full of soft dry grass underneath the snow. They were alone, or nearly so. Demane, Sipho, Roland and Allen were all tucked into the curve of Temeraire's haunch, under a little lean-to which Demane and Roland had worked out of a tent and a few sticks. But all four were fast asleep. Arkady at last had stopped telling stories, and was now busily making up to Iskierka, in order to sleep near the heat she gave off. Temeraire had sniffed a little in disdain, and curled his own tail about the lean-to, just to be sure his crew would sleep warm, and dry besides.

He did not at once understand what Laurence was apologizing for, until Laurence had explained a little. 'Forgive me,' he repeated. 'Bad enough that I used myself so; but to have used you likewise, is unpardonable—'

'But Laurence,' Temeraire said, at once glad and baffled, 'it was *my* fault, surely. It was my notion we should go to France in the first place. Only, I did not know that they should take your capital, and your rank; and I am so sorry—'

'I am not,' Laurence said. 'I should give more than that, and count it cheap, to preserve my conscience. I am ashamed to have submitted to despair so far as to ever have thought differently.'

Temeraire did not wish to argue. Laurence sounded like himself again, if still rather drawn, and that was worth anything; but privately he could not help resent that conscience seemed so very expensive, and yet had no substantial form which one might admire, and show off to one's company.

'But,' he said, heroically, 'I did mean what I said, dear Laurence, about the talon-sheaths, and I do wish you would sell them, and buy some new things for yourself. I would like my conscience to be just as clear.'

Laurence replied with a touch of amusement, 'I am sorry to have neglected my dress, if it has given you so wretched a notion of my finances, but I am not so wholly impoverished.' More gently he added, 'There will be no more pavilions, I am afraid, but I hope I need not be an embarrassment to you.'

'You would never be,' Temeraire said, and nudged Laurence with his nose.

Laurence stroked his muzzle. 'I do not know what our course will be hereafter,' he said. 'I owe apologies, more than this, and must make them; and then I must write to Wellesley—I know not how, but I must tell him we will not continue in this manner. There will be no more of this massacre without quarter. We will manage our prisoners somehow; and we will seek out rather than flee from any force which has a gun, or a few dragons.'

Temeraire had not known how worried he had been, until the source of the distress had lifted. His spirits rose effervescently at Laurence's words. 'How happy I am to hear it,' he said, adding, 'and I am sure we will take a great many 'prizes.' However brave a face Laurence wished to put on it, Temeraire felt this could not be anything but reassuring.

'More likely,' Laurence said, 'Wellesley will order me to come back and be hanged at once.'

'If he does, you shall not go,' Temeraire said indignantly, flaring his ruff.

'No,' Laurence said, after a moment. 'I shall not.'

Sir,

I must beg your leave to acquaint you with an Alteration in the methods of our company, to which I hope you will not object, for humanity's sake, despite some increase in Inconvenience and in Danger, which all those officers in His Majesty's service presently reporting to me, and those dragons likewise, have gladly agreed to support, venturing rather their persons than their conscience.

The letter was written with difficulty, and was carried by Gherni.

They established their new camp between North Seaton and Newbiggin-by-the-Sea, and began to put up a stockade manned with volunteers from the countryside. 'We are making a nice honey-pot for them to rescue,' Sutton commented, as the dragons cheerfully tore up trees: they had no guns to defend the walls.

'Then at least they will have spent the time and effort to come for them, which they would otherwise use to bring fresh troops over from France,' Laurence said. In any case, no-one objected; it shamed him again to see how greatly relieved the other officers and dragons both were by the alteration in their practice. He expected daily an answer from Wellesley, relieving him of the command, and wondered what he should say to the other captains when it came; or if Wellesley had found some other officer to carry on the work.

But no letter came. Three days later a great noise arose in the morning around their camp. Many ferals burst in upon them eager with news, and before their combined chatter could be worked out, the great dragons of the Corps were already landing everywhere, laden with men. One company after another were put off onto the ground, with supplies and artillery, then the dragons leapt away again with scarcely more than a call of greeting. Above them more dragons were flying past, the entire British army was on the move.

Wellesley arrived a little past noon, and commandeered the derelict barn, where the crews had been sleeping, for his headquarters. 'Out, the rest of you,' he said, jerking his head at the crew and even the aides sweeping the floor, fixing Laurence in place with a cold look. 'Cleverly done, Laurence,' Wellesley said, when they were alone. 'Not so simple after all, are you?'

Laurence was silent, uncertain, until Wellesley added, 'I will not waste my breath asking who on my staff passed you the news, but you will understand me: if you have the infernal gall to waste my time *now*, with some damned attempt at extortion, I will shoot you myself.'

And then Laurence understood. Wellesley thought his letter had been timed deliberately, on the eve of his southward advance, to establish Wellesley's responsibility for the slaughter of the French irregulars.

'I will not hear a damned word about pardon from you,' Wellesley said, 'not a one. In three days' time we will meet Bonaparte, and if I win, no one will give a damn whatever accusations you like to make. And of course,' he added, icily, 'you will be well looked-after in the event of a loss. Rowley!' he bellowed. 'Get my desk in here, and call in the general staff.'

302

Officers began to pour in, struggling under tables and maps and chairs. Laurence was at once pressed away from Wellesley as they thronged around him, and any reply he might have made was lost in the crowd.

He urgently wished to push through, to seize Wellesley and to argue; but he forced himself to be still. It did not matter. He could make no denial Wellesley would believe. In any case, that Wellesley thought him a blackguard for refusing to continue, rather than for having begun at all, made little difference; Laurence had earned the condemnation, and he might as well bear it for the wrong cause.

'Emily,' he said, turning instead, and beckoned her into the building. She had been peering in at the door cautiously, to one side of the stampede. 'Take Demane and go and get those hayloft doors open,' he told her, 'so that Temeraire and the other dragons can hear.'

He went outside. It was already becoming impossibly cramped upon the ground, though more trees had been uprooted and a broad avenue opened up to the road. Every dragon who had landed and dropped off their men soon jostled for space at the hayloft.

'We shan't manage like this,' Jane said, Excidium having landed after a warning hiss cleared him a place. 'Only dragons over the rank of lieutenant may stay: the rest of you must go on with the rest of the army and get the news from your officers or your captains. We have had to give them all ranks, thanks to your Temeraire's splendid scheme,' she added dryly to Laurence. 'The rest of them turned sulky and wanted epaulets of their own. Frivolous creatures.' She patted Excidium, who looked rather smug with two epaulets of deep fire-orange, to match the edges of his massive wings.

They had scarcely made a little order, and crammed themselves into the barn, before Wellesley began. His aides put up a map of Chatham roads, and the mouth of the Thames where it spilled into the Channel, with all the small towns and villages thereabout. Their positions were marked, and a low murmur went about: their backs would be to the sea.

'Well, gentlemen, I see you like our position less than I hope our friend Bonaparte will do,' Wellesley said. 'The Navy and the Corps have all but cut off his connection to the Continent, and the countryside has risen. He loses now a hundred men a day, and each week two dragons, for lack of supply. He can ill afford to refuse us a pitched battle if we offer it to him on what I trust he will think reasonable terms.'

The terms seemed indeed reasonable, from the French perspective. Laurence wondered if Wellesley meant to stiffen the backs of the soldiers by denying them any avenue of retreat save through the French troops before them.

'Colonels Featherstone and Bree, you will take the centre. Your position is the most essential: you must hold, until you are signalled,' Wellesley said. 'Yield before the moment is ripe and he will split our forces, and destroy us at his leisure. You are not to advance, under any circumstances. You are only to form square and hold. Colonel Rethlow, you will back them with the artillery.

'The cavalry will take position on either flank, with the rest of our infantry positioned here, and here,' he indicated, 'and the Corps will hold off any French attempt to charge our centre from aloft. All our design, gentlemen, as I hope you gather,' he went on, 'is to hold fast while they spend the best part of their strength, and divert their attacks from our centre until the signal is given.

'The order of march then sounded, we will gradually withdraw along either flank—' Two of the aides heaved up a fresh map, with new positions marked, marking the French the at very centre. '—and cut him off from his aerial support and whatever reserves he may have yet held back. Then we launch our attack against his rear. General Paget, it will be your task to ensure that Bonaparte remains within our circle. General Ollen, your artillery will be directed towards his reserves, rather than the main body of his force, to keep them from rejoining him.

'Our aim, gentlemen, is the capture of this tyrant, and an end to his perpetual war mongering. I will be satisfied with nothing less, and I assure you their Lordships have agreed with my judgment.'

Having given this brief and unsettling plan of battle, he concluded and dismissed them all, adding, 'Colonel Featherstone, a word with you.' He drew the man aside privately, thus blocking many other officers of the general staff, who plainly wanted a word.

Laurence went out to Temeraire, who had rather regretfully submitted to being rigged out in carrying-harness. 'We are taking this company,' he said, as Laurence came, 'or so he tells me.' The infantry officer nodded to Laurence, a little stiffly, and touched his hat.

'Very good,' Laurence answered, and stifled his doubts. To risk dividing their forces, yielding the centre to Napoleon and then directing all their force deliberately between him and his reserve, seemed a terrible risk to run. If it made Napoleon's capture more likely, the plan also made it likelier that the French would simply overrun them. But Wellesley was not a fool, and if he meant to tolerate the weaknesses and dangers of his planned course, he had good cause. He had certainly taken pains to evade any questions, and any protests which might have been made against him to the ministers, by delaying the conference until the deployment already had begun. There was nothing for it now, but to trust him.

The degree of excitement which Temeraire felt, expressed itself nearly as pain: his expanded ruff drew a pounding tightness all along the line of his neck. He tried now and again to curl himself for a little rest, but it was impossible. No more wretched raids, no more hiding, no more carrying about anyone; they would have a real battle at last.

Their coverts were also established on the coast, but on the flanks of the battlefield, to north and south. From their camp Temeraire could see the dotted lines of fishing huts scattered around them, showing a few distant yellow candle-gleams. The rocky coastline was a dark mass against the faintly lighter sky, and the steady ongoing roar of the surf was behind them. It was still dark. The voices of the Fleur de Nuits, scouting their positions, echoed overhead. Occasionally a flare was shot off to blind them, or a few dragons chosen by lot went up to chase a few of them away.

Laurence rose a little before dawn, and climbed down from Temeraire's back, to look out towards the battlefield.

'Is Napoleon there?' Temeraire asked Laurence, eagerly. 'Have they come?'

'Yes,' Laurence said. 'They are in pickets. Put your head down and you will see them.'

Temeraire lowered his head and tipped it so he aimed one eye along the ground. Against the deep grey of the lightning sky, he could see the tiny narrow lines of the pickets on top of a hill. The narrow posts were little more than sticks, each leaning a little in one direction or another, and the lumpy dark shapes at their base, the sleeping soldiers kept in their columns. Overhead, the stars were dimming: a thick grey fog was rolling in from the water, as the sky grew paler.

'It is time,' Laurence said. Fellowes stirred behind Temeraire's leg, and yawning rose to see to the harness.

Temeraire rumbled softly, deep in his throat, and called, 'Majestatis, Ballista; it is time to get everyone up.'

'I still do not like this plan,' Perscitia said, fretfully, as they all ate the fresh cattle, saved for this morning. 'I do not see what the use is in fighting so hard to keep them from the centre, and then letting them have it after all; why not give it to them at once? And are you quite sure they are there?'

The question was not as odd as it seemed. The fog had grown so thick they could see nothing from the ground but the trees about the clearing: the presence of their own army had to be taken on faith, much less the enemy's.

'Yes, I am quite sure,' Temeraire said. 'Laurence pointed them out to me, just before morning. We will see them better once we are aloft, I am sure.'

Rain fell in a thin icy drizzle as they went up. They had drawn lots to see who should have which shift, as Admiral Roland had insisted that they should not all fight at once, and Temeraire could see the sense in keeping some back, when the battle might be very long. He was however, very relieved to be leading the first rank, and hoped privately that the fog might last; and that perhaps Laurence would not notice when it was midday and time for their own rest.

He could not see much better from above after all. Pockets of mist sat like seething cauldrons in every low valley, and great towering clouds were rolling majestically in from the sea, so high they engulfed him as much as the ground below, and filled with gusts of sharp rain that pattered noisily on his wings. As they flew on towards the battlefield, he began to glimpse the soldiers of their companies on the march, all arranged a little differently, like patches of cloth in odd sizes, some long like ribbons and only five men across, others great crowds upon the field.

All of the shapes rippled smoothly over the ground, columns of white and black and blue and red, gliding over the hills, and down into the valleys to be swallowed up in the fog. Even so, he could still hear the strange noise they made marching along. It was less a thumping, which he

307

might have expected, than a regular hiss as their clothing or their boots brushed against one another. The wet ground muffled their steps. The trumpets sounded, a joyful encouraging noise no matter who had blown them; and the cannon spoke in orange flame to announce that the battle had been joined, somewhere.

The French dragons were somewhere farther back, Temeraire supposed, peering uselessly; trees lashed with fogbanks barred his view of the French rear. 'There,' Laurence called, and Temeraire followed the line of his arm to see their own centre established.

Temeraire was pleased that, to his eye, their force was by far the more handsome. A great many of the Frenchmen wore long drab coats, with scarcely a touch of colour, or otherwise white breeches and white shirts—none too clean Temeraire noted—with very ordinary dark blue coats. He much preferred the vivid red coats which dominated their own army. Several companies of soldiers in the centre wore colourful, patterned skirts, and of course their union flag was by far the more interesting.

'And if they *do* have eagles,' Temeraire said to Laurence, 'all the better for us to take them away. Laurence, do you not like those skirts they are wearing, over there?'

'Those are the Scots Greys cavalry,' Laurence said, looking through his glass, 'and those are the Coldstream Guard, beside them. If anyone can hold the centre, they will; but good God. Bonaparte will pound them without mercy.'

'We will keep the dragons off,' Temeraire said. 'I am only a little worried that at the end we are meant to encircle Bonaparte, and not his aerial support. What if Lien should escape?' Privately, Temeraire felt it was rather peculiar to take so many pains to capture Napoleon and not Lien, who was a good deal larger, and possessed the divine wind.

'Let us hope for such success as will make that a matter

for concern,' Laurence said. 'But if Bonaparte is taken, she will surrender, I expect. Although she may realize he cannot be held hostage for her behaviour in the usual manner.'

'Here they come,' Majestatis called, wheeling around. Through the sheen of rain, Temeraire could see the dark shadows of the French dragons coming on. Below them the front lines of the British infantry began to form into their large bristling squares to receive the charge. Soldiers stood shoulder-to-shoulder, about an open centre. The front rank knelt with bayonets outward, the second aiming over their heads, and the third pointed upwards. Long pole-arms were thrust deeply into the ground just behind them, steadied by their bearers: the gleaming broad fan-shaped blades straight up, and the narrower pikes angled backwards, to catch any dragon attempting to strike at the line of the square from behind.

The French dragons were coming with bombs and nets, to try and overcome such measures; they had also stolen Perscitia's trick of uprooting trees, which they plainly meant to use broom-like to sweep gaps into the squares at a distance.

'Now, Temeraire,' Laurence called urgently, and Temeraire dashed ahead to meet the French skirmishers, roaring with delight. A Roi-de-Vitesse came out of the fog. He was armed with a tall, slender birch tree, white and bare-branched. He dove to avoid Temeraire's charge, making determinedly for the front lines of the first square. His crew fired a spray of rifle-fire up at Temeraire's belly as they passed. A quick hot sting of pain—he had been hit, but Temeraire only sniffed when Laurence asked; it was nothing, nothing at all.

He threw himself over with an elegant, corkscrewing twist, and plunged low in pursuit of the smaller French dragon. Dimly aware of the bayonets looming ahead, gleaming and silver as the fog swirled away from them, Temeraire heard Laurence say something to Demane about the bombs, but

309

the French dragon filled most of his view. It was very quick, but Temeraire stretched his wings, cupped all the air he could and flung himself after. He would not let it at the square; he would not be outrun, and with a lunge, he got near enough to put his claws into the other dragon's tail.

The Roi-de-Vitesse squalled and tried to jerk away. Temeraire hooked his talons and beat backwards furiously, while a couple of small bombs were lobbed over his shoulder, at the French dragon's crew as they tried to bring their rifle-fire to bear again. 'Tenez-vous bien,' the dragon cried to his crew, squirming to throw off the bombs and flailing his birch as best he could with Temeraire's grip upon him.

Temeraire only just stifled an undignified yelp as the tree-top fetched him a sharp slap across the neck and belly. The branches were springy and stung painfully. But he kept his head, despite the very unpleasant sensation, and managed to seize hold of the tree in his jaws and wrest it away. Disarmed, the French beast gave over his attempt and flew away hurriedly for the safety of his own covert, his bleeding tail dripping behind him.

'Ha,' Temeraire called after the vanquished beast, and curling his talons about the trunk, he lashed the air experimentally a few times. 'Laurence, perhaps we might go at their ranks, with this?' he proposed, over his shoulder. He could see a company of French soldiers emerging slowly from the mist, and he was quite sure the tree would answer nicely in reverse.

'We must stay near the squares,' Laurence answered, 'and not advance. Pray call those Reapers back, on your left. They have already let themselves be lured too far.'

Temeraire sighed a little, but he threw the birch tree into the sea, and turned to corral Chalcedony and the others. They were darting at a Grand Chevalier, lunging in at her head and nipping at her flanks, but the big dragon, rather than turning on them in earnest or fleeing properly, was slyly retreating a little by little, luring them back towards the French lines so the smaller dragons could slip past and make their own attempts against the squares.

'You are meant to be an officer, it is your duty to keep everyone else from flying off,' Temeraire said sternly to Chalcedony, when he had rounded them and they were all flying back towards the squares.

'Well, Cantarella has the epaulet,' Chalcedony said, a rather craven defence.

'Oh!' Cantarella said, and nipped the edge of his wing. He yelped and twisted away. 'Very well, then I am in command now, you have all heard him say as much,' she declared, and hitched her epaulet forward. It was a bit sodden with rain, but still noticeable against her pale yellow and white. 'You may be sure *I* will not let us go off field again.'

They did not have to go far afield, anyway, to have all the fighting they desired. the French were coming steadily after them, and Temeraire wheeled to meet them with a will.

By midday, they were driven further aloft. The French had established an artillery emplacement at the centre, with a shield of pepper guns and several of the cannon elevated to strike at any dragon dipping low.

The air was colder and cleaner as they rose out of range, and more clouds streamed past to divorce them from the noise and fury of the battlefield below. Their own struggle was quieter, the whistling air and the muffling clouds stealing all but fragments of roaring, and the occasional pop-pop of rifle fire. The French had abandoned their trees and netting, encumbering them too greatly against a determined aerial defence. Laurence felt more discouraged than pleased, however, by the speed with which the experiment had been adopted, tried, and cast off.

He could feel Temeraire's energy flagging. They had been fighting now for six hours, and there was little chance to pause and rest. Many of the soldiers below were lying upon the ground, out of the way of cannon-fire; Wellesley had ordered they might do so, when not engaged. There was nowhere similar for the dragons to land, except the coverts where they had slept, a mile away. Behind the British lines there was only the roar of the sea, invisible beneath the blanketing fog, and on either flank the cavalry horses stood nervously shifting, pawing at the earth.

The French had abandoned cavalry entirely. It ought to give away an advantage: dragons would not be risked on charges in the face of artillery, as the cold calculation of warfare allowed horses to be, and the British horses were all hooded now, blinders cupping their eyes so they could only see straight ahead, with fragrant sachets over their nostrils so they could not smell the dragons. A little past noon, Laurence heard the drumming of the first charge below.

The heavy British cavalry were splendid in their rush, all of them shouting furiously and waving scimitars, the standard flying out behind them. They were sent at a battalion of the French infantry, a manoeuvre to gain some breathing room. Nearly every French company now pressed steady fire against the Coldstream Guards, which Napoleon had evidently marked as the linchpins of the British centre. The French battalion did not break, instead they formed square themselves; a peculiar square, double-sized, with a great empty gap in the centre.

The cavalry committed to their charge. They flew across the gap, in the face of the steady musketry, horses falling with terrible human shrieks, men flung off and crushed beneath the hooves of their own mounts. 'Laurence, where is that Pou de Ciel going?' Temeraire said urgently, pointing. One of the small drab French dragons had broken away from the skirmish and was diving quickly toward its own lines.

The Pou de Ciel landed directly within the French square, and doing so, brought to life the relative nature of their size. Pou de Ciel were a lightweight breed, just barely combat weight, and this one was perhaps only six or seven tons; yet it loomed hugely over the ranks of soldiers, its great taloned claws flexing behind the silver rows of bayonets as it roared with a red mouth full of teeth.

Even hooded and perfumed, the horses would not run directly at a dragon. The cavalry-charge wavered, and broke. The horses' necks bowed deeply, or pulled frantically away to either side, as they fell into a stumbling gait and fought the reins. One, out in front recoiled too late and slid on its hind legs as it came too close. The Pou de Ciel leaned over and snatched the horse off the ground with one clawed forehand, shook the rider unceremoniously off onto the ground, and opening its jaws wide took off the flailing horse's head with one bite; the French dragons had likely been on short commons for a while now.

The effect of sight upon the remaining cavalry was pronounced; the horses were immediately given their way, and wheeled away back to the British lines, most never having come within ten yards of the infantry square at all. The Pou de Ciel leapt away as soon as the cavalry had fled, before British artillery could be brought to bear against it, having had a little rest and a little supper besides.

Further to the rear of the French army, Laurence saw more of their dragons dropping down for a rest, out of artillery-range and amidst the infantry companies, who did not flinch.

'Well, I do not need a rest,' Temeraire said bravely, 'but if I did, there are Ballista and Requiescat coming now, with the fresh shift. I suppose I would not mind setting down for just a minute, perhaps,' he added, 'and a little something to eat.'

'I think we cannot,' Laurence said, grimly. 'He is sending in his reserves.' The fog was thinning now a little, blowing away from the land. Far to the rear of the French lines dragons were leaping into the air, one after another. And now the advantage would tell: none of the French dragons, with their short and frequent rests, were withdrawing. There would be no rest for Temeraire, or any of the British dragons who had been aloft and fighting since first light.

Temeraire pulled up abruptly, so Laurence was flung against his leather straps. A determined crowd of six little Garde de Lyons charged him in a body, and began belabouring his head and neck wildly, shrieking in exaggerated voices, batting with wings and claws.

Temeraire backwinged with two mighty strokes and roared to scatter them. The tremor of the divine wind knocked them back, but in those few moments, the enormous Grand Chevalier they had seen earlier came crashing past, and threw herself at the square of the Coldstream Guards.

The pikes and bayonets were stiffened, but she did not come down upon them directly. Instead she struck the ground before the front ranks, so heavily many of the men were flung off their feet, and turning round roared full in all their faces. It was a moral assault only, but a dragon the size of a large barn roaring less than ten paces away might make the bravest man blanch. Bayonets wavered and dipped, and then twenty riflemen stood up on her back and fired a terrible and concentrated volley into the stunned ranks.

A knot of men fell, opening a vulnerable gap in the wall of the square, and the dragon thrust her massive foreleg into the open space and swept it along the line, all the way to the corner of the square, crushing and knocking down men and pikes like blades of grass. Temeraire roared furiously and dived towards her, but one of the Garde de Lyon flung itself into his path.

'That,' Temeraire said furiously, 'is quite enough; the soldiers are smaller still than you.' He seized the little dragon's neck in his jaws and with a jerk of his head broke it in a single dreadful snap. He let the beast fall out of the sky, a little scrap of scarlet and blue, his small handful of crewmen scattering like falling leaves through the air.

However, the Garde de Lyon had bought the necessary time with its life. Below, the Grand Chevalier had got off the ground again and with an escort of joyfully roaring Pêcheurs and Pou de Ciels was already flying back to the shelter of her lines. 'The coward,' Temeraire said bitterly, watching her escape behind the cover of French artillery. The square was trying desperately to re-form, some soldiers even crawling back to their places on hands and knees, too dazed yet to stand, dragging their muskets along behind them.

Laurence heard the horns, thin and reedy, and everywhere the French were suddenly advancing. The knot of fishing huts on the British left flank, now came suddenly under a savage bombardment. The fresh enemy dragons flung themselves over it, casting down loads of munitions, until a rush of infantry poured over the low encircling fences and charged into the huts, one after another. Black smoke poured out of the windows as the British colours came down.

If they meant to give up the centre, it must be soon. But Wellesley gave no order. He observed the battle from a ridge on the right flank, where a few tents had been erected for the headquarters. At the moment he was looking out to sea, gauging perhaps the weather, which had begun at last to clear, before sweeping his glass back towards the French rear. Laurence followed his line of sight with his own glass, and saw Napoleon's standard in the thinning mist, and the Emperor himself in his plain grey coat and black hat, mounted on a white horse and backed by the gleaming and polished ranks of his Guard.

As he watched, Napoleon raised a hand, and with a single economical gesture set ten thousand men in motion. The word ran along the French lines, and one after another of those marshalled companies began their steady march forward, into the British centre. The Emperor turned towards the fishing huts, just taken, and the Guard followed in steady ranks as his company shifted forward.

On either flank, the dragons of the Corps were fighting fiercely to hold off the advance, but they too were tired. On the right, the great Flamme de Gloire, Accendare, loosed a torrent of flame against Lily's formation, and to his horror Laurence saw Messoria recoil, her wing blackened and smoking. She did not fall out of the sky, but reeled heavily against little Nitidus, fouling his flight, sending a few of his men tumbling down through the sky.

Two of Accendare's wingmen darted in to press the advantage, and boarders leaped across to Lily's back. She twisted and plunged, trying to shake them loose, and in the opening a spectacular gold, blue and red Honneur d'Or went through the shield, diving towards the massed ranks of British cavalry with a great roar, his crew fired off flares from his shoulders as he spread his wings wide.

The horses shrilled and bucked in terror, and stampeded madly straight ahead, pouring into the open field, and providing the French with a shield against the British artillery. The advancing ranks of the French infantry broke now into a steady jog, their bayonets fixed low as they came. Over the French camp, dragons formed into line: heavyweights and middleweights, with a screen of lightweights and courier beasts before them. Together they began a slow, measured advance, one wing-beat after another.

* * *

'Laurence, if we do not give them the centre now, I think they will take it themselves,' Temeraire said, doubtfully. Still Wellesley did not give the order. The signal-flags on the hill, when Temeraire could get a glimpse of them through the fog, still showed *hold fast*.

'I know,' Laurence said. 'We must keep off the advance, as long as we can. If you will break their line at scattered points, and engage the heavyweights—'

'Wait, wait,' Perscitia cried shrilly from a distance, and Temeraire looked over, surprised to see her flapping madly towards them. She looked very odd. Her artillery crew were upon her back, tied on with ropes; they in turn were helping to hold on to enormous bundles of carrying-harnesses, which had been used to bring the army hence. The harnesses had been made hastily of silk and linen, Dresses, curtains and tablecloths all sacrificed to the cause, many in bright colours, so she looked as though she were wearing an enormous fringed skirt dangling over her sides and legs, just barely shy of her wings.

'We are not going to retreat!' Temeraire said, indignantly. 'We have not lost the battle; and we shan't, either,' he added determinedly.

'No, no,' she said, panting, as she came up to them. The harnesses were really so hopelessly tangled up that they could not have been picked in less than an hour. 'Take—' she said, gulping for breath, and waggled some of them at him.

Dubiously he took a bundle of it in his claws, and discovered it was wet; and it did not smell very nice, either, like the smell when grog was passed out, aboard a ship. 'What have you done with them?' he said, and then, 'Ow,' jerking his head back; there was also something sharp and bitter, which stung his nose.

'Liquor,' Perscitia said, finding her breath, as other dragons came and took more of the bundles from her, 'and also some tar, I think; and there is some pepper on them too, so do not sniff them. Where is Iskierka? She must—Oh, there you are. No,' she said, resisting as Iskierka reached for the cloth, 'you shan't take one, you must set them all alight, as we drop them—'

'Oh, that is easy,' Iskierka said. The Anglewings each snatched a bundle, and the Grey Coppers, and a good many of the ferals: all the quicker dragons, the little ones.

'Hurry, hurry,' Temeraire called. The French dragons were coming on slow, but they were coming, and down below their infantry was already engaged in a dreadful struggle, bayonet-to-bayonet, which was spilling blood over the field and weakening the British squares. the French design plainly meant to leave them vulnerable to aerial attack.

He led them high aloft. Then, spreading out along in parallel to the French line they let the bundles go. Iskierka shot after them eagerly, flames licking from her jaws in one burst after another. The unravelling bundles caught with bright blue and yellow flames as they fell through the air.

The French dragons recoiled from the fireballs dropping into their faces. 'Now, at once,' Laurence said urgently, pointing at the weaknesses in their line. 'That Chanson de Guerre, and that Defendeur-Brave—'

'Ballista, do you see?' Temeraire called, and she waved her tail like a flag to show she had heard. A swarm of Yellow Reapers dashed after her as she charged the marbled yellow-brown Chanson de Guerre. 'Quickly, with me,' Temeraire said, to the lightweights, 'and do you want to come with us?' he asked Perscitia.

'No, I do not,' she said, hastily circling away, 'and anyway,' she called back over her shoulder, 'I must go see if I can make more of those bundles; although I think I have used all the spirits—'

Temeraire did not have time to listen to any more, they

were hurrying down straight for the Defendeur, who had swerved to avoid a particularly large fireball, that left a thick trail of smoke behind it. His flank lay exposed for a moment, unprotected by the line, and the Grey Copper Rictus darted in and opened a great gash along the line of his shoulder, nearly severing one strap of his harness.

The Defendeur bellowed in pain and hunched himself towards the wound. It was a wide gaping slice starkly red against the golden-brown and green of his hide. 'Hah!' Rictus called, and then squalled as the Defendeur snapped out his hook-ended tail and caught him full in the belly: a more dreadful and dangerous wound, on so much smaller a beast, and Rictus was borne crying away by one of the Anglewings.

But he had opened an avenue for attack, and Velocita flung herself at the Defendeur's rear, baiting his slashing tail and swerving this way and that, so that the other Anglewings and the Grey Coppers could make darting attempts on the Defendeur's head. When all of the riflemen had been flung off their feet, Minnow threw herself into the melee, landed upon the big dragon's back, and snatched away one of the men in her talons.

'There, that's your captain,' she called, waving the poor man, and the French dragon roared furiously and went after her in a rush, bowling over one of the Anglewings and breaking the French line completely, as Minnow raced away towards the British clearings with her prisoner.

'That is a little hard,' Temeraire said, feeling rather sorry for the poor dragon, and making a note that Minnow should never again ride upon his own back while Laurence was there. He had not thought she was quite so unscrupulous as to steal in the middle of a fight. But he could not deny it had been very handy luring the big dragon away, as now he could clear away great swaths of middleweights, just by roaring to either side of the gap the heavyweight had left.

Requiescat was engaged with the Grand Chevalier in the next section of the line. Although he had a little edge in weight, her advantage in having a crew was telling against him. A steady rifle-fire was peppering his massive sides and had left a great many small holes visible in his wings, and she cleverly took every opportunity to position herself higher aloft, where he was forced to dodge the bombs her bell-men flung against him. Temeraire saw that on their flank, the harnessed dragons of the Corps were only just barely holding off the advancing right wing of l'Armée de l'Air, and realized that they would soon be forced into a tangled mess.

'There are ships coming,' Majestatis said, looping nearby.

'What?' Temeraire said.

'Ships,' Majestatis said laconically. 'Out to sea. You can see them if you go over that cloud.'

And then the trumpets were at last sounding the order to yield the centre, with a shrill note, and there was no time to look. The squares below were falling back into column and marching away, and Temeraire made sure that everyone was flying away properly, to either flank as they were meant to do. 'Remember, we are to meet again behind their lines!' he called urgently, nipping an over-excited Anglewing who had started to fly the wrong way.

The French soldiers were charging forward more quickly now, and their dragons were stooping. 'Surely we ought not just fly away? They will have our men in a moment,' Temeraire said urgently over his shoulder to Laurence.

'Go!' Laurence said; he was looking through his glass at the sea. 'Go at once! You must get clear of the centre, and aloft—'

Temeraire pulled away, with a last anxious look over his shoulder; but as he did, he was startled to see the last of the Coldstream Guards throwing themselves flat upon the ground instead of marching away further. Then a roar of thunder erupted from the fog-bank, with smoke and orange flame.

He broke the top of the cloud-bank and in that moment saw them: sixteen ships of the line, and the enormous gold-blazoned *Victory* at their head, with Admiral Nelson's flag flying from the mast. They unleashed their full broadsides directly into the front rank of the French dragons and men, clouds of black smoke enveloping them even as the last of the fog spilled off their sails and prows.

The French dragons came down in shocking numbers. The heavyweights, were struck one after another, with cannonballs; wings shattered and bones cracked, they came down into their own infantry below them. Only a few managed, with faltering beats, to carry themselves out over the remaining laggard lines of British infantry and smash them. The great Grand Chevalier dragged so far along the ground that she ended at last in the surf, shattered and still, her head rising and falling limply with the break as the waves crashed upon her shoulders.

Temeraire felt a queer, confusing shudder of sympathy, wanting to bring his wings forward, as if to protect his own breast. The trumpets were blowing again, and the British artillery on the flanks opened a deadly hail of canister-shot against the rear and flanks of the French infantry, chasing them forward into the endless rain of cannon-fire from the ships.

'Temeraire!' Laurence called. Excidium was already roaring out the signal, and they were not yet in place! Temeraire flung himself hastily back, he no longer felt tired: the urgency of the moment trembled along his wings. He gathered the others who also had been distracted by the dreadful spectacle, and they flew to join the dragons of the Corps in a great single body, nearly a hundred of them in all, and as one they roared and charged the French reserves.

The French soldiers were already reeling from so visible a disaster. The falling dragons could be seen for a good mile, and the wind was blowing harder now, clearing the clouds. Nelson's flagship was plainly visible off shore, and the fleet in line-of-battle ranged alongside *Victory*: the *Minotaur* and the *Prince of Wales*, and all the rest of the ships returned from Copenhagen, and some six prizes beside them, pounding away now at the shore.

The French broke at the attack from their rear, and fled; but there was nowhere to run but into the waiting maw, a withering crossfire of Navy and Army guns ready to receive them. The British infantry marched at a steady trot into the emptied space, and Temeraire heard Lien at last. She was calling frantically as the infantry divided her and the last French aerial reserves from Napoleon and his Guard.

Napoleon had seen the trap, of course, and the retreat was sounding furiously from every French trumpet; but too late. The order of the French ranks had dissolved into one mass of terrified men, and the dragons carried by their momentum came falling into the hail of cannon-fire. Wellesley had committed all his reserves now, companies which had been held off to either flank, emerged from the trees and fog with their artillery and sent up a wall of hot iron to prevent the French forces from retreating or regrouping.

The tightening noose closed upon Bonaparte. 'Temeraire, the Corps will help the infantry hold the line,' Laurence called. 'We must keep off any who break through.'

Temeraire could now see Lien clearly. She was yet on the ground, calling to direct the French dragons to try one thing after another, intent only on breaking someone through to rescue Napoleon and other survivors who might be rescued from the wrack and ruin.

'Of course she would not come herself,' Temeraire said, contemptuously, as a great cloud of little dragons came racing forward. She had even sent in the couriers. 'Velocita, you and all the other Anglewings, fall back to meet them, and you too, Moncey. Cantarella, when they have got them confused, you harry them forward, into the range of the ships.'

The little dragons managed to dart through and past the heavyweights, but quickly came up against the pack of Anglewings, too agile to easily be passed. Velocita and the others slashed and snapped at the little dragons, chivvying them along, breaking up the knot and dividing the dragons from one another to leave them easy prey for the pouncing Yellow Reapers. Recoiling from so many larger dragons, they were herded straight into the crossfire. 'Temeraire, you must call Chalcedony back,' Laurence said, sharply.

'Where?' Temeraire said, looking round. But he was too late. Chalcedony had pursued one little Pou-de-Ciel too far, and with a dreadful hollow thump, one of the indiscriminate cannonballs took him directly in the chest. He seemed to fold around the blow, and then fell without a sound.

The little Pou de Ciel fluttered raggedly on, managed to thread the rain of iron, and broke out again into the open sky. It did not turn back for another attempt, but flew out across the Channel, towards France.

A handful of others had also got through. A few even had collected a handful of desperate soldiers from the ground, and were straggling away over the water with them onboard. But none had got near to Napoleon The British infantry were now advancing on his position. The Guard had pulled into square around him, a mortal shield.

Lien had seen the failure, and his peril. She suddenly gave a loud shrilling call, and took to the air.

'Oh!' Temeraire cried, eagerly, but she did not approach, instead she turned away and fled over the fields, with a scattered handful of French dragons behind her: her honour guard of Petit Chevaliers, and a few half-blind Fleur-de-Nuits, with eyeshades. 'Oh, oh!' Temeraire said, jouncing in the air with indignation, 'oh, how cowardly, she is leaving him behind—'

'She will be going after the ships,' Laurence said. 'Quickly Temeraire, turn so they can see you. Allen, the signal flags, *warning to ships, wing to northeast*—spell out for them, *Celestial*; Nelson will understand—'

'Shall we go and help them?' Temeraire said hopefully, hovering while Allen waved the flags urgently. It still looked to him as though Lien had run away. And he was sure that if she did mean to head for the ships, it would just be a ruse: what she really wanted was to be out of the fighting. He was sure that she would flee as soon as she made some small gesture. 'If she does mean to run away, we ought to stop her. I was worried all along that she might escape.'

'If we engage, the British ships will not be able to fire upon her,' Laurence said. 'There, they have been warned, do you see? He is directing some of their fire against her. Can you come about the other side? If she tries to flee towards France, we may then intercept her course.'

It was a fine and elegant sight to watch the flank of the British line-of-battle turning gracefully, one after another, to present their broadsides to the dragons coming around. But Lien went nowhere near the ships' range; she had stopped far distant, a small white figure against the grey sky, and now was hovering over the waves while the remnants of the French aerial forces wheeled above her in tight circles. She roared. The echoes of the divine wind carried over the water, even at such a distance, and a fine mist of wave spray steamed away from her in clouds of white.

'Have you any notion of what she is doing?' Laurence asked, looking out at her through his glass.

'Perhaps she has gone mad, over losing *another*

324

companion,' Temeraire offered. He did not really think so, but he did not see what good it could possibly do her, to roar at the water so. 'It is not as though water holds shape; even if she breaks it, it will just come back together, so—' He flicked his tail, uncertainly. 'She is going nearer the ships now, though,' he added, 'so they will be able to shoot her, soon, in any case.'

Lien was indeed gradually approaching the ships, still roaring madly at the waves. She flew so low now the waves were nearly lapping at her belly, rearing up to reach for her after every roar.

'Those waves are ten foot above the rest of the swell,' Laurence said. 'Mr. Allen, a signal for the ships: *storm anchors*, not in our code, in the Navy's—Yes, the red and white, and then the green, and then the red circle. Temeraire, I do not know what she is about, but I think we cannot hazard her trying it. Go after her, and quickly now—'

Temeraire scarcely waited for the word and threw himself joyously forward. The waves did not seem so very high; they would not have reached over the sides of the tall ships, and he had been to sea enough to know they might manage much higher. But if they should be struck by many such waves, one after another, perhaps they would not be able to fire their guns, and then Lien might come near enough to use the divine wind upon them.

Privately he cared only that at last he would have a chance at Lien; who had only sat about watching while everyone else was hurt and killed. But even as he approached, Lien stopped chasing the waves she had raised. Instead, she wheeled some dozen wing-beats back from them. Temeraire was close enough to see the trembling of her breast, and the way her wings wavered. She was very tired. Temeraire pressed on with new urgency. He would have her now, she could not fly away quickly enough.

Lien hovered a moment, drawing great breaths, and then charged after the waves once more. She swept low and level across the water, roaring so loudly that the cannon, still speaking behind Temeraire, were drowned out. A fresh swell rose ahead of her in response, not so high as the others, but low and smooth and moving very fast. Spent by the effort, she fell silent and hung in the air trembling. Her head was almost limp, but the swell ran on without her, to outpace and catch the elevated waves. As it met them, the waves seemed almost to stutter and collapse into it, one after another melting into the whole.

Temeraire heeled back, startled. With scarce warning the wave had reared high enough to block Lien out, thrusting itself directly in his way. His wing-tip cut a line of spray in its face as he wheeled away just in time to keep from being caught by its rising crest. He thought, at first, to climb higher aloft and go over the wave; but he had no time. Behind him the swell was rising, a dark green-glossy wall of water so vast that now small curlers of foam were breaking upon its face as well as its crest, and he was racing it towards the ships.

'Temeraire!' Laurence was crying out, 'Temeraire, can you break it—'

Temeraire darted a look over his shoulder: the wave was still growing. He had never seen anything so vast, and a shudder trembled along the tip of his tail. They had weathered a typhoon once, in the Indian Ocean; a swirling wrath of clouds overhead, and the *Allegiance* climbing and falling with each terrible rising wave. But this was another thing entirely; almost unworldly in its monstrous size. But Lien had made it, raised it with the divine wind, and so surely he could break it.

The wave came on after them, swift and dreadfully silent for all its great size. With frantic wing-beats he pulled away, trying to gain a little more room in which to turn around. The ships were so close now that he could read their names off their prows, and see men in their rigging. Temeraire was dripping with the spray, his wings streaming as he flew and flew. He could not gain enough elevation, and he had not time to draw much breath, but he had gained all the ground there was to be gained; he turned himself around, and roared out, with all his might.

'Dear God have mercy,' Laurence said, or thought he said, when he had wiped the salt from his eyes and looked back.

Temeraire had broken them through a hole in the wave. For an instant, a great watery hollow stood open like a window, where through they could still see a glimpse of *Victory* with her pennants, and all the line-of-battle, their white sails gleaming like pearl against the thunderstorm colour of the ocean. And then doom was upon them.

The great *Neptune*, broadside to the wave, fired her guns in a flaming golden roar before she was struck, a last shout of defiance; then she was gone. The ships facing into the wave rose up its shining face, their prows driving sea-foam gouges into the monster; climbing bravely until one after another they were overturned in cataracts of white and swallowed into the green.

The wave slouched onward, subsiding gradually as it ran. One solitary ship, the *Superb*, still bobbed at anchor, all her masts snapped and water pouring from her sides; two frigates, who had dropped their anchors in time, were on their beam-ends and struggling to right themselves before they sank. A few human specks in the water were clinging to wreckage. Nothing else remained of fourteen ships of the line.

No cannon spoke, nor guns; even the small knots of fighting stilled. The last of the French dragons came flying into the silence. They made a desperate arrow-head lunge into the sudden gap in the cross-fire, and the Guard, packed around Napoleon, ran forward to meet them.

'Temeraire!' Laurence called; a frantic trumpet-signal was blowing the alarm. Temeraire struggled wearily to turn, calling out to the other dragons. Already a small, lithe Chasseur-Vocifère was leaping away from the ground, and Napoleon was on her back.

Temeraire made for the party, but four of the French dragons wheeled to meet them. They were small Pêcheur-Rayés but valiant, clawing and shrieking heedless of how they themselves were cut about. Ballista dived into the fray, lashing a couple of them across the heads with her tail, and Requiescat charged in to join them, roaring in fury; but the Chasseur was away, fleeing across the Channel, and after her went five others burdened with dozens of Guardsmen. They were clear.

Across the water, Lien, was being supported away over the water by her escort, a couple of Petit Chevaliers, labouring mightily to keep her in the air.

The last of the French dragons broke away and fled. The men still upon the field threw down their guns, and most of them sank to their knees, or to all fours, broken with exhaustion. Nineteen eagle standards lay trampled and mired in the blood-churned mud, amid twenty thousand corpses.

The day was won.

Chapter Sixteen

'Laurence, I will do you credit; I have never in my life met any man more desirable to hang, and less convenient,' Wellesley said.

'Oh, and after everything we have done,' Temeraire said, indignantly.

'It was no more than you ought, and less than some,' Wellesley fired back. 'It is a damned pity you could not get yourself decently killed on the field.'

Laurence put a restraining hand on Temeraire's forearm. 'Yes, sir; and the same could be said of many other.'

Wellesley—or rather Wellington now that he had taken the new name with the ducal coronet that was his reward—snorted. They sat on the portico of Temeraire's own pavilion on his first opportunity to take up residence. Laurence had built it for him months before, but their journey to Africa and their ensuing imprisonment had intervened, and in the interim it had become a general residence. Even now, a few other dragons napped in corners, and nearby Perscitia lectured her former militia. She had brought the men along with her after the battle, those who could be bribed with a share of her treasure—for their skills in the mixing of mortar: they were putting up another pavilion.

A tremendous crash heralded the arrival of another load of bricks. Requiescat assisted the construction, and fired with enthusiasm, had carried alone what looked to be nearly five tons.

Wellington looked broodingly at the heap, and at the foundations for the next pavilion, which were being excavated by Minnow and half a dozen of her fellows: earth was flying at a prodigious rate. 'Where are you getting that brick?'

'We have bought it,' Perscitia said, overhearing his question, 'so you needn't try and complain that we are stealing. We have sold our eagles and have capital.'

'And God help us all,' Wellington said, tapping his fingers against his thigh. 'You ought to be made to pay damages out of it. Do you know I almost had a mutiny on my hands the next day? Not one drop of beer or rum to be found, among a hundred thousand men, and a good ten thousand casualties—'

'If you did not like it,' Perscitia said, 'you ought to have managed the battle more neatly; then I should not have needed to find a way to stop those French dragons for so long.'

This was not a little outrageous, considering that Wellington had managed to stage a battle of two hundred thousand men, three hundred dragons, and two dozen ships-of-the-line; and successfully hold worse ground against a better-trained and better-equipped army than his own, until the fog had loosened its grip enough for the ships to make their way in close enough to shore to begin the bombardment: nearly three hours longer than planned. 'Damn your impudence,' he growled; but Perscitia only flipped her wings at him a little, and loftily went back to her pavilion.

It was mid-morning on the seventeenth of March. Some three weeks had passed since the battle and its immediate aftermath. Lassitude and confusion mingled over so great a triumph and disaster. The survivors had, man and beast sunk,

330

to the ground and slept where they stood, uneasily, listening to the chorus of the low sighs of the dying upon the field; men awoke with cries whenever a greater wave came crashing upon the rocky shore.

The next day, without direction, they had begun the immense effort of clearing away the dead. Temeraire and his cohort had attended to the dragons. Not all were dead; many lingered, broken and slowly bleeding, dull-eyed and surrounded by the shattered bodies of their crew. Some were coaxed with much nudging and support back onto their feet, to limp away over the ground to the surgeons' clearing. Others, worse injured, could only be given a merciful end. Some of the aviators had survived, too, shielded from the worst of the impact by their dragon's body, and had to be taken away to join the other prisoners.

Chalcedony's body lay stretched upon a green hill; whole, it seemed, until they turned him over and saw the shattered red ruin of his chest. The Yellow Reapers nudged their shoulders beneath him, and in a knot carefully lifted him up to carry off the field.

'But where will we take him?' Gladius said, much subdued.

'We will take him to the old quarantine-grounds,' Temeraire said, 'near Dover, where the sick dragons were buried.'

They had laid Chalcedony and their other dead to rest in another of the great barrow-mounds rising in the quarantine valley. Early green shoots were climbing valiantly from the softening cover of snow, and the earth smelt richly moist as the dragons turned it over to raise the mound.

They had flown on to Dover looking for food, more from habit than any conscious decision, but habit served well enough. Many dragons of the Corps had returned to their own clearings, and the ground-crews and herdsmen were bringing in what cattle could be rounded up and shared out.

A week later Lloyd, the grounds-keeper from the old Wales

breeding ground, appeared at Temeraire's pavilion looking bedraggled and leading a string of cattle.

'Why, Lloyd,' Temeraire said, 'where have you got these cows from?' He did not wait for an answer to begin eating.

'The pens in London,' Lloyd said, accepting a cup of tea with gratitude, though he looked around first for spirits. 'Well, and they were ours first, weren't they,' he added with a self-righteous air, so perhaps their provenance was best not inquired after very far.

The dragons from Dover came every so often, and looked wistfully at the work going forward. 'I do not see why we cannot have one at the covert, too,' Maximus said, rumbling in dissatisfaction. 'Iskierka does.'

'Do I have a few thousand pounds to spare on erecting you a temple?' Berkley said. 'Nonsense, all this complaining; you have slept outside your entire life and never once taken an ounce of harm from it,' but shortly after a collection had quietly been taken up, among the officers, and a friendly rivalry began among the dragons to see whose should be completed first.

Through such visitors, Laurence had some word from London: the King had retired to Kensington, and the Prince of Wales made regent; Bonaparte successfully escaped to Paris, though with his tail between his legs. The newspapers were full of patriotic fervour and mourning for Nelson and the lost seamen, reputed martyrs for their nation.

All the while, no one sought to limit their freedom, nor paid them any official notice, but Laurence had known the situation an ephemeral one. The wheels of government might be some time restoring their course after so great a disruption, but inevitably they would fall into the cart tracks. Laurence's treason could not be ignored.

Wellington's arrival had surprised him only because it was Wellington and not Jane sent to demand his surrender; it did not encourage him. 'Sir,' Laurence said, 'I hope you will speak freely.'

'Laurence is not going to prison, or to be hanged,' Temeraire put in, 'and if that is what you came for, you may go away again. Come back with an army and take him, if you can.'

'We are not going to start a pitched battle against you and your pack of rogues, if that is what you imply,' Wellington said. 'I know about your damned little pact. That Longwing and Regal Copper, are going about Dover telling everyone that if we should come against you, they will fight with you, and so should every other dragon, or their captains will likely be taken away next.'

Laurence looked at Temeraire, who had the grace to look slightly abashed, but not greatly. He retorted, 'You haven't any right to complain if I do not trust you; you have tried to take Laurence before, and where is our pay? And the coverts, which you promised to open to us.'

'That is enough,' Wellington said. 'You had my word, and my word is good. You will have your coverts and your pay, and no later than any other scoundrel who stood up under fire. It will be half a year before the Government can pay off all its arrears, and you will have to lump it until then. You are not starving, at least, which is more than many an Englishman can say.'

'Well, then,' Temeraire said, a little mollified, 'I am sorry if I was rude, but if you will keep your promises and you do not mean to try and put Laurence in prison, what do you want?'

'What I want—' Wellington said, '—or rather, what His Majesty's Government wants, is to be shot of you. Submit to the King's justice, and your sentence will be commuted to transportation and labour.'

Temeraire snorted, at the word *justice*, and with much suspicion had the sentence explained to him. The Government

333

meant for Laurence to be sent abroad to the colony of New South Wales. 'But that is on the other side of the world! It is as bad as putting you in prison again!' Temeraire protested. 'I will certainly not let them send you so far away from me.'

'No,' Laurence said, watching Wellington's face. 'That, I imagine, is not their intention. Sir, it cannot be wise to send Temeraire away, not when the French have Lien. Whatever you may think of me, it is too high a price.'

'You are a little dull today, Laurence,' Wellington said. 'The *price* is giving your life, and their Lordships think it a cheap way to be rid of a dragon, who, if he takes it into his head, can sink half the shipping in Dover Harbour.'

Temeraire flared out his ruff. 'That is very rude,' he said. 'I would never do anything so cruel to the fishermen, and the merchants. Whyever would I?'

The story of Lien's feat had crossed the country like wildfire, carried with news of victory and Nelson's death by the victorious soldiers marching back to London and their homes. It had not gained much in the telling, there was not much more to gain, either in horror or in amazement. But Laurence was dismayed to find the fear it had whipped up, thus transferred to such irrational argument, and said so. 'If this *is* a dreadful weapon, we cannot forget that the French possess it also. To ignore it does no good, anymore than melting down your own cannon because the French had fired one upon you.'

'When they have built a cannon which chooses to turn, now and again, and fire into our faces instead, and then finds means to persuade all their other cannon to do the same, I will gladly concede,' Wellington said. 'No, Laurence, you have convinced me entirely that the beasts are sapient, but I will be damned if I will let you make them political. We can defend against one solitary beast, but not your Whiggish rabblerousing among ten thousand of them.'

'But if you agree we are intelligent, not that it is not perfectly obvious, then you cannot deny we have every right to be political,' Temeraire said.

'I can and will deny any man, or beast, the right to tear apart the foundations of our state,' Wellington said. 'Rights be damned; we will never hear the end of it.'

When he had gone, Temeraire looked sidelong at Laurence. 'I am sure no one can make us go, if we do not like to,' he said, 'and I do not care what Wellesley thinks, or Wellington, even if he is a duke now.'

Laurence put a hand on Temeraire's foreleg and looked out over the valley. It was a view much improved over the last summer, with the verdant growth over the undulating barrow-mounds, and the sheep and cattle Lloyd had gathered dotting the green hills as they browsed. It was all England and home laid out before him, creeping out from under the shadow; and now he must leave it, forever, for a distant, dry country. 'We must go,' he said.

'I am sending a few eggs on your transport,' Jane said. 'They need some beasts in New South Wales, to forward the settlement.' She sat down upon the edge of a boulder; they had walked a little way from the pavilion, to have some privacy, and now stood on a hillside where they had a view all the way to the sea: grey mist hanging over the water, and at its edges a little glitter of sunlight and a few white sails.

'Can they be spared?' Laurence asked.

'More easily than they can be kept,' Jane said. 'Before you brought us your cure, we thought we might have to replace the entire population of the Isles. Now there are more eggs than we will be able to feed in a year, after all this plundering and bad management. As for our friend across the way,' she added, tossing a pebble over the side of the cliff, vaguely in the direction of France, 'Bonaparte lost forty

335

beasts in his adventures here. He will not come over again shortly, and we will be ready for him if he does.'

He nodded and sat down beside her. Jane rubbed her hands together and blew upon them: there was still a chill in the air. Below, Excidium was inspecting the foundations with interest, Perscitia cajoling him to spray a channel for her through some of the stones, to allow water to run off more easily.

'I am afraid, Laurence, you will be an official prisoner; it is understood you shan't be put in irons, or anything which should distress Temeraire, but so far as formality—'

'I could expect nothing else.'

She sighed. 'At any rate, I have had some work persuading them, but there will be crews for the new hatchlings going along too, of course; so I have managed that you will have your handful also, among them.'

'You will not send Emily, surely,' Laurence said.

'I would rather risk her health than her spirit.' Jane said. 'She will do better to be as far away from my station as she can. I suppose you have not yet heard, they have named me Admiral of the Air,' and she laughed. 'Wellesley—Wellington, I must say now—is a damned hard-headed bastard, but do you know, he insisted on it; and that they make me a peer or some such nonsense, only they are still arguing over how to manage it, without letting me also sit in the Lords.'

'I congratulate you most heartily,' Laurence said, and shook her hand. 'But Jane, we will be halfway across the world; I do not even know what we will do there—'

'They will find out some work for you, I have no doubt,' Jane said. 'They mean to find a way into the interior; dragons will make easy work of that. And if nothing else, you may help them clear land. It is a waste, of course,' she added, 'and I hope we do not have cause to regret it, but I will tell you honestly, Laurence, I am glad you will go. I have not liked to think what should happen if you did not.'

'I would not raise civil war,' he said.

'You would not. I am not so sanguine about him,' Jane said, looking down at Temeraire, presently settling some sort of squabble between Cantarella and Perscitia; half the Yellow Reapers had dived into the quarrel on Cantarella's side at once. 'But as for Emily: I do not mean to give anyone opportunity to whisper of special treatment, or try to work on me through her, either for good or ill. With three or four beasts established, there will be enough scope for her to advance a while, and ships come and go often enough. I am only worried for Catherine.'

Riley and the *Allegiance* would be their transport, as so often before. Catherine, of course, could not be spared even if she had wished to go. 'Only I do not know what to do about the boy,' Catherine said. 'I do not like to let him go—'

'I do not see why,' Lily muttered, not very quietly.

'—but if he is to go to sea, I suppose he had better begin as he will go on; and if he should prefer the Corps someday, there will be dragons enough, so perhaps he ought to be with his father for now,' Catherine finished, at dinner that evening. She and Berkley had come out to see him off, as of course Laurence could not come to the covert to dine while legally a prisoner. They sat together in the pavilion around a small convenient card-table, eating roast mutton and bread, and sheltered from the wind by the dragons dozing comfortably around them.

Laurence with some reluctance said, 'Harcourt, under ordinary circumstances, I would not presume to offer advice on such a point; but you must recall she will be a prison-ship for the journey; she will be carrying prisoners.' The ordinary transports ran twice a year; the *Allegiance* would go out of turn, but she was so vast that a great many convicts could be crammed into her decks.

337

'I suppose they will not be allowed to wander the ship,' she said, surprised, and he had to convey some sense of the natural order of a prison-ship: the dreadful frequency of scurvy and fever and dysentery, the misery and regular danger of rebellion.

He was sorry to find his descriptions borne out when they came to the *Allegiance* the next morning, at Sheerness Dockyard. It was not pleasant to see their familiar and faithful transport in such a state. Her crew was a surly crowd of pressed landsmen, some of them not far removed from the wretches who could be heard—and smelled—beneath, clanking restlessly in their restraining irons. Nearly every able seaman had been plundered away by ships with nobler duties and captains with more influence than Riley, having perhaps been tainted by too much association with Laurence. A grating was already rigged; fresh bloodstains beneath it showed that it had lately seen use. The bo'sun and his mates were shoving the men to their work.

Across the harbour, another vessel was making ready to go down the Thames on the same wind that would keep the *Allegiance* in port a while longer. She made a stark contrast: a sailing barge, flat-bottomed and small next to the massive dragon transport, and manned to precision by a handful of sailors all in black; even her sails were dyed black, and her sides had been freshly painted, so there was no waterline to mar her side. A great casket, black and gold-painted, was gently and respectfully being conveyed onto her, while her officers stood at attention.

'That is Nelson's coffin,' Laurence said, when Temeraire inquired quietly. A hush had fallen over all the ship, and even the most bitter of the impressed landsmen had been silenced while the casket was in view—by the fists of their fellows if not by a sense of decorum. Tears showed on hardened faces, and Laurence could hear one man sobbing like a child, somewhere up in the rigging. A confused prickling of tears stood in his own eyes.

338

Nelson had given Britain mastery of the sea at Trafalgar. From Copenhagen he had brought back eighteen prizes and secured the passages of the Baltic Sea. The month before the battle at Shoeburyness had been joined, he had with his fleet swept the Channel clean of French shipping and beaten away at the regular French flights, so Napoleon should have no reinforcements. The ships had concealed their flags and painted over their names, to conceal his return, and for love of him, not one man out of five thousand sailors had deserted, even while the ships hid in home ports.

His personal sins might have been excused, though Nelson had selfishly exposed his wife to the misery of his flagrant unfaithfulness, and his friend Lord Hamilton to the astonished censure of the world. Lady Hamilton had rescued her reputation, by her heroic spy-work in the occupation, though it did not fully redeem Nelson's choice. But even if these venial matters were passed-over for so much victory and sacrifice, there were worse evils held to Nelson's account. He had defended slavery, and without a qualm advocated the hideous murder of thousands of dragons, allies and neutrals as well as their enemies, by the spreading of the plague. These evils Laurence could never forgive, and whose consequence he would personally bear the rest of his life.

Yet for a moment, Laurence could feel nothing but wrenching misery, watching the barge heave off the dock, its black sails filling; it was a grief unburdened by judgment; a grief he might have felt wholeheartedly, in another life. Guns were firing as the barge passed: an impromptu thunder of salutes. The *Allegiance*'s ragged crew managed to contribute a meaningful roar or two to the procession, though they could not yet fire a broadside in unison.

The barge vanished swiftly over the horizon, carried inland by wind and tide. Distantly the salutes blasted on, like a receding storm, and at last faded entirely. The *Allegiance* groaned softly at her anchors, and the unhappy life of the ship resumed behind him. Laurence breathed again. He had not wept, in the end.

Temeraire had watched the procession with interest; now he stretched his wings—cautiously keeping them in line with the wind and not abreast of it—and asked, 'Will we leave soon?'

'When the captain and the passengers are come aboard,' Laurence said. 'In a few days perhaps, if the wind turns fair.'

They, of course, had been required aboard earlier as they were not passengers but prisoners; and even if Laurence had been disposed to forget their official status, the first lieutenant, Lord Purbeck, was not. A guard, two Marines armed with muskets, had been placed on the steps to the dragon-deck, and when Laurence looked for his things, he found them stowed in a small, dark cabin beside the stern ladder way, two decks down: as near to the gaol-deck as was practical, without being right in it, and full of the stench. His guard looked as though they would have liked to keep him in it; until he said, 'You may go up, then, and explain to Temeraire that I am not allowed to come to him.'

The aviators began to come aboard irregularly: they were not an assembled crew with their own dragon, but were drifting over from Dover covert, in twos and threes. They included two of the captains Jane had sent: both of them older men lately consigned to earth by the death of their dragons, in the dreadful epidemic, long before anyone had looked for such an event. They were experienced men who might otherwise have looked for long careers ahead of them. They would take another man aboard in Gibraltar; three eggs were to be sent with them.

These were delivered, with great care and attention, by a party of three dragons. The eggs, swaddled in cotton wadding and lowered down into a nest built for them over the galley, were not what anyone would call a real prize: one a Yellow Reaper, and one an unfortunate cross between a Chequered

Nettle and a Parnassian, which had produced a shockingly small egg that looked more likely to produce a Winchester than a heavyweight. The third, delivered by Arkady, was his own: or so he smugly informed them, and had lately been produced by Wringe. He was not at all sorry to see the egg go, convinced it was an especial honour to have it sent to a wide-open and unclaimed territory. Although he stayed a long time lecturing Temeraire sternly on his duty of oversight and care, and extracting the promise that Temeraire would make sure the egg was not touched by anyone at all, and that only someone very rich should be permitted to become the captain.

'I am glad to see you again, before we go,' Laurence said, to Tharkay, awkwardly. They had not spoken since that day in the camp, when Tharkay had cut him to the bone; Laurence scarcely knew whether to apologize or to express his gratitude.

'You need not bid me farewell, just yet; I am coming,' Tharkay said. 'Captain Riley has been good enough to invite me as his guest.'

'I did not know you were acquainted,' Laurence said, as near as he could come to questioning.

'I did not,' Tharkay said, 'but Captain Harcourt was good enough to introduce me. I am well in pocket, at present, thanks to your admiral's generosity,' he added, seeing that Laurence was surprised, 'and I have never been to Terra Australis. The journey tempts me.'

Wanderlust might drive a man across the ocean or to the furthest edge of the world; it would not drive him aboard a ship with one he despised, when funds would have allowed him to choose his passage. 'Then I am glad we shall be shipmates,' Laurence said. It was as far as he could trust himself to go, without giving mortification to himself or any other.

Riley came aboard late, grim, and alone, with the tide already making a noise against *Allegiance*'s sides; he did not come to greet Laurence, of course, but neither did he say a word to the two captains, nor to Tharkay, technically at least his guest. He went directly to his cabin, and came out only to weigh anchor and make sail; before sequestering himself again. Purbeck knew his work, and managed despite the very awkward crew to get them out of the harbour, with only the least direction. And then the black waters of the Channel were slipping away behind them.

Temeraire put his head over the side and studied the waves, as he said to Laurence, 'I only wish I knew how she did it. Might I practice, to work it out?' But Laurence with some effort dissuaded him, although Temeraire protested he would only make the waves go *away* from the ship. Even so, Laurence did not think Riley or the sailors would like it.

Temeraire sighed, and settled himself again. It was bad enough to be facing so long a sea-journey again, when all his friends were building pavilions, and soon to have pay, but it was worse still to be sent to such a strange and unfriendly country, which had no dragons at all. He was sure that if it were at all nice, some dragons would have gone there before; so it must be wholly dreadful, and he was particularly anxious about the eggs. Not that he would let anything happen to them, of course, but it was a heavy responsibility, and none of them his own. It did not seem very fair.

'Will it be very long?' he asked Laurence the next morning, already feeling discouraged by the monotony of the horizon. He was gloomily unsurprised to hear they should be sailing for seven months, or longer.

'We must put in at Gibraltar and then at St. Helena,' Laurence said, 'as we cannot put in at the Cape anymore; and then likely again at New Amsterdam.'

'And you are sure we might not just as well go to China?' Temeraire asked. 'We might fly there overland—' but Laurence did not wish to do it.

'I do not mean to be a martyr,' he said, 'but the law must be the law for everyone; and it has already bent for me a great deal, and for you; however grudgingly. Though our actions were just, I cannot easily forget that others, who had a claim on our loyalty and our service, have suffered by them, and that our enemies thereby have profited. We have left England behind safer than she was, and free, thank God. I need not reproach myself for that. But I would gladly do what honourable work I might find, in her service, to repay the debt I owe, even if I may only do it indirect.'

Temeraire would have objected strongly if anyone else had suggested that Laurence owed more than he had given; but he could not very well quarrel with Laurence himself on the subject, when *he* owed Laurence a debt, too. Only, he wished they were not going so very far. Already the days had begun to drag intolerably.

'Wing, two points off the larboard stern,' the lookout cried, and Temeraire roused hopefully. Perhaps it would be a battle; or perhaps Volly, coming to call them back to England; or Maximus and Lily, come to bear him company, so they should all go together.

'It is Iskierka,' he said disgruntled, when she had come close enough to see the thin cloud of steam trailing her. She was flying a little sluggishly and tired, and she thumped down upon the dragondeck in much disarray. She did not wear her full harness and none of her crew was aboard, only Granby latched on to her neck-strap.

'What are you doing here?' Temeraire demanded, while she thirstily drank two barrels of his water.

She settled herself more comfortably, looping her massive coils over the deck, some of them dangling over the sides. Temeraire could not help but notice that in reaching her full length she had grown longer than he was. 'I am coming with you,' she announced.

'No, you are not,' Temeraire said. '*We* are transported, *you* are not. You had better go back at once.'

'Well, I cannot,' she said. 'I am too tired to fly back now, and by tomorrow morning it will be too far; so we may as well go on.'

'I do not see what you want to come for, anyway,' Temeraire said.

'I told you that you might give me an egg, when we had won,' Iskierka said, 'so I have come to keep my promise.'

'But I do not want to give you an egg, at all!' Temeraire said. 'I do not want you aboard the ship, either: you take up too much room, and you are damp.'

'I do not take any more room than you; at least, not *much* more,' Iskierka said, to add insult to injury, 'and I am warmer; so you needn't quarrel.'

'And,' Temeraire said, 'you are disobeying orders again, I am sure of it: Granby would never let you come.'

'Oh, well,' she said, 'one cannot always be obeying orders. When will we be there?'

'It is this dratted egg,' Granby said to Laurence. 'She is set on it having fire, *and* the divine wind. I have tried and tried to tell her it don't work so, but she will not listen, and now here we are.'

'You may take her off at Gibraltar,' Laurence suggested.

'Oh yes, if she will choose to go,' Granby said, and sat down upon an emptied cask of water, limp with defeat.

Iskierka, having eaten a pig, had already gone to sleep; her steadily issuing cloud of vapour spilling over the bow and trailing away along either side of the ship. Temeraire had pushed her to one half the dragondeck, as best he could, and now sat coiled up and disgruntled, with his ruff flattened against his neck.

'You may be glad of the company before we have crossed the line,' Laurence said, by way of comfort.

344

'I will not, even if I am very bored; any more than I would be glad of a typhoon,' Temeraire said, broodingly. 'And I am sure she will be a bad influence upon the eggs.'

Laurence looked at Iskierka and at Granby, who was presently drowning his sorrow in a glass of rum. Tharkay had come on deck and prudently caught one of the runners, to send for a bottle. 'At least you need not fear for their safety,' he suggested.

'Unless she should set the ship alight,' Temeraire said, a good deal too loudly for the comfort of any sailor within earshot, which simply omitted those two decks below, or in the stern.

'Then I am afraid you must study philosophy,' Laurence said, 'and learn to bear the misfortune. I hope the arrangement is at least preferable to the breeding-grounds.'

'Oh! anything might be better than that, and still be dreadful,' Temeraire said, and with a sigh settled his head down forward. 'Pray, Laurence; let us have the *Principia Mathematica*, as there is nothing better.'

'Again?' Laurence said, but sent Roland down for the book. She returned scowling at the state of his quarters, but with a shake of his head he dissuaded her from any word to Temeraire. 'Where shall I begin?' he asked, but did not immediately hear the answer. he looked down his fingers caught on the delicate pages of the book, and he traced the embossed lines of the heavy cover, leather stamped with gilt. It was the same book under his hands, with the salt wind in his face, and Temeraire at his side; nothing had changed outwardly, and yet he felt as wholly altered as if he had been reborn, since the last time he had set foot upon the deck of a ship. It seemed that a tide, coming in high and fast, had swept clean the sand.

'Laurence?' Temeraire said. 'Would you prefer another?'

'No, my dear,' Laurence said. 'This will do very well.'